AVENGING HOME

A. AMERICAN

AUTHOR'S NOTE

I WANT TO TAKE A MOMENT to thank you, the reader, for hanging in there so long. It's been a long ride to get here and I cannot thank you enough for sticking with me. Some of you have expressed your desire to see a satisfying ending to the series. As much as you've enjoyed it, for some, it's time to move on. I can appreciate that. So if you're one of those readers, Avenging Home is the end of the line for you. There is a satisfying end to this addition to The Survivalist series. For the rest of you, well, you'll see.

I want to acknowledge my editor, Mike, for all his hard work. I know Enforcing Home had some issues. Those however were not his fault. They were mine alone. This time though, there's been a massive effort to ensure an error free read for you guys. Thank you Mike for all your hard work and undying support and encouragement.

I also want to take a moment and thank a group of you that have been following this adventure since Going Home was being written online. Those were wild days and more fun than I can really explain. It was an amazing experience to post new pieces of the book each night and follow the discussions online the next day. Not to mention your unceasing, persistent and damn near nagging desire to see it published. If it wasn't for you guys I would never have published Going Home and we certainly wouldn't be here today with Avenging Home. Thank you, from the bottom of my heart.

Now, if you're one of those readers that want more of The Survivalist and are among the many that ask how many more books will be in the series, the answer is, I don't know. But after reading Avenging Home I think you'll get an idea of what's about to happen and just how long it could take to explain it all. I hope you enjoy this work. I've put a lot into it.

PROLOGUE

M EL SAT BY TAYLOR'S SIDE until Doc finally said we could take her home. Three long days spent away from home. But she was home now. With the loss of Jeff, something I still hadn't completely processed yet, it looked like we were in for a dark period. We knew the DHS was once again out there. That they'd managed to escape from their transport was very concerning. I had not voiced my concerns on the topic to anyone. I was worried things were not going our way and we could be in for some hard times. But we had enough to deal with.

The bombing delayed having the medical staff come take a look Tyler and Brandy. We wanted to get the kids out of the house if we could, but couldn't run the risk if they were sick. There was plenty to do yet. Cecil needed help getting the crops into the ground at the new farm. There were the prisoners to be dealt with; and to take that task out of my hands, we needed to find a judge.

With so much to do, our days became busy. Everyone pitched in and worked hard but it seemed as if there just weren't enough hours in the day. And we had yet to take the fight back to DHS. I wasn't content to sit around and wait for them to come to us. I wanted to strike first. Sarge tempered my thoughts, however, insisting we needed to take a cautious approach. We simply couldn't afford any more losses. And on that point, I agreed with him.

CHAPTER 1

T HAD WIPED SWEAT FROM HIS brow as he cranked the wheel of the tractor around to make another pass. The ground was hard and it was taking time to break it. It took long hard days in the scorching Florida summer heat to bush hog the field. Then the hard work started. Thad looked over at Cecil in the seat of his tractor. He was looking back over his shoulder at the cloud of dust kicked up by the disc. Cecil looked over and smiled, taking off his hat in salute. Thad smiled and nodded back.

The field was a mass of gray mounds and clumps of upturned grass. Long-legged Sandhill Cranes and Egrets with their wispy white feathers worked the field picking bugs and grubs from the freshly turned earth. It had been a banner few days for the birds, and more and more had come to join the buffet. When the field was being cut, the birds followed the tractors closely to snap up the countless grasshoppers fleeing from the machines.

Taking a break, Thad stopped his tractor under a large oak on the edge of the field and climbed off. He looked at Perez and shook his head. "I ain't keeping you awake, am I?"

Ian laughed. "Not hardly. Takes a lot more than that rattle trap to wake him up."

Perez replied by adjusting his hat. "Keep it down, would ya?"

Thad filled a cup from the water keg and took a long drink.

He winced and shook his head. "Damn that's cold." Smiling, he added, "Gives me a brain freeze and makes my teeth hurt."

"Yeah. It's almost too cold," Ian replied.

Smiling, Thad replied, "No it ain't. I can take the pain."

Cecil pulled up and shut his machine down. Thad refilled the cup and handed it to him as he walked up. Cecil drained it in one long gulp. "Thanks, Thad. That sure is good."

Thad looked out across the field dotted with the occasional pine tree. "What do you think?"

Cecil took his hat off and wiped his forehead with the back of his hand. "I think it's hotter than hell full of lawyers." He looked out across the field and added, "I think we need to make one more pass. That ground is pretty hard. Probably never been tilled before. We need to break it good and deep to give the crops the best chance we can."

Thad looked up at the sun. It was past its apex and beginning its descent. But there was still plenty of time. He looked at blue drum strapped to the top of his disc. "I'm glad we added the weight; we'd never got this broke up if we hadn't."

"Soon as I saw your disc rolling on the grass, I knew we'd have to do something. I've always liked using the barrels. Makes it easy to add or remove weight," Cecil replied.

The two men grabbed another quick drink of water and mounted their respective tractors. Cecil led the way and Thad fell in behind him, offset to catch new ground. They worked the entire field in this formation in an ever-tightening ring. The two men wound around the scattered trees, turning the thick layer of needles into the earth.

Thad looked back as he passed one of the large long leaf pines. The soil was darker here, the constant addition of fallen needles creating mulch around the base of the tree. But this soil would be acidic as a result and would either have to be dealt with or planted accordingly. They worked into early evening to take advantage of the cooler temps as the sun dipped towards the horizon. When Cecil raised his disc and headed towards the tree line where their security detail sought cover from the scorching day, Thad raised his disc and followed the older man. He was happy the day was over. He was hot, dirty, thirsty and tired.

Perez was sitting on the hood of the Hummer smoking as they pulled up. Cecil got off his machine and stretched his back. Bending forwards and back, he let out a couple of moans.

"How you feeling?" Perez asked.

"Old," Cecil replied. Stepping over and leaning on the hood of the truck, he held out his hand. "Give me one of them things."

Perez cocked his head to the side. "You don't want one of these; they're bad for you."

"At my age everything's bad for you," Cecil replied, gesturing with his hand for a smoke.

Perez smiled and handed one over. "You wanna start a tab?"

Thad leaned against the truck and looked at Jamie sitting in the driver's seat. Her foot was propped up on the door and her hat was pulled down over her eyes. Thad smiled and asked, "You ready to go home?"

Jamie sat up, straightening her hat. "Pfft, if we were going home and not to that damn armory." She looked up at him. "How much longer until you guys are done?"

Thad looked out across the field. "I think we're done with the tractors. Just need to get some bodies out here and try to rake as much of the grass out as possible."

Cecil pushed the brim of his hat up and spit from between his teeth. "And that is going to be a bear of a job. But if we don't, it'll be nearly impossible to keep up with later."

Perez laughed. "You really think you're going to get them town folks out here in this sun to rake this shit?"

"If they wanna eat, they're going to have to." He looked at Perez. "You don't work, you don't eat."

Ian laughed. "Shit, Perez. You're going to be one hungry beaner."

Perez leaned back on the hood. "I'm in the Army, Ian. Remember? I do more before five AM than most people do all day."

Ian laughed. "Yeah, you're an army of one alright."

Taking a drag from his smoke, Perez replied, "And don't you forget it either."

Cecil straightened up. "If y'all are done jacking yer jaws, let's head to town."

Jamie quickly started the Hummer and slammed her door shut. Ian looked down from his perch in the turret. "You in a hurry there, sweet cheeks?"

Jamie drew her knife from its sheath and pushed the spine of the blade up between Ian's legs. "You call me that again, and I'll cut your nuts off like a hog."

Ian squirmed away from the blade. "Easy woman!" Thad laughed and headed back towards his tractor, shaking his head.

Jamie followed the two tractors for the short ride back to town. Being far too valuable, the tractors were brought back to town every night. Security had yet to be established at the farm, so nothing could be left there yet. Cecil waved over his shoulder as he passed the armory on his way home. Thad turned into the parking lot and shut the old machine down. Jamie parked the Hummer and got out and asked Thad if he were hungry.

Replying with his signature smile, "Yes ma'am."

She looked over her shoulder at the hall. "If you want to

hang out here, I'll grab you some chow. Unless you want to go in there."

"I'd appreciate it, Jamie. Don't really feel like going in there."

Scrunching her face, Jamie replied, "Me neither. Smells like feet and ass in there." She looked at the building and some of the soldiers coming out and added, "sweaty balls."

Ian was pulling his gear from the truck and cackled.

Thad laughed heartily. "Miss Jamie!"

She gave him a deadpan look and nodded at the building. "Go in there and tell me I'm wrong."

"I'll take your word for it that it smells like a locker room, Miss Jamie," He said as he tried to put a more appropriate name to the discussion. Thad was still a very polite man and easily embarrassed by such talk around women, let alone from one.

"Come on, Thad. Let's go grab us a spot to sleep while she gets us some grub," Ian said.

Jamie shouted over her shoulder. "I ain't getting you shit, sweet cheeks!"

"Awe come on. I was just kidding!" Ian called back.

Jamie gave him the finger over her shoulder. "I'm not, asshole!"

Ian, Perez and Thad found themselves an unoccupied truck to take up residence in for the night. It was certainly better than staying in the main hall or one of the tents with everyone else. Of course, if it came to that, they would. But given the opportunity, it was always preferable to be away from the masses. After stowing their gear in the truck, Perez said he'd go find Jamie and let her know where they were.

Thad looked at the truck. "Tell you what, if we're all going to be here for the night, I'm going to sleep under the truck and give you guys more room in here."

"Sounds like a good idea. "I might join you down there tonight."

Jamie and Perez showed up with an armload of MREs. Jamie tossed one to Thad, and Perez gave one to Ian. Ian looked at the bag and scrunched his nose. "Ah man, you've got to be kidding me."

"This is it for tonight," Jamie replied as she climbed up into the truck to claim her spot.

Thad looked at the brown bag in his hand. "I wish we were home. Whatever they're having has to be better than this."

"Look on the bright side, we get to go home tomorrow," Ian said as he tore his bag open.

I stood in the door of Taylor's room watching Mel. She wouldn't leave Taylor's side and took her job as head nurse seriously. Taylor was awake now and getting better daily. She had no recollection of the bombing beyond being in town. I was happy about that, as the entire scene had been horrible. Little Bit also saw it as her duty to nurse her sister, and probably pestered her more than she would have liked. But Taylor never complained, and actually tried to make her little sister feel as though she were important.

Mel hadn't blamed me for what took place. At least she'd never said as much to me. Even though, I couldn't help but feel responsible. After all, I'd allowed them to go to town. But did that really make it my fault? In a normal world, these girls would be coming and going as they pleased. And was it the right thing to do to try and keep them cooped up out here? In the end, it was really a matter of physics. Time and space came together at that time, at that place.

Nonetheless, I still felt a level of responsibility that I would never shake. For every time I looked at my beautiful daughter, there would be reminders staring back at me. Thankfully, she didn't have many wounds to her face. But there were some, and they were profound. Taylor knew her face had been scarred, but she didn't know to what extent. Mel and I had discussed the matter and agreed not to let her have the mirror she requested daily. Telling her instead, that when she was strong enough to get up and go to the bathroom, she could see for herself.

Taylor saw me and smiled. "Morning, Dad."

Holding up my hand, "Morning kiddo. How are you feeling today?"

She pushed herself up on her pillows. "Better. I'm feeling better. I'm actually really hungry."

Mel quickly rose. "You want me to get you something?"

"Do we have anything?" Taylor asked.

Mel smiled. "I'm sure I can come up with something."

"I've got to get out to the bunker. I'll check on you later," I said as I headed towards the door.

Lee Ann was in the living room putting her shoes on. I stopped in front of her. "Where are you headed?"

Without looking up, she replied, "Over to Jess's."

I was more worried about her than I was Taylor. Since the bombing, she, Jess and Fred had become thick as thieves. They were always together and generally discussing their mutual burgeoning hate. They wanted vengeance; and I was afraid that when the time came, I wouldn't be able to prevent them from taking part. I wanted it too, more than anyone. I too had a hate burning inside. But I did my best to temper it and not let it show, because I didn't want to fan the flames that were threatening to consume those girls.

"What are you guys up to today?" I asked.

She shrugged as she finished her last knot and stood up. "I don't know. Probably just hang out until we have to take our turn at the bunker."

I stepped over and wrapped my arm around her. "Alright, keep your eyes open."

She didn't smile. She didn't frown. She stared back blankly and replied, "I hope they do come."

This was what I feared. I pulled her in tight. "Baby girl, be careful what you wish for. Things are hard enough now. Let's not go wishing for more to deal with."

To placate me, she smiled. "I know, Dad. I'm just kinda sayin'."

I went to the kitchen and found Mel scrambling a couple of eggs. She had the very last can of Red Feather cheese sitting on the counter, its top already pulled open. I picked the can up, looked at it, then lifted it up to smell the cheddar inside.

"Ah, that smells good."

Mel took the can from me. "It's for Taylor."

Smiling, I replied, "I know. I wouldn't eat it if you offered it to me. Let her enjoy it. She was always looking for a reason to open that can anyway."

She didn't look up from the eggs she was stirring around in the pan, so I grabbed her hand. "You okay?"

Mel looked up and smiled. "I'm fine."

"You sure?"

Nodding and returning to the eggs in the pan, she replied. "Yeah, what are you doing today?"

"I have to go on guard duty and meet with Sarge later today."

"You going anywhere?"

"No, I'll be here all day."

She smiled again. "Good, then I'll see you later."

Before I left the kitchen, Little Bit wandered in. "What's that smell?" She asked, craning her neck to see into the pan.

Mel smiled at her. "Scrambled eggs with cheese. You want some?"

She bounced up and down. "With cheese? Yes, I want some! Where did we get cheese? I love cheese!"

"Let me fix a plate for Taylor, and you take it to her; then come back and I'll have a plate for you on the table."

Little Bit held her hands out. With wide eyes, she licked her lips when Mel handed her the plate and she sniffed the yellow pile.

"Go on now. Take that to your sister. Here's a fork too."

I patted Mel on the ass and kissed her cheek. "I'll see you later, baby."

She smiled and winked, then asked if I wanted a glass of tea.

"What kind of question is that?" I replied.

She took a red Solo cup and filled it with tea. The girls were still going through the houses in the neighborhood and bringing things home, and these came in pretty handy. As she handed me the cup, I smiled. "Thanks, babe."

She smiled. "I gotta take care of you."

"And you do a fine job of it," I replied, and gave her a kiss before collecting my gear.

In the living room, I grabbed my Florida atlas. I'd gone through my topo maps, but didn't have one that covered the area where the Elk's Camp was located. Sarge asked for a map, and this was the best I could do. Tucking the book under my arm, I left the house. It was really warm out, even though the sun was barely up. *Ugh, it's going to be a hot one.* Looking up, I could see the large puffy nimbus clouds that predicted rain at some point today.

Our location in Florida was interesting. We were almost

equidistant from the east and west coasts. That meant that the sea breeze from either side collided right over us; and in the heat of the afternoon, usually brought some pretty strong thunderstorms. And today looked as though it would live up to it.

I sipped my tea on the short walk to the bunker and found Danny was already there when I arrived. We were to relieve Ted and Mike. Danny was leaning on the bunker talking to Ted, but I didn't see Mike.

"Morning, boys." I greeted them.

Ted looked over his shoulder. "What's up, Morg?"

Looking around, I asked, "Where's Mike?"

Ted jerked his head in the direction of the latrine. "The king is on his throne."

"Ah, should have known. How's it going, Danny?"

Danny looked up towards the sky. "It's going to be hot today."

Swallowing a sip of tea, I replied, "Gotta love summer in the Sunshine State."

"Looks like it's going to be liquid sunshine today," Ted added.

"It'll cool things off," I replied.

"That'll make you feel like a new man!" Mike shouted. We all turned to see Mike standing beside the thatched hut, stretching. "Feel like I lost five pounds dropping some heat, boys!"

Ted was shaking his head. "Thanks for that. My day is complete."

Mike smiled. "Well, that's me!" He pounded his chest with his fists. "I'm a giver!"

"Cept no one wants it," Ted replied.

Mike hoisted his plate carrier over his head and dropped it on his shoulders. "Now that's just inconsiderate, Teddy."

"You are a true knucklehead," Ted replied.

I laid the atlas out on the roof of the bunker and flipped through it until I found the page with the area of the camp and pointed it out to Ted.

"Take this with you and give it to the old man," I said.

"Yeah, he wants to get an idea of where it is. You coming over later?"

"When we're relieved, we'll be over. Thad's bringing that guy back from town today, and we need to have a talk with him," I replied.

Ted snorted. "Not like he's going to tell us anything we don't already know."

I shrugged. "Well, there's always his buddy."

We'd caught another man the next day. Some residents of Eustis brought him to the armory. It was a two man team that set the bomb. The guy we caught immediately after the blast was the one that actually set it. This was the other half of that team.

"Someone willing to do something like that probably isn't going to tell you anything."

I nodded and looked at him. "Maybe. But I still need to have a talk with him."

Ted picked up the book and looked at me. "Talk, huh? Is that what you're going to do? Talk to him?" I didn't reply as Ted called to Mike. "Come on, Mikey. I'm tired."

"On my way, boss! On my way!" Mike shouted as he ran to catch up.

"That guy needs Ritalin," Danny said with a smile.

"That, or he's cooking meth someplace," I said with a chuckle.

"Morning, lads!"

Danny and I both jumped and looked over to see Dalton coming out of the woods.

"Damn, man. You slink around like some kind of frickin cat or ninja." Danny said.

I laughed. "Yeah, a ninja cat."

Dalton pressed his hands to his thighs and bowed. "Watashi wa ninja nekodesu."

"Watashi what?" Danny asked.

Dalton smiled. "Just what you said. I am the ninja cat."

I was surprised. "You speak Japanese?"

"A little. Enough to get by."

Danny looked up. "Man, it's already getting hot."

"Mmm, yes. I think it's going to be a scorcher," Dalton replied with a cockney accent.

"Yeah, we need some kind of shade out here," I replied, then looked into the bunker opening. "And I don't want to hang out in there all day."

"We should put up a tarp here on the backside," Danny said.

"I'll go cut some poles if you guys want," Dalton offered.

"That'd be great. If you go to my shed, the smaller one, there's a blue ten by ten tarp in there. Grab it and some rope or something to tie it down," Danny replied.

"Right O!" Dalton shouted and took off.

I laughed. "That dude just ain't right."

"Seems to be a common thread around here lately."

While we waited for Dalton to come back, we wasted no time flipping a quarter and trying to call it. You could only spend so much time looking around. Dalton returned with an armload of poles, the tarp and some cordage.

Dropping the poles, "I tried to get long ones so they would be taller than the roof of the bunker so we could stand under it back here and see over the top."

"Sounds good to me. Some shade will be nice," Danny replied.

We got to work driving the poles and lashing the tarp. We staked out the poles to draw the tarp taught. We decided to make it flat so that when it rained it would pool some water that we could then direct off and collect. Not that we really needed the water, but why waste it?

CHAPTER 2

MORNING COULDN'T COME SOON ENOUGH for Thad. He just didn't like being at the armory. So when he woke up, he was ready to go.

Thad went to the back of the truck and looked in. "Hey, you guys ready to go?"

Perez was lying on his back with his hat pulled down over his eyes. "It's too early for this crap."

Thad smiled and grabbed Perez's boot. "Come on, grumpy. Get up. I'm ready to go home."

Jamie got up and started packing her gear. "Shake a leg, old man. Let's get the hell out of here before they try and rope us into some kind of BS."

Perez groaned and sat up, the hat falling into his lap. He looked bleary-eyed at Thad and shook his head. Fumbling around in his pockets, he produced a cigarette, lit it and took a long drag. He spent the next several minutes coughing.

"Them things gonna kill you, Perez," Thad said.

Still coughing, Perez waved him off. Ian rolled out from under the truck and started putting his gear together. He looked up in the back of the truck and smiled.

Ian winked at Jamie. "You and you're boyfriend have a good night?" While trying to catch his breath, Perez gave him the finger in reply.

Jamie was stuffing her poncho liner in her pack. "Keep it up, Ian."

Grinning, Thad looked at Ian. "She gonna get you one of these days."

Ian laughed. "She's harmless." Then Jamie's pack hit him in the side of the head and knocked him on his ass.

When he looked up, Jamie was looking down at him from the back of the truck. "How's that for harmless?"

Ian pushed the pack off his chest. As he was getting up, he said, "You've got anger issues, woman."

Jamie let out a loud laugh and looked at Thad. "You think I've got anger issues?"

Thad shook his head. "No, ma'am." Then he laughed as well.

"See, Ian? Thad doesn't agree with you."

Then Shane with the Eustis PD walked up. "Morning, guys."

"Hey, Shane. How's it going?" Thad asked.

"Good. It'll be better when you guys take that prisoner with you. You're taking him today, aren't you?"

"I'm not. I'm riding a tractor home. They might though," Thad said, nodding at Ian.

"Yeah. You get him trussed up and we'll come get him shortly," Ian said.

"Thank God. People around here are pretty pissed. We spend all our time trying to keep people away. They want to lynch his ass. They're pissed at the other one too, but the guy that actually set it, they want his head on a pole."

Ian snorted. "Just let them know there's something far worse in store for him. When that old man gets ahold of him, he'll wish he were dead."

"I think Morgan wants a piece of him too," Thad added.

Ian shouldered his pack. "I don't think Morgan has same mean streak the old man does."

Thad shook his head slightly. "Don't underestimate the man."

Shane ran a hand through his hair. "I just want this one gone. I've got another over there now, and some people want this guy's scalp too. I just want one of them gone. Tell Morgan I need to talk to him about this guy when he gets a chance."

"What'd he do?" Thad asked.

"It was a domestic thing with his girlfriend. He got drunk and thought she was talking to some dude. Shit got out of hand, and she's dead," Shane said.

"Damn, why?"

"He was drunk. Guess he got some booze from that old guy at the market before he was blasted all over the place."

Shaking his head, Thad asked, "His excuse is he was drunk?"

Shane shrugged. "That's what he's saying. Says he didn't mean to. His family brought him in to keep her family from killing him."

"I'll tell Morgan. He'll get with you the next time he comes to town," Thad said.

"Y'all get the hell out of the way so I can get out of here," Perez grumbled.

Thad stepped back and Perez flopped out of the truck, dragging his pack on the ground behind him. "I'll be at the truck when you're ready." He looked at Ian. "And I'm driving. You ride up there in that damn perch."

Jamie hopped out beside him. "I'll drive. Perez, you can sleep."

Perez smiled. "I love you."

Jamie laughed. "I love you too, Poppie. Give me a cigarette." Perez shook one out of the pack and handed it over, then lit it for her.

Ian was shaking his head. "I think you're gay for him."

Jamie took a long drag as she walked towards Ian. Once close enough, she blew the smoke in his face. "In your dreams. I'm going to go find the engineers and see when they're going to meet Morgan."

"I'll be over at the PD waiting for you guys. I'll open the roll-up door so you can pull in. We bring that guy outside and someone's liable to take a shot at him," Shane said.

Jamie went into the armory and found Livingston. "Hey, Lt. When are those engineers going to meet Morgan at the plant? He asked me to find out." Then she looked around. "How the hell did you guys get the lights on in here?"

Livingston smiled as he looked around. "Those clever engineers hooked us up to the generator running the clinic. They said they'd meet him tomorrow. But today we're sending a couple of trucks with you guys so the doc can look at those people you think have TB."

She nodded. "Ok, tell them to meet us over at the PD. We're going to load that guy to take him with us today."

"And what does the good Sheriff have in mind for him?" Livingston asked.

Jamie shrugged. "Probably best not to ask questions you don't want answers to."

"I'm assuming then we'll probably never see him again."

"What do you want me to say? I have no idea what they plan to do. If you guys need him for something, keep him here."

Livingston looked towards the police station. "No, you guys take him. He's causing us enough trouble just being here."

"I'll tell Morgan to meet the engineers tomorrow. What time?"

"Around noon I guess. Sure would be nice if they could get that plant on line," Livingston added.

"I'm not holding my breath. We'll be over there," Jamie

said, nodding towards the police station. And then she headed to the truck.

Perez was already asleep in the truck when she got there. Ian was up in the turret setting up the machinegun. Jamie climbed in behind the wheel and asked Ian if he was ready.

"I was born ready. Let's get the hell out of here," Ian replied.

Thad was sitting in the PD parking lot when she pulled in. Shane and Shawn were standing in the open roll-up door. It was pretty early, so there was no lynch mob. Jamie pulled the truck into the vehicle sally port. Shawn stayed by the door as Shane went in and returned with their prisoner. Per their request, he'd put a blindfold on the man, and he was both cuffed and shackled with a belly chain, preventing him use of his hands. He didn't say anything as Shane stuffed him into the back of the truck.

Once he was in, Shane looked at Jamie. "He's all yours."

Jamie gave him a thumbs up. "Thanks. We're out of here."

She backed the truck out and stopped beside Thad. "We're waiting on some medics."

"That's good. They need to check on Tyler and Brandy. Maybe we can get them kids out of that house."

The two Hummers they were waiting on pulled up and Jamie pulled out in the lead. Thad started the tractor and pulled out behind the last truck.

I saw the Hummers round the corner with Thad behind them on the tractor. Jamie pulled up beside the bunker and stopped. Looking in, I saw the prisoner secured in the back.

"That him?" I asked. Though I knew who it was.

She nodded, "Yeah. Where do you want him?"

"Take him to Sarge's."

She jabbed a thumb over her shoulder. "They're here to check out Tyler and Brandy."

"Good, about time. I'll call and get Doc over there."

"And the engineers want to meet at the plant tomorrow around noon."

"Ok, good. Maybe we can get that plant up and running. Tell Sarge I'll be over as soon as this is taken care of," I said.

She nodded and turned to head to Sarge's house. The next truck pulled up and I told him where to go, pointing out Tyler and Brandy's house.

"I'll meet you over there in a few minutes. I want to get Doc over there too."

The driver nodded. "We'll meet you there."

I asked Dalton if he could hang out at the bunker. He gave me a thumbs up, and I nodded as I pulled the mic for my radio up.

"Hey, Doc. Can you meet me at Tyler and Brandy's place? The medics from town are here to check them out."

On my way.

"Later we need to get everyone together and talk," Dalton said as I started to walk away. Stopping, I asked him what was up. "I found some more tracks, and I think another observation point. Haven't found anyone in it yet, but there's a lot of traffic on the trail. We're being watched again."

"They're going to come eventually," I replied.

"No doubt, but I'd like to be ready for them."

"Alright. Soon as we handle this, we'll go talk to the guys. Maybe we can get the girls to relieve you guys so we can all talk," I said, and then headed for Tyler's.

At Tyler's, the folks from the clinic were hanging out around the truck. Shortly after I got there, Doc pulled up in Sarge's Hummer. The driveway was crowded with the three big trucks.

One of the doctors walked up to Doc. "You think these folks are positive?"

Doc nodded. "Yeah, I'm pretty sure. But without a test I can't be a hundred percent."

The doctor held up a box. "Well, I brought some so we can be."

Surprised, Doc said, "I didn't know you guys had any."

"After hearing what was going on, I had some sent out with an evac helo. One of the people from town was in pretty bad shape, and I convinced Eglin to fly them out. They sent the skin tests on the bird."

Doc examined the box. "This is great."

"So this will tell us for certain if they have it?" I asked.

Doc nodded. "Oh yeah. It takes three days to determine the result, but we'll know."

The doctor looked at Doc. "Let's get to it then."

They went over to the Hummer and the doctor handed out Tyvek suits and booties. The three people going in suited up, the doctor, Doc and a nurse. They put on rubber gloves, tucking the sleeves into them, and pulled the booties over their boots. Lastly, they put large respirators on their faces before going in.

They were inside for what seemed like an eternity. Finally, the door opened and they came out. Once in the yard, one of the Guardsmen pulled a small pump sprayer from the truck. Putting on a respirator of his own, he started to spray each of them down. Once they were rinsed off, they pulled the suits off and piled them up, along with the masks and booties. Once everyone was out of their suits, the soldier poured a jar of fuel on the pile and tossed a match on it, sending a flame leaping into the sky with a plume of black smoke.

"Is all that really necessary?" I asked.

"TB isn't anything to fool with. The last thing you want is for this to take hold. You guys did the right thing by isolating them. Let's just hope you did it soon enough," the doctor said.

"Roll up your sleeve, Morg. We're going to test you too," Doc said.

"Me? Why?"

"We're going to do a few random tests. You interact with about everyone here. So if anyone had it, you certainly could," Doc said.

His statement scared me. "But I feel fine."

Doc smiled. "It's not that big a deal. We just want to make sure there are no other cases."

I rolled up the sleeve on my left arm and held it out. He produced the preloaded needle and inserted it just under the skin. He slowly pressed the plunger, and whatever it was went under my skin. I was looking at the spot when I asked, "How do you know if it's positive?"

"If it's positive, it swells up real big." Doc replied.

Still looking at the spot, I responded. "Great, I'll be staring at this thing for the next three days."

"Don't let it eat you up, Morg. I seriously doubt you have it. You'd be coughing your guts up if you did," Doc said.

I glanced at the spot again. "That really doesn't makes me feel better. Can you give me a ride to the house? I need to talk with the old man."

Doc nodded. "Sure, let me talk with these guys and we'll head that way."

Doc spoke with the other medical folks for a moment and climbed into the truck. I was already in the passenger seat waiting on him. We followed the other trucks out of the yard and past the bunker. They waved at Danny and Dalton as we passed, but I didn't even notice them. I was a little distracted about the guest waiting for me at Sarge's.

Doc looked over at me. "What's your plan for the dude at the house?"

Shrugging, I replied, "I don't know. See what he can tell us about the Elk's Camp. I want to know how many of those guys there are."

"Hmm." He looked back over at me. "You sure you're up for this?"

Looking back, I asked, "What do you mean?"

"This isn't pretty stuff, ya know."

Turning my attention back to the road, "I'm fine. Don't worry about me."

We pulled up to the house and I got my first look at the guy. The garage door was open and he was tied to a chair in the middle of it. Sarge, Mike, Ted, Thad and the girls were there. So far, he looked untouched. But then I couldn't see his head with the sack on it.

Getting out, I asked Sarge, "He tell you anything yet?"

The old man shook his head. "No, we haven't got that far yet. Just exchanging pleasantries."

As I walked up to the garage, I looked at Lee Ann. "Why don't you guys take off. I don't think you need to see this."

She was staring at the man and didn't look at me when she replied. "No. We're going to stay."

I looked at Jess and Fred, but Jess just crossed her arms as if to say, *we're not going anywhere.*

Shaking my head, I said, "Suit yourself," and looked at Sarge. "Let's get this done."

Sarge walked into the garage as Aric was coming out of the house with another chair. The old man pointed to the floor in front of the other chair and Aric set it down. Sarge spun it around and straddled it, resting his arms on the chair back. He reached over and pulled the sack off the guy's head. The man blinked, looking down to try and avoid the light coming through the door.

Sarge gave him a minute, then said, "I guess you know what comes next. We're going to ask you some questions. You're going to try and be tough and not answer. But this will be a lot easier if you just answer them. We're going to find out what we want one way or another." He lowered his head to see the man's eyes. "And all I have is time. This don't have to end today."

Everyone stood in silence for a minute letting the man take it all in. He looked around, taking each person in. After a moment, he simply looked back down at the floor without commenting. But Sarge was right there in his face and didn't let him have time to collect his thoughts.

"So let's kick this off," Sarge said. The man raised his eyes and Sarge started his questions. "I'll start with what we already know. You guys are holed up at the Elk's Camp." That statement caught the man off guard and he couldn't hide it. "You thought we didn't know that, didn't you? Well, we know some more. We also know there's some DHS turds and some of their lackeys." This time the man stared back, but it obviously came as a surprise to him.

The man looked around, sat back in the chair and swallowed. "Sounds like you already know everything."

Sarge nodded. "Well, we can always know more. Like, how many men are in the camp?"

The man shrugged. "More than one, less than a million."

Wagging a finger in his face, Sarge said. "Now, see that kind of smart ass shit is what's going to make this more unpleasant than it needs to be. So I'll give you another chance. How many?"

He simply slumped in the chair without replying. I walked

over to the work bench and picked up a small tack hammer. Moving over beside the man, he was eyeing me up. I twirled the hammer in my hand and said, "I'm not nearly as diplomatic as he is." Looking at Sarge, I added, "and that's saying something."

Sarge smiled. "I know he means business. After all, you really hurt one of his daughters with that little bomb of yours."

The man shrugged. "I don't know what you're talking about."

"Yes you do! I saw you!" Jess shouted.

The man looked up as Mike and Ted moved towards the girls. They were already on their way into the garage. While his attention was distracted, and to let the girls know this wasn't going to be that easy on him, I tapped the guy on the head with the hammer. Not a really hard hit, more like when you bang your head on a cabinet or something. But it was enough, and he let out a yelp.

Sarge laughed. "That smarts, don't it?"

The man was shouting something. Probably because he really wanted to rub his head. To reinforce that this was just the beginning, I tapped him a little harder this time. He squealed again and rocked back and forth in the chair. This time though, he had more to say.

"You're all dead! We're going to kill you all!"

"You're in no position to be making threats, my friend," Sarge said calmly.

The man was now wild-eyed. "Screw you! We know who you guys are." He looked at me. "We know who you are, Morgan. He then looked at Sarge and added, "and you, Linus."

While he was still looking at me, I tapped him on the head three times in rapid succession. I was trying not to hit him too hard, just hard enough to really smart. He started to scream and rock in the chair.

"Don't worry. If the lumps get too tall, I'll just tap 'em back down like in the old Bugs Bunny cartoons."

His eyes were watering now as he looked up at me. "Do not hit me again! I swear to God if you hit me again—"

I cut him off by tapping him on the head again. "Or what?" Then I tapped him again, "Or what?" And again, followed with the same question.

He was screaming out in pain. While none of the blows was particularly hard, the accumulated blows were starting to add up.

Sarge grabbed his chin and lifted it. The man's eyes were squeezed tightly closed. "If you want that man to stop hitting you, you'd better start talking." When the guy looked over at me, I raised the hammer as though I was going to whack him again. Then he screamed, "Okay, okay!"

Sarge smiled and winked at me. "That's more like it. So, back to the question. How many guys are over there?"

"There's about 53 of us, plus some women and kids. There, you happy now?" The guy answered and shook his head.

Sarge reached over and rubbed his head. "That shit smarts, don't it? How do you know our names?"

This time there was a smile on his face when he looked up. "We're the federal government. You don't think we know who you clowns are?"

Just to remind him where he was, I gave him a slightly harder tap on the head. He jolted as though he'd been shocked, and started to scream again. "You're dead! You're a fucking dead man!"

"You're awful sure of yourself. There's only fifty of you guys. Hell, with the National Guard, we've got more men than you do. What the hell makes you think you can take us? We could hit your camp and take it out," Sarge said.

With his eyes still tightly shut, he replied, "Maybe for now; but there are big changes in store for you assholes." He opened his eyes, "big changes."

"What kind of changes?" Sarge asked.

But there was no answer this time. He simply sat back in the chair and sniffed loudly. His eyes were tearing up badly. And as a result of that, his nose was running.

Using the hammer, I pushed the side of his head. "What kind of changes?" He didn't answer, so I pushed harder and asked again. He didn't answer, only glaring up at me. So I gave another rapid round of taps to his noggin, the last one having the most force yet. He went into a fit in the chair, rocking, gyrating and screaming, but still didn't answer.

Sarge looked over at Ted. "Hand me those tin snips right there, Teddy." Ted handed them over and Sarge grabbed the guy by his face. "I'm going to ask you one more time what kind of changes are coming and you better answer me."

The guy answered by spitting in Sarge's face. Sarge took a moment to take out a handkerchief and wipe his face. Looking at the man, he said, "That was a mistake." The guy glared back with half a sneer. In one quick motion, Sarge reached up with the snips and cut through the septum of the man's nose. His eyes went wide and he began to scream as blood poured from his nose. Sarge followed it up with a severe punch to his nose, snapping his head back and cutting off the scream.

When he brought his head back up, he looked around, dazed for a moment. Then he settled on me, and in a calm voice, he said, "Next time were going to kill all your daughters. All three of them, and that pretty wife of yours too."

I smashed him in the head with the hammer so hard it broke the handle. Drawing my pistol, I gripped the barrel like a handle and started to beat him as I screamed profanities. Savage blows rained down on the man's skull as blood splattered me. Sarge jumped from the chair and tried to stop me, but I gave him a hard shove, sending him sprawling to the ground as I continued to beat the man. The magazine popped out at some point, then I was grabbed on either side and pulled away. I fought against Mike and Ted as they pulled me back. We eventually fell to the floor in a struggling heap.

I was still screaming. I wanted to kill the man. I wanted to beat him, beat him to death with my own hands. I was trying to get back up and the garage was full of shouts and screams. I'd totally forgotten the girls were there. A sudden gunshot brought all of us back around. I stopped and looked up. Ted and Mike were still on me, but I could clearly see Lee Ann standing in front of the man. Her H&K was extended out in front of her in one hand. A small wisp of smoke was coming out of the barrel. I looked at the man's bloody face and a small hole just above his left eye.

Lee Ann stood there for a moment, then lowered the weapon. She looked at the man as blood oozed from him. "No you're not," was all she said before turning and walking out of the garage.

Sarge threw his hands up. "Damn it, Morgan! We needed to get more info from him!"

I rose to my feet in a daze. I was in shock seeing Lee Ann shoot the man. I looked around the garage. There was blood splattered all over the place. It was on the ceiling, on the back wall and the floor in front of him. Sarge was still fuming, but I pushed past him and followed my daughter outside. She was leaning on the front of the truck.

"Why'd you do that?" I asked.

She shrugged. "He said he was going to kill us. Kill mom.

He already hurt Taylor real bad." She looked up at me. "I'm not going to let anyone hurt us again."

Looking at her, I said, "But you shot him, like it was nothing."

"He wasn't the first." She looked up at me. "And he won't be the last."

I shook my head and wrapped my arms around her. "Baby, don't let this eat you up. Trust me, I know what it's like, and it isn't good." I felt her nod her head. "You're too young and sweet for this kind of thing."

She pulled back a little. "I'm not going to be a victim. I'm not going to let anyone hurt us. Just like you."

I pulled her in again. "Just don't let it take control of you, baby. This is ugly stuff, and you're too beautiful to let it take charge."

"Don't worry, dad. It's not like I enjoy it. I know you don't either. But if it has to be done, I'll do it."

I kissed the top of her head. "Why don't you guys take off. Maybe go relieve the guys at the barricade for a while. I'll come by later." I let go of her and wiped tears from my eyes. Jess, Fred and Aric were staring at us. Lee Ann motioned to them and they walked off together.

Thad was standing outside the garage. He'd been there the whole time but never said a word. He walked up and put his hand on my shoulder. "I'm going with them. I'm going to go have a talk with her."

I nodded as he followed the group off and turned my attention to the man in the garage. The 9mm didn't do much damage on the entry. But the beating certainly did. And the exit wound of the mushroomed projectile took out the back of his head. Mike and Ted were staring at the body, and Sarge was sitting on a stool shaking his head.

"Damn it, Morgan. I really wanted to know what the hell he was talking about, changes coming," Sarge said.

Still looking at the body, I replied, "Sorry. It wasn't a conscious decision. When he said they were going to kill my girls and Mel, I snapped."

He let out a long breath. "I don't blame you." He then let out a little chuckle. "Hell, if you hadn't done it, I would've."

"Guess we'll have to wait and see what he was talking about," Ted said.

Sarge jumped to his feet. "Like hell! We know where they are, and they know where we are. But they don't know we know where they are, so we're going to pay them an unexpected visit."

"You don't think we should leave? We know they're going to come back. Hell, they know your names now," Ted replied.

"I'm not going anywhere. We're not going to run again. All I want is to be left the hell alone. No way in hell am I going to tell my family we have to run into hiding again," I added.

Sarge shook his head. "No. We ain't running again. We're going to take it to *them* this time."

"What are you thinking?" Mike asked.

Sarge lifted his hat and scratched his head as he thought. "We're going to take that Goose and knock out as many trucks as we can. Use the sixty millimeter tube to keep 'em in their holes and apply some very accurate rifle fire on any fucker that sticks his head up."

Mike smiled like a jackass eating briars as he rubbed his hands together. "Aww hell, I'm gonna blow some shit up!"

"When do you want to do this?" Ted asked.

"As soon as possible," Sarge said.

"I have to meet with the engineers at the power plant tomorrow," I said.

Sarge nodded. "Alright, that's important. We need to try

and get that thing up and running if we can. We'll plan the attack for a couple days from now."

"What do you want to do with him?" Mike asked, pointing at the body.

Sarge glanced at him. "We'll take him with us tomorrow and leave him where they can find him."

Mike grinned devilishly. "Can I leave them a little something?"

Sarge looked over as a smile slowly spread across his face. "Mikey, I think that's a fine idea."

Ted rolled his eyes and moaned. "Oh hell." Then he looked at Sarge. "Why do you encourage him?"

Sarge guffawed. "As damn annoying as he is, he does have his uses."

"Yeah. When it absolutely, positively has to be destroyed, just call Mikey!" Mike shouted.

Waving Mike towards the body, Ted said, "Come on demo dork. Help me get this guy outta here."

"You need a hand?" I asked.

Ted shook his head. "No, we've got this."

"Sarge, you should come with me. Dalton said he's found heavy tracks somewhere and wanted to show us," I said.

He nodded, "Let's go."

We walked over to the barricade to find everyone still there. Dalton was talking with Fred, Jess and Aric, and Thad was talking with Lee Ann. Their relationship was still pretty strong and I was glad to see them together.

"So where's these tracks, Dalton?" Sarge asked.

Dalton pointed to the east. "Back over there. You wanna go take a look?"

"Yeah, let's go take a look see."

"I'll come with you," Danny said.

"Me too," Aric added.

We followed Dalton down the road past Danny's place. It reminded me of the trailer back there and what happened. It seemed everywhere I looked in this neighborhood, it reminded me of a body. As we got close to the end of the road, Dalton turned and pressed a finger close to his lips.

"Let's be real quiet. I don't know when these guys have been coming in here, so they could be here now."

Everyone gripped their weapons a little tighter and started to scan the area around us as we followed Dalton. He slowly led us through the brush. He'd stop often and look and listen, and we'd naturally follow suit. After a short walk into the woods behind our community, Dalton stopped and waved Sarge forward. I moved up as well.

Dalton knelt down and pointed to a patch of dirt and spoke in a whisper. "You can see here where they've been coming and going."

Sarge looked at the tracks, scanning the area around them. After a moment, he whispered, "You can tell they're trying to walk on the pine needles." Pointing, he said, "Look at the distance of this stride. Here's the left boot and here's the right." He looked around the area. "Sneaky bastards."

Dalton pointed down the trail. "It goes to the south there and turns west going back over behind Danny's house."

Sarge examined the ground again and looked at Dalton. "Let's go back. I want you to get with Mike and bring him out here. You two set up some surprises for these assholes."

Dalton smiled. "I like the way you think."

Sarge looked back and started motioning. "Everyone, back out real careful."

Once we were back on the road to the bunker, Sarge said,

"These dickheads think they've got us. But we're going to hit them before they can hit us."

Dalton raised his brow. "Taking the fight to them? What's your plan?" Sarge went over what he'd said back at the garage.

"How many people are going on this?" Aric asked.

Sarge glanced over at him. "You looking to get some scalps for yer belt?"

Aric worked his arm and nodded. "I think I'm ready to get in the game, coach."

Sarge smiled. "That's my man."

"I need to go to the power plant tomorrow. Anyone want to come with me?" I asked.

"I'll go," Aric said.

Looking sideways at him, I asked, "You getting tired of being cooped up around here?"

He nodded. "Kinda. Plus, it's about time I started doing my part around here. The arm's better now and I can help out more, and I want to."

"Good deal. We're going to go meet with the engineers at the plant and see if it's possible to get it up and running."

"Some power would be a wonderful thing," Sarge said.

I grunted. "Yeah, well even if the plant will run, there will be a shit ton of work to get the power out. We'll have to check all the lines and open or cut a number of them to get it where we want. Then we're going to have to hope the transformers are still good."

"Let's see if the plant will run first," Sarge said.

As we got back to the bunker, I replied, "That's the plan."

Dalton left to go get Mike so they could play demo man together. Thad was with Lee Ann talking, and I wandered over to them.

"How's it going?" I asked.

Thad looked at her, "We're good."

I smiled, "Glad to hear it."

Lee Ann looked at me and grinned. "I'm OK."

"Hey, Morg. I've got an idea on something I want to do," Thad said.

"What is it?" I asked.

"It's getting harder to feed the pigs. I want to go out behind the pasture there and string some hot wire around as much land back there as we can, and let the pigs loose."

Nodding, I replied, "Let them fend for themselves. Good idea. We'll just need wire and insulators."

"I've already got it all. Been going through all the places around here and piling them up. We've got enough to wire a hundred acres probably."

"When do you want to start?" I asked.

"How about after lunch?"

The girls were going to take on duty at the bunker for the rest of the afternoon. Thad, Danny and I were going to go grab something to eat real quick, then go get started on the pig project. Sarge said he'd join us. After all, Miss Kay was at Danny's.

CHAPTER 3

MEL, BOBBY AND MISS KAY were sitting on the back porch when we got to the house. Mary was out in the garden and Thad quickly excused himself to join her there. Mel smiled and looked at Miss Kay. "I think there's a relationship in the works there."

Miss Kay giggled just as Sarge walked out onto the porch. Bobbie smiled. "Speaking of relationships."

Miss Kay reached over and swatted her on the arm. Mel and Bobbie were laughing as Sarge announced, "Good afternoon, ladies." He looked around. "What's so funny?"

Mel tried to get herself under control as she replied, "Nothing, nothing. We were just talking about something is all."

Sarge narrowed his eyes. "Mmm, something huh? It's been my experience that a bunch of women sitting around are never *just talking*."

As Mel and Bobbie started to laugh again, Miss Kay got up and told Sarge to take a seat. I looked at Mel with a questioning glance. She waved me off. Guess I'll hear about it later. We took seats at one of the picnic tables as Miss Kay carried a large pot out and set it on the table. Bobbie went in and came back out with a stack of bowls, and we were each handed a steaming bowl of soup.

After blowing the steam off, I took a bite. "This is really good. What is it?"

"Just a vegetable stew," Miss Kay replied.

Looking at the bowl, I asked, "No meat?"

"We're running really low on meat," Mel said.

"I can't hunt the squirrels anymore. There's nothing left to hunt now," Little Bit said. She was sitting on the floor working on a large puzzle.

"Oh there's always something to hunt, kiddo," I said.

"Yeah. We'll find something," Danny added.

"This sure is a good stew, Miss Kay," Sarge said.

"Thank you, Linus," she replied with a smile.

"You guys need to figure something out about meat," Bobbie said.

"Thad, you gonna eat?" Danny called out.

Thad looked up and smiled. He spoke to Mary and headed for the porch. As he took a seat, he said, "Sorry, I just gotta tend my plants."

"Yeah. You're tending something," I replied with a smile.

Thad visibly blushed and I laughed at him. He shook his head and said, "You a mess Morgan," and set to the bowl of stew in front of him. After a couple of bites, he looked up at the ladies. "This is really good."

"Miss Kay cooked it. We just prepared the veggies," Mel said.

Nodding his head, Thad said, "Whoever did, it's good. You ladies surely do make the most of what we have."

"So you guys are going to string some fence today?" Sarge asked.

"Just hot wire. Give them pigs some place to forage," Thad said.

Sarge nodded and scooped another spoon full. "Out behind

that pasture in the woods?" Thad nodded and Sarge added, "I'll send someone over to provide security for you guys."

"That would be good," Danny said.

Finishing up lunch, I gave Mel a kiss as she was filling a bowl with stew. "Is that for Taylor?" I asked.

She nodded. "Yeah, she's sleeping. I'll take her some lunch."

"How's she feeling?"

Setting the bowl on the counter Mel replied, "She was in good spirits before taking her nap."

And that made me feel good too, very good.

She turned around. "You going to be here for dinner?"

"Of course. We're just going to be putting up some wire. I'll be over by Thad's house."

She smiled, "Wonderful."

"Thank you ladies for the lunch. It was delicious as always," Sarge said as he picked up his carbine.

"You're welcome, guys," Bobbie said. Then she added, "go find us some meat."

"Some meat would be nice," Miss Kay said.

Slinging my carbine I said, "I'll see what we can do."

We headed off to get started stringing the wire. It would make it a lot easier dealing with the pigs, not having to feed them in the pen. We stopped by my place so I could grab a machete and an axe before heading over to Thad's. At the barn, Thad pointed out a large pile of yellow plastic insulators and a couple rolls of wire.

"I been scrounging them all over the neighborhood. There's still a lot out there I didn't get."

"Yeah. Almost everyone around here used it in one form or another," Danny said.

Hearing us at the barn, the pigs started making a ruckus,

squealing and banging into the sides of the pen. I looked in at them. "Looks like they're hungry."

Thad smiled. "They're always hungry. They're pigs." He then pointed out a large sow, "Look how low her belly is. She's going to drop a litter any day."

Danny laughed. "Looks like she could use a skateboard under that belly."

I picked up a bucket full of insulators and said, "Well, let's get to it."

Thad went to get a couple hammers and Danny grabbed the wire. We walked out to the back of the pasture and looked the woods over. When Thad showed up, I asked him what he was thinking.

He pointed to the south. "The woods go back there for a couple hundred yards before turning to pasture again. I was thinking of clearing a line right off the edge of the fence there and running straight through, then cut across the edge of pasture. Then cut a line back on the other side and we'll have them hemmed in."

"You want to keep the wire about a foot off the ground?" Danny asked.

Thad nodded. "That'd be plenty. They only need to touch it once or twice before they figure it out."

Pulling the machete out of its sheath, I said, "I'll start cutting a line."

And so we got to work. I started clearing brush with the machete. It wasn't always a straight line as I would weave back and forth to allow for large trees. They would make good places to nail in the insulators. Thad and Danny worked behind me hanging those. The bush in the area wasn't very thick and made the job of clearing it pretty easy. The hardest part was actually the edge of the pasture.

I made it through the wood line without too much trouble. But once at the transition line between the woods and pasture, the grass proved to be quite thick. It took a lot of chopping to clear it and the other brush. It was hard work, but I actually enjoyed it. It kept my mind off things that had taken place earlier, something I still haven't really processed. But lately, I enjoyed any kind of work that put a tool other than a firearm in my hand.

I was on my knees hacking at the tall grass when Jamie walked up. I looked up to her holding a sickle and looking at me with a smirk on her face.

"Wouldn't this be a lot easier?"

I shook my head. "I guess it would. Didn't even think about trying to get a better tool."

She tossed it to me. "I watched you for a while and finally took pity on you and asked Thad if he knew where one was."

With a smirk of my own, I asked, "Just how long did you watch before taking pity on me?"

"Till I started to get tired," she replied with a laugh.

Picking up the curved blade, I said, "Hope I didn't wear you out."

It certainly made the job of cutting the grass a lot easier. Thad and Danny caught up to me because of the slow going and pitched in to help. With Jamie and Ian hanging around to keep an eye on us, we finished up the line and had insulators hung all the way around the patch of woods by early evening.

Thad wiped his forehead with a rag as he looked down the cleared line. "We'll string the wire tomorrow and let those hogs loose."

Ian looked around the patch of woods. "Is there anything in there they can eat?"

"Oh yeah, plenty," Danny replied.

Ian shook his head. "I don't see anything."

"You get out there and root around and you'll find plenty," Thad offered.

Jamie laughed. "Yeah, Ian. Get out there and root around. Want me to help rub you face in the dirt?"

Ian snorted, "You wish."

Jamie smiled, "You have no idea how much."

Now I had to laugh. "Why don't you two just go ahead and bump uglies and get it over with."

Jamie looked as though she'd just seen a unicorn. Ian, however, broke out in a raucous laugh, bending over and holding his stomach. Jamie's face narrowed and she glared at me but didn't say anything. It made me laugh. Shrugging, I said, "Just sayin'."

Thad started to laugh as well, until Jamie cut her eyes to him. The smile on his face faded as he started collecting tools and headed for the barn. Danny was smiling and shaking his head as we followed Thad's lead. We left Ian and Jamie to stew. Well, Jamie was certainly stewing.

"I'm going to the house and get cleaned up before dinner," Danny said.

"Sounds good to me," I replied.

We met Thad at the barn where he was putting tools away as the pigs complained. He turned as we walked up. "What are you two going to do now?"

"Go take a shower before dinner," Danny replied.

Thad smiled. "Me too. That water tower is the best thing since sliced bread."

I snorted. "You got sliced bread you're holding out?"

Thad laughed. "I wish. I guess the water tower is better than sliced bread since we ain't got any."

"How's the water temp?" Danny asked.

"It's perfect. It's warm, but not too hot. Perfect."

"Bet it gets a little colder in the winter," I said.

"I been thinking about that. I'm going to look around for all the black spray paint I can find and paint the tank. During the winter it'll help keep it warm," Thad said.

"Better than nothing," Danny added.

With a nod I said, "Alright, lads. I'm off. See you at dinner."

Thad went in the house and grabbed a change of clothes and a towel before heading down the hall to the bathroom. He could hear the water running when he got to the door and knocked.

"I'll be done in a minute," Jess's voice called back.

Thad smiled and went back out to the living room and sat down on the couch. Since the water tower was installed, the girls were showering every day. Thad kept an eye on the tank; and just as he'd suspected, the level dropped dramatically the first couple of days before seeming to slow some. He was going to have to fill it soon, like tomorrow probably. But there was still sufficient pressure for a shower and to fill the toilets.

He sat on the couch for what seemed like an eternity. Getting a little annoyed, he got up and started down the hall. Just then, the bathroom door opened and Jess stepped out wrapped in a towel with another one wrapped around her head.

She smiled sheepishly. "Sorry, it just feels so good!"

Thad smiled. It was his natural response. "I know it does, but you know I have to fill that thing."

Bobbing her head, she replied, "I know, I know. It just feels so good. The water is warmer than at Danny's, and I can take one every day."

His smile broadening a little as he replied, "And you can help fill that tank tomorrow too."

Jess stepped over and, standing on her tip toes, she wrapped her arms around his neck. "I love you too, Thad." Then she kissed him on the cheek before quickly heading to her room.

Blushing, Thad replied, "I love you too."

"I know you do!" She shouted back as she shut the door.

Smiling and shaking his head, Thad went into the bathroom. He'd take a little longer with his shower too. After all, it was really warm water.

We stopped by the bunker as we passed. The girls were gone and Mike and Ted were there with Dalton now.

"You guys on for a while?" I asked.

Ted nodded. "Yeah, me and Tweedle Dumb here."

"Guess that makes you Tweedle Dee then," Mike shot back.

Looking over his shoulder, Ted said, "Yeah. I got the D and the umb."

Mike shrugged, "You are a subject matter expert on dumb."

Ted laughed. "After spending so many years with your dumbass, I am indeed."

I laughed and looked at Dalton. "So what's that make you?"

He jumped up on top of the bunker and struck a pose with his hands on his hips. "Why, the Mad Hatter of course!" And he followed it with a maniacal laugh.

Ted looked up at him. "Yes, yes you are."

Laughing, I added, "Indeed."

Danny pointed to a long green tube leaned against the side of the bunker. "What's that?"

Mike smiled. "That's a Goose. It's a recoilless rifle. It blows shit up."

Danny was impressed. "Nice."

"Yeah, those assholes show up with another MRAP and I'm turning it into scrap metal," Mike replied.

"It's nice to have something to deal with them," I added.

Ted nudged the weapon with the toe of his boot. "This will more than deal with them."

"Let's just hope we don't need to," Danny said.

We all agreed to that sentiment. We said goodbye and headed home. I wanted to check on Taylor and hang out with her a little while. As we walked, I looked at the little raised spot on my arm where the TB shot was given. Danny looked over and asked, "How's it looking?"

I shrugged. "Hell if I know. Looks swollen to me, but I wouldn't know good from bad."

"Doc check it lately?"

"Going to have him look at it at dinner."

"Hopefully it's good news."

I shrugged. "I don't think I have it. I mean, I don't feel sick. I'm not coughing or anything. I'm sure it's fine. But it's still kinda creepy waiting."

Danny grunted. "No shit. I wouldn't want to."

I looked sideways at him. "You know, if it's positive, then everyone's going to have to be tested. If they have enough tests."

Danny cut his eyes at me. "Then you better be negative."

Laughing, I replied, "I'm pretty negative these days."

Danny laughed. "Yeah, I guess." Then with a serious tone, he added, "But you better be negative."

I laughed as I slapped him on the back, and we parted ways at my driveway. Little Bit was sitting on the porch with the dogs when I walked up. Meat Head's tail thumped the porch as she scratched his belly. Drake barely lifted his eyes to acknowledge my arrival. At least Little Sister got up after stretching and wandered over for her obligatory scratching.

"Look at these lazy dogs," I said with a smile.

Little Bit looked up. "They're so cute."

"They're lazy!" I replied with a laugh.

She lay on the floor and snuggled up to Meat Head and smiled. "I like it."

Grinning, I shook my head. "How can you snuggle up to that smelly hound?"

Meat Head rolled his head over and licked her face. "He doesn't smell that bad." I laughed and went inside.

Mel was sitting in the living room and looked up from a book. In the Before she never read. It just wasn't normal for her to sit and read. Now, however, she and Bobbie scoured the houses for books, and both of them were always reading. If they weren't reading, then they were talking about books. I guess that was a bit of a return to the old ways. Books were now, once again, a distraction. An escape from the harsh realities of daily life. They seemed to really get into the romance novels. Little Bit also spent a lot of time reading, though she preferred adventure stories with fairies and dragons. I had a stack of books too, though I'd already read most of mine from before. For the rest of the group, they weren't much fun to read. Books on edible plants and the Fox Fire series weren't nearly as exciting as romantic interludes on a sailboat or the trials of a fairy princess.

"What'cha reading there, babe?" I asked as I sat on the couch.

Folding the book closed, she laid it cover-down in her lap. With a smile, she replied, "Nothing you'd be interested in."

I reached and turned the book over to expose the cover,

depicting some muscled hunk with no shirt on. With a laugh, I said, "Not going to learn much in there that'll help us out."

She turned her book over. "That's your job."

"How's Taylor?" I asked.

"Good, she's reading some vampire book."

I rolled my eyes. "Oh God. I remember those things. Back into that huh?"

"She can't really do much right now. It's good for her."

Standing up, I said, "I'm going to check on her."

Mel opened her book. "Good. I need to see what Blake does."

Shaking my head, I wandered down the hall. Stopping at her door, I tapped on it. "Come in."

I opened the door and was met with a smile. "Hey, Dad!"

I sat on the edge of her bed and ran my hand over her head. "Hey, kiddo. How are you feeling today?"

She perked up. "I'm feeling really good today. I walked to the bathroom by myself. Mom was there, but I didn't let her help me. I did it all by myself."

I leaned over and hugged her. "That's awesome. You'll be out of this bed regularly in no time."

"I can't wait. I'm so sick of being here." She laid her book down and looked at me. "I want to get up and get back to normal."

"You will. Just don't rush it."

She rolled her eyes. "I just want to be able to get out of bed and sit on the couch or maybe on the porch. Plus, I want to be able to walk over to Bobbie's when we eat. It sucks being in here all alone."

"Well, you spend a couple of days walking around the house and we'll get you over to Bobbie's."

She smiled. "Thanks, Dad."

Before I could reply, there was a sudden flurry of voices in the living room. I looked down the hall to see Lee Ann, Fred and Jess. Mel was talking to them. I looked at Taylor. "I'll get out of here, looks like you have visitors."

"Yeah, we're going to play Scrabble. Can I go out to the dining room so we can play on the table?"

"Of course," I replied with a smile as I left the room.

Walking into the living room, Jess looked at me. "Hey, Morgan."

I looked at her, then around the room. "What's that smell?"

She smiled. "It's perfume, if you must know."

"You know you can shower now, right?" I replied.

With her hands on her hips, she shot back. "For your information, I did!" Flipping her hair, she replied in a dismissive tone. "A girl can still dress up."

It was then I noticed she was wearing a dress. I'd never seen her in a dress. For the first time, she actually looked like a woman, a pretty damned fine one at that.

"Wow, I just noticed."

"Doesn't she look beautiful?" Mel asked.

I nodded. "Yeah," and my mind started turning. "What are you two up to?" I asked, looking at Fred. She was in a dress too. With cowboy boots, no less.

Fred started laughing. Twirling her skirt, she said, "We just felt pretty today."

"Where's Aric?"

"This is a girl's night," Jess said as she waltzed past me.

Fred followed her. "Yeah."

Little Bit came out of her room in a dress too. "Daddy, it's girl's night!"

"What the hell's going on here?" I asked, shaking my head.

Mel stood up and headed for the bedroom. "You heard them. Its girl's night. So you need to find someplace to go."

Jess laughed. "Yeah, don't go away mad. Just go away."

I walked into the kitchen mumbling to myself about my house being taken over and being asked to make myself scarce in no uncertain terms. I went to the fridge and poured myself a cup of tea before heading for the bedroom as well. Mel was beside the bed pulling a dress of her own up over one shoulder.

I gave her a little whistle. "Maybe you should do girl's night more often," I said as I moved towards her.

She stopped me with a hand on my chest. "I don't think so, mister. This is girl's night. And I don't mean the porno kind either."

I looked her up and down. She looked amazing in the dress, standing barefoot in our room.

"Aw, come on," I pleaded.

She pulled the dress over her other shoulder and turned. Lifting her hair, she said, "Zip me up."

I stepped close to her and slowly pulled the zipper up her back. She spun around and gave me a kiss, then asked what I was doing.

"I'm going to take shower."

She looked down at me and with a devilish grin and said, "Looks like you could use one, a cold one."

"You're evil, woman."

She leaned in close and whispered in my ear. "I know. Now hurry up and get out of here."

As she left the room, I heard Bobbie come in the front door. It was turning into an estrogen fest out there. But I had to smile. They were just having fun. Like little girls, they were all playing dress-up. There was no reason now to ever dress up or try to look good, but they obviously needed it. It gave me an idea, one that would take some time to put together, but I think everyone would like.

I showered and dressed in clean clothes. Looking at the laundry pile, I knew it would soon be time to get the wash done. It was a bit of a chore not using the machine. We could run the generator for it, but it was a waste of precious fuel. Mel fought tooth and nail for a long time about it, but finally gave in. Of course, I had to help. It was a lot of work. I wish I'd invested in one of the numerous wash systems I'd looked at before. They seemed a little expensive at the time; and I always thought, *I can build that*. But I never did. Now I would gladly pay twice the price for one.

Coming out of the bedroom, I was met with laughter. The ladies were in the living room cueing up a video on the laptop. I was saying my goodbyes, looking to make a hasty escape when another woman appeared from the hallway leading to the bathroom. I didn't recognize her and stared for a moment. Like the others, she too was in a pretty dress and cowboy boots.

She crossed her arms over her chest and cocked her hips to the side. "What?" She asked.

Then I realized it was Jamie. I'd never even imagined her in something other than the BDUs she always wore, but she looked amazing. Still surprised, I simply replied, "Uh, nothin'."

"Then quit staring at me like a slack-jawed fool," she said as she passed me.

I smiled and turned to the door. Pausing, I turned back around. "You ladies all look beautiful tonight." I thought it was a nice gesture. But I was met with shouts, various objects thrown in my direction and several orders to *Get out!* Still smiling, I left the house to the ladies.

I made my way over to Danny's house. He was sitting on the front porch. "Come on up and grab a chair," he said, motioning to the rocker beside him.

"Did you see any of them?" I asked as I sat down.

"Just Bobbie, when she was leaving."

"You should see my house. They're all in there, even Jamie. And they're all dressed up. Makeup and everything."

"Yeah, Bobbie said they wanted a girl's night."

Shaking my head, I replied, "Seems like a waste. There's some hot ass women over there." Then I looked at Danny. "Who knew?"

Danny laughed. "Probably a good thing. Could you imagine some of these guys around here seeing them all dolled up?"

"Yeah, I guess." I replied. Then a smirk appeared on my face. "I imagine it would be hard on Mike's face. I have a feeling he knows what it's like to be slapped."

"Ian too. I think Jamie would take him down, dress and all."

Then I laughed. "He'd probably try to piss her off just to get her to do it. She looked good. They all did. You should see the dress Mel was wearing."

"Let 'em have their fun."

The door opened and Miss Kay stuck her head out. "You boys hungry?"

Standing up, I replied, "Yes, ma'am!"

"Well, come on in here and let's get you fed."

As we followed her into the house, I asked, "Why aren't you over there at the party?"

Mary was standing in the kitchen. "We had to make sure you guys got your supper."

Over her shoulder, Miss Kay added, "Someone has to do it."

"We could have fended for ourselves," Danny said.

Miss Kay turned and smiled. "Oh, I'm sure you could have, but it wasn't a bother."

The way she said it though, led me to believe she didn't really think we could! Tonight's dinner was the leftovers from lunch. Nothing ever went to waste. When a meal was prepared, it was eaten until it was gone. We were soon joined by Thad and Dalton. And about the time Danny and I finished our meal, Sarge, Perez and Ian showed up.

"You're late. We ate it all," Thad said as they came through the door.

"Just couldn't wait, could you?" Sarge fired back.

"Like one big dog does another," I replied.

Sarge grunted. "Big dog, my ass." He came up beside me at the table. "Move your ass, pup." I smiled and picked up my bowl to make room for him.

"Don't let him bother you, Linus. You know I have some for you," Miss Kay said as she set a bowl in front of him.

Sarge smiled at her. "I know you do. I always let the kids eat before I do."

Thad smiled. "Who you callin' a kid, little man?"

Chewing a mouthful of stew, Sarge pointed his spoon at Thad. "It ain't the size of the dog in the fight. It's the size of the fight in the dog."

Still smiling, Thad raised his arm, making a muscle. "This dog's got plenty of fight."

Sarge nodded. "I know you do. I'd just have to shoot your big ass." Thad's smile quickly faded and he laughed, blowing stew out his nose and mouth.

We all started to laugh as Perez wiped the mess from his arm, having caught most of it. "Ay yos mios!" Perez groaned.

Sarge was laughing at Perez and said, "How many times I gotta tell you, *English!* You chili chomper!"

"Usted vieja cabra," Perez shot back.

Sarge laughed even harder now and looked across the table, doing his best impression of a goat, "Baaa aa baa aa!"

In a calm almost quiet voice, Dalton said, "La cabra siempre tira al monte."

"See, he knows!" Sarge shouted.

"What the hell did you say?" Danny asked.

"The goat always seeks out the mountain heights," Dalton replied, giving Sarge a nod.

Shaking my head, I said, "You suck any harder and your eyes'll cross."

Dalton busted out into a deep laugh, joined by several others. Even Sarge laughed, adding, "Don't let him fool you. Never underestimate the value of ass-kissing."

Perez leaned over and patted his ass cheek. "Come here, old man. I've got some work for you."

Sarge snorted. "Pick a spot, Beaner. You're all ass!"

The reply got a smile from Perez. Shaking his head, he turned his attention back to his meal.

I carried my bowl into the kitchen. Mary took it from me. "I'll take care of this."

"You don't have to clean up after me. Why aren't you over there?" I asked.

"We're going over in a bit. We just wanted to make sure dinner was taken care of."

"Good. You two need to go have some fun too," I replied.

"Where you going Morgan?" Sarge called.

"Headed to the bunker to relieve the guys so they can come eat."

"Alright. I'll stop by later. Need to talk about tomorrow."

Danny was on duty with me and we walked to the bunker together. I could hear slaps and Mike bitching as we got closer. As we walked up, he jumped down from the roof of the bunker. "Thank God, you're here!"

"What's eatin' your ass?" I asked.

Collecting his gear, he replied, "Oh, you'll see soon enough."

"Mosquitos are driving him nuts tonight; and in turn, he's driving me nuts," Ted said.

Mike slapped at another of the blood suckers. "I've never seen them like this before."

"They are pretty bad," Ted added as he slammed his palm against his forehead.

"You guys go get something to eat. We'll take it from here," Danny said.

"You have my pity," Ted said as they headed off.

Danny slapped at his arm. "Damn, they are bad."

I was waving the little bastards away from my head, "Yeah they are. Let me go get something that will help."

I walked back up the road towards my house. I knew what I was looking for grew just a little ways away. Finding the Beautyberry bush, I cut several leafy stems and carried them back to the bunker. I handed several of them to Danny.

"Here, strip the leaves like this and crush them up. Rub it on your face and neck, your arms too." I was going through the motions as I said it. The leaves have a pungent odor that mosquitos don't like. While not as effective as chemical repellants, it's certainly better than nothing.

"How well does this work?" Danny asked.

"It's better than nothing," I said. Then I took another couple of stems and crushed the leaves, leaving them on the stalk. Taking off my boonie hat, I wove the thin stems into the nylon webbing. "Hang it around your head too."

Danny did the same as I had, though he made a wreath to lay over his ball cap. It did help keep them off our faces and neck. Our arms though were a different story.

"I need to remember to wear long sleeves," Danny said.

As I rolled my sleeves down, I said, "It doesn't help much. They bite right through it."

We settled into trying to ignore the bugs while at the same time trying to keep them off us. They would be bad for a while and begin to taper off later. In an effort to distract myself, I pulled out the little AM/FM/shortwave radio from a pocket on my vest. I'd started carrying it around and scanning through the bands every now and then. On a clear night like this, I could usually pick up several foreign stations. Though I'd yet to find anything broadcast from here. To increase the reception of the small radio, I would string a wire antenna into a tree. It was in a small reel and had a clip to connect it to the telescoping antenna on the radio. Beside the bunker was a small persimmon tree. We'd left it because Danny and I both knew this tree bore fruit.

With the antenna up, I sat on the roof of the bunker and turned the little radio on. As I started scanning through the bands, I heard Doc's voice from the darkness.

"Hey, Morgan. Let me take a look at your arm."

"Where the hell have you been hiding?" I asked as I rolled my sleeve up.

"I was at the house," he replied as I stretched my arm out. He took my arm and turned on a small light to inspect the test site. Doc pulled a small paper marked with measurements and laid it on my arm. He looked up and smiled. "Looks like you're in the clear. It hasn't grown any, so you're good to go."

I let out the breath I didn't know I was holding. "Thanks, Doc. I was really worried."

"Can't say I blame you. But you're out of the woods."

"Good!" Danny said from the other side of the bunker.

"You going to hang out?" I asked.

Wiping a mosquito from his ear, Doc replied, "Yeah, why not. Got nothing else to do." He looked at the little radio and asked, "What's that?"

Picking it up, I replied, "It's a small shortwave. I like to scan the bands and see what I can hear."

"Pick anything up?"

As I turned the radio on, I said, "Lots of foreign stuff. Nothing to speak of, though."

I set the radio on one of the bands and pressed the scan button, and the radio began scrolling through the frequencies. After a moment, it stopped on one, but it was rapid-fire Spanish. "Figures," I said, and pressed the scan button again. It continued on for a bit and found several more Spanish stations, one German and what I think was French, but in a strange accent.

With no luck on that band, I switched the radio to another and pressed the scan button again. This time it hit a station that was actually in English. Not just English, but from the way it sounded, it was someone with a Midwestern accent.

…..are moving against the DHS in the suburbs of Atlanta. Doc slapped me on the arm and pointed at the radio as the voice continued. *In intense house to house fighting, the Marines are gaining ground. The fighting is intense as it is now apparent the Feds armed street gangs that were fighting alongside them.*

In the south, the Navy has secured the Exxon/Mobile refinery in Baton Rouge. Pumping continues on offshore rigs with assistance from Navy Seabees and auxiliary ships providing power to the rigs. With the addition of the production capacity of the Baton Rouge plant, the fuel limitations are now easing, allowing additional strikes against Federal targets. However, the plant is not up to full capacity as a result of sabotage that caused moderate damage and several casualties among plant workers. The injured were airlifted to Fort Polk and are being treated by the 115th Combat Support Hospital. God bless the men and woman of our armed forces, fighting the good fight on behalf of the people of this nation.

You're listening to John Jacob Schmidt on the Radio Free

Redoubt, broadcasting to all of you in occupied territory, as well as those outside the wire. Bringing you the news you need in these uncertain times. On the international front, the UN Security Council today released a statement saying that the deteriorating situation in North America is becoming a humanitarian crisis. The Secretary General of the UN, Hussein Torboko, has asked the Security Council to consider a resolution to send UN peace keepers to the US in an attempt to quell the violence. The UK ambassador to the UN objected vehemently to the proposal, as did the Canadians and Australians. However, before the motion was even brought to the floor for discussion, the Russians and Chinese both said they were willing to assist the US, "in this, their greatest time of need." Marine General Bill Puller replied to the UN in unequivocal terms, stating that any foreign troops setting foot on US soil will be seen as an invading force and dealt with accordingly.

I was stunned by what I was hearing. We'd been in the dark for so long about what the rest of the world was doing, and now all of a sudden we hear the Chinese and Russians want to invade! Apparently, I wasn't the only one surprised. At some point, Danny came over and said exactly what I was thinking, "What the hell?"

Doc was a little more certain in his response. "Fuck them! Those bastards try that shit and we'll be shooting blue helmets as well as black ones!"

The broadcast continued. *I don't think they will like their reception. Tune in at 2100 hours for our next update.*

A woman's voice then came on. *Good evening, patriots. Prepare for a message.* After a ten-second pause, she continued. *The Maple Tree sings a lullaby. The Maple Tree sings a lullaby...* She then proceeded to read off a series of numbers.

...29185 39458 89085 57723 31931 94832 49495 22840

As the woman repeated the message a second time, I asked

Doc if we should have copied it. When she finished the message, AC/DC's Thunderstruck came on.

"Yeah, probably," Doc replied.

"Who the hell is this?" Danny asked.

"I don't know," Doc replied. "But they're obviously sending coded messages to someone."

"You think you can decode it?" Danny asked.

Shaking his head, Doc responded. "Without the code sheet, I don't think even the NSA could decode it."

"I know who they are. I used to listen to Radio Free Redoubt. They ran AmRRON radio nets around the country. This is exactly the kind of thing they trained for back then. We'll have to start checking for their broadcasts. Don't know why I haven't come across this until now," I said.

Doc's face was suddenly illuminated in a bright orange glow. We all looked towards the source of the light and saw a large ball of flame rising into the sky as a loud boom hit us. Doc realized what we were looking at first.

"That's Tyler and Brandy's place. It's on fire!"

As Doc was about to run towards the house, a large caliber machinegun began firing at the bunker. The heavy bullets slammed into the log structure sending us diving to the ground.

Danny shouted, "What the hell's going on?"

I crawled into the bunker and chanced a peek out one of the firing ports. "There's a truck down there, one of those armored ones!"

Doc came crawling in and shouted at Danny. "Get the Goose and toss it in here!"

Small arms fire began to sound from behind us. I could hear numerous weapons firing and started to worry about Mel and the girls. Then I heard the unmistakable sound of two shotgun blasts in rapid succession. That had to be Thad and his coach gun. Danny tossed the Gustav into the bunker and I heard him start cussing. I looked back to see him and Dalton trying to get free of one another.

Dalton looked into the bunker. "They're coming in from the back too, but I think they're under control." As he spoke, there was a large explosion to the back of the neighborhood. Dalton smiled. "That'll teach the bastards!"

Mel and the rest of the girls were watching Dirty Dancing on my laptop. There were oil lamps and candles set around the living room, and they were busy talking and laughing over the movie when they heard the boom. Jamie was instantly on her feet, carbine in hand as she moved towards the front door.

"What was that?" Bobbie asked.

As Jamie got to the front door and looked out the window, she shouted. "Fire! Brandy's house is on fire!"

She was reaching for the door knob when the sliding glass door leading to the back porch shattered, sending glass flying into the dinning room. Little Bit screamed and pulled a pillow from the sofa over her head. Jamie spun as two men came through the opening. She began firing as she brought the weapon up to her shoulder. The lead man went down, and the one behind him stumbled over the body and fired at the same time, sending a wild spray of bullets into the house. Drywall dust and insulation rained down.

Jamie fell back against the door and onto the floor as the man tried to regain his feet. Lee Ann ran into the kitchen from the opposite side while the man's attention was focused on the entry into the living room. She raised her H&K and squeezed the trigger, letting out a long burst of 9mm. Mel got to her feet and she, Fred and Jess rounded the corner to the kitchen at the same moment a third man appeared in the shattered glass door. The second man was on the floor, riddled with bullets. The three women all raised their pistols and fired in unison, sending a hail of lead into the man in the door. He never had a chance to pull the trigger.

Mel looked over her shoulder and shouted at Mary. "Get Ashley to the bathroom!"

Mary quickly grabbed her with one hand and Miss Kay by the other and ran towards the bathroom.

Thad, Sarge, Mike and Ted were all sitting on the back porch of Danny's house after dinner talking. Miss Kay and Mary had left to hang out with the rest of the ladies and watch a movie. It was dark, having turned off the lanterns to conserve fuel. They were talking about the need to hit the Elk's Camp and how Sarge thought it should be done, when they heard the boom. They were instantly on their feet and ran to the front of the house. They were coming out of Danny's gate onto the road when they ran directly into a group of six raiders. In the darkness, none had seen the other until they collided in the road.

Mike, being younger and faster, had crashed into two men of the group, them falling to the ground in a heap of flailing arms and legs. Ted hit the light from his carbine to reveal the other four men, who were obviously caught off guard. He began to fire as Thad pulled the coach gun from his back scabbard. Sarge began firing on the men with Ted, who were shooting back in a panic. But this was all taking place at contact range; they could physically touch one another.

The two men Mike ran into were fighting with him. One of

the men had a grip on Mike's carbine and was jerking it to keep him from getting his feet under him. With the single-point sling wrapped around him, it was as good as a handle. Mike fumbled for the quick release, trying to disconnect himself from the weapon. The second man charged Mike and wrapped him in a bear hug from behind. Thad stepped up and swung the coach gun at the crown of the man's head with all the force he could muster, which was considerable. He split the man's skull and he collapsed. As the body hit the ground, Thad fired one barrel into the man's face.

At the same moment, Mike finally found the release and the weapon came free. Both he and the man he struggled with fell back away from one another. Mike drew his pistol as he fell and fired when his ass hit the ground. Thad swung the old shotgun around, holding it at arm's length, and pulled the second trigger, sending a load of number four buck into the man's chest, along with the hail of .45 rounds Mike was raining into the man.

Thad dropped the shotgun and drew his pistol, spinning around and looking for more targets. Ted and Sarge were back to back doing the same. Six bodies were on the ground around them. Mike got to his feet and picked up his carbine.

"Anybody hit?" Sarge asked.

Everyone patted themselves and replied in the negative. In the light from Ted's carbine, Thad said, "Ted, your head's bleeding."

Ted reached up and felt the warm wetness on the side of his head. Sarge grabbed his chin, turning Ted's head to the side. "You're alright. Shot the top of your ear off." He patted Ted's shoulder. "You're one lucky son of a bitch."

Ted was pawing at his ear. "What do you mean, shot it off? Is it gone?"

"Hell yeah, it's gone. Come on. We'll worry about that later," Sarge said as he started towards Tyler's place.

Ted searched the ground with his light. "We've got to find it!"

"For what? Not like we can put it back on. What are you going to do? Make a damn necklace out of it?" Sarge shot back.

Ted was in mild shock. "Fuck that! It's my ear!"

Sarge grabbed Ted by his plate carrier. "Get yer head outta yer ass! This shit ain't over, and you know there's no medicine in a gun fight! We'll tend to your grape when this shit's over. Now get yer ass in gear!"

Mike ran past Ted and slapped him on the shoulder. "Come on, Teddy. Let's get these fuckers!"

Ted looked down at the men on the ground. "Shot my ear off, you sons of bitches!" And he proceeded to stomp one of the bodies in the face. Ted looked up with a wild expression, let out a scream, and then took off after Mike.

Thad picked up the coach gun and broke the action open. The two spent shells ejected and he dropped in two more. Sarge looked at him. "You OK, Thad?"

Thad nodded and was about to reply when there was an explosion from the back of the neighborhood. Sarge looked in the direction of the sound and said, "That's Dalton's IED. Let's go take a look." Thad nodded, and they moved down the road in the direction of the explosion.

Mel looked around the house. "Is everyone OK? Is anyone hurt?"

Taylor was on the floor searching frantically. "Where's my gun? I can't find my gun!"

"I think we're alright," Jess said.

Mel looked at Lee Ann. "Go check on Ashley. They're in the bathroom." Lee Ann nodded as she methodically removed the magazine from her H&K and placed a fresh one in. She pulled the bolt back slightly and checked to make sure it was chambered, and walked to the bathroom.

"Aww shit," Jamie said. She was lying on the floor in front of the door looking at her blood-covered hand.

"Oh God, Jamie's hurt!" Fred yelled.

They rushed to her side. "Are you OK? Where is it?" Jess asked.

Mel looked around. "We need to blow these lights out. Taylor, can you take care of that for us?"

Taylor was getting to her feet, having found her weapon on the floor under pillows from the sofa. She began extinguishing the candles and lanterns. Fred reached over and took one oil lamp from the top of a bookshelf and brought it over beside Jamie.

"Let me see it," she said as she moved Jamie's hand.

"Son of a bitch! I really liked this dress! First time I wear dress, and I get fuckin' shot!" Jamie shouted.

Miss Kay came out of the hallway, tripping over the piles of pillows on the floor. "Who's hurt?"

"Jess, get my vest. There's a blowout kit on it," Jamie said.

Mel could hear Little Bit crying in the bathroom. She looked at Fred. "I have to go check on Ashley." Fred nodded and Mel left.

Little Bit and Mary were in the bathtub. Mary had her arms wrapped around the small girl as they both cried. Mel knelt down beside the tub. "Are you OK?" She asked as Little Bit reached out and wrapped her arms around her mother. Mel then looked at Mary. "Are you alright?"

Mary wiped tears from her face and sniffled. "Guess I'm not very brave."

Mel put her hand on Mary's. "You're as brave as any of us." Mel smiled and Mary smiled back.

"Can you help me out of here?" Mary asked as she tried to extract herself from the tub.

Mel picked up Little Bit and offered a hand to Mary and helped pull her from the tub.

Doc pulled the Gustav over and prepared it to fire. He peeked up over the side of the bunker. "I can't really see the damn thing. I'm just going to aim below the muzzle flashes!" He shouldered the weapon while crouching, then stood up enough for the weapon to clear the side of the bunker. I was standing beside him when he shouted. "Back blast, clear!" Dalton grabbed me and jerked me to the ground as Doc fired. Inside the bunker, the blast and concussion were intense. My ears rang, and the small space was choked with dust. I didn't hear the resulting explosion, and could barely breathe.

Doc dropped the weapon and stumbled towards the rear exit. Dalton pushed me out the doorway before coming out himself. He looked around for a moment then stuck his head back in. He reappeared, dragging Danny by the leg. We were all covered in dust and dirt. It was in our eyes, our ears and mouths. I was blinking trying to get the dust out of my eyes and pulled a canteen from the vest and started to wash them out.

Dalton grabbed the canteen from me and poured water on his face as well. Danny was complaining about his eyes, so Dalton knelt down and pulled Danny's hands from his face. "Don't rub your eyes. You'll just make it worse." He began pouring water on Danny's face, "Blink. Blink your eyes."

"I can't."

Dalton lifted one of his eyelids and poured water directly into the eye.

Doc was coughing up dust as well and trying to clear his eyes.

"Did you hit it?" I asked, trying to blink the crap from my own eyes.

"I think so. They aren't shooting anymore."

"We need to go check on Tyler and Brandy," I said.

Dalton handed me the canteen. "Here, keep trying to wash his eyes out. I'll go."

All the while, AC/DC still blared from the small radio. The song was just over five minutes long and it was only now coming to an end. That five minutes seemed like an eternity.

There was a sudden burst of gunfire. I looked over the top of the bunker to see a burning hulk at the end of the road. What appeared to be one rifle was firing up there somewhere, but I couldn't tell where.

"Someone is still up there," I said.

Doc looked over. "I don't think they're shooting at us though."

I strained to see where the sporadic gunfire was coming from, but couldn't find it. I slid back down beside Danny. "How are your eyes doing?"

Danny shook his head, blinking hard. "They're getting better."

Lee Ann came running up. "Dad, you need to come home. Jamie is hurt."

Looking over while still wiping the crust from his eyes, Doc asked, "Did she get shot?"

Lee Ann nodded as Doc and I were both getting to our feet. We took off running as fast as we could. Hanging with these military guys and a young, healthy teenager made me feel like shit. While I was in better shape now than before the Day, I still couldn't stick with them. Doc left me in his wake.

As I came up on the porch, Jamie was laid out in front of the door. The dress that was so pretty before was now covered in blood and pulled up onto her chest. Doc was looking at a dressing covering a wound in her abdomen.

"Did it exit?" Doc asked.

"I don't know," Jamie replied.

"We didn't even look," Jess said.

"I'm gonna roll you over and take a look. It's going to hurt." Jamie gritted her teeth and nodded. Doc gave instructions to Jess and Fred on how to roll her onto her side. Working together, they gently rolled her to her side. Jamie let out a yelp, and Doc quickly ran a hand along her back and looked. It was smeared with blood.

"Looks like it went through. We need to get another dressing on it," Doc said as he started digging through his bag. Finding the bandage, he and the girls applied another dressing to the exit.

"I'm starting to get cold," Jamie said.

"I know. Just hang in there for another minute and we'll get you fixed up," Doc quickly said. Looking at Fred, he said, "Get some blankets."

Fred gabbed blankets from the girls' beds and brought them back. They wrapped Jamie up and moved her into the living room. Doc took a space blanket from his bag and unfolded it, laying it out on the sofa. Then he had the girls help him get Jamie laid out on it. They elevated her feet with some pillows, and she started to feel a little better. Doc then started an IV, giving her a precious supply of fluid.

"We need to get to town," Doc said.

"There's no way we can go tonight," I said.

"Will she be alright until morning?" Jess asked.

"I can hear you," Jaimie moaned.

"Yeah. She can make it until morning, but we need to leave as early as possible."

Seeing that Jamie was taken care of, I went to Mel. She was sitting on the edge of Little Bit's bed with her. A faint glow from the lantern in the living room barely lit the space. I sat down on the side of the bed and wrapped my arm around them.

"You guys alright?" I asked.

Mel nodded. "Yeah. We're fine. She's just scared.

Little Bit peaked at me. "They came into the house."

I was thunderstruck. "What?"

"They came in through the sliding glass door. Didn't you see it?" Mel asked.

I leapt to me feet. "Hell no, I didn't see it!"

Mel grabbed my arm. "They're dead."

I looked at her. "They? How many?"

She held up three fingers but said nothing. I looked out the door, then back to her. "I'll go check on it."

As I was walking out of the bedroom, I heard Sarge's voice in the living room. Glancing in, I saw him and Thad, and went the other way into the kitchen. There were two bodies on the kitchen floor and another lying just outside the shattered glass door. They were dead alright, and the floor was covered in blood.

I grabbed one of the bodies by the feet and dragged it out onto the back porch. As I dropped the legs onto the deck, Thad came through the door with the second one.

"Thanks, man," I said.

Thad nodded. "No problem. There's six more on the road down by Danny's house."

"Six? Holy shit."

Thad smiled. "There's more out back where Dalton set up

his little trap. Whatever he put out there, it sure worked. There's pieces of them hanging in the trees. They're splattered all over the place."

Doing some quick math, I said, "So somewhere between twelve and fifteen of theirs are dead."

"And only one wounded on our side," Thad said.

"We just got lucky is all. It can't last forever."

"Come on, Morg. We're doing pretty good. We're holding our own."

"What happened with the six down the road?" I asked.

"We came running out the gate at Danny's and ran slap into them. Mike and Ted crashed into them and they all went flailing to the ground. Me and Sarge got to work on them, and we killed 'em all."

Nodding, I noted again. "We're lucky."

Thad gripped my shoulder. "I'll take lucky any day, Morgan."

Seeing just how lucky we'd been really weighed on me. Shaking my head, I said, "But what if our luck runs out. We've got to fix this once and for all. If this keeps going, luck isn't going to cut it."

We went back in the house. Mel had put Little Bit to bed. Mel said she was upset because she didn't have her blanket. It was on Jamie at the moment. She finally settled down when Mel gave her one of my poncho liners. As we were talking, Dalton stuck his head in the door and nodded for me to follow him.

Once outside, I saw he had a grim look. "What is it?"

He pointed to the bench on my porch. I looked and saw Jace and Edie sitting there. It took a moment for it to sink in. But looking in the direction of their house, I could see the fire that still raged there.

"Is there any chance?" I asked. His reply was a slow shaking of his head. I looked at Thad. "Still think we're lucky?"

CHAPTER 4

THAD AND I STOOD STARING at the scorched and smoking remains of the house. It was early and a heavy fog blanketed the ground, giving the entire scene a spooky feel. The air was heavy with an acrid odor of fire and loss. Little was left, the frame of the mobile home really the only thing recognizable. Thad leaned on a shovel as he surveyed the scene. Of all things that have happened to this point, I'm sure this was the hardest thing for him to look at. But he revealed nothing as we stood in silence.

"I'm not looking forward to this," I said.

"It's an unpleasant thing," Thad replied.

"At least they got the kids out."

Thad glanced over. "How are the kids?"

"They're at Bobbie's. She's taking care of them. Doc checked the skin pop on them earlier and said Jace was positive for antibodies, but didn't appear to be sick. Said there's a chance he was able to fight it off. Edie was negative."

"That's good. But now those babies have to grow up without their momma and daddy," Thad lamented.

"That may be true, but they're not going to be alone," I replied. Then I looked at Thad. "They're a part of our family now, and we'll raise them, all of us." Thad nodded and I added, "you're a big uncle now, again."

Thad smiled. "Guess that makes Sarge the crazy grandpa then."

Laughing, I replied, "Yeah, ole mean ass grandpa."

Thad chuckled and turned his attention to the grizzly task before us. "You ready to do this?"

Letting out a long breath, I responded. "No."

"Me neither. But let's get it done."

With gloved hands, we worked our way into the remains of the house. It didn't look like we'd find their bodies; the fire was intense and left little. We picked through the debris carefully, respectfully. It was an unpleasant task. As we worked, Sarge showed up with several of the guys.

"You find them?" Sarge asked.

I was knelt down picking my way through a large black pile. "Not yet."

"I doubt you will. That fire was hot."

I rose to my feet. "We've got to get those bastards. This is twice now. They need to pay in a big way."

Sarge nodded. "They will. We're going to stomp their dicks in the dirt."

Looking at Ted, I asked, "How's the ear?"

Ted reached up and rubbed the bandage over his ear. "Fucking gone."

Mike gave him a little punch on the shoulder. "Come on, man. Chicks dig scars." Ted glared back in reply.

"Speaking of chicks, how's Jamie?" Thad asked.

"She's doing OK, but Doc wants to get her to town. Which is why we're here, you're supposed to meet the engineers at the power plant," Sarge said.

"I know. I just wanted to find them."

"We'll get some other folks over here to continue the search. We need to get on the road."

"Go ahead, Morgan. We'll take care of this," Thad said.

Wiping sweat from my face, I said, "I also have to close up the broken sliding glass door. Not to mention clean all the blood off my kitchen floor."

Thad smiled. "I'll take care of that too. I'll just get a door from one of the other houses around here. They're pretty standard, and we should find one that will fit."

I left Thad with Mike and Ted to keep looking. We went over to my house where Sarge's Hummer was waiting. Doc came out the door holding one end of a collapsible stretcher. Ian had the other end and Jamie was lying on it with her eyes closed, wrapped in a blanket. Aric was inside the truck and helped pull her inside. She winced a couple of times as it wasn't the easiest thing to get her inside.

Once she was in, Ian sat down beside her and wiped a couple loose strands of hair from her face. He smiled and said, "You're going to be alright. You've got to come back so I can see what you look like in that dress."

Without opening her eyes, she replied, "Pshh, fat chance. Are you coming with me?"

"You want me to?"

"You need adult supervision. Someone needs to keep an eye on you."

Ian smiled again. "Alright. I'll go so you can keep an eye on me."

I asked Aric where he was last night. I hadn't seen him since the shooting began.

He nodded at Ian. "I was with him. When the shooting started, we moved to flank the truck. Then the damn thing blew up. Almost killed us. A couple of guys got out of it and we shot their asses."

"Oh, ok. That was you guys shooting up there. We didn't know who it was," I said.

"It was us alright. I just wish we had been down here to help deal with all these assholes," Ian added.

Looking around, he asked, "Where's Perez?"

Ian snorted. "Oh man, he's sick. Got the shits real bad. You thought he was a pain in the ass before. Holy hell. He's the biggest freaking baby I've ever seen."

"Is he alright?" I asked.

Ian nodded. "Yeah. Doc checked on him. He'll get over it."

"Tell him to suck it up," Sarge said.

"What was the explosion back there?" I asked, pointing to the rear of the neighborhood with my chin.

"That was a couple trying to get out I think. They hit Dalton's surprise. There's pieces of them hanging in the trees back there," Sarge replied.

"Let's get this on the road. We need to get Jamie to the clinic," Doc said.

Whispering, I asked, "How's she doing, Doc?"

"She's alright, but might need surgery. That's why I want to get her to the clinic. There's only so much I can do here."

We loaded up. Doc sat in the back with Jamie and Ian took the turret. I drove and Sarge rode shotgun. We didn't want to take too many people from the neighborhood. We didn't know what these guys may try next. As I pulled around two bodies lying in the road next to the still-smoking truck, Sarge said, "Good work, Ian."

This truck was like the others, an MRAP. I shook my head, thinking back to the days in the Before when people would look at you like you were crazy for being upset that the DHS was acquiring such equipment. But I have to admit, even I didn't foresee this.

I pushed the speed on the old truck, not wanting to waste time getting Jamie to the clinic. It was odd seeing the market in Altoona busy with people trading. They surely had heard the shooting last night. Maybe they didn't care. Not that I expected anything from them. After all, they had more pressing issues, like feeding themselves and their families.

As we came into Umatilla, I noticed the old Kangaroo there was busy as well. I briefly saw a sign that said milk. It intrigued me, and I made a mental note to stop by on the way back. As we passed the old Golden Gem plant, I hoped we'd be able to get the turbine running. And I really hoped these engineers knew something about it. The car barricade was opened as we approached, and I was able to pass straight through. Pulling up in front of the clinic, the staff was there waiting for us. Jamie was quickly unloaded and taken inside. I watched the doors close behind Doc as he followed her in. There was nothing I could do in there, and I'd only be in the way. After a brief moment, Doc came back out the door and handed me the bloody blankets.

I looked at them and instantly recognized one of them. It was Little Bit's. It was originally made for Taylor by one of my aunts and was passed down to each new baby girl. It was a mess now, but somehow we'd have to clean it up. Little Bit would surely want it back. It also made me think of my aunt up there in Jacksonville. She was alone, my uncle having passed away a couple years ago. He was a good man, retired Coastie. I always enjoyed visiting them as a kid. They had three sons, and I'm sure those boys were taking care of her. I hoped so anyway. It really drove home the idea of not taking your loved ones for granted. You never know when the last time you see them will be THE last time you see them.

"Let's go to the armory and find those engineers," Sarge said.

We pulled up to the back gate and parked. As we were

getting out, Cecil walked up. "Mornin', fellers. I hear you guys had a hard night."

Sarge nodded. "You could say that. But they got the worst end of it."

"That's good. Something needs done with 'em though or this is just going to keep happening."

Sarge spit in the dirt. "And we're going to do just that."

As they were talking, Shane with the Eustis PD came up. "Hey, Morgan. What are we going to do with the kid we have locked up? It's getting to be a pain in the ass having to watch him and the guy from the other night."

"You're going to have to watch them for now. We've got bigger fish to fry at the moment. Anything else going on?" I asked.

He shook his head. "No. It's actually been kind of quiet." As we were talking, a guy with a neatly trimmed beard ran up.

"Hey, Shane. I fed the prisoners. You need anything else?"

"Not right now. Thanks." Shane replied.

"I've got a couple of things I need to do. I'll be back later."

As he walked off, I asked, "Who's that?"

"Oh, that's Micah Revelle. He wants to join the PD. He helps out with little things, takes some of the work off us," Shane replied.

"He from around here?" I asked.

"No, I don't think so. He came in a few days ago. Seems eager enough and does whatever we ask."

I looked at the guy as he walked off. Something about him just didn't sit well with me. Looking back at Shane, I said, "Keep an eye on him."

"Micah? He's fine. You don't have to worry about him."

"I have to worry about everyone."

Sarge returned and said the engineers would meet at the

barricade out of town. They went to get their truck. Cecil was going to ride with us. We mounted up and pulled out onto the road. I drove down to the Lake Eustis canal and we got out to wait. I waved at the guys on the barricade when gunfire erupted right behind me. I dove to the ground as Ian opened up with the SAW from the turret.

Looking up, I shouted. "What is it?"

Pausing for an instant, Ian shouted back. "I don't know!" And he went back to work with the machinegun.

I got up and saw Sarge firing wildly into the water of the canal. Sarge was screaming his ass off as he pumped round after round into the water. I looked at Ian and waved, "Cease fire! Cease fire!"

He stopped and looked over the smoking weapon at me. "What is it?"

"Hell if I know."

I turned back towards Sarge just as he jumped off the road into the water. "What the hell?" I said as I stepped up and peered over the edge. There was Sarge in the water shouting to himself.

"I got your ass! I got your big ass!" He looked up at me. "Morgan, get yer ass down here!"

I sat on the edge of the road and dropped into the water. "What is it?"

Sarge heaved, and an alligator's head bobbed out of the water. "I got his ass! I finally got me a lizard!"

"All that for a damn gator?" I asked.

"What is it?" Ian shouted.

"I got me a big ass lizard!" Sarge shouted back.

"You're out of your damn mind," I said.

"All that for a gator?" Ian asked from the road. I looked up to see him standing over us.

"I think the old man has lost his mind," I said.

"Quit yer belly aching and help me drag this thing out of here," Sarge barked. He was smiling from ear to ear.

"You want to put that in the truck?" Ian asked.

"Hell yeah. We need the meat, and this is my lizard! And I'm taking it!" Sarge shot back.

I helped Sarge drag the beast from the water. But we needed Ian's help to get the nearly nine-foot reptile up to the road.

"Damn this thing is heavy!" Ian grunted.

Sarge was almost vibrating with excitement. He looked at Ian wide-eyed, "I know! It's huge, ain't it!"

Ian shook his head. "What the hell are you going to do with it?"

Sarge looked at him like he was an idiot. "We're going to eat it, dipshit. What did you think we're going to do with it!"

As we dropped the gator on the back of the truck, two Hummers came skidding to a stop beside us. Sheffield and Livingston hopped out with several Guardsmen. Sheffield looked around. "What the hell's going on?"

Putting his foot on the gator's head, Sarge replied, "I killed me one big ass gator."

Sheffield looked down, then at Sarge. "All that shooting was for this?" He then looked up at Ian. "What the hell were you shooting at?

Ian shrugged. "When he started shooting over there, I thought we were under attack, and I opened up on the tree line."

Livingston chuckled. "So he killed a gator and you killed some trees?"

Ian smiled. "I guess, yeah."

Sheffield shook his head and looked at Sarge. "Here's your engineers. Don't you need to be getting to the plant?"

Sarge waved him off. "We're going, we're going. Just as soon as we load this lizard up."

Sheffield huffed and looked at Baker. "I'll see you guys later. Try and get back before dark."

She nodded and Sheffield got back in his truck. Livingston looked at me. "You really need to keep an eye on him."

I shrugged. "We need the meat."

Livingston walked away, shaking his head. After he was in the truck and they were driving back towards the armory, Ian looked at Sarge and said, "I get the feeling the captain doesn't like you much."

Cecil laughed. "Ya think?"

Sarge snorted. "He can kiss my ass if he don't like me. He can't be first, but he can be next. Get on the end of this lizard," Sarge said, motioning to the gator's tail.

Cecil snickered. "I bet you was hell on the brass when you was still in."

As we hefted the gator, Sarge groaned. "You wouldn't believe half of it."

Once Sarge's trophy was loaded in the back of the Hummer, we mounted up and pulled out with the engineers following us.

As we drove, I asked Sarge, "Did Doc tell you about the radio transmission we heard last night?"

Surprised, Sarge looked over. "No, he didn't. What was it?"

"Smells like shit back here!" Cecil shouted.

I laughed, but answered Sarge. "It was some guys up in Idaho called the Radio Free Redoubt. They gave some news about the Marine Corps fighting in Atlanta. They also said the UN was considering sending in peacekeepers."

Sarge snorted. "Peacekeepers! What are they going to send? Bunch of candy ass Belgians? Or worse yet, the French? We'll kick the shit out of those boys."

"Actually, they said the Russians and Chinese were all about it."

Cecil leaned forward. "The Russians and Chinese, you say?" Then I looked at Sarge. "You actually going to eat this smelly ass thing?"

"Hell yeah I am!" Sarge shouted.

Trying to keep the conversation on track, I replied, "That's what they said. I don't know how they'd have that kind of info."

"They're probably being fed the info from the DOD," Cecil said.

"They also gave out some kind of coded message. Something about a maple tree, followed by a bunch of numbers," I said.

Again, Cecil leaned forward. "A maple tree? How many numbers?" Then he looked at Sarge. "I wanna switch seats."

I shrugged. "I don't know. A bunch."

"Pull yer skirt down and quit yer bellyaching. What sort of format were they in?" Sarge asked.

"I don't know. There were a lot of them," I said.

"You mean you fucking booger eaters didn't write it down?" Sarge boomed.

I glanced sideways at him. "Calm down. No, we didn't. We couldn't decode it anyway."

"Well, we can't now for damn sure!" Sarge shot back.

"We may have been able to. I know who you're talking about, and it sounds like they're using one-time pads," Cecil said.

Sarge spun around in his seat to face Cecil. "What do you know about one-time pads?"

Cecil smiled. "You an Elmer, Linus?"

"What the hell's an Elmer?" I asked.

"It's a HAM radio operator," Cecil said.

I laughed and said, "Be vewy vewy qwiet. I'm hunting wadios. Uh uh uh uh."

Sarge slapped me in the back of head. "Shut up and let the grownups talk."

"Hey!" I shouted. But Sarge ignored me and spoke to Cecil. "You think you got the pads, Cecil?"

"They used to run drills using one-time pads. I attended HAM Fest and picked up a stack of pads from a friend of mine there. Morgan, what frequency did you pick it up on?"

"Somewhere around 6800 megahertz, I think."

"That's about right for a pirate radio station," Cecil replied.

"Pirate radio?" I asked.

"Not really pirate now; but back in the day they would have been a pirate station. They probably practiced on ten or fifteen watts. But when the shit hit the fan, they ramped up their output. No one to stop them now," Cecil said.

"We need to keep people on the radios from now on, and write down any and all transmissions we hear," Sarge said.

At the plant, we all dismounted, and the engineers introduced themselves.

"I'm Scott Westpfahl," a man with a neat beard said, offering his hand.

I took it. "Morgan Carter. And this is First Sergeant Mitchell and this is Cecil." Everyone shook hands, and Scott continued the introductions.

"This is Doc Baker." He motioned to a very attractive red-headed woman with blue eyes.

Going to have to keep Mike away from her, I thought.

"Doc? I thought you were an engineer?" Sarge said.

She smiled. "I have my doctorate."

Using a Gomer Pyle style voice, Scott said, "It means she's really smart."

She smiled. "Watch it, Westpfahl."

Scott continued. "This is Terry Lane." Terry nodded and shook everyone's hand. "And this is Eric Beach."

Beach was a young guy. He offered his hand, saying "Beach, like the ocean."

Shaking his hand, I asked. "What other kind is there?"

He offered a nervous smile. "Well, the tree. Ya know."

Sarge snorted. "You ain't from around here, are you?"

Beach looked a little nervous. I put my hand on his shoulder. "Don't worry about him. Just don't get your hands too close to his mouth." I had to smile when he looked at his hands and pulled them in a little closer to his body.

"Well, you brainiacs think you can get this heap up and running?" Sarge asked.

"Let's take a look at things. One thing we're going to need for sure is a generator. We're going to need power to even test much of this," Terry said.

"You guys know anything about gas turbines?" Cecil asked.

"I've got some experience with them and Baker there worked in the utility industry, so she's familiar with it," Terry replied.

"I'm no stranger to them," Scott said.

Sarge looked at Beach. "What about you?"

"I've studied them," he replied.

Sarge cocked his head. "What kind of engineer are you?"

Beach stuttered. "I'm a, a......."

Sarge cut him off. "Huma, huma, huma. Spit it out!"

"I'm an engineering student."

"Holy Mary, mother of God. Student! We need engineers!" Sarge barked.

Laughing, I put my hand on Sarge's shoulder. "Leave him alone, grumpy."

"What's your plan to get power here?" Baker asked.

"I'm guessing you need three-phase 480." I said. Scott nodded. "I know where a thirty-five KV generator is. We'll have to get it moved over here. It used to run the Eustis Police station."

"That's on the small side, but it would probably get the job done," Terry said.

Sarge looked at Cecil. "Folks, Cecil here performed maintenance on this place when it was running, so he's a wealth of info for you. Cecil, why don't you show these guys around this thing and see if there is any kind of obvious defects."

Cecil nodded. "Come on, and I'll give the nickel tour."

Cecil led them off into the plant while Sarge and I hung out at the truck. I had enough on my plate. These guys were going to have to get this done.

I was getting anxious and asked Sarge, "What are we going to do about those bastards who attacked us?"

He was leaning over the hood of the truck and motioned with his hands. "I don't think we'll have a problem with these brainiacs."

"You know what I'm talking about."

Sarge nodded. "I know, Morgan. We're going to have to talk to Sheffield. We're going to need their help to do this all the way. And it IS going to be…. all the way."

Nodding, I said, "No quarter. Kill them all."

"I'm worried though," Sarge said. "There's no way to take these guys on without casualties." He paused and fiddled with an oak leaf stuck behind the wiper blade on the windshield. After a moment, he looked back at me. "And I don't want to lose any of you."

"You're not the only one. But how many more times are these guys going to hit us before someone dies? Taylor is still recovering, and now Jamie is in the clinic. I think we've used all our luck. We've at least got to take away their ability to drive up and start shooting," I replied.

Sarge nodded. "I've been thinking on that. They're far

enough away that if they didn't have wheels, it would be a lot harder for them to get here."

"Not to mention they wouldn't be able to bring in heavy weapons."

Sarge flipped the leaf out onto the hood. "But now we may have a real problem from what you heard on the radio. If the UN is talking about sending in peacekeepers, you can bet your ass it's because our turd-in-chief is asking for help. He's probably getting desperate and is willing to take any help he can get."

I thumped the hood. "But he's got to know those clowns aren't going to come over here and lose soldiers just to *help* out. They're going to want something in return."

"I'd like to talk to the General and see what the hell's going on. How legit this threat is. If there is a real possibility of them coming, then we've really got to take those guys at the Elk's Camp out before they show up, or we'll damn sure have our hands full." Sarge said.

Cecil and the engineers walked out of the plant talking.

"Well, what's the verdict?" I asked.

"Nothing in there is obviously damaged." Scott said.

Terry jabbed a thumb over his shoulder. "The switches out in the substation are open on both sides, the lines coming from the plant as well as to the distribution. That means the transformers there are probably good too. We may actually have a chance at this."

"You get us that generator and we can start testing," Baker said.

Nodding, I replied, "I'll get on that today."

"Something else for your to-do list, Morgan," Cecil said. "We need to get to work planting. I need Thad and some other bodies."

"I know. We've just had our hands full the last couple of

days. I'll get Thad to come down tomorrow. See what you can find for bodies in town. Talk to Sheffield. He's supposed to provide security for you. Then get with Shawn and tell him to get the prisoners ready to send out there as well. They can work off their sentences out there," I said.

"You going to let the boy that killed that girl work it off?" Cecil asked.

Shaking my head, I said, "No. But he's going to work until it's time for him to be put in the dirt."

Cecil nodded, "Good."

"When do you think you'll have the generator here?" Scott asked.

I shrugged. "Don't know. We'll have to figure out how to move it first. It's sitting on the ground, and we'll need to get it loaded on a trailer and drag it over. I'll let you guys know when it's here. Once it's here though, there will need to be a constant presence to guard it. We won't be able to leave it unattended."

"That won't be a problem. We'll just move into the offices or something and set up house. I'll ask Sheffield for a couple of bodies to help with security as well," Scott replied.

"It's settled then," Sarge said and he looked at Cecil. "You gotta tower at your place?"

Cecil shook his head. "No. I run a dipole."

"We should still be able to reach each other. How many watts are you pushing?"

"I can push a hundred watts. But I have to be careful because it takes a long time for me to recharge the batteries."

While Sarge and Cecil talked radio stuff, I asked Scott's crew what they thought of how we would get the power into town.

"It's going to take a lot of work," Baker said. "We're going to have to open a lot of sidelines and hope the transformers are good."

"The local power company has a lay-down yard on the west side of town. There are probably some stored there," I said.

"Hopefully there are enough of them," Terry said.

"Enough jawin'. We've got shit to do, so let's all get to it," Sarge barked. He always was delicate. "Cecil's riding back with the engineers. Let's get going so you can sort out moving this generator."

Looking at Cecil, I said, "I'll get Thad over tomorrow. He'll enjoy the time working in the dirt."

"I'll be expecting him," Cecil replied with a smile.

"Terry. I'll let you guys know when the generator is headed your way," I said.

"We'll be ready. In the meantime, we're going to check out that out that lay-down yard and see if there are any stored transformers, and whether they're any good," Terry replied.

As we got back in the Hummer, Ian slammed his fist on the roof. "Hurry up. That thing is starting to smell like hell!"

"Quit your whining! That's no way to talk about your dinner," Sarge replied.

As we rode, Sarge and I talked about the generator move for a while. Getting the beast on the trailer would be the hardest part, but I'm sure we would figure something out.

"What were you and Cecil talking about?" I asked.

"We were setting up a frequency to stay in touch on HF."

"Good. Someone else we can stay in touch with up there." I cocked my head and looked at him. "You know, I really like Cecil. He's good people."

Sarge chuckled. "He is. Like me, he calls it how he sees it. He's also got a lot of experience in different things. Good man to know."

As the Kangaroo in Altoona came into view, I was relieved to see Mario's buggy. It would save me a trip out to his place.

"Mario's there. I'm going to stop in and ask about the generator."

Sarge looked sideways at me. "Ask? You promised something you don't have?"

"He'll let us use it. Besides, we need it and he's not using it."

Sarge let out a devilish laugh. "You're starting to think too much like me."

I wheeled up beside Mario's table and stopped. Shelly smiled and waved as I got out.

"Hey guys! How are you doing?" She asked.

Mario was busy haggling over a deal. That was the way of things now. Bickering was back in style. A trader would offer a price and the customer would counter, usually fifty percent of the first asking price. The typical deal would come in somewhere in the middle of the two. But there were exceptions on both sides.

"We're good, Shelly. How's business?" I asked.

She looked down at the table stacked with jars, candles and blocks of wax. "Great. Everyone wants this stuff."

Mario finished up with his customer and walked over. "But not everyone has things of worth to offer."

"Oh stop it," Shelly said, offering him a light slap on the shoulder.

"What brings you fellas down here?" Mario asked.

"We need a favor," Sarge said.

"Always happy to help if we can. What is it?" Mario asked.

Ian hopped out of the truck. "I'm going to prowl around the market." He wandered off to look over the offerings.

"That old generator from the Eustis PD. We need to borrow it for a while," I said.

Mario shrugged. "It's yours. What are you going to do with it?"

"We've got some engineers in town to see if we can get the power house at the old Golden Gem plant up and running."

Mario's eyebrows went up. "Really? Think you have a shot at it?"

"We won't know until we try. Even if we get it running, there's a ton of work that will still be needed."

"To say the least," Mario replied. I could see the wheels in his head turning.

"We got hit again last night. Keep your eyes open and let us know if you see any DHS folks around," Sarge said.

"Did anyone get hurt?" Shelly asked.

Sarge nodded slightly. "Jamie was hit. She's up at the clinic now."

"How bad?" Mario asked.

"It's not good. But it could have been worse," Sarge replied.

"We also lost two people. You haven't met them. Tyler and Brandy. They were quarantined because they had TB. The house was set on fire. They got the kids out, two little ones, but they didn't make it," I said.

Shelly covered her mouth. "Oh, that's horrible."

Mario was shaking his head. "Burned. I couldn't imagine a worse thing." He looked at me. "Sorry, I was just—" I waved him off.

"It's alright. Tough for everyone," I said.

"We're here to help. Whatever we can," Shelly said.

Looking at Mario I asked, "You think we can get that generator on a trailer?"

"I'm sure we'll figure something out," Mario replied.

"How about tomorrow?"

"Alright. Say nine o'clock?"

"We'll be there. And we'll bring some of the knuckle draggers with us to help," Sarge replied.

"I've got some machinery that will help as well. I don't think it will be too big a deal," Mario said.

We talked for a while longer, sharing with Mario and Shelly the info about the radio broadcast. They were both HAMs as well, and wanted the frequency. Shelly said they spent most nights trying to find broadcasts. They'd found a few, but never reliably. Shelly said they would start monitoring the frequency as well.

"Be sure and write down any coded messages you hear," Sarge said.

"You really think the Russians and Chinese will come?" Mario asked.

Sarge shrugged. "I don't know. It'd be a hell of a thing if they did. We think we've got problems now dealing with these bumbling idiots with the DHS. But the Russians, they're some mean bastards. Tough, well-armed."

"What about the Chinese?" Shelly asked.

"Mean little fuckers. What they lack in quality weapons, they make up for in sheer numbers."

"We'll worry about that when the time comes," I said.

Sarge took a very serious tone. "If it comes to that, we'll have more to worry about than you can imagine."

"If what you said is right, we could be truly screwed," Mario said.

"Keep yer ears open," Sarge said and turned around. "Ian! Saddle up!"

"I'll see you guys tomorrow," I said.

As we walked back to the truck, Mario said, "What the hell?"

Sarge beamed. "Got me a gator!"

Mario and Shelly walked over and looked in the back of the Hummer. "It's a big one," Shelly said.

"I like gator meat," Mario said with a smile.

"You want some of it?" Sarge asked.

Mario politely hesitated. "Well, yeah. But I couldn't take it from you."

Sarge slapped him on the back. "Of course you can! We'll bring it over in the morning."

Smiling even wider Mario replied, "I mean, if you insist."

Shelly laughed. "Oh, whatever. We'd love some. He's trying to act all bashful."

"Let's get home and butcher this big lizard, and then we'll bring some meat over."

We said our goodbyes as Ian ran up and climbed into the truck. Getting back in, we made the short ride to the neighborhood. Pulling in, I stopped at the bunker. Aric, Fred and Jess were there on duty.

"How's Jamie?" Jess asked as I rolled to a stop.

With a slight shrug, I said, "She's at the clinic. Doc stayed with her."

Sarge leaned forward. "She'll be alright. She's a tough girl. Doc won't let anything happen to her."

Jess smiled weakly. "I hope so. I miss her already." She looked up at Ian and squinted against the sun. "Several of us do."

Ian smiled but didn't say anything for a moment. "She's too mean to kill. They'll have to do better than that."

"We've got a lizard to gut," Sarge said.

"I see that," Aric said, looking in the back of the truck. "It's huge."

"It's dinner!" Sarge shot back.

"We're having gator meat for dinner?" Fred asked.

"Looks that way. You like it?" I asked.

She twisted her face, "Don't know. I've never had it."

"It's good. I like it fried," Aric said with a smile.

"Well I'm sure Miss Kay will do something wonderful with it," Sarge replied.

We'll see you guys at dinner," I said and pulled off.

We took the beast to Danny's house. Thad and Mary were in the garden working when we pulled in. Danny came out as I backed the truck up towards the sheds.

"What's up?" Danny asked as we were getting out.

"I took care of the meat issue for a little while," Sarge replied with a smile.

Danny walked around to the back of the Hummer and opened it. "Damn, that's a nice looking gator."

"I want to keep the skin as nice as we can," Sarge said.

"Sounds good to me. I've never done a gator before. Should be fun," Danny said.

Not wanting to, but knowing I must, I asked Danny about the recovery at Tyler and Brandy's.

Danny looked at the ground. "We couldn't find much. But what we found, we buried out back by Jeff."

"What about them youngins?" Sarge asked.

"They're in the house with Bobbie and Kay. Jace said Tyler pushed them out the window but was too weak to get himself out. I guess Brandy was too weak to even try."

Sarge shook his head. "That's a hell of a thing."

"At least the kids are ok," I said.

"They're shook up and not really saying much. But Kay and Bobbie are in there fussing over them," Danny said.

"It's sad, but what's done, is done," Sarge said. He then looked at the gator. "Right now, we've got work to do."

I looked at him. "This is far from done."

He stared at me for a moment. "It ain't over, Morgan."

I looked off into the woods behind him. "We can't lose

any more." Looking back at him, I added, "I'm not burying anyone else."

"Don't worry, Morg. They'll pay for what they've done." He reached out and gripped my shoulder. "Pay for all of them."

Danny set up three sawhorses and laid out a couple pieces of plywood on it to make it long enough so we could work the whole animal. Once it was on the makeshift bench, we looked the beast over. Sarge asked Ian to go get Mike and Ted.

"No problem," Ian said as he headed off.

I took my vest off and laid it on a stump by the shed and pulled the ESEE from its sheath. Looking at the gator, I said, "Well, I guess we start at the beginning."

"Whoa whoa whoa," Sarge said. He looked at me and asked. "You ever skinned a gator?"

"No." I replied. Then I looked around. "What is that banging?" I'd heard it when we first arrived. It seemed to have some sort of rhythm, starting and stopping.

Danny looked around too. "I was wondering the same thing."

"Then keep yer dick skinners off it 'till I tell you what to do." He asked Danny for a razor knife. Danny grabbed one from a tool box in the shed and brought it back out. Sarge took the tool and looked at us. "The hide on one of these is the most valuable part."

"Can we eat it?" I asked with a grin.

Sarge pursed his lips and shook his head. "Just shut up and pay attention." He took the razor and traced a line on the gator's back. "You skin these from the top down. You don't split the belly open like on most critters." Using the razor knife, he made a cut just outside the large bumps on the gator's back, starting just behind the head. As he worked, he continued to explain what he was doing.

"These knots are called scoots. We're going to make another cut on the other side as well until they meet at the tail." After the second cut on the opposite side, he began to peel the hide back, running the blade of his knife along the meat. "Here, Danny. Pull back on this so I can cut it," Sarge said. Danny did as instructed.

As they worked on that section, Thad walked up. Seeing the gator, he stopped short. "Oh, hell no!"

Chuckling, I said, "Come on Thad. It ain't a snake."

Keeping his distance from the gator, Thad walked around the scene. "No it ain't no snake. It's a damn crocodile! A snake will bite you, but a crocodile will eat your ass!" Danny and I both laughed at him.

Sarge snorted. "Yeah? Well, *we're* going to eat this crocodile! Actually, it's an alligator. There aren't any crocs in this part of the world." As Sarge said that, Danny lifted the back section of hide from the gator.

"That thing's a damn monster," Thad said.

Sarge smiled broadly. "Yeah, but it so gooooood!"

Thad eyed him. "What's it taste like?"

Sarge straightened up. "Gator, of course! That whole *it tastes like chicken* is chicken shit! If you wanted something that taste like chicken, then eat chicken!" Sarge looked at me. "Alright, Morgan. Pay attention." Sarge made another cut on the top of one of the gator's legs from just above the foot up to where the hide was missing. "I want you and Danny to start skinning these legs back."

After he made the cut, I used my knife to start peeling back the skin. It had an interesting feel, reminded me of vinyl.

I looked at Thad. "Danny said you guys took care of Tyler and Brandy."

"Wasn't much to take care of. But we did what we could."

"We're going to make it right, Thad," Sarge said.

"Ain't going to make any difference to them," Thad said.

"Maybe not," I said. "But it will to us if we don't have to dig any more graves."

Thad nodded. "That will make a difference.

Sarge looked up at Thad. "You know there's four legs. Get your ass over here and start working on that other'n there." Thad's brow furrowed as he stared at the animal. Sarge cackled. "Quit being a pussy and get over here. It's dead for fuck sake!" He was trying to bring Thad out of the dark hole he was on the edge of. The guy's seen some horrible crap, and no doubt this was wearing on him.

Thad removed the gun scabbard from his back and stepped up to the table. Drawing his knife, he poked at the gator, as if he expected it to jump off the table. It made all of us laugh. Thad hesitantly touched the gator with one finger. After a moment, he was running his hands over the gator's skin.

"I ain't never touched one before. Feels kind of like plastic," Thad said.

Finally, past his apprehension, Thad got to work. With a skilled hand, he made short work of the leg he was working on and quickly moved on. Under Sarge's tutelage, we had the top side of the beast skinned in no time and had to roll it over to continue the process. Just as we'd flipped it, Ian showed up with Mike and Ted in tow.

"Holy hell!" Mike shouted when he saw what we were doing. "The old poacher finally got him a gator!"

Without looking up, Sarge barked, "I ain't no poacher!"

Looking down at the reptile, Mike said, "It's your lie. You tell it."

"Shit. What's a poacher anyway? You gotta ask the State for permission to feed yourself? Think about it. What's the natural way for a man to eat? He has to hunt or fish. He has to go get his meat. But in today's ass-backwards world, that's illegal, less'n you go to the State and get permission. They see hunting as a privilege and not a right. Instead they say you have to go buy your meat from a store, on Styrofoam trays wrapped in plastic. You got to have a license to do any damn thing." Sarge looked up, "'Cept to vote."

Ted snorted. "The one thing there should be a license for."

"And an IQ test," Mike added.

Sarge looked at Mike. "That'd keep you from ever seeing a polling booth." The comment got a round of laughs from all of us.

Mike snorted. "Pffft, I've forgot more than you know."

"Shit. You're so damn ignorant, you don't even know what you don't know!" Sarge shouted.

Mike looked at the gator and Thad. "You know what you're doing?"

"I'm following his lead," Thad said with a smile.

"Careful with that, Thad. He's led us into some shitty situations," Ted said.

Sarge cut his eyes at him. "Yeah, but I always brought your asses out."

Ted nodded slowly. "That you did. That you did."

Sarge then looked at Mike. "And hell yes, I know what I'm doing!"

"I think you've done this before," Mike said.

Sarge nodded his head slightly. "Once or twice."

Danny was working the hide from the tail and asked, "Ever have a license?"

Sarge looked up, and holding his trigger finger up and, working it back and forth, he said, "Yeah, right here. This is all the license I need."

Mike grunted. "Told you he was a poacher."

An interesting thing about a gator is it has a perpetually erect penis. And on occasion when that nerve is hit, it will shoot out as if on a spring. As Sarge was cutting around one of the back legs he hit that nerve in the gator and its penis suddenly shot out. It caused all of us to jump back, except the old man. He quickly grabbed a hold of it and sliced it off.

Mike was wide-eyed. "What the hell is that?" He shouted.

Sarge grinned and threw it at Mike's face. "It's a dick, Dick."

The phallus hit him on the chin as he jumped back. We all started to laugh as he thrashed about, wiping his chin vigorously. "What the fuck, man!"

Ted was doubled over laughing. Pointing at Mike, he said, "You just got tea-bagged by a gator, a dead gator no less!" Sarge erupted into laughter and had to stop work.

Mike looked down at the member lying in the dirt and picked it up. He eyed Sarge, though only briefly, before taking a quick step towards Ted who was still laughing uproariously. Before Ted saw him, Mike slapped Ted in the face with it. The laughter ceased as Ted went into a spitting fit.

"Dude! I had my fucking mouth open!"

"Oh, that's just wrong!" Ian shouted.

That was it. We were all now immobilized with laughter. Even Mike got his chance for a good laugh, reminding me so much of Goose from Top Gun. Once we all had ourselves under control, we got back to work. Now that the hide was off, it was time to get serious.

Sarge was sharpening his knife on a folding diamond hone as he talked about the next phase of the process.

"All right, girls. Listen up. A gator has basically two kinds of meat, white and dark."

"No wonder they say it tastes like chicken," Ted said.

"Shut up, Teddy. Or I'll shove that gator cock in your mouth again," Sarge replied. Ted's brow wrinkled and he turned his head slightly and spit. "Didn't take you for a spitter," Sarge added.

Mike started to laugh until Sarge said, "You really want my attention, Mikey?" Suddenly, Mike found something very interesting in the trees behind us.

"Now, where was I?" Sarge asked.

"Two kinds of meat," I said.

"Right. So the jowl meat and the jelly roll from the tail are the white meats. The rest is dark meat."

"Jelly roll?" Thad asked.

Sarge smiled. "Yeah, jelly roll. Let me show you."

Working on the tail, he separated the meat from the bone. At the base of the tail he pulled the muscle back and reached down inside and pulled out a smooth tube of meat and cut it free. Removing the beautiful piece of nearly translucent muscle, Sarge held it up and said, "This is the finest piece of eating on these things. It's a tenderloin, and there's another one on the other side."

Sarge laid the piece of flesh down and went to work on the other side. In the blink of an eye, he had the other one out. Picking up the two pieces of meat, Sarge said, "Now go ahead and bone out the rest of the critter. Don't open it up. It don't need to be gutted. Just cut the meat off it."

"Where are you going?" I asked.

"To give these to Miss Kay so she can get started on supper," Sarge replied.

He then looked at Mike and Ted. "I want you two to get out there to the Elk's Camp and get a lay of the land. We need some range cards. I want a place to set the mortar up. Get us some ranges so we can drop some heat on those bastards. I also want you to find out where the vehicles are stored so we can hit as many of them as possible too."

"I'm going with them," Ian said.

Sarge looked at him. "I know you want to, but I want you to stay here. Those bastards could come back, and we need to keep as much manpower here as we can. But don't worry. You'll get your chance, Ian. I'll make sure you get some scalps for your belt."

Ian nodded. "Alright. But when the time comes, don't even think about keeping me out of the fight."

"I wouldn't dream of it," Sarge said.

"When are you thinking of hitting them?" I asked.

"We need some intel first. See what their strength is and work up a plan. When we do this, we're all in. There will be no half measures," Sarge said.

"No half measures," Danny repeated.

I was looking at Ian and could tell there was a fire in him. "I say you let Ian go. Three of them stand a better chance of getting out if they run into anything."

Ian looked at me, then at Sarge. Sarge crossed his arms and eyed Ian. "You want some get-back, don't you?" Ian nodded. "Alright, go with them. Just remember, this isn't the time to start any shit. This is recon only."

"Cross my heart," Ian replied.

"Alright, go with 'em."

"We'll get it done, boss," Ted said.

"You boys be careful," Sarge said.

"Damn sure, be careful," I added, then asked, "How's Perez?"

Ian smiled. "He's getting better. He's sore all over now. The shits are gone though."

"I hope you guys are staying away from him," Sarge said.

Ian nodded. "We are. We just slide some food under the

door to him. Doc gave us a bottle of alcohol to wipe things down with, and we've been doing that. I don't want to get sick."

"You better not. You ain't got permission. Now git. You got lots of stuff to do," Sarge said.

The three men nodded and quickly left to get their gear together. As we stood there, the hammering started again.

"What the hell is *that!*" I said. Then I looked around. "You smell smoke?"

Thad looked off in the direction of the sound. "Someone is hammering on something; and yeah, I smell it."

"You guys got this? I want to go see what the hell that is," I said.

Thad nodded. "Sure. Ain't no big deal."

"I'm taking these pieces of meat inside, and I'll be back. Thad, you and Danny cut them Jowls out. That's good meat," Sarge said as he headed for the house.

CHAPTER 5

I FOUND THE SOURCE OF THE hammering under a lean-to type shed behind one of the houses on the block. There was a large fire burning in front of it. As I approached the shed, I called out. "Yo!"

A shirtless Dalton came out of the small shed. In his right hand he held a five pound hammer. He was sweating and covered in soot. "Allo, allo," he said with a broad smile.

"What the hell are you doing? What's all the racket?"

He smiled and beckoned me towards the shed. "Follow me and I'll show you, laddie."

Under the tin roof of the shed was a crude forge. The fire bed was actually an old wheelbarrow pan. One of the shallow ones that makes you wonder what in the hell its purpose is. I could carry more in a five gallon bucket. He'd removed the handles and wheel and had it set up on what was once a cast iron patio table. Lying on the ground was a foot bellow, the kind used to blow up inflatable mattresses when camping or when you had company you didn't particularly care for.

"What do you think? Took me a couple of days to get it all sorted out, but it's working good now," Dalton said, beaming with pride.

I nodded. "Looks good. But uhm, why didn't you just

drag an old Webber grill or something over here from one of the houses?"

Dalton blinked at me, then looked at the forge. Shrugging, he said, "Hell, anyone could do that."

Sitting beside the forge was a small anvil. Pointing at it, I asked, "Where in the hell did you find that?"

"Like everything else, in a barn behind one of the houses. It was covered with rust, but it still serves its purpose just fine."

The old anvil was indeed covered in rust. Thick chunks formed a ring around its base, having been loosed during hammering. Dalton had also scrounged an assortment of ad hoc smithing tools.

Picking up a large pair of channel locks, I said, "Looks like you've got about everything you need. What are you making?"

Taking the channel locks, he plucked an axe head, or what was once an axe head, from the bed of coals. Laying it on the anvil, he gripped the hammer, cut me an evil grin and said, "Tomahawks!" And then he slammed the hammer into the red hot steel with a shower of sparks. He hammered on it for several strokes before plunging it back into the coals. Looking at me with an eye squinted shut and the opposite eyebrow arched, he shouted. "Air, lad! I need air! Doddle not! Make ye self useful!"

I looked down at the foot bellow and stepped down on it. The coals began to glow a bright red. Dalton called for more air, and I continued to pump the bellows. His enthusiasm was infectious, and soon I was laughing.

"You're nuts!" I shouted.

He leaned in close to my face. "We're working iron!"

I stayed with him for a while, working the bellow while he reshaped the axe head. As we worked, I asked about the large fire.

Dalton pointed at it. "Making charcoal. See that can there? It's full of chunks of wood. Cook it down to coal."

Nodding, I said, "Like a gasifier."

"Yeah. Same principal, except we're not collecting the gas."

Looking back into the fire pit, I asked, "So you're making charcoal to burn in here?"

Dalton adjusted the head in the coals. "Yep. This burns hotter and there's no real flame. Makes it a lot easier."

Looking at him, I asked, "Why?"

Dalton took the axe head from the coals and laid it on the anvil. Shrugging, he said, "Every boy needs a hobby." Then he smiled and added, "idle hands are the devil's playground."

Mike squatted in the tall grass observing the cluster of small concrete block cabins through a pair of binoculars. "This side sucks," he said as he as he slowly dropped back down.

Ted looked around. "Yeah. We're downhill. Not where I'd want to be when the bullets started flying."

"We need to find the trucks," Mike said.

"Alright. Let's move to the west and go around and see what we can find," Ted replied.

"I think we need a little security," Ian said as his eyes darted around. "I don't like this."

As a Marine, Ian was accustomed to taking the fight to the enemy. Kicking in doors and smoking bad guys with speed and violence of action. He was not comfortable with the whole sneaking and peaking thing. He'd tried out for Force Recon, but it quickly became clear he wasn't cut out for it. He wasn't the right guy for precision warfare. He was a hammer, and everything to him looked like a nail. Not that he wasn't good at what he did. Two Purple Hearts and a Bronze Star were acknowledgements of his past deeds.

"I'm going to provide rear security. I'll shadow you guys so no one sneaks up on our six," Ian added.

Ted nodded. "Alright. Good idea. There's a lot of goons running around. If you see something, let us know. These radios are encrypted, so they won't be able to listen in even if they knew we were here."

Ian nodded and gave a thumbs up.

"Quick radio check," Mike said and keyed his mic. Ted and Ian both heard the squelch break and nodded. Then each did the same.

"Alright. Keep your eyes open," Ted said as he and Mike moved off.

The camp had several very nice features. One was a military-style confidence course on the northeast side. There were twin pools, mirrors of one another sitting together just off the dining hall. Behind it was a series of ball fields. A large auditorium was the crowning component of the facility.

Mike and Ted moved around the ball field slowly and cautiously. The place was full of people, and they'd seen two roving patrols already. While they hadn't been noticed, it was enough to keep them on their toes. The patrols seemed lackadaisical at best, with those in the element walking with weapons slung and talking amongst themselves. Mike noted their discipline, or lack of it, on his pad.

The Elk's Camp is situated on over four hundred acres of rolling hills and scattered oak trees. It opened in 1991 to serve kids, and has been continually upgraded to be one of the finest youth camps in the state. At least it was. Now, the fifty plus cabins house elements of the DHS and those working with them.

It was early evening, and Ted and Mike kept to the tree lines and thicker brush. Lack of maintenance since the Day meant overgrown grass, weeds and brush. Something they used to their advantage. Once the sun went down, they would be able to move a little freer, but would see less. Ted halted and moved slowly to the edge of the trees on the west side of the ball field. It was a thin line of screening vegetation, so they had to be cautious. Lying prone, Ted scanned the main road of the camp, then passed the binoculars to Mike. "There's the trucks."

The area was busy with people, but in a very organized fashion. There were only a couple of open fires they could see, which made them wonder where the camp occupants were cooking. But there were two large buildings that could easily handle that. Not to mention this was a large camp. There had to be a kitchen someplace. The people they saw were for the most part not carrying long arms. While many had pistols on their sides, only a few were seen with a rifle. Either they were practicing some discipline in camp or they were confident they were safe, and it wasn't deemed necessary.

Ian moved into the tree line as well, staying a hundred or so yards away. He raised up on his elbows and looked towards Mike and Ted. Seeing the tops of their heads and confirming where they were, he dropped back down and settled in behind his rifle. Ian scanned the area around the pools through the ACOG mounted on his carbine.

He observed the black-clad Stormtroopers. As the peak of the chevron on the optic crossed a head, he would whisper *boom,* and move on to the next one and repeat it. He wanted to shoot these bastards. While Ian was always in this fight, things were now personal. He wanted retribution. He wanted their heads.

Mike adjusted the glass and looked at the line of the vehicles sitting on the main road. Just to the south was a large metal building with its rollup door open and what appeared to be a truck getting serviced.

"That's the motor pool there," Mike said.

Ted nodded. "Yeah. They've got some hardware there."

"Even with the four we've killed. Where'd they get all of them?"

"What are they doing over there?" Ted asked, pointing to a couple of MRAPs sitting behind the metal building.

"They're painting them," he said. And then he looked at the other trucks.

"Makes sense. Can't believe they went with white to begin with," Ted replied.

"Makes for good targets."

"Those trucks are well within range for the Goose. We could put a hurt on them from anywhere along here," Ted said.

Mike swung the binoculars around. "The best place would be that little hut out there in the ball field. We'd have a great view of nearly everything out here."

"That thing would be a fucking bullet magnet," Ted hissed.

"Only if they could see it. How many phosphorus rounds did the old man get?"

Ted thumped Mike in the side of the head. "How the hell are you going to see the trucks if you start dropping Willie Pete rounds? If they can't see you, you can't see them."

"Calm down, peckerwood. What I was thinking was hitting them with some sixty millimeter rounds first. Set the tube up over there where we came in. Drop some HE Quick on them. And when they start running around like chickens, we start hitting trucks from over here. If they get their shit together and figure out we're here, then we drop phosphorus on them to blind 'em and set shit on fire." Mike took the optic from his face and looked at Ted. "It would be fucking epic!" He hissed.

Ted took the binoculars and scanned the area. His head slowly started to nod. "You know, Mikey, you're a sick and twisted little shit, but I think you've nailed it."

Giggling to himself, he said, "I know! Throw in a couple of shooters with scoped rifles from a couple different places, and we could raise some hell here!"

"Maybe. But there's a bunch of swinging dicks out there. Gotta be more than a hundred."

Mike rolled back over and looked out over the field. "True. Let's knock 'em in the dirt."

The sun was dropping and the light was fading. Ted looked up into the sky and said, "Sharpen your pencil and finish the sketch. Get all the ranges down. After it's good and dark, we'll sneak out of here." Just as the words left his mouth, there was the sudden rumble of a diesel engine. Lights quickly came on around the compound, illuminating the whole area. It caused both men to press themselves closer to the earth, if that were possible.

"What the fuck?" Mike mumbled. "You think they made us?"

Ted lifted his head. "No, I think they're scared of the dark."

Mike lifted his head. "Ya think? Jeeze, could they have any more damn light?"

"I think we need to be very careful getting out of here."

Ian's voice came over the radio. *"What the hell's going on?"*

"Think they're scared of the dark. We're good here," Ted replied.

"This makes me nervous. Let's get the hell out of here."

"We're with you. Let's back out to the west, and get these trees between us and them before we start to head out."

Ian's reply was terse. *"Moving."*

"Let's head straight back out of here, and find him," Mike whispered.

"Lead the way, Tonto." Ted replied.

I left Dalton and got back to Danny's just as the guys were wrapping up work on the gator. Thad was looking at what was left of the creature, knife in hand. "Should we cut its heart out?"

Sarge walked up then. "No. You don't want to eat organ meat from one of these. Tastes like the north end of a southbound pole cat." As he was talking, Little Bit walked up and leaned against me. I ran my hand through her hair as we listened.

"Is it bad for you?" Thad asked.

"Naw. It'll keep you alive. Just tastes like shit."

"Little ears there, Grandpa Lumpy Lap," I said.

Sarge looked at her and smiled. "Oh. Sorry, Lil' Bit. I didn't see you there." Looking at me, he added, "I just meant they aren't very good; no predator organs are."

Nodding, I said, "Yeah. I kind of got that from the whole north end south end thing."

"Then what are we going to do with the rest of this creature?" Danny asked.

Little Bit walked over to the gator and lifted its snout open, exposing the big teeth. Squinting, she looked at me. "Can I have the teeth?"

I couldn't help but smile. Sarge and Thad both laughed. "You want those teeth?" Sarge asked as he pulled a Leatherman from his vest. She smiled and nodded. "Hold its mouth open and I'll get 'em for ya."

Her nose wrinkled as she watched the old man wrench

them out, one tooth at a time. She picked one of the large teeth up and looked closely at it, tapping the tip of it with her finger.

"What are you going to do with 'em?" Thad asked.

She shrugged. "I don't know."

"I'll go get the tractor so we can get this thing out of here," Thad said.

"Guess we should bury it," Danny said.

"I was thinking of dumping it out there where the hogs could get to it. Let them get what they want off it, and the buzzards will finish what they leave."

"Is that a good idea? We're going to be eating them one day," Danny said.

"Ain't going to hurt us none. Let 'em have it," Sarge said as Thad left to get the tractor.

Little Bit was talking about the pigs eating the gator. She thought it was kind of funny because a gator would usually eat a pig. Now it was the other way around.

"Is that enough teeth for you, missy?" Sarge asked as he dropped another tooth on the pile.

She smiled. "Yes. Thank you, mister Sarge."

Danny went into the shed and came out with an old peanut butter jar. "Here, we'll put them in this until we think of something to do with them."

"Need to dry them out, Danny," Sarge said.

"Yeah they're kinda stinky," Little Bit added.

Hearing the banging again, Sarge asked, "What's all that infernal banging?"

"Oh, Dalton made himself a forge. He's over there hammering out tomahawks," I said.

Sarge's bushy eyebrows shot up. "Really? A forge, you say?"

"Yeah. It's quite the setup. Actually pretty impressive."

"He's making tomahawks?" Danny asked.

I nodded. "Yeah. He's got some old axe heads over there that he's reforming into hawks. They look pretty good too. He's got a whole operation set up over there. He's making charcoal and using that to fire the forge."

"I got to see this," Sarge said. "If you boys got this, I'm going over to check it out."

"We got it. When Thad gets back with that tractor, I'm going over with him to let the hogs out," I said.

"I wanna go watch the pigs eat the gator!" Little Bit shouted.

Rubbing her head, I said, "You can come."

"I'll see you boys at supper," Sarge said as he walked off.

When Thad returned with the tractor, Danny and I wrestled what was left of Sarge's lizard into the bucket. Danny said he wanted to go in and check on the kids and left us. Little Bit wanted to go along, and Thad said she could ride in his lap, so I hoisted her up to him. Once she was settled in, I straddled the three-point hitch, and held onto the headache bar. Little Bit thought she was a big shot because Thad let her steer the machine down the dirt road.

Once at his place, I hopped off as he pulled up to the gate that led into the pasture, and opened it. He pulled through and drove towards the back of the field near where the new wire was strung, and he dumped the load. While he was doing that, I let the hogs out. They were very happy to get out of the barn. They took off running as if the barn were trying to eat them. I walked out to where Thad and Little Bit were, following the pigs.

As I walked up, Thad pointed to a sow. "That one's about to drop, like today or tomorrow."

Pointing to another, I added, "That one too. We'll be covered up in piglets soon."

Little Bit squealed. "I can't wait for the babies!" Looking up at me, she asked, "Can I have one as a pet?"

Smiling, I said, "We'll see."

"Aw, Come on, Daddy. You know Mom would like it too. We could house train it and everything!"

Thad started to laugh and chimed in. "Yeah. Come on, Dad. It'll be house-trained and everything."

With a glaring smirk, I replied, "You're not helping."

Thad nodded. "I know." And he broke out into that deep laugh.

"Look. They're sniffing the gator but they aren't eating it," Little Bit said. The pigs were cautiously approaching the carcass and sniffing at it, but not one had yet touched it.

"They probably recognize it as some kind of predator," Thad said.

"Give 'em a day. I say they'll eat it," I said.

"We need to tend to something in a bit, over there across the road from Danny's house."

I nodded. "Whenever you're ready."

"I'll come down in a bit," Thad said.

Grabbing Little Bit by the shoulder, I said, "Come on, kiddo. We gotta head home and check on your mom and sister."

"Okay."

"I'll see you at supper, Thad."

He nodded. "I think after supper we need to take a moment out at Brandy and Tyler's grave."

It wasn't a happy thought, but certainly one we should address. It was an all too frequently occurring event, standing by the grave of fallen friends.

"We should," I said with a nod as I turned to walk away with Little Bit in tow.

Danny found Bobbie in the house with the kids. They were sitting on the couch together, curled up tight beside her and fast asleep. He looked at her and smiled. Bobbie ran her hand through Edie's hair and smiled as well.

"How are they doing?" Danny whispered.

"They're ok. They seem tired, exhausted. If they're not sleeping, they're eating. They don't seem to fill up. Kay's been feeding them fresh bread all day."

Danny looked around. "Where is she?"

Pointing to the downstairs bedroom door, she said," Taking a nap."

Danny eyed the place more carefully. "I think you guys are all onto something here. Think I'll join you." He sat down into a recliner that he'd salvaged from one of the nearby houses. It wasn't his old one, but it was a decent replacement. Grabbing the handle on the side, he rocked back and stretched his feet out. The sound woke little Jace up. He sat up and rubbed his eyes and looked around. Seeing Danny, he climbed down off the couch and walked over to him. Danny helped the little boy into his lap where he quickly made himself comfortable and was asleep almost instantly. Danny brushed hair from the boy's face as he broke out into a smile.

While the events leading to this little union were tragic, they were not without some happiness. The kids were still very young, and Danny promised himself there and then to raise the two children as his own, something he'd always wanted. Sad though it was to happen this way, he would do his best to make the most of the situation. For the kids and himself. He glanced over at Bobbie and saw she'd drifted off to sleep as well. Laying his head back, he closed his eyes and soon joined them.

Taylor was in the living room with Mel when we came in the door. She looked up and smiled halfheartedly. "What's up, kiddo?" I asked.

"I'm worried about Jamie. Have you heard anything?"

"No, not yet. But I have to go to town tomorrow. I'll check on her then."

She perked up a little at that. "Can I come?"

Mel started to say something. I knew what it would be, so I cut her off. "Not yet. You're not strong enough for that yet. Give it some time and you'll get back to normal."

Her shoulders dropped. "It's just sitting in the truck. I can do that."

"Unless something happens. I don't want you out there and something goes wrong and you're not fully mobile."

Mel gripped her leg. "We just don't want you to get hurt again, sweetie."

Still moping, she replied, "I know."

Moving closer to her, I stuck my hand out. "Look, as soon as you're back up to speed, I'll get you out of here and take you for a ride. Deal?"

She reached out and gave my hand a perfunctory brush. "Deal."

Little Bit came out of her room with a checkerboard and set it on the coffee table. "Taylor, you wanna play checkers?"

Taylor reached out and pulled the table closer to the couch. "Sure, why not."

I went to the kitchen for a glass of tea. Mel came in as I was taking a long drink.

"What are you doing for the rest of the day?" She asked.

"I'm going to take some of the gator meat over to Gina and Dylan. They can use it, and will probably trade us some veggies for it. What are you guys up to?"

"Nothing really. Can I come with you?"

Setting the cup down, I smiled and said, "Hey baby, you wanna go for a ride in my new car?"

"Yeah, I'd like to get out of here for a while."

I looked into the living room. "You think they'll be alright?"

"We aren't going to be gone long, are we?"

"No. Just go over there and come back," I said.

"They'll be fine. They're playing checkers."

"Alright then. Let's take a ride. Let me go over and get some of the meat, and I'll be back."

"I'll be waiting when you get back."

I went over to Danny's and tapped on the door before walking in. They were stretched out snoozing. Danny looked up and I whispered what I was doing. He gave me a thumbs up, and I went to the kitchen and pulled the meat out of the small fridge. There was quite a lot, and I took a few pounds and placed it in a double plastic grocery bag. Funny, that even now the bags were still around. With my trade goods in hand, I tiptoed out and quietly closed the door.

Mel was out by the Suburban when I got there and asked what Danny and Bobbie were doing. I told her they were napping with the kids.

"That's good. It'll be as good for them as for those two poor kids," she said.

"Yeah. Danny's always wanted kids."

"Even Bobbie is happy. She was doing Edie's hair earlier when we were over there."

We pulled out onto the road and headed towards the bunker. The girls were walking down the road with Aric and I stopped beside them. "What you guys up to?"

"Nothing. Sarge and Dalton took over, so we're going to take a break," Jess said.

"Where are you guys going?" Lee Ann asked.

"To trade some meat for some veggies," I said.

"Can I come?"

"Sure, hop in."

She looked at the group. "I'll catch up with you guys later."

"Ok," Fred said and looked at Aric. "I think we're going to take a nap."

Lee Ann got in and we headed off. Mel spun around in her seat. "You alright?"

Lee Ann smiled. "Yeah. I'm fine."

"Have you met Gina before?"

"I don't think so."

"You'll like them. Both of you will. They're good people," I said.

Once out on Hwy 19, I decided to go up to the store and see what was going on there. Plus, I thought Mel and Lee Ann would enjoy getting out and browsing the offerings. As we drove, we passed a couple pulling a wagon down the road. They waved as we passed, and Mel waved back. She looked at the wagon and asked, "Where are they going?"

People could still be seen walking down the road. Though it was different now. We didn't see so many looking like refugees. The people we saw now looked more like they were out trying to make a living in one way or another. They didn't have the same hopeless look to them, and they moved with some semblance of purpose. It was a nice change.

"Probably the same place we are," I replied.

"Where are we going?" Lee Ann asked.

"Up to the Kangaroo store. Thought we would check out the market and see what's going on."

"Oh really! I haven't been there before," Mel said.

We pulled into the parking lot and parked, and got out to

check the trade offerings. I was seeing a change in what people were offering, and mentioned it to Mel. More actually useable items were being offered up. Lots of food items in various forms were on display. Clothes, shoes and boots were popular items, as well as hand tools. Without electricity, they were the only really useful items for the kind of work now common.

"What did they have before?" Mel asked.

"You name it. Lots of electronics. Lots of stuff that was valuable before, but is useless now."

"Hey, Dad. Look, they have butter," Lee Ann said.

"Where?" Mel asked.

Lee Ann pointed to a table, and we walked over. A couple in their late fifties I guessed had a table set up with jars of butter and farmer's cheese, honey and other food stuffs. Mel quickly picked one of the jars up and inspected it.

"That's fresh honey butter." The woman said.

"What kind of cows do you have?" Mel asked.

"We've got a small herd of Jerseys."

"How have you managed to keep them?" I asked.

"We're kind of out in the boonies. But me and my son keep watch on them. The dogs help too," the man replied.

"You're lucky. Anyone with livestock has an advantage now."

"Yeah, but it's a lot of work. We have to move them around to graze and bring them in to milk. I've got fields in hay that I'm going to have to put up by hand. It's a huge task," he emphasized.

"How much is the butter?" Mel asked.

"Well, that depends. What'cha trading?" The woman asked.

Mel looked at me. I smiled. "How about a couple pounds of fresh gator meat for a jar of butter and some cheese."

"Gator meat, you say?" The man asked.

"Yeah, we just butchered it."

Rubbing his chin, the man said, "Let me see it."

I went to the truck and separated the doubled grocery bags, then split the meat into the two bags and carried it back over to the man. Opening the bag, I showed him the cubed meat. He inspected it and said, "That works for me. A change in diet is always nice."

"Oh, thank you. This will be really nice," Mel said.

"You're welcome. Come back anytime," the woman said.

"Do you have any milk?" I asked.

"We do, but we're out. Folks with little ones really want the milk. But we have it every morning," the man replied.

"I'll check back then," I said with a wave as we walked off.

With her treasures in hand, Mel said, "Let's see what else we can find," and led the way through the market.

I stopped by the stall of the man I'd talked with before. He'd set up a nice wet wheel to sharpen tools. Now, in addition to the sharpening tools, there was an assortment of various other tools offered for sale.

"How's business?" I asked.

The old man wiped his hands on a rag and came out from behind his grinder. "Good, good. Can I interest you in an axe or a saw?"

"No thanks. I'm good there. Just wanted to see how business was going," I replied.

"Oh, it's pretty good." He patted his belly. "I ain't getting fat, but it's keeping me in vittles."

I laughed. "That's about all you can hope for these days."

"Yes sir, it sure is. Come see me when you need some sharpening done."

"I will," I said as I turned to leave.

I found Mel and Lee Ann looking at some jewelry and told them I wanted to get to Gina's before it got dark. I was kind of curious why Mario wasn't here, but I'd be seeing him tomorrow anyway. As we got back in the truck, Mel was looking at the jar of butter.

"This is going to be so good with the bread Kay makes."

"I want to try that cheese. What kind is it?" Lee Ann asked.

"It's a soft cheese. But I bet it's good," Mel said looking at the bag containing the cheese.

As I turned onto Gina's road, Mel commented on the oak trees hanging over the road and how nice it looked.

"Yeah, it's like old Florida," I said as I pulled up to the gate at Gina's.

Dylan came out from around the side of the house. He smiled and waved when he saw us. "Hey, Morgan!"

"Gina, Morgan's here!" Dylan called out.

Gina came out of the house, a big smile spread across her face when she saw Mel. Coming out on the porch, she said, "You must be Mel."

Mel greeted her with a hug. "It's nice to meet you finally!"

Holding Mel's hand, she asked, "Would you like a cup of tea?"

"That would be wonderful. Come on, Lee Ann. Let's go inside," Mel said, waving. Lee Ann followed them into the house as the two chatted away.

Dylan looked at me and smiled. "I'm glad you brought them. I think she gets tired of talking to me."

Slapping him on the shoulder, I said, "It ain't just you buddy."

Dylan jerked his head. "Hey, come here. I've got something for you."

I followed him back to the greenhouse. It was warm and humid inside. Everything was damp, even the ground felt spongy. It was like entering a jungle. If a monkey were to drop down onto my shoulders, I wouldn't be surprised. Well, not much anyway.

Dylan pointed to a large basket on a bench sitting along one wall. "You take these with you. We've canned all we are able, and got nowhere to put any more of them."

Walking towards the basket, I asked, "What is it?" Seeing over the top of the basket, it was full of tomatoes, red, green and yellow peppers and onions. "Wow, Dylan. That's a lot of veggies, man. You sure?"

With a dismissive wave, he said, "Hell yes. If I have to blanch one more mater, I'm going to lose my mind. We can eat canned maters every day for every meal for a year!"

"I really appreciate this. It's a lot of produce. I've got something for you too. I was hoping to make a trade, but this is way more than I expected. Come out to the truck."

He followed me out to the truck and grabbed the bag of meat and held it out. He took and opened it, "What is it?"

"It's gator meat. The old man killed one. We butchered it today. It's fresh," I said.

"Oh, man! I love gator meat. Thanks, Morgan. I can't say how much we appreciate you bringing this kind of thing over to us. I mean, we've got plenty of veggies, but no meat. So this really helps out a lot."

"We try to get what we can, and I always think of you guys," I replied.

"Let me take this into Gina. She's gonna love it!"

"I'll go get the basket and load it in the truck."

As I was stowing the basket in the back of the truck, everyone came outside. Gina and Mel were still chatting away.

"Thank you guys so much for the meat. I can't tell you how much we appreciate it," Gina said.

7 0 Avenging
Home

8 Home invasion

9 conflicted
home

10 Home
Coming

11 engineering
home

"Don't worry about it. Remember what I said about the butter too. You should go up there and trade for some." Mel said.

Gina looked at Dylan. "Mel said there's someone at the Kangaroo selling butter and cheese. Can we go up there and trade for some? Butter would be so good."

"Of course. We'll go tomorrow."

"We have to go guys," I said.

"Mel, thank you so much for coming by. It's nice to talk to another lady," Gina said. Looking at Dylan, she continued. "I love Batman, but we've been together so long there really isn't much to say to one another anymore."

Dylan snorted. "You sure talk an awful lot for someone with nothing to say!"

Lee Ann started to laugh, giving a little snort. Gina smiled. "You just wait. You'll see someday. I bet your momma and daddy run out of things to say."

"You're half right, Gina," I said. Mel backhanded my shoulder. "Use your words, honey," I said.

Dylan laughed and Gina shook her finger at me. "You better watch it, mister."

I gave Gina a hug and shook Dylan's hand, thanking them for what they'd done for us. This was yet another in a long list of lopsided trades. Gina hugged Mel and Lee Ann as well, telling them both to come back soon.

Once we were in the truck and headed back towards home, Mel said how much she liked Gina.

"She's so sweet."

"They're nice people for sure. Every time we do any trades with them, they give far more than they get," I said.

"We need to help them as much as we can," Mel said.

"I like her. She's really funny." Lee Ann said. "I'd like to go visit with her."

I looked at her in the mirror. "You and the girls should drop in on her. It would do her good. It's close enough to walk to."

"Or, we could use the four wheelers."

I smiled. "Or you could use the four wheelers."

We took the food we'd collected to Danny's house. Lee Ann went off to find Fred and Jess. Miss Kay was puttering around in the kitchen when we came in. Her face beamed when she saw me carrying the large basket of produce.

"What do you have there, Morgan?" She asked as I set the basket on the island.

"We did some trading and got some good veggies."

Mel set the butter and cheese down. "We also got these."

Kay snatched the jar of butter up. "Butter? Where'd you find butter?"

"There's a couple trading it down at the market. They said they have milk too, but were out," Mel replied.

Kay's mouth fell open. "Milk, I'd love some milk." She turned her attention to the basket. "Look at all these tomatoes. There's more here than we can eat, so I'll can them. I'll also make up some sauce. This will be so good."

"You want some help?" Mel asked.

"Of course dear! Come, let's get a kettle on. I've got an idea for dinner." Kay looked at me. "Shoo, shoo, you get out of here. We've got work to do."

"Alright, I'll leave you ladies to it. I'm going to check on Taylor."

"Bring her over here. She'd enjoy this," Mel said.

Walking out on the back porch, I saw Danny out by the pond with Jace, Edie and Little Bit. It brought a smile to my face seeing those kids in such a normal activity. Not to mention, Little Bit had her young friends back. Looking out at the garden,

I saw Thad and Mary out there. They were laughing as they worked on the beds. Such a peaceful scene belying our reality.

I wandered over to the house and found Taylor asleep on the sofa and woke her up. "Hey, kiddo. Come on. Let's go over to Danny's. Mom and Kay are going to be canning a bunch of veggies and mom wants you to help."

She sat up, rubbing her eyes. "Really? Like in jars?"

"Yeah. Come on."

She got ready and I held her arm as we walked over to Danny's. She got around pretty well, and was able to walk; but she was a little wobbly on her feet, so I held on to her despite her protests.

"You can let go, Dad. I can walk."

"I know you can. Just making sure you don't topple over," I said.

Once she was up on the porch, I gave her a hug and told her I would see her later. Wandering over to the garden, I interrupted Thad and Mary.

"Hey, Thad. Tomorrow we have to go to town with the tractor. We need to get those fields planted." Then I looked at Mary and smiled. "Hi, Mary."

She shaded her eyes with a gloved hand covered in soil. It was a pink gardening glove. Made me wonder where in the hell she came up with them. "Hi, Morgan."

Thad stood. "Yeah, we need to get those seeds in the ground. I'll be ready when you are."

"We've got to stop by Mario's place on the way and load a generator on a trailer I'm taking, then drop it off at the power plant."

"Sounds good to me. When you want to leave?"

"After breakfast I guess."

Thad smiled. "I'll be ready. You wanna go handle that business across the road?"

I didn't. I really didn't. But it needed to be done. "Yeah, let's get it done."

Thad left the garden and walked towards me. I stepped off the porch to meet him. He nodded towards the pasture across the road. "Tractor's already over there."

We crossed the dirt road and walked out into the pasture. The bodies were laid out in a row, ready for burial. I stopped at the end of the line and looked down. "There's a lot of them."

"Yeah, there's a bunch."

Waving a finger over them, I asked, "Anyone go through their stuff yet?"

Thad shook his head. "No, but Sarge said he wanted to before we put 'em in the ground."

Digging around in my vest, I pulled out a pair of nitrile gloves. "Let's do it then."

Putting on the gloves, I started at one end of the line. These guys were pretty well equipped. Each had a rifle and a pistol. The pistols were mounted in either a thigh rig or on their load-bearing kit, usually a vest with DHS in big white letters on the back. It was kind of surreal to be stripping the bodies of dead federal personnel. I've always been a law-abiding person, and this was just over the top.

I removed all equipment from the bodies and handed it back to Thad. He piled it according to what it was. Rifles in one pile; vest, packs and the like in another. I also went through their pockets and removed whatever was there. On a couple of them I found personal effects like photos. I looked at them, seeing the faces that meant something to these men starring back at me. In each case, I placed them back into a pocket.

There was also the assortment of knives, and oddly enough,

cigarettes and lighters. Finding a full pack on one body, I tossed it to Thad. "Wonder where they're getting these."

Thad checked it out. "They're European. Someone, somewhere is sending stuff over."

"We'll give them to Perez when we see him."

There was no real intelligence, not that I could see. But we would still need to go through their kits to see if there was anything. When I was done, I stepped back, stripping the gloves off my hands and tossing them onto one of the bodies. We stood looking at the bodies for a moment, then Thad said something that caught me off guard.

"What about their boots?"

I hadn't even thought about that. Never occurred to me. But they were surely a resource, and one we shouldn't just bury in a hole.

"I guess we should take them. I mean, it's a shame to just bury useful stuff. Someone could certainly use them."

After stripping the boots from all of the bodies, Thad went to work digging the hole. It took a long trench, which was actually easier to dig as Thad could drive down into it to scoop out the earth. Once the hole was big enough, we dragged them into it. Wearing leather gloves, I grabbed each by the feet and pulled them down into the trench. As soon as they were all in the pit, Thad started immediately pushing dirt in on them.

Once they were covered, we loaded all the gear into the bucket of the tractor. Thad said he'd take it all to the old man's house so he could go through it and make sure we didn't miss anything. The weapons would end up in our inventory, which was now immense. But these weapons were really nice, and I was going to trade mine for one of them. These carbines were all select fire, which mine wasn't. I'd already set one aside with an ACOG on it. I liked the optic, and it would make for a nice replacement. Thad left to go deliver the goods, and I walked out to the road.

I wanted to go talk to Sarge before dinner, and took a walk down to the bunker. Passing the scorched remains of Brandy and Tyler's house, I stopped at the gate and stared at what was left. I thought about Thad and Danny digging through those ashes trying to find them. I shuddered to think about what they found. I've been so lucky. We've been so lucky, but I was being selfish and thinking more about my family and the fact that I hadn't lost any of them yet.

But it's been close. Lee Ann and then Taylor. Our luck couldn't hold out forever. The law of averages simply assures that our luck will eventually give out, and someone close to me will die. The thought crushed me. Just imagining burying one of my girls or Mel was more than I could bear. Trying to wipe the thought from my mind, I continued down to the bunker.

Sarge and Dalton were there resting over the top of the structure. As I closed on them, I was about to call out to them when Dalton spun around. His ankles were crossed and his arms were spread out behind him on the log. He smiled and his face resembled the Joker.

"Alow, you cheeky basta'd!" He shouted.

It was just what I needed. The horrible thoughts rolling around in my head were gone in an instant. Not that the replacement image was any better. Shaking my head, I replied, "You simply are not right in the head."

Sarge snorted. "And that's saying something around here. The bar's been set pretty damn high."

"Well we all have a gift!" Dalton replied.

Looking at Sarge, I asked. "You heard from the guys yet?"

He shook his head. "Nah. I won't worry about them until late tonight. If they aren't here before the sun comes up, then something's wrong. You never know what you'll get when you turn them two loose."

In a heavy hillbilly drawl, Dalton asked, "Prone ta wanderin', are they?"

"Wanderin'!" Sarge shouted. "Hell, once at Camp Rhino I sent those two idiots over to Camp Gibraltar to handle a little deal I had with some lads from the 102nd Royal electricians and engineers."

"What sort of deal?" Dalton asked with a raised eyebrow.

Sarge waved him off. "That's not important. What is important is that those two booger eaters called me from Darwin, Australia four days later!"

I laughed. "How in the hell did they get there?"

"I still have no damn idea! But I played hell getting them back! I had to use up a lot of hard-earned favors to get their asses returned."

Dalton was leaning against the bunker rubbing his chin. "But you did get them back."

"Damn right I did. I take care of my own. Besides, the last place you want to be is in my pocket."

I glanced down at his trousers and made a distasteful face. "Yeah, I think not. I bet it's sticky in there."

Dalton laughed. "And hot and steamy."

Sarge jammed his fist into the pocket and made an act of rummaging around. "Want some candy, little boys?"

Dalton turned his head and clenched his eyes shut. "Oh, the thought of it!"

"When the guys get back, you sort out how we're going to deal with those assholes over at that camp. I've got other issues to deal with. I'm going to town in the morning. Taking Thad to get with Cecil so they can get to work. Plus, I've got to get that generator over to the plant," I said.

"I'm looking forward to the chance to school some of those fools," Dalton said. He then produced a tomahawk from someplace and proceeded to swing and swirl the damn thing. I expected any minute he'd bury it in his forehead; but after a few seconds of the show, I realized he knew what he was doing.

"Let me see that thing," Sarge said, holding his hand out.

Dalton held the instrument up for a moment and inspected it before handing it over to the old man. The hammer marks were clearly evident on the head. The head was finely shaped in the fashion of the Cherokee with a small hammer head on the poll. The heel and toe were mirrors of one another, dropping slightly to increase the face of the bit. Sarge hefted the weapon, checking the balance and weight. He made a couple of swipes in rapid succession and smiled.

"You do some fine work, Dalton," Sarge said, and offered the hawk to me.

I took it and quickly noticed the excellent balance of the weapon as well. While I wasn't exactly a hand to hand pro, I still appreciated the quality. "That's nice. But I don't know much about using one of these," I said as the images of my Gerber hatchet sticking upright in Thomas's head popped into my mind.

Dalton grabbed my hand and held them up while working them to the base of the handle, wrapping his hands around mine. He looked me straight in the eye. "Give it firm purchase here. It knows the rest of the way."

Dalton reached into the bunker and pulled out a bag. Opening it, he took out two additional hawks and inspected them. He looked at a long-bearded hawk, then at Sarge and smiled.

"I think this one fits you." Kinda nasty." And he handed it to the old man.

Sarge held it up and smiled. "I like the way you think, son."

"It never jams. Never runs out of ammo, and goes off every time you swing it. If it's a little dull, just push harder," Dalton said.

Sarge smiled again. "Don't use your musket if you can kill 'em with your hatchet."

Dalton nodded. "And keep it scoured at all times."

Dalton handed me one much like the first in classic Cherokee style. "Thanks, this is really nice." I held it up and added, "Hope I never need to use it."

Dalton smiled. "You know what they say. Violence is never the answer. Except when it is; and then it's the only answer."

"Bullshit!" Sarge shouted. "Violence is always the answer. Those blathering idiots that say violence is never the answer, are always the first ones to resort to it. I just don't give them the chance to compromise their morals. Hit 'em first, and hit 'em fucking hard."

Dalton broke out into a Cheshire Cat smile. Depending on the circumstances, it could be viewed as mischievous or malevolent. Either way, it was creepy. "Now, I like the way you think, Pop."

Sarge wagged the bearded hawk at Dalton. "You call me Pop again and I'll compromise your morals."

Dalton stuck the tip of his finger in his mouth and swiveled his hips. "I didn't know you cared."

A crimson line crept out of Sarge's collar and up over his ears. The two hairy ass caterpillars on his brow merged into one. "You little shit!" Sarge shouted as his foot shot out for Dalton's backside. Dalton cackled as he leapt out of the way.

"Little? He's twice the size of you." I said with a chuckle.

"And he'll take twice the ass whoopin' too!"

"I'll leave you two to play nice with one another," I said.

That night for dinner, Kate and Mel made a goulash of sorts with the gator and the veggies. But the real highlight was the fresh baked bread slathered in melted butter. It was Mana from heaven. A taste that you fully don't appreciate until its wanton absence is finally abated. We had a quiet dinner. While everyone enjoyed the meal, there was an overlying weight on everyone's mood. As soon as all were done with their meal, we filed out to the pond behind Danny's house.

In an all too familiar custom, we gathered around the freshly disturbed earth. A plot too small to contain the bodies of our two friends bore grim evidence of their fate. As before, Thad placed a cross over their resting place. He'd inscribed their names on it together. A fine carving of a vine intertwined the two names.

Jace and Edie clung close to Danny and Bobbie. Little Bit stood beside Mel holding her hand. It was so quiet, not even the wind blew. After a moment of inner reflection, I broke the silence.

"I'm sorry, my friends. You won't be forgotten."

"We'll carry you in our hearts forever," Mary said.

Each in turn said their piece. Once everyone had said what they could, we headed back towards the house. Mel was holding one of my hands and Little Bit, the other. Taylor was beside her, walking under her own power. She looked over and asked me, "Dad, why did you say you're sorry?"

Looking at the ground, I said, "Because I let them down and they died as a result."

Mel looked at me. "How did you let them down?"

"The fact that they're dead. Those guys got in here. We're supposed to be defending ourselves, and they keep showing up and killing people," I replied despondently.

"That's not all on your shoulders. Everyone here is part of it. You can't blame yourself," Mel said.

I wanted to reply. To ask how many more of us would die before we got it under control. But feeling Little Bit's small hand in my own, brought my mind around, and I thought better of it. I didn't want to scare her or cause her to lose sleep with nightmares of what may never come. Far too young was she to burden her heart with such.

CHAPTER 6

I TOOK THE LATE SHIFT AT the bunker with Aric. I wanted to be awake at midnight for the radio transmissions that should be on the air. Aric said he just wanted some time away from all those women. Certainly couldn't blame him for that. I took the little radio out and extended the antenna. After tossing the little wire extension up into the small oak tree, I connected it to the radio.

"What's with that?" Aric asked.

"I picked up a radio transmission the other night. And we should be able to pick one up tonight."

"What'd you hear? Was it local?"

Shaking my head, "Wasn't local. I think they were in Idaho. And what they had to say wasn't too comforting."

"Like what?" Aric asked.

I took a minute to explain what I'd heard, and we talked about the possibilities. None of them was very good. But I reminded him I'd only heard it once, and there was no way to confirm any of it. It could all be a hoax or psyop by the feds or some other unknown entity. Then again, it could be correct.

"What time does it come on?" He asked.

Looking at my watch, "In about half an hour." But just in case, I turned the radio on and lowered the volume on the static. "So how are things with you and Fred?"

He smiled. "It's good. She's a really great gal."

I leaned over the top of the bunker, "That's terrific. I'm happy for both of you."

He let out a long breath. "I just hope someday we can settle down in a little place of our own." He was staring off into the darkness. "Not like before, ya know. Just a small place and a simple life. I'd like some livestock and a garden. A big garden. I'd like to look out my window and see Fred kneeling in the garden with our little girl filling a basket with the bounty of the land."

I chuckled. "Nostalgic much?"

He smiled lightly, a little embarrassed. "It just appeals to me, you know. Before, I was all about a big house, expensive cars and living what we all thought was the good life." Looking over, he added, "I've learned what's really important."

"I guess we've all learned a little something," I said.

I picked up the NVG and scanned the road and the areas around and behind us. There was nothing to see, fortunately, so I laid them down and checked my watch. I was eager to hear the radio come to life.

"How's Jess doing? You guys spend so much time together I hardly ever see her."

His head wobbled back and forth. "She's good. I mean, I think she want's someone in her life, you know."

With a smile, I said, "I guess it is hard." I stood up. "But there are some options around here." I couldn't help myself, and laughed at the thought.

Aric snickered. "Yeah, we've talked about it. If you could mash Ted and Mike together, it'd be the perfect guy for her. Mike is young, and she thinks he's good looking. But Ted is far more mature and has a better temperament."

Now I laughed. "Ted is more mature, huh? I guess compared to Mike a two year old is more mature."

"Exactly."

Just then, the static on the radio dropped out as a transmitter came on the air somewhere out there. Aric and I both focused intently on the radio.

A man's voice came over the radio. It was crystal clear and loud. I actually turned the volume down slightly.

You're listening John Jacob Schmidt on the Radio Free Redoubt, broadcasting to all of you in occupied territory as well as those outside the wire. Bringing you the news you need in these uncertain times. Good evening, patriots. We're happy to report to you tonight that the Marine Corps has secured the Hartsfield-Jackson airport in Atlanta. In intense fighting, the Marines pushed aside the resistance. One Marine claiming, 'it was a slaughter. We killed them by the dozens.' With the airfield now in their hands, the Air Force has begun airlifting in reinforcements, equipment and much-needed supplies for the people of Atlanta. Those brave Marines deserve our appreciation and prayers.

On a sad note, we've received word that Baltimore is burning. The reports claim it looks as if the entire city is ablaze in a fire storm. Refugees are said to stretch for miles, moving north and south on I-95 as well as west on I-70. Conditions are said to be horrific. The source of the fire is currently debated, with the Federal troops claiming the military started it by bombing the city. Brigadier General Dawson claims that operatives of the Federal forces started the fire as an act of retribution for an ambush that resulted in the death of several troopers.

On the west coast, conditions in San Francisco are deteriorating rapidly. As the city pulled together in the initial aftermath of the event, that solidarity has become fractured in recent weeks as resources dwindle. The city has been broken up into distinct districts, and the roads blocked and movement heavily restricted according to the neighborhood you live in. There are unconfirmed reports of hundreds of dead in street fighting.

In the southwest, the war with Mexico is heating up.

Hearing that, I looked at Aric. "I wondered what they were up to. I knew they'd try to take advantage of the situation."

As the broadcast continued, I took a Write in the Rain notebook from my pocket. I was surely going to miss those things when I used the last one. I wanted to be ready for the message this time. While listening, I was processing what I'd heard. I worked for a time at the BWI airport, and spent some time in Baltimore. I was imagining that city on fire.

What I remembered of Baltimore was that it was a crowded city. I'm sure there were a lot fewer people now, but still quite a crowd. The thought of being caught in a place like that was horrible to me, terrifying. I'd been fortunate about where I was when things went down. I could have just as easily been in Atlanta.

As Mexican nationals continue to stream south, American citizens are prevented from crossing the border. There are reports of hundreds shot dead trying to cross the border to the south. The Texas National Guard as well as elements of the Third Armored Cavalry Regiment, repulsed an attempted cross-border foray by Mexican troops. Even in their weakened state, the Texans were far more than the Mexicans could handle. However, the Mexicans have gained ground in southern California, New Mexico and Arizona. In all but California, their advance has been checked through the judicious use of air strikes by Air Force, Marine and Army aviators. Again, it cannot be said enough. The men and women of our armed forces deserve our sincerest appreciation and prayers. Keep up the good fight!

On the international front, the UN Security Council is

currently debating the resolution to send in peacekeepers. From what we're hearing here in the Redoubt, there would appear to be considerable pressure on the UN to send in troops. Though the ambassador from the UK claims those urging the use of force are in reality asking for permission to invade. The Department of Defense has made its position very clear. Any vessels attempting to reach the shores of the US will be met with force. In unequivocal terms, they were told they'd be sent to the bottom of the sea. We can only hope cooler heads prevail. God bless the United States of America.

And with that the transmission ended. The message I was expecting never happened. I waited, expecting any minute to hear it. After a couple of minutes, I turned the radio off.

"Holy hell," Aric said.

"No shit. Can you imagine a city like Baltimore burning?"

He looked at me. "Can you imagine the Mexicans shooting Americans? I mean, you remember all that shit their government did? They encouraged their people to come over here! Remember how those illegals were always portrayed as poor little victims? That Asshole-in-Chief tied the hands of the Border Patrol, and those pricks in the Justice Department wouldn't prosecute them. Hell, they had a standing policy to let them go when they were caught!"

"Oh, I remember. And look how they act when the shoe's on the other foot. Wonder where all those whiney liberals are now. They were so against guns. Makes me wonder how many of them had wished they had one just before they died."

Aric snorted. "Shit. A lot of them had guns pretty damn quick. Hell, I bet a bunch of them already had them!"

Looking down my nose, I said, "Only to protect themselves from people like us of course."

"Yeah, just like politicians surrounded by armed security telling us we couldn't have guns. It drove me nuts."

I laughed. "I find your attitude very interesting considering where you came from. I mean, you were part of the machine. How did you reconcile your personal views with what you were doing?" I could tell the question hurt him, but I was genuinely curious about it.

Aric spun around and leaned against the bunker. Crossing his arms, he let out a breath. "It wasn't easy." He looked directly at me. "But I fell into a position I didn't want to be in. I had to survive and I wasn't prepared for what happened. I should have been. I should have been prepping all along. But I didn't. Like I said, I was hung up on the idea of the good life and chasing what we were always told was the American Dream. But it was all bullshit. That whole consumer-driven idea was only the dream of bankers. Not us. "

Nodding, I said, "You're right about that. That's why I never went into debt. Not that there weren't things I wanted or needed. I just avoided the use of credit. I figured if I couldn't pay cash for it, I didn't need it. The only loans I had were the house and my truck payment. Neither of which I now have. So what's the point? I like the good life. I like a nice house and air conditioning. Vacations and going out to eat. But in the end, those are all just distractions from the things that really matter. The things that preserve life."

He nodded. "I know. So I got caught with my pants around my ankles. I had to do something. And when the DHS offered me a spot, I took it. But it was wrong, and I knew it. I compromised my morals by doing what I was told. I told myself it was for the best, and these people needed our help whether they wanted it or not."

I grunted. "The old line of, *we know what's best for the people.*"

"Yeah, exactly! That's really how they think. They look at us like cattle; and it goes all the way to the top. People for labor were accounted for just like fuel. They were seen as a consumable commodity."

"In the Before, we were seen as ATMs. Now, just a strong back. What you're saying reminds me of the way the Nazis dealt with the Jews and others they considered undesirable. One of the first steps of this process is to dehumanize people. If you can get folks to view others as less than human, then it's much easier to abuse them."

He pointed at me, wagging his finger. "You know, that's exactly what they are doing now. They call anyone with an independent streak or patriotic views Bubbas or Rednecks. They're very, what's the word, vehement in their hate for them."

I smiled. "For me. And now for you. What do they call the rest of the people?"

"Useful Slugs, for those that are capable of working. They look at them as some kind of investment. What's the least we can put into them to get what we need out of them. And for those that aren't able to work or bring some skill to the table, they're just called Eaters. They're seen as a drain, no return on the investment."

"See, just what I was saying. And it'll get worse before it gets better."

Aric rubbed his chin. "Of course those aren't the official terms. I'm trying to remember them. I think there was Able Bodied Manual, Semi-Skilled and Skilled. Then there was something like Infirm. And for the real undesirables, it was Radical with several levels running from Potential to Extreme. And you know what's really bad? Nearly all of them had standing KOS, Kill On Site orders."

That was a shock? I asked. "Really? Kill on site?"

Aric nodded. "Yeah. When we showed up, if anyone started mouthing off about Constitutional Rights or anything along those lines, they would pop them right there in front of the rest. It usually ended any debate, and most fell in line. But it didn't always go that way. There were some hellacious gun fights, and the DHS didn't always win."

I saw an opportunity and took it.

"And what did you do in such situations?"

He quickly shook his head. "Oh, I was never involved in any of that. I was on a team that scavenged. Of course, to the government everything is theirs and they have the right to take it. That's what bothers me. That's what I lose sleep over. Having participated in taking people's property. Their food, weapons and even clothes." He stopped talking and looked at the ground as he pushed the dirt around with the toe of his boot. "The worst one was when we found a family that was pretty prepared. They really had it together. We took everything from them. They had a small baby and this guy had done the math and stored enough diapers in the proper sizes to get his kid through until he was potty trained." Aric looked at me. "We took it all. They left him one box of diapers. We took all the formula, everything."

Shaking my head, I asked, "What was their rationale? Why would they take something like diapers from someone?"

"They took it because they wouldn't come into the camp. It was to punish them. I knew the guy was a prepper and very patriotic, but he played it cool and didn't say anything. So we just took everything. He has no idea how close to death his family was."

"Or maybe he did, and that's why he didn't say anything," I replied.

"Yeah, probably. But they took it all to the camp. I mean, we needed it there too. There were lots of kids to take care of and a lot of people were helped, and that's what I kept telling myself. That's how I justified it."

"Just like how the Jews had to surrender their property to the State. It's the same thing. Or maybe they were fans of Marx, you know. From each according to his ability, to each according to his need," I said.

Aric nodded. "I know that now."

We spent the rest of the night in silence. I was lost in thoughts of what was going in. Sure, the news in Baltimore and Arizona was bad, but it didn't have any impact on me or my family. But the thought of Russian or Chinese troops showing up, that would certainly have an impact on us. Hell, on everyone in the country. Because I'm quite sure that, contrary to their stated goals of wanting *help us in our time of need*, it's just as much bullshit as I think it is.

The fact they were so eager is disturbing. It's like they've been waiting for the chance. Now that they think we're weakened, they're going to pounce. But I have a feeling they underestimate us. The Russians know full well what a determined people can do. They crushed the Germans in Stalingrad with sheer numbers. So when you consider private ownership of guns was not possible there, one can only imagine what the people of this nation would be capable of.

I was relieved by Dalton and Danny around two in the morning. I needed a little sleep before taking on the task of moving the generator, among other things. But it was a restless sleep. I kept waking up with images of Russian or Chinese troops kicking in the door of my house and dragging my family out of the house. Not like they would. I'm sure they'd have bigger issues to deal with. We're no more than a blip in the big picture.

However, the thoughts were there, and I found myself

several times watching Mel sleep. Sometime around five AM, I decided it wasn't worth it anymore. I got dressed and went out to the kitchen for some tea. I had work to do today, and I may as well get ready for it. After pouring a cup of tea, I nosed around in the cupboards. I was curious how much more sugar we had. I found the container Mel kept it in. It was full. So I went looking for the bucket. I found it in one of the lower cabinets and pulled it out. I could tell just from the weight it was too light. Pulling the top off proved my fear. It was less than half full. Oh, the thought of not having tea once again! But it wasn't like I could run to the store and buy a bag. Oh well, it is what it is.

I went outside and tripped over the dogs lying on the porch. It never ceased to amaze me that they found it necessary to lie right in front of the door. There's a whole porch there, but inevitably one of them would be right in front of the door! Meathead looked up at me when the door hit his belly. He didn't move though. Instead, he simply dropped his head back onto the deck. So I used the door to scoot him out of the way.

At my neighbor's house was the trailer I planned on using for the generator. I went out and started the old Suburban. As it belched smoke, I gave it a minute to wake up. The pause also gave me a minute to think about my old neighbors and what happened to them. I know they went to the camp, but I didn't see them there. It was odd that after the camp was abandoned, no one came back. What happened to them? Where else would they have gone?

I pulled out onto the road and drove towards my old house near the end of the road. As I passed the bunker, I stopped for a minute and talked with Dalton and Danny, telling them what I was doing. After a bit of small talk, I continued down the road.

It was kind of odd to be driving around in the dark. I couldn't remember the last time I'd done it.

As I came to the house, I pulled through the open gate and drove towards the garage that sat off to the side. Turning the truck around, I backed up to the trailer and got out. The trailer had sat for a long time, so I inspected the tires carefully. They were in very good shape, probably fairly new. Continuing the inspection, I heard a thud and looked up. The sound came from the house. I squatted down behind the trailer and waited. I heard a shuffling sound and the floor creak, but nothing more. Someone was in there.

I went to the truck and got my carbine and slowly moved towards the back of the house. Another thud, louder this time, confirmed someone was in the house. I picked up my pace and made it to the back door and found it standing open. Now I wished I had my NVG with me. Unfortunately, I didn't and would have to rely on the light on the carbine. I always hated the thought of trying to clear a house. Especially at night with a light. It always seemed to me that turning one of these things on was turning on a *shoot here* light.

Standing off to the side of the open door, my pulse began to pick up - I could hear it in my ears. I cautiously stepped up onto the concrete steps. Each subsequent step took considerable effort, I was scared to death. But eventually I was in the threshold of the door, staring into the inky blackness of the house's interior. I had the carbine up to my shoulder and waited, listening.

Hearing a bump to the right, I turned and started to walk through the kitchen. There was a stinks to high heaven, water your eyes stink. I couldn't quite place it. As I took one slow step after another, my foot met some resistance. I placed weight on my right foot and stepped into something soft that felt as though it was mashing out either side under my step. I looked down but couldn't see anything. But whatever it was, it was substantial. With my head still looking down, there was a sudden noise in front of me. Instinctively, I hit the switch for the light on my rifle.

The intense LED light filled the kitchen and stunned my eyes. But the presence of a huge black bear a mere couple of feet from me in the confines of the kitchen shocked me. *Shit!* I shouted and tried to back pedal to get some space between me and the bruin. But my right foot slipped on whatever I was standing in, and I fell back, landing hard on my ass.

For his part, the bear let out a loud growl, groan or some kind of unholy sound. How my bowels didn't let go, I have no idea. But as soon as my ass landed on the floor, I started shooting while trying to scramble away from the beast. The blast and concussion from the weapon was deafening. Being on the floor between the cabinets in the kitchen, there was no place for the muzzle blast to go except through my head it seemed.

I kept firing as I tried to gain some purchase on the floor. But it was as if I only had one foot to work with, because the right one simply found no traction. To my great fortune, it must have been the first or second round that killed the bear. That didn't stop me from shooting, however, as I continued to fire round after round. Once my senses returned to me, I stopped shooting. Smoke lingered in the beam of my light, and the smell of burnt powder hung heavy, mixing with the existing stench.

As I was getting to my feet, there was a crash behind me. I spun to see Dalton coming through the door. His face was wild and he was breathing hard. His AK was at his shoulder and he was scanning the house.

"What the hell's going on!" He shouted.

Giving him a little wave, "It's ok."

Weapon still shouldered, he asked, "What are you shooting at?"

I turned sideways and pointed to the opposite end of the kitchen. "That."

There was more noise outside, and Mike burst through the door with Doc right behind him.

"What the hell's going on in here?" Doc asked, looking around.

Dalton laughed. "Ole Morg got himself a bear!"

"No shit? A bear?" Mike asked and leaned in to see.

Doc looked at me. "You alright?"

I looked myself up and down. "Yeah, I guess so."

He pointed to my leg. "What's on your leg? Is that blood?"

I pointed the light at the floor and looked at my leg. Dalton stepped in and inspected it. Running his finger across my pants, he brought it up to his nose. "No, that'd be bear shit." Then he wiped it back on my pants.

"Oh thanks," I said.

The floor was covered in bear scat. That soft pile I stepped in was now spread all over the kitchen floor, and me.

Mike pinched his nose. "Damn, you stink!"

"What the hell are you doing over here?" Doc asked.

I told them I was getting the trailer to put the generator on when I heard a bump inside. I thought it was a person and went to investigate.

"And found a bear," Doc said. I nodded.

"Hey, Morg. Next time, just step over the pile of bear poop. Don't roll around in it." Mike said.

Dalton laughed. "Gotta say, I ain't never seen it done like that before."

"You guys can kiss my ass," I said.

"Let's drag this thing out of here," Dalton said.

We got to work and pulled the beast out the back door. Sarge was there with Ted and Thad when we got it out to the concrete slab behind the house.

"Hot damn, boys!" Sarge shouted. "That's one fine looking bear."

"I'm surprised there's any left," Doc said. "I figured they'd be hunted out by now."

Sarge nodded. "Me too. But we got us one now." He looked at me and said, "Nice work." Then wrinkled his nose and looked me over. "Why are you covered in bear shit?"

"He was rolling around in it in there," Mike said. I gave him the finger and he smiled.

Looking at Sarge, I said, "I'll see your gator and raise you one bear."

Sarge smiled. "Hell of a job, son. Let's get this thing out of here. We got some butchering to do."

Thad was standing off to the side not saying much. I stepped over to him. "What'da think?"

His arms were crossed over his chest as he inspected the bear. After a moment, he said, "I think you white people is crazy for messin' with these wild animals."

I started to laugh. "That's pretty good, Thad."

He smiled. "But now that it's dead, I'll deal with it."

I went with Mike and got the trailer connected to the truck and backed it over closer to the bear. We picked it up and loaded it onto the trailer and headed towards Danny's house. Mike and Ted went to relieve Danny so he could come to the house and help with the butchering. Thad and Dalton rode with me.

Looking at Thad, I said, "You know you have to go with me this morning."

"Yeah, I know. I'd like to work on that bear, but we got work to do."

"Don't fret, lads. I'll skin the beast!" Dalton shouted from the back seat.

Thad looked over his shoulder. "Take good care of that hide."

"But of course! I'll make me a furry kilt of it!"

I started to laugh. "Now there's an image I don't need in my mind."

Laughing, Thad added, "I know, right!"

After unloading the bear at Danny's, we left him and Dalton. Thad went to get the tractor while I got the truck back out onto the road. Sarge took forever, but finally came out of the house carrying a plastic shopping bag.

"What the hell were you doing?" I asked as he climbed in beside me.

He held the bag up. "Getting Mario some lizard meat."

With a smirk, I replied, "You were just making time with Miss Kay."

"Just shut up and drive!"

Smiling, I pulled off. I made a quick pit stop at the house to change my pants. I stunk to high heaven and wasn't about to spend all day covered in bear shit. We met up with Thad on the road and headed out towards town. As we passed the road to the house Ian shared with Perez and Jamie, I saw Perez slumped against a fence post. Rolling up, I asked, "Well, look who's still alive."

Perez took a drag on a cigarette and started to hack and cough while giving me the finger. Once he finally got it under control, he looked up with watering eyes and asked, "You headed to town?"

"Yeah, we're on our way there now."

Slinging his rifle over his shoulder, he said, "Good, I'm going too."

Sarge looked at him. "You look like shit. I think you should stay here."

"Tough shit, Top. I'm going to check on Jamie." Perez replied as he climbed in the backseat. Once in the back of the truck, Perez slumped over and almost immediately fell asleep.

I had to keep an eye on Thad on the tractor to make sure I didn't leave him. I was glancing back at Thad when I heard Sarge ask, "What's that?"

I looked down the road past the bullet holes in my windshield - I still hadn't forgiven Danny for that. And I saw something lying in the road. As we got a little closer, I said, "Looks like a person."

"Sure is. Let's stop and check him out."

I stopped short of the body and we got out. I looked back at Thad and waved him forward. He pulled the tractor around the truck as I walked over to the body.

"Somebody did a hell of a number on his head," Sarge said.

"Yeah, I used to joke about striking someone repeatedly about the head and neck. Shit. Someone did it to this poor guy," I said.

Thad shut the tractor down and pronounced, "Damn! He took one hell of an ass whoopin."

Sarge rolled the body over on its back. The man's face was severely beaten. So bad, the nose sat at an extreme angle. Both eye sockets were probably shattered from the looks of them. His jaw also appeared to be broken.

"This was personal," Sarge said.

"That, or whoever did it just enjoyed it," Thad said.

Sarge looked around. The road was covered in blood. Bloody footprints were in a large circular area around the body. "Looks like it was a hell of a fight."

"He ain't got no shoes," Thad said.

The man's bare feet were rather clean compared to the soiled clothes he wore. Someone relieved him of his footwear. It was a stark image, to imagine this man being beaten to death over a pair of shoes. It harkened back to the days when inner city kids would jack one another up over a pair of whatever was *the* sneaker of the day. But this wasn't done over envy or some sense of fashion. This was more than likely done for need. Someone didn't have shoes, or theirs weren't in as good a condition, and they decided to take this guy's.

Sarge looked at me. "What do you want to do with him?"

"Let's get him out of the road and we'll pick him up on the way back I guess."

"Just put him in the bucket. I'll bury him out at the farm," Thad said.

We agreed that was the best idea, and Sarge and I hefted the body into the bucket when Thad pulled it over. I couldn't just leave the man there. While I knew nothing about him, it was the proper thing to do. We got back in the truck and headed for Mario's.

Looking over at Sarge, I said, "Wonder what Mario's going to think with us pulling up with this corpse in the bucket."

Sarge laughed. "Well, I told him we'd bring him some meat today."

"Oh, that's just wrong."

We stopped at the gate and I honked the horn and waited. After a couple of minutes, I hit the horn again. Not long after, I saw a side by side come out from behind the warehouse. Mario stopped at the gate and opened it. I pulled through and watched in the mirror as Thad came through with the tractor. I couldn't help but smile when I saw him crane his neck to look in the bucket. The feet sticking out the side of the bucket gave no doubt what was in it.

I saw him say something to Thad and point at the bucket. Thad shrugged and replied as he rolled through the gate. Once Mario secured the gate, he walked up.

"What the hell is that?" He asked, pointing at the feet sticking out of the bucket.

Before I could reply, Sarge leaned forward. "Told you I'd bring you some meat today!"

Mario pointed at the tractor. "That don't look like a gator to me."

Sarge started to laugh and slapped the dash of the truck. I shook my head. "Just ignore him. We found him on the road. Couldn't just leave him there."

With a quick shake of his head, Mario replied, "You ain't leaving him here either."

Waving him off, I said, "No, no. I just need to get the generator on the trailer. We'll deal with him later."

"Alright then. Follow me, I've got the backhoe over at the generator. Shouldn't be too hard to load it up."

We followed him around the warehouse to a small lean-to structure. The generator was out from under the structure, Mario having used the backhoe to pull it out. Once he was off the ATV, I asked him where he wanted me, and pulled the truck in as he indicated.

Sarge got out and walked around the generator, looking it over. "You sure this thing's gonna run?"

Mario smiled. "Hell yeah." Stepping up to it, he flipped one switch and then another. The generator rumbled to life, coughing thick black smoke for an instant before settling into a loud rumble. "She's great!" Mario shouted over the roar of the machine. Since it was just sitting on the ground, it vibrated furiously.

Sarge gave him the *kill it* signal, and Mario shut it off. "Have you checked the output?" Sarge asked.

Mario nodded. "Yeah, it's about 487 volts."

"That's good enough," I said.

"Let's get this contraption loaded up then," Sarge barked.

Mario explained his plan. He would lift the front of the generator up with a chain connected to the bucket of the backhoe. Then I was to back the trailer under it and he would set it down and move to the back of the generator and using the bucket again, lift it from the bottom and push it up and onto the trailer. Sounded pretty easy.

Mario lifted the front of the generator and Sarge guided me back. Sarge gave me the signal to stop, and I waited as Mario lowered the generator onto the end of the trailer. That's when things went sideways. While the trailer was more than sufficient to handle the load, having all of it on the very end wasn't working out. The front of the trailer rose steadily as he lowered the load. It was putting a lot of pressure on the hitch itself. Sarge yelled at Mario to hold up. I got out to see what was going on.

"This ain't going to work. It's putting too much pressure on the hitch," Sarge said.

Thad stepped over and looked at the problem. "I could come over here with the tractor and put pressure up here on the front. That should be enough for him to get off it."

Sarge nodded. "Alright, let's try it."

Thad pulled the tractor up and lowered the bucket down onto the tongue of the trailer. He forced the trailer back down but had to roll the bucket down a little to get enough pressure. Sarge called to Mario, and he let off the load entirely. It worked and the trailer sat fairly level. Sarge climbed up and quickly unhooked the chain, and Mario moved the machine to the back of the generator and slid the bucket under it.

Picking up the ass end of the machine, he started to push it forward. The generator was mounted on a frame made of four-inch I-beam. The deck of the trailer was diamond plate; and as Mario started to push, it slid rather easily across the bed. That is until it hit a small piece of weld we hadn't noticed. When it hit the weld, the whole trailer and generator shuddered hard. The body in Thad's bucket rolled out and ended up with the upper torso on the ground and the legs on the trailer.

Mario stopped and asked what was going on. Sarge quickly told him, and Mario jumped off the machine and disappeared into his warehouse. He returned with a long pry bar and handed it to Sarge, who jumped up onto the trailer and jammed the edge of the bar under the I-beam and put some pressure on it. Mario was back in the hoe and gave it a little push.

The generator came free and moved forward quickly, throwing Sarge off balance. In trying to catch himself, he tripped over the dead guy's legs and fell off the trailer in a barrage of curses. I ran around the trailer to help him up, but he was in no mood for it.

He shoved me away. "Get off me you fucking potato head!" Sarge shouted when I tried to help. I laughed and stepped back.

"Be careful, old man. You don't want to break a hip." I shot back, trying not to laugh. He wasn't hurt, so I wasn't worried about him now.

He got to his feet and dusted himself off. "I'll break your fucking hip!" He shouted. Then, looking at the corpse he had tripped over, he shouted, "Get on the other end of this sack of shit!" I helped Sarge get the body back into the bucket, and Thad backed away.

"Taken down by a dead man," I said. "I think you're slipping."

Sarge pointed at me. "Keep it up, peckerhead." I laughed,

but decided it was probably best to leave the grumpy old bastard alone. Best for me that is.

Mario brought out some chains and binders, and we secured the generator to the trailer. It wasn't long before it was properly secured and we were ready to go. Sarge stepped back and inspected the load.

"That went better than I thought it would," he said.

Mario huffed. "What? It went exactly like I expected."

"Shit, I'm happy. I didn't know what to expect," I said.

"Me too. It's on the trailer. That's all I expected," Thad said with a chuckle.

Sarge shook Mario's hand. "Thanks for the help, Mario. Hopefully, those engineers can get that generator running."

"Not a problem. Glad to do my part," Mario replied.

I grabbed the bag of gator meat from the truck and brought it over. "Here, Mario. Here's some of the old man's lizard."

Mario smiled. "Thanks. This'll be good."

"Hope you enjoy it," Sarge said, then looked at Thad. "You and your buddy there ready to go?"

Thad smiled. "I am, and he's always ready."

"You two are messed up," I said as I got in the truck and gave Mario a wave.

Sarge climbed in beside me. "What's eatin' your ass?"

"Me? Nothing. Let's get this thing delivered and go to town so we can check on Jamie."

"Yeah. I need to set up a time to sit down with Sheffield," Sarge replied. "You're going to need to be there as well. But we'll also need Mikey and Ted to be there."

Sarge called the armory on the radio to let them know we were on our way to the plant with the generator. One more stop before we could get into town. I was eager to check on Jamie. Not to mention we needed to get the farm up and running.

Thad and Cecil would oversee the work, but we needed more bodies out there. That meant we needed either volunteers, or needed to make some volunteers.

Pulling up to the plant, I drove around to the building that held the controls for the plant. The power would have to go in there first, so it was only logical. The engineers weren't there yet, so we got out and looked around.

"Where do you think it needs to go?" Sarge asked.

"Let me look around," I said.

"I hope you know, 'cause I ain't going to be no help on this," Thad said.

Going inside, I looked at the banks of breakers and motor control centers or MCCs. I found the main for what looked to contain most of the pump motors and other associated components of the plant. But there was another one on the other side of the room, and the two weren't directly connected. Trying to rig power between the two would be a real pain in the ass. There had to be a better way.

Going outside, I started looking for transformers. The power for the operation of the plant would be tied in with the main grid somewhere. There would also be a switchgear someplace that would allow the plant to swap between grid power and the plant's own output. If I could find that, then we would have one point of connection, making it a lot easier.

"What are you looking for?" Sarge asked.

"A transformer, a big one," I replied.

Sarge walked with me as I went around the corner of the building. And there it was. A giant green transformer sat just outside the back of the building. Considering the power of an EMP and the fact that this thing was tied to the grid, it was probably no good. But that was alright. Our generator would produce the same voltage that this thing did on its secondary side. Power came into the transformer at line voltage of 7200 volts, and was stepped down to 480 volts. The generator produced the same 480 volts.

Trying the handle on the big green box, I said, "Right here. This is where we need to put the generator. We need to get into this transformer so the engineers can connect to the wire going into the building."

"I'll go get the truck," Sarge said as he disappeared back around the building.

There was a padlock on the doors of the transformer. It was the typical power company lock they all seemed to use down here. One of the round ones with a stamped metal body designed primarily to keep honest people honest. Getting it off would be no great feat.

Sarge drove around the corner with a Hummer following him. I was glad to see the engineers because I wanted to get going on the other tasks for the day. So I smiled when Scott and Baker climbed out of the truck.

"Well, I hope we weren't interrupting anything important this morning," I said.

Baker nodded at Scott. "Just his beauty sleep."

Sarge snorted. "And he needs it from the look of that pumpkin on his shoulders."

"Hey!" Scott said. "Didn't your mother ever teach you if don't have something nice to say, don't say anything at all?"

Sarge smiled. "Where do you think I got my sparkling personality from?"

Thad laughed. "You was raised by a rabid dog?"

Sarge pointed at Thad and shouted. "I'll have you know the test for rabies came back negative!" He winked and added. "Now, where were we?"

I told Baker and Scott to follow me and took them around

back to the transformer. Leaning against it, I said, "This is the transformer for the plant's controls. I figured this would be the best place. But if you guys find a better way, by all means, go for it."

Scott looked the piece of equipment over and said, "It probably will be, but we'll take a look around just to make sure."

"Then we'll unhook the trailer and leave it here," I said.

"How are you going to keep someone from stealing it?" Thad asked.

"Once we start work, we'll be staying here with a squad to provide security. But for now, we may just drag it back to town at night," Baker said.

"Whatever blows yer skirt up," Sarge replied and smiled at Baker. Her only reply was to roll her eyes and shake her head.

"Alright then. We'll leave you two with it," I said.

Sarge looked around and asked, "Where's that snot-nosed student of yours?"

"He's back at the armory finishing up a little job. We didn't need him today," Scott said.

"You don't need him unless you need a doorstop," Sarge snorted.

"Don't be so hard on him. He's a good kid. Smart too," Baker said.

"Glad he's your problem," Sarge said. "You guys ready to go?"

Thad nodded and headed for the tractor while we walked over to the truck and disconnected the trailer. Fortunately, the jack on the tongue of the trailer was stout and had handled the load with no issues. When Thad drove around to join us, Baker saw the legs hanging out of the bucket and nearly shouted. "What the hell is that?"

Sarge looked over and flatly replied, "Oh, that. That's just roadkill."

She looked at me for more, but I waved her off. "Don't worry. I won't let him eat it."

The look on her face made me laugh. It almost looked as though she thought the old man capable of it. We said goodbye and left. The field Thad and Cecil were working wasn't far from here, and we needed to get him over there. As we headed up nineteen, Sarge pointed at a couple of guys on the side of the road at a small tote-the-note car lot. They were messing around under the hood of an old station wagon of some kind. They stopped their work and looked up as we passed.

"Probably trying to get it to run," Sarge said.

"Or scavenging parts," I replied.

As if to reaffirm the fact there were still machines in operation, a motorcycle passed us heading back towards Umatilla. Neither of the two riders wore helmets, and the passenger was trying to manage a large bundle of some sort. It looked like pictures and video I'd seen from places like India and Pakistan where the motorbike was the primary form of transportation for many. And people would load them with all sorts of junk that would cause a state trooper an immediate erection.

At the field, Cecil was already at work. He had a plow connected to his tractor and was out cutting rows. Another plow sat waiting for Thad's tractor. Seeing us pull in, he took off his hat and waved. We pulled over to the plow and waited for him. When he completed the pass he was on, he came over and shut the machine down.

Looking at the bucket of Thad's tractor, he cocked his head to the side and asked, "What's his story?"

Sarge glanced over and said, "His story is that his story is over. Found him on the road. Someone beat the hell out of him."

Cecil walked over and looked in. Letting out a whistle, he said, "They damn sure did." Then he looked at Sarge. "What are you going to do with him?"

Sarge shrugged. "Bury his ass somewhere."

Cecil looked out over the field. "I'm sure we got a spot out here that'll work."

I was struck by the casualness of the conversation. Here was a dead man that we'd found on the road and tossed into the bucket of a tractor. We then drove all over the country with the corpse before ending up here where Cecil just took it in with no more surprise than if it were a dead cat. Contrasted against how things worked in the Before, it was stark.

There would have been a road closure with highly skilled people coming out to examine the body and looking for evidence of the crime. The body would have been inspected by the medical examiner, who would determine the cause of death. The body would then be kept in a cooler until the family was notified and arrangements were made. Then someone in a big Cadillac would show up to take the body, covered in a nice velvet blanket, to another building. And there it would be cleaned, dressed and placed in a box.

Elsewhere, someone would lay a slab of granite on a machine and punch in the appropriate words, and the machine would forever etch into the stone the words that would sit for all eternity over the grave of this man. Family and friends would gather as a service was held before the box with the body in it. And then it would finally be lowered on small winches into a hole dug by a machine. The exposed dirt would be covered with cheap green indoor/outdoor carpet so as not to upset anyone with the reality of the situation. Once the bereaved had departed the burial site, the machine would return to fill in the hole.

There were so many moving parts. So many people and

machines involved. Now, one tractor and a couple of men. Nothing more. And hardly any notice, and certainly no surprise. Not for those that found him or those that would intern him. But maybe this was the better way. It was certainly closer to the natural way. But then we couldn't really use the natural way of just leaving one where they fell until nature took its course. As much for health reasons as for the fact that no one wanted to see a body in public any more now than before. Though I would imagine that there were millions lying where they fell. Or rather their bones. But the killing and dying was by no measure over.

"You get anywhere on your help?" I asked. Cecil had an expression that reminded me of my grandfather. His chin would drop to the chest and folds of skin would show around it, and he'd smirk as if to say, *what do you think.* He did it now, but said nothing. "So we're going to have to find you some bodies then?"

Cecil smiled and pointed at the bucket. "Not more of this."

Sarge snorted. "Hell, Cecil. If you want live ones, we'll get you live ones!"

"They would be more productive," Cecil replied.

"Shit Cecil. Worms gotta eat too!" Sarge shouted and slapped the hood of the truck. "You need anything before we leave?"

"I just need some able-bodied people what aren't afraid of hard work."

I walked around to the driver's side of the truck and said, "They can get over their fear."

Cecil grinned. "Make 'em too tired to be scared."

As Sarge climbed in beside me, he added, "Pain is just fear leaving the body! You know, like when that bear scared the crap out of you this morning."

"Yeah. Well, me one. Bear None."

Sarge laughed. "True. That thing is going to be good eatin'!"

I drove up to the armory and parked. Looking back at Perez, he was still asleep. "Hey, Perez! We're here."

He sat up groggily and looked bleary-eyed out the window. He started to cough, and I quickly jumped out of the truck. Sarge also exited the truck with haste and looked back. "Damn it, Perez. You get me sick, and I'll beat your ass!"

Perez gave him a dismissive wave. "Yeah, yeah." Smiling, he added, "Wouldn't be hard right now."

Perez extracted himself from the truck and slung his weapon as he trudged towards the clinic. I followed Sarge into the armory to talk to Sheffield. We ran into Livingston first and told him we needed to talk. Livingston pointed us towards the conference room and went off to find the Captain. Sarge and I went in, and I dropped into a chair. Sarge, of course, went to the head of the table and took a seat.

I was shaking my head. "You just can't stop screwing with him, can you?"

Sarge swiveled the chair back and forth. "It's only right that the smartest man in the room be sitting here."

I was shaking my head when Sheffield and Livingston came into the room. "What's up, guys?" Sheffield asked as he took a seat. I was surprised he didn't say anything about the seating arrangement, considering the earlier pissing contest between these two.

"We need to come up with a plan to hit those assholes at the Elk's Camp. My guys did some recon out there, so we know where everything is. This is going to take a coordinated effort to get rid of these guys," Sarge said.

Sheffield was drumming his fingers on the table. "How many people do they have?"

"Over a hundred."

"Holy shit," Livingston said. Then he looked at Sheffield. "I don't like those numbers."

"No doubt it's going to be a hell of a fight, but we've got to do it. They shot up the market in Altoona and bombed the one here. They've hit us a couple of times. We have to take them out," Sarge said.

Sheffield nodded. "We do. But I don't want to lose half my people doing it."

"Nor do I, Captain. I want to bring Mike and Ted up here and go over the lay of the land and come up with a plan. I've got some ideas, but we need to talk about it," Sarge said.

"We definitely need to discuss it," Sheffield said.

Perez made his way to the clinic and walked in. He found Doc and asked where Jamie was. Doc looked at him. "You still look like shit. Come in here and let me check you out."

"Fuck it, Doc. I'm fine. Believe it or not, I'm better than I was. I just want to check on Jamie."

Doc eyed him for a minute before giving up. He knew Perez wouldn't cooperate. "Alright. But if you start to feel worse, let me know. Come on. She's over here."

Doc led Perez over to a curtained treatment area. Jamie was sitting up in a bed and smiled when she saw Perez.

"Hey, Poppie!" She said with a smile on her face.

"Ola chica. How are you feeling?" Perez asked.

Jamie shrugged and lifted the gown she wore to expose a bandage around her abdomen. "Not bad, considering. These docs here are pretty damn good."

"Good. I'd hate to have to shoot a bunch of doctors."

Jamie smiled. "You here to take me home?"

"If you're ready, I'm willing," Perez replied and sniffed loudly.

Jamie cocked her head to the side. "You look like hell. You alright?"

Perez chuckled. "Thanks for noticing. I'm fine. Just been sick."

"So you want me to come home to take care of you, huh?" Jamie asked with a smile.

Perez shrugged. "Somebody's got to do it."

Doc cleared his throat. "You should stay here another day or two."

Jamie looked at him. "Why? They're not doing anything to me. I can sit at home as good as I can sit here."

Perez looked at Doc. "Yeah. Besides, you'll be there."

"Whatever. I'm ready to get the hell out of here anyway."

"Okay. We'll get the guys up here and start working out a plan," Sarge said.

"Let's move on to the farm. We need labor. Have you guys talked to anyone around here?" I asked.

Livingston shook his head. "No. We were leaving that up to Cecil for the most part."

"Cecil said he wasn't having any luck. We need people out in the fields if we want to grow any food over there," I replied.

"I guess we need to wander over to the park and see if we can get any volunteers," Sarge said.

Looking at Sheffield, I asked, "You got a bullhorn?"

"Actually, we do," Livingston replied, and left the room.

"You going to go over and see if you can those people to work out in the sun breaking their backs for no pay?" Sheffield asked.

I threw my hands up. "How do these people expect to eat?

We're going to grow this food for everyone. And if you don't contribute, you won't eat."

Sheffield drummed the table with his fingers again and smiled. "Good luck with that."

Livingston returned with the bullhorn and set it on the table. Sarge picked it up and hit the trigger, speaking into it. "Does it work?" The thing was loud and caused everyone to flinch. Sheffield gave him a look and shook his head.

I picked up the bullhorn and walked out. Sarge followed me, muttering something about *I gotta see this.* I walked down to the park and up onto the stage of the clam shell. The park was crowded with people either offering trades or looking for them. Plus, there was the usual assortment of people just hanging out. I guess with no job and nothing to do, a lot of people just didn't know what to do with themselves.

Looking at the bullhorn, I said, "Here goes nothing." and I pulled the speaker trigger.

"Hey, folks. Can I get your attention for a minute?" I gave people a minute to wander closer, or as was the case with a number of them, at least turn their heads. "We're starting to plant crops outside of town. We've got a big section of land tilled and plowed and we're ready to start planting. But we need help. This food is for all of us, so all of us need to pitch in. If you would please step up over here, we can get transportation and the like organized."

I waited to see what sort of response I would get. I was met with silence as the crowd looked around at their fellows. They did move closer and start to mumble amongst themselves. After a minute, a man stepped up.

"So what do we get out of it?" He asked.

"You get food. How about not starving to death?" I replied.

"Well, seems like this farm would happen with me or

without me. If I didn't work, I could just wait for someone else to do it and then still get my share, couldn't I?"

"What share? You wouldn't have a share." Keying the horn again, I said, "If you do not contribute to the farm, you will not be given food. There is no freeloading. You wanna eat, you work."

The man smiled. "That's what I wanted to hear. I'm in."

And with that, several others came to the edge of the stage and said they wanted to work as well. There were still many out there that made no move to offer up their labor, and they began to congregate and talk amongst themselves. After a moment, one of the group stepped forward.

"How can you expect us to spend every day working on this farm? We still gotta eat. It'll be months before any of those crops are ready. How are we going to feed ourselves today?"

Using the bullhorn again, I answered the man. "No one needs to be out there every day. Two or three days a week for a few hours will get it done if everyone pitches in. We're not wanting to work anyone like a slave. But the simple fact is we need people in the fields; and if everyone just does a little, then we can get a lot done. We'll provide transportation out and back and water kegs at the farm."

The statement was met with more nods and even more people came up and offered to help. There were still a few holdouts, but there always will be. Hell, if you were giving away sacks of money, someone would complain they were too heavy.

Sarge stepped up and crossed his arms. "That went way better than I thought it would."

I laughed. "No shit. I didn't expect it to be this easy."

Keying the horn again, I said, "Anyone going to the farm needs to be at the armory at seven tomorrow morning. We'll have trucks ready to take you, and get your names and info then."

As we walked off the stage, Sarge started to laugh. I looked at him and asked what he thought was so funny. He slapped his leg. "There's going to a damn mob at the armory in the morning. Sheffield's going to be pissed."

It made me laugh. "Yeah, he probably will be. Let's go tell him so he can't say we didn't warn him."

We were mobbed with people when we came off the stage. Questions were hurled at us by a dozen or so people. I put my hands up. "We'll try and answer your questions tomorrow. Just know that this is for all of us."

We pushed through the crowd and made our way back to the armory. I saw Livingston as we came through the gate, and called him over.

"You're going to have a crowd here in the morning about seven. We need to have trucks ready to take people to the farm. You also need to establish the security detail for them while they're out there. I don't think we need overnight security yet; but when crops start coming up, we'll need it for sure."

Livingston looked over at the park. "Wow. I didn't think you'd get any takers."

"Hunger will do that to a man," Sarge said.

Livingston smiled. "If they're hungry, maybe they'll work then."

"They're going to have to," I said.

Livingston nodded. "I'll get it put together. We'll be ready."

We left and headed to the clinic to check on Jamie. We were intercepted by Shane with the PD. "Hey, Morgan. I got a guy over here that I need to talk to you about."

"This your murderer?" I asked.

"Yeah. What are we supposed to do with him?"

"Hang him!" Sarge shouted.

"Probably." I said. "But let's go over and talk to him."

As we walked, he told me what he knew of the situation. The guy was drunk and his girlfriend ended up dead. No one is sure exactly how, but she had bruises on her face and marks on her neck like she'd been choked. His family brought him to the station to keep her family from killing him.

"Sounds like a good time," Sarge said.

As we got closer to the station, I saw three people standing out front talking to Sean Meador, Shane's second in command of the police.

"This is Dave Rosa's mom," Sean said.

Looking at her, I said. "And Dave is the guy that killed the girl?"

"It's not his fault! He was drunk; and if that man wasn't selling liquor over there, he wouldn't have been drunk—," she started to protest. But I cut her off.

Holding up my hand, I asked, "Did he kill her?"

She'd paused, but picked right back up. "Yes he did, but he was drunk….." I cut her off again.

"And what do you think that has to do with this?"

She stared at me for a moment before taking off again. "If he wasn't drunk, it wouldn't have happened. He didn't mean to do it. Dave's a good boy an….."

I stopped her once again. I was getting a little pissed with her argument. "Look, drunk or not, he killed someone and has to pay for that. Unlike before, there is no *not guilty by reason of insanity or drunkenness,*" I said - the last part with a heavy dose of sarcasm.

Even back in the Before, I was so damned tired of people committing horrible ass crimes and being able to walk away from them relatively unscathed because of a bunch of bleeding hearts. If a dog killed someone, for whatever reason, it would be put down. If a bear or some other predator were to kill a person, it would be hunted to the ends of the Earth and put down. But for some reason, our thinking had changed. It was deemed better to keep some people confined for the rest of their lives. Or worse yet, to actually be released back into society after committing these horrible crimes.

Pointing towards the market, she started again. "But if that man wasn't selling liquor….." I'd had enough.

I stepped towards her and shouted. "Your son will accept responsibility for what he's done! And the man selling liquor isn't an issue anymore, now is he?"

She immediately cowed away from me, which was fine with me. Looking at Shane, I jerked my head and he followed me towards the door to the PD. As I walked away, a young man that was with the woman, and as yet, hadn't said a word, spoke up.

"You kill my brother, and you won't be able to close your eyes, ever."

I spun on my heels and headed straight for him. He glared at me as I approached. I could see the hate on his face, and I could also tell that at the moment he meant what he said. As I got closer to him he stepped forward with his chest pumped up. He was young, maybe sixteen, and obviously foolish. Once close enough to him, I slammed the butt of my carbine into his nose. It busted like a ripe grape, and a geyser of blood flowed from it as he collapsed.

His mother moved towards me and I drew my pistol as I stepped forward, the kid now on the ground. I pointed the pistol at the woman and shouted. "Back off!" She froze in her tracks and took a step back. I grabbed the kid by his shirt and lifted him from the ground.

Jamming the pistol in his face with as much calm as I could muster, I said, "Just like your brother has to take responsibility for his actions. You're going to learn your words have consequences." Looking at him, I asked, "You threatening me? You think you're going to get me?"

His mother was pleading. "Please don't hurt him! He didn't mean anything. He's just a boy!"

"A boy will kill you as fast as any man!" I shouted back. Looking back at the kid, I said, "And I do not plan on looking over my shoulder!"

Holding his shaking hands in front of his face, the kid pleaded. "Please mister! I didn't mean anything by it. I'm just upset!"

I stared into his eyes as my finger lay on the side of the pistol's trigger. Pointing with the muzzle, I said, "I'm going to believe you, for now. You're young and dumber than a sack of dog shit. But you better believe if I ever catch you looking sideways at me, I'll kill your ass. Understand me?"

The kid nodded, and I released my hold on his shirt. He dropped back to the pavement as I stepped off him. His mother rushed to his side and knelt down, lifting his head into her lap. Holstering my pistol, I looked at the two others there with them. They wouldn't make eye contact, so I headed back for the PD.

Shane looked at me. Raising his eyebrows, he said, "Feel better?"

"I don't deal well with threats," I replied as I passed him.

He looked back at the boy and said, "Could'a fooled me." And he followed me inside.

I found Sarge talking to Sean. He looked up. "Well? What's it going to be?"

"He's killed someone. There's only one solution for him. But we'll use him for a bit first. I'm going to have him put to work for a while." Looking at Sean, I added, "We need to come up with some sort of jury system or something. We need a judge."

Sarge smiled. "I was wondering when you'd get around to that."

"It would be best. But I don't know who we'd use," Sean replied.

"If we ever want to get this community put back together, we have to. You've got to know someone around here," I said.

Sean let out a long breath and looked at the floor. Looking up, he said. "I'll have to think about it for a bit."

"Let me know when you come up with some names, and we'll talk to them. In the meantime, we need some chain. From now on, people caught for petty shit will be put to work on the farm. Have the two prisoners chained and at the armory by seven for transport to the farm."

Sarge's bushy eyebrows went up. "Chain gang?" I nodded. "That's a good idea."

"We're going to use Sheffield's people out at the farm. Just like any other form of detention, escape attempts will be dealt with in one manner."

"Gun line," Sarge grunted.

"That's a good idea. Make it clear where the line is and what the consequences are," Sean added.

"Just like at Angola in Louisiana. That old prison didn't have a fence. Just a line painted on the ground. No warning shots."

"I'll find some chain and locks and get it ready," Sean said.

"I'm going over to the clinic to check on Jamie. We'll see you guys in the morning," I said.

"I'm glad to see you're starting to think about things like a judge and jury," Sarge said as he glanced over at me.

"It needs to be done," I replied and looked at him. "Bad as it sounds though, the real reason is I don't want to be responsible for everything. I don't want to be the one making those decisions all the time."

Sarge shook his head. "Don't blame you a bit, Morgan. I sure as hell wouldn't want to be making those calls either."

Sarge and I went to the clinic to see what Jamie's status was. She didn't look so good the last time I saw her, and I was worried. But when Sarge and I got to the clinic, we were surprised to see her dressed and ready to go. Ian was with her, along with Doc.

"You look fit as a fiddle," Sarge said with a smile.

"I don't feel like a fiddle," She replied with half a smile.

I looked at Doc. "Well, Doc. What's the word?"

He didn't look too happy. "I think she should stay here another day or two, but she wants to go home, and there is no real reason for her to stay here. She can heal just as well at home."

"Damn right I can," Jamie added.

"Alright then. Let's get loaded up and on the road.

CHAPTER 7

D ANNY AND DALTON WORKED ON the bear for a couple of hours. Danny was being meticulous with the hide. He'd always wanted a bear hide, and this was probably the only chance he'd have with one. The two men worked carefully but quickly to remove the hide. Dalton worked on the head, completely skinning it out.

Holding up one of the paws, Danny asked, "What about these?"

Dalton held the foot up and looked at it. "If you want, I'll do 'em. I've never done it before, but I watched a guy out at the Rabbitstick gathering in Idaho once."

"Well, that's a hundred percent more than I have, so go at it."

"Let's get this thing skinned and quartered and I'll tend to those later. When we open this thing up, I want to get the gallbladder out intact."

Unsure why, Danny asked, "What for? What are you going to do with that?"

Dalton looked at him curiously. "Medicine."

"Medicine?" Danny asked.

In a stoic voice of a TV Indian, Dalton replied, "Hmm, big medicine."

Danny laughed. "Whatever you say, Tonto."

They continued working on the carcass. When it was nearly skinned out, Dalton turned his attention to the feet. He used his small Bark River neck knife and made a slit along the edge of the pad on the bottom of the foot. He then meticulously skinned each digit. It took some time to do all four feet, but when he was done, the feet were intact. It would only take a couple of stitches to reconnect the pad where he made the cut, and the bear-skin rug would have all four feet.

Danny held one of the feet up and looked at it. "That's really cool. I didn't think you'd be able to get it done that quick."

"Seemed to me to take forever," Dalton said as he wiped his brow.

Danny rolled the hide up and set it aside. Looking at Dalton, Danny said, "You ready to open this thing up?"

Dalton nodded. "Yeah, I'll do the cutting so I can get that gallbladder out."

Dalton made a slit in the belly of the animal and inserted his finger into the animal's abdomen and laid the tip of the blade against it. Using his finger as a guide, he ran the tip of the blade down the animal's middle, exposing the internal organs. Once it was open, he reached in and ran his hand along the liver and found the gallbladder. Using the small knife, he pinched the top of the gallbladder and cut it free.

Taking it out, he held it up to show Danny. "Here it is."

Danny wrinkled his nose. "Doesn't look like medicine to me."

Dalton looked at it. "Maybe not. But in Asian medicine this is used a lot. Sadly, thousands of bears were kept in captivity in China where they were milked for this. Only reason I'm taking it out is to respect the animal by using everything we can from it. I would never buy this."

Cocking his head to the side, Danny asked, "How do you milk a bear's gallbladder?"

Dalton shook his head. "It's sad. They surgically insert a tube so they can do it. The bears are kept in a cage that keeps them from moving, at all, for up to twenty years. It's really pathetic."

Danny spit in the dirt. "Damn Chinese."

With Dalton's prized gallbladder now out of the bear, they set to work quartering the rest of the animal up. The tenderloin was cut out and set aside as the prime cut it was. Then, all that remained was breaking the rest of the animal down. That work didn't take long, and soon the meat was ready to be taken into the house. They took a few extra minutes to remove as much fat from the carcass as possible.

Holding a piece up, Dalton said, "This is like gold. It's the hardest thing to come by in nature."

"Yeah, it's hard to produce this," Danny replied.

Nodding, Dalton said, "Takes lots of calories, and this bear did the work for us."

Dalton grabbed the two hind quarters to carry inside. Danny asked if he could use Dalton's neck knife. He wanted to remove the meat from between the ribs. "I don't want to waste any of it."

"Right on, go ahead. I'll take these in and I'll be back."

Going inside, Miss Kay and Bobbie were ready. They had Danny's meat tubs and large cutting board sitting on the island.

Coming through the door, Dalton shouted, "Did someone order some meat!"

Clasping her hands in front of her face, Kay said, "Oh, look at all that!"

Bobbie was standing behind the island, knife in hand. She slapped the cutting board. "Bring that over here!"

Dalton dropped the two quarters onto the cutting board. "Here you go, ladies. More to come!"

"Keep it coming," Kay said as she grabbed one of the legs, rolled it over and examined it. After giving it a once over, she went to work with her knife.

Dalton brought the other two quarters in and returned to help Danny with what was left. Danny picked through the gut pile and removed the kidneys. He cut them in half and carried them over to the chicken feeder bucket and dropped them in. It wouldn't take long for the flies to find them and lay eggs. Then the chickens would enjoy the extra protein provided by the developing larvae.

All that remained now was the gut pile. They'd wait for Thad to get back with the tractor to haul it over to the pig pen.

Thad and Cecil worked on the field for several hours. With two tractors they were able to get the first section rowed out and ready to plant. The two men stopped their tractors under the oaks and inspected their work.

"I think we're ready," Cecil said.

Thad nodded. "Yeah. They get some folks out here and we'll be able to get this planted in no time."

"I'm going to head back to town. I've got a couple of things I want to do before we kick this off."

Thad nodded. "Me too. I'll head home today as well. Morgan killed a bear and I want to go see it."

Cecil smiled. "Can't believe there's still a bear around."

Thad laughed. "There's on less now."

Cecil laughed at the comment as he climbed up onto his tractor. "I'll see you tomorrow."

Thad waved as he mounted his machine. "In the morning, Cecil."

The two men parted ways at highway nineteen, with Cecil headed south and Thad north. It wouldn't take long to get back home. He got there just in time to find the gut pile of the bear, all that was left. Danny told him it needed taken care of and Thad said he'd take it to the pigs and scooped it up.

Thad drove the tractor over to his place. Getting the tractor through the gate, he drove out towards where the gator was dropped, and dumped the bucket. The gator was gone, hardly anything remained. Thad shut the tractor down and climbed off. He was looking for the pigs. He took a couple of steps towards the back of the field when a single gunshot rang out. It came from the direction where he was looking. Thad waited a minute to see if there would be more. Then he saw the pigs come running out of the woods headed for the barn. When there wasn't another shot, he started to walk towards the sound to find its source. As he walked, he pulled the shotgun from the scabbard on his back.

Gripping the shotgun, he moved to the wood line and listened. He could hear voices, cussing. Thad moved off to his left so as not to approach the voices directly. He cautiously found his way through the woods, made easier by the fact that the pigs were doing a fine job of under-brushing the area. Drawing closer, the voices got louder.

Thad took a knee behind a large oak tree and listened. He could distinctly hear two voices. They were bitching at one another about getting a pig loaded quickly and getting the hell out of there. Rising to his feet, Thad moved to a Sabal Palm between him and the voices. Pulling a frond back revealed a truck sitting in the field bordering the pigs' hot-wired enclosure.

It was a familiar truck. Thad instantly recognized the old green pick-up.

Knowing who was out there caused a rage to begin building in Thad, and he moved quickly towards the back of the truck. Two men were standing at the rear of the truck, gutting a pig. She was just too heavy for the two of them to pick up.

"Holly shit! It's full of babies!" One of the men said.

"Shh. Be quiet, dickhead!" His friend countered. "You wanna die?"

"There ain't no one out here. We watched 'em leave headed to town. You wanna go get another?"

"We ain't got this one yet. Hurry up," his friend countered.

Thad crept forward. Both men had their backs to him. He looked for the weapon and saw a shotgun leaning against the tire of the truck. Thad waited until the men went to pick up the pig. Once one was on either end and they lifted the sow from the ground Thad stepped out and leveled his Daddy's old coach gun at them.

The two men were straining to get the hog up onto the tailgate when Thad said, "Now y'all just keep that pig off the ground and don't even think about moving."

Both men's heads swiveled around in surprise. They were looking down the double barrels of his shotgun. They started to lower the hog when Thad motioned with the barrel of the gun, and told them to keep it up off the ground.

"Come on mister, this thing is heavy!" One of them complained.

"I bet it is. She's a big sow. You killed the biggest one we got." Then he motioned with the barrel at the ten piglets lying lifeless on the ground. "Plus her litter."

"You've got a bunch of hogs. You ain't going to miss one," one of the men moaned.

"Maybe, but I'll damn sure miss eleven pigs." Motioning with the barrel of the gun, he said, "Now you two carry that hog up to the house."

"What?" One of the men said.

"You heard me!" Thad shouted. "Now get moving. And if that pig touches the ground, I'll unload all of this buckshot in your face! Now move!"

Though Thad kept threatening them with the shotgun, the weight of the sow was simply impossible for the two men to carry. They just couldn't keep it off the ground. And it wasn't long before they were dragging it on its back through the woods. Reaching the cleared pasture behind the barn, the men dropped the hog and doubled over breathing hard, spent from the effort. Dalton was there looking around and walked over to Thad.

"I heard a shot," he said and looked at the pig. "What a shame."

"Yeah it is. Lost the litter too," Thad replied.

Thad pointed at one of the men, "This one's name is Tommy Harrell. I don't know that one."

Tommy squinted at Thad, "You know me?"

"Yeah. I know you. You don't remember running into me out in the woods one day with your girlfriend do you?"

Tommy thought for a minute and slowly started to nod his head. A smile started to spread across his face. "Yeah, I remember you now. You were burying my nigger."

Dalton was standing close to Tommy. His right hand flew out lightning quick and connected with Tommy's nose snapping his head back and staggering him. "Watch your mouth," Dalton said as he looked at his hand. "Shit!" Tommy exclaimed.

"That's right. Now you remember me. You killed the wrong hog today," Thad said.

Dalton looked at Thad, "What's this all about?"

"We found a young black kid hanging from a tree. This piece of shit showed up with two girls. They were showing him off it to them. At least they thought they were. We buried the boy but Morgan let this asshole go."

The other man with Tommy was getting scared. He looked at Thad, "I didn't have anything to do with that mister."

Thad glared at him, "You still guilty of stealing my hog."

"So we got a real piece of shit here then," Dalton said.

"To say the least."

Looking at the two men, Dalton drew his Glock. "Alright, you fuckers. On your faces."

Still holding his nose, Tommy said, "What?"

Dalton stepped forward, placing his foot between Tommy's feet. Cupping the man's neck, Dalton shoved him, sending him to the ground with a thud. He looked at the other man who was starting to squat.

"What are you going to do to us? I'm really sorry. It was Tommy's idea!" He said.

Lying on his back, Tommy said, "Shut up, Robert. You pussy!"

Dalton stepped up and kicked Tommy's hip. "Roll over on your face." Then he pointed the Glock at Robert. "You too. On your face."

When the men rolled over, Dalton knelt on their heads and searched both men. He took a knife from each of them and tossed them over behind Thad. Now that he knew they weren't armed, he stood up and looked at Thad and asked, "What do you want to do with them?"

Thad stepped up to Tommy. "You killed that boy, didn't you?" At first Tommy wouldn't reply, so Thad kicked him. "Didn't you!"

Tommy looked up, "You can't prove it."

"Prove it! I don't need to prove anything! I know you did it!"

Turning his face back to the ground, Tommy muttered, "Can't prove it."

Thad snapped. The shotgun spit thunder and fire as the load of buckshot smashed into Tommy's head. He was so close, it crushed it like a bat hitting a melon.

Dalton jumped back. "Damn Thad!" And he looked down at his pants to see them covered with blood, bone and tissue.

Robert started to scream, "Oh Jesus, oh Jesus! Please don't shoot me! I didn't do it! Tommy and some other guys did!"

Thad looked at Dalton. "I told you he did it. I knew he did. I knew that day he did." Thad looked at the body. "And now he's gotten what he deserves."

"If he did what you say, then he certainly got what he deserved," Dalton replied.

Thad motioned with the barrel to Robert. "You heard him, he did it."

Dalton looked at the second man. "What are we going to do with him?"

"We'll give him to Morgan. I think he's got a chain gang going. He can work his crime off."

"Just don't kill me. Please don't kill me!" Robert begged.

"We just have to figure out what to do with him until Morgan gets back," Thad said.

Dalton looked at Robert. "You know how to butcher a hog? I mean, you killed one, so I assume you do."

Robert looked up and nodded. "Yeah, I know how. I'll butcher it for you. I'll do anything you want."

"I'll go get the tractor," Thad said.

I stopped at the bunker as I came up to it. Jess, Fred and Aric were there. The girls ran up to her window.

"How are you?" Jess asked.

"So glad you're back!" Fred said.

Jamie stuck her hand out the widow and both women reached for it. "I'm alright. Just glad to be home."

Jess looked at me. "Are you taking her home?"

Nodding, I replied, "We are. She needs to rest."

"Can you get someone over here so we can leave?" Fred asked.

Sarge climbed out of the truck. "You girls go on. I'll stay here."

"I'll stay too," Aric said.

Jess and Fred ran around the truck and climbed in. At the house, they helped get Jamie inside and comfortable. Doc stayed to make sure she was alright. I told Jamie to let me know if she needed anything and I'd drop in on her later. She waved at me from the sofa, where she'd been planted by the girls. Perez took up residence in a chair beside her and put his feet up.

"You staying here?" Jess asked.

Pulling his hat down over his eyes, Perez nodded. "Yep."

Jess looked at Doc. "Should he be here since he's sick?" She looked at Perez. "Sorry, I just don't want her to get sick."

Perez waved her off. "I'm alright."

"Whatever he had isn't contagious now, I don't think," Doc said.

From under his hat, Perez added, "Plus, I ain't leaving."

Doc shook his head. "Jamie, I'll be back to check on you. If you should start to bleed or anything, let me know. But I think you'll be alright. You got lucky. Real lucky."

Placing her hand over the wound, she said, "Yeah I won the frickin' lottery."

With a very serious expression, "You did. You won the best prize you could, life."

Doc walked out with me. I asked if he wanted a ride, and he said he'd walk. I told him I wanted to get home and see what was going on. See how the bear was going. We parted ways and I drove the truck down to the house. When I pulled up, I saw Dalton, Danny and Thad over at Danny's and walked over to see what was going on. When I came around the corner of the shop, I saw another man. I was surprised to see they were butchering a hog.

"Why are you guys doing that? We just got that bear," I said.

Dalton looked up. "Well. We didn't kill it." Pointing at the strange man, he said, "He did." The young guy looked scared to death.

"What the hell did you do that for?" I asked. He didn't reply.

"Him and his buddy was trying to poach a pig. I heard the shot and went to see what was going on," Thad said.

I looked around. "Where's the other one?"

Thad crossed his big arms over his chest. "You remember that boy we found hanging in the tree? The one we buried?" I nodded and he continued. "Remember the two guys that showed up?" Again, I nodded. "I knew that day they killed that kid. I wanted to kill them then. The day finally came for one of them."

"You sure he did it?" I asked.

Thad pointed at the other man. "He said they did. And yeah, I'm sure."

Shrugging, I said, "Sounds like it all worked out. What are we going to do with him?" I asked. He was working on the pig and glanced up at me, then at the others.

"That's up to you," Dalton said. "You're the Sheriff."

"Well, I guess we'll take him to town and put him on the

chain gang for a while." I looked at the young man. "There's a price to pay for stealing. And your price is working on the farm on a chain gang."

Still working a knife on the hog, the man asked, "For how long?"

I looked at the pig. "Is that one of the sows that was carrying a litter?"

"She had ten piglets in her. They're all dead," Thad said.

"So, you killed eleven pigs. You better get friendly with that chain that's going on your ankle. You'll be there for a while."

"What the hell are we going to do with all this meat? We've got the bear, the gator and now this," Danny said.

"We'll have to pack everything we can into the freezer I guess," I said.

"There ain't nearly enough room," Danny said.

"Can it," Dalton said.

"Now there's a good idea. We'll have to talk to Kay and see how many jars she has. That'd be the best way to keep it," Thad said.

"Go check with her. Plus, we'll take a big piece over to Gina, and maybe take some up to the armory in the morning," I said.

Thad smiled. "They'd like that. I'll go see what we've got for jars and lids."

"What do you want to do with this guy when we're done here?" Dalton asked.

"Secure him somewhere, I guess." I took a pair of cuffs from my vest and tossed them to him.

"Will do," Dalton said.

"Hey Thad, where are the piglets she was carrying?" I asked.

"They're out back where they were butchering her. Why?"

"I want to get them and feed them to the dogs."

Thad nodded. "That's a good idea. I'll get 'em. Better than just letting the buzzards eat 'em."

I left the guys and went home. I wanted to check on Mel and the girls. The dogs were lying in the driveway when I walked up. Little Sister got up and came up to me wagging her tail. I squatted down to rub her head. She curled around as I scratched her head and back. Seeing some attention being doled out, Meathead and Drake came over as well. The three dogs jostled for position in the scratching line. I noticed all of them looked a little thin. They needed more to eat. The piglets certainly wouldn't go to waste.

I was happy to find Mel and the girls in the living room. They were piled up on the sofa and loveseat watching a movie on the laptop. Mel looked up as I came in and smiled. Taylor quickly sat up. "You killed a bear?"

I nodded. "Yeah. He surprised me and I shot it. So, we'll have a really good dinner tonight."

"It's a big bear!" Little Bit shouted as she bounced on the edge of the sofa. "Were you scared?"

Laughing, I said, "Yeah I was. He was in a house and made a noise. I went to see what it was and ran into him."

"Oooooohhhh. I would have been so scared!"

I walked over and rubbed her head. "I was too, kiddo."

"You going to sit with us?" Mel asked.

I moved over to the sofa and Little Bit wormed out of the way to make room. Sitting down, I asked, "What are we watching?"

"Willey Wonka!" Little Bit shouted.

I leaned back and put my arm around Mel and Little Bit. Looking at Lee Ann, I smiled. She was curled up on the end of the loveseat, half asleep. Reaching out with my boot, I nudged her knee. She opened her eyes and smiled before quickly drifting off again.

Mel patted my shoulder. "Go take this stuff off."

I looked down at the vest bulging with magazines and other gear. I stood up and took it off, setting in on the floor beside the carbine I'd leaned against the end of the sofa. It was good to take it off. I always felt as if I'd float away, taking all the weight off. Between the carbine, magazines, knife, pistol mags and pistol, it was heavy. But I'd become so accustomed to wearing it, I never noticed, that is until I took it off. Then, what really stood out was its absence. Its presence was now normal to me, and that was a sobering thought.

But with the hardware now off, I wrapped my arms around Mel and Little Bit once again and put my feet up on the ottoman. It was time to relax while Willey Wonka, played by Johnny Depp, carried on. As ridiculous as the movie was, it was a very nice distraction.

I half dozed and half watched the movie. After a while, Little Bit said she was hungry. Mel got up and went into the kitchen. I heard her in there puttering around but had no idea what she was doing. We didn't keep much food at all at the house as everyone generally ate together. But after a couple of minutes, she returned with a plate. On it were five slices of Kay's bread with a little butter and a lot of honey on them. She set the plate down on the coffee table to cries of delight from the girls.

Little Bit and Taylor were instantly on a piece each. It even woke Lee Ann up, and she quickly grabbed one. Mel handed one to me, and I started trying to fold it in a manner that would keep the honey on the bread. Far easier said than done. And since I'd pretty much given up shaving weeks ago I had quite the beard going. You just don't realize the amount of food that ends up on your chin until you have a beard. And honey in a beard is a real pain in the ass. Mel was laughing at me as I tried to eat the piece of bread as honey would squirt out from between the folds despite my best efforts.

Licking the sticky substance from my fingers, I said, "You did this on purpose."

She laughed as she too tried to find some control on her piece of bread. "Well, I may have put a little extra on yours. But it's only because I love you!"

I snorted. "It's only because you think it's so funny!"

Little Bit finished hers in record time and was sitting sideways on the sofa watching me. I looked at her out of the corner of my eye. "What?"

Beaming as only a happy child can, she said, "It's so good!"

I took another bite of my piece and held the rest out. "You want it?"

In a sad attempt at looking bashful, she said, "Yeah." And I handed it to her. Her face lit up. "Thanks Dad!"

I spent the afternoon with Mel and the girls. We watched a couple of movies and relaxed. Having something like movies on DVD was a huge bonus. Having something familiar, something that was really frivolous and allowed everyone to escape was important. We did this sort of thing in the Before but really had taken it for granted. And back then it had to be in a theater with overpriced sodas and popcorn. Now, we're all sitting here watching the movie on a seventeen-inch laptop and eating bread with butter and honey. And it costs nothing, yet was worth so much more.

At dinner time, we shut the computer off and headed for Danny's. Taylor insisted in walking on her own, unassisted. She was beyond us fretting over her. So we let her go on her own, but stayed close. While slow, she was certainly getting better. It showed in the way she carried herself. She was taking the whole thing well overall.

She surprised both Mel and me when she finally got in front of a mirror. She looked at herself and turned her head from side to side examining the injuries to her face and head. After a moment, a long moment that Mel and I both held our breath for, she said, "It ain't that bad. My hair will cover most it and makeup will cover the rest." She actually turned and smiled at us after saying that. Mel moved in and hugged her. I stayed a little more stoic however, not wanting her to think I thought it was more that she did. Instead, I just smiled.

As we walked up on the porch, the air was full of a mouthwatering aroma. It was a rich and hearty smell, and I for couldn't wait to get inside. Opening the door, the odor wrapped around us, and Little Bit shouted. "MM mm, something smells good!"

"Yeah it does," Taylor said.

Miss Kay was in the kitchen stirring a large kettle. Seeing us come in, she said, "Come on in and get yourself a bowl of my bear stew!"

And we did just that. Everyone filed through the kitchen and got their bowl before going out to the porch to sit and eat. Fresh baked bread was sliced and laid out on plates. The butter was there as well, waiting to be spread. We took our seats with Thad and Mary who were already there.

"How is it, Thad?" I asked as I sat down.

His head was low over the bowl with a spoon in one hand and a piece of bread in the other. He looked up, shook his head and said, "You don't want none."

I laughed. "That good, huh?" And I slid into my seat.

Mary smiled. "It's really good, Morgan."

Little Bit was already at work on hers and announced, "Miss Kay, this is super good! Can I have more?"

Mike, Ted and Dalton came through the door. They were carrying on like a bunch of kids getting out of school. Miss Kay shushed them, and after filling their bowls, ran them out to the porch. They were taking their seats as Jess came in. She went to the kitchen and said she wanted dinner for her, Fred and Jamie to go. They were going to eat with her at home.

"What is it?" Jess asked, "It smells wonderful."

Dunking a large ladle into the steaming pot, Kay replied, "Just a little stew I threw together."

"Don't let her fool you," Bobbie said. "She worked hard on it, and it's really good."

Kay filled a large plastic bowl with stew and put a lid on it. She then put a half a loaf of bread in a bag with the stew and handed it to Jess.

"Here you go, honey. Let me know what the girls think of it," Kay said.

Jess smiled. "I know it's good. Thanks, Kay."

We sat around and talked a bit. I was happy to see Lee Ann laughing at Mike and Dalton who were carrying on. Mary was sitting with Thad and they were talking quietly. Mel and Bobbie were talking with one another and I was trying to get through my dinner so I could head to the barricade. Tonight Danny and I were on duty, and I'm sure Sarge would want to be relieved.

Danny was sitting with Jace and Edie at the table in the kitchen. Little Bit sat with them as well, and they were all laughing. Danny was feeding Edie like a baby, playing airplane with the spoon. She was giggling loudly and the other kids were as well. Each time he'd get a spoonful, all three kids would open their mouths like a nest of baby birds. They were having a good time.

As soon as I finished my meal, I returned my bowl to the sink and gave Mel a kiss, telling her I'd be back later. Danny told the kids he had to go. They complained but settled down to their dinner quickly.

"You need any help tonight?" Thad asked.

"Nah. We got it," I replied.

"Just let me know," he said with a smile.

After telling the girls goodbye, we left the house. As we walked the short distance to the bunker, we talked about the kids. I'd asked Danny how they were doing.

"They're actually doing pretty good. I'm surprised how well they're handling things."

"Are they asking about their mom and dad?"

Danny shook his head. "No. It's kind of weird. They know they're dead and say they're in heaven. They cry sometimes, but not very often. Bobbie and Edie are really close. They spend a lot of time together. And little Jace just wants to follow me around. It's kinda cool."

"It's a sad thing, but I'm glad they're dealing with it."

Danny smiled. "I think they're going to be fine."

Sarge and Aric were sitting on top of the bunker when we got there. In his usual pleasant style, he let us know he was happy to see us.

Looking at his wrist where there was no watch, he shouted. "About damn time!"

"Look, old man. I'm right on time," I replied.

Sarge snorted. "On time, huh? What the hell would you know about being on time? I bet your ass was late to your own birth."

I laughed. "Whenever I show up, is exactly when I'm supposed to be there."

"Well, I'm glad to see you," Aric said as he hopped off the bunker.

"You guys better hurry before Mike and the guys eat all that bear stew Kay made," Danny said.

"Those snot-nosed runts better save me some!" Sarge shouted.

Aric waved at him. "Come on, let's go get us some. I'm starving!"

Sarge looked over at me. "Tomorrow we're going to town with Mike and Ted to work up the plan to hit the Elk's Camp."

I nodded. "Good. We need to go early so I can drop that pig thief off with Cecil."

Sarge shook his head. "Damn shame losing that hog like that. Thad said he shot one of them. Said he'd hung a boy out in the woods somewhere."

"Yeah. We found the guy hanging and buried him. It really messed Thad up, but I guess he finally dealt with that demon."

Sarge was nodding his head while he thought. "I'm guessing he's going on the chain gang?" I nodded and he asked, "How long you going to keep him there?"

Shrugging, I said, "I don't know. He's got to work off eleven hogs."

"A damn shame," Sarge said.

"They won't go to waste. Thad collected them and we'll feed them to the dogs," I said.

"Them dogs been eating pretty good lately," Sarge said.

"If you're going to stay here and bullshit I'm going to get me some dinner," Aric said.

Sarge twisted his face and replied, "Oh quit yer bellyaching." Looking at me, he said, "I'll see you in the morning." I took the small radio from its pocket on my vest and pulled the antenna out. Sarge added, "You better write down any messages you hear."

Taking a pad and pen out, I smiled and said, "Way ahead of you."

Sarge snorted. "If you was ahead of me, we'd have the last message." Then he looked at Danny. "Will you please keep him in line."

Danny shrugged. "Many better than me have tried and failed."

Sarge laughed as he and Aric headed for the house and a warm bowl of stew. Danny and I settled into the normal routine of preparing for the maddening onslaught of mosquitoes. But this time, I had a secret weapon. Reaching into my shirt pocket, I pulled out a small wadded mosquito head net. I'd found it in one of the boxes from the shed. It was a cheap piece of fine mesh with elastic around the top and bottom. I pulled it over my boonie hat and pushed it down into my collar.

"That's much better," I said as I rolled down my sleeves and put on a pair of gloves.

Danny looked at me. "You suck."

Smiling, I said, "Hey man, don't hate the player."

We tried to get comfortable and took turns scanning the country with the NVGs. We talked a little about the kids and the forthcoming confrontation with the DHS. Neither of us was particularly excited about it. It was certain people would die. It was simply too big a group to take on and not expect casualties.

"What about the girls?" Danny asked. "You going to let them go?"

"I don't want to, but I know they won't be left behind either. And as much as I hate to say it, we'll need every trigger-puller we can muster."

Danny grunted. "That's what I'm afraid of."

"Let's just hope the old man comes up with some sort of amazing plan. You know he doesn't like a fair fight."

The night wore on and clouds moved in, blocking out the stars that filled the sky in unfathomable numbers. When it was time for the radio broadcast, I turned the little radio on. Static poured from the small speaker and I wondered aloud if there would be a broadcast or not. But just when I felt there wouldn't be, the speaker crackled and the Star Spangled Banner began to play. I set the radio on the bunker and leaned beside it to take in the news.

You're listening John Jacob Schmidt on the Radio Free Redoubt broadcasting to all of you in occupied territory as well as those outside the wire. Bringing you the news you need in these uncertain times. We have urgent news for all you patriots out there tonight. The UN Security Council rejected the resolution to send peacekeepers here. This is good news. The fact the international community joined together to renounce sending armed forces into the US is positive for us. Several nations agreed instead to send aid in the form of food, medicine and clothing. Unfortunately, however, the Russians and Chinese have stated they will act unilaterally and send troops here at the request of the president.

The request was made after the president released launch codes to NORAD with instructions to launch against the patriotic forces of our military. Upon receiving the launch codes, NORAD placed themselves under the command of General Buster Peters of the Air Force, who is a steadfast patriot and firmly set against the plans of the Federalists. The voice chuckled. *Oh, to have been a fly on the wall of whatever hole that bastard president of ours is hiding in when he got that message!*

Sadly, intense fighting is raging in the ports of Long Beach and several other California ports between the thug Federalists and noble Patriot military forces, in what we can only assume is an attempt to prepare a beachhead for the arrival of the invaders. But now that we have control of our nuclear arsenal, those commies will have to think twice about actually trying to land troops.

The language being used was striking. While I'd only heard a couple of these broadcasts, there was certainly a change in the language being used. We were now the Patriotic forces fighting against the Federalist forces. But I guess it had to happen at some time. Eventually there would be a drawing of sides and the propaganda machine was now beginning to move. And while I firmly agreed with the portrayal of the Federalists as thugs, I had to keep in mind that it was still propaganda and must be digested as such.

On the home-front, great strides have been made against the Federal forces. With the liberation of Denver, the western states, with a few exceptions, are now all firmly under the control of the Patriot Military. Of course, California is still heavily contested. And with the news from China and Russia, we can only expect things to get worse there before they get better.

Guerrilla fighters in the Carolinas and Tennessee have pushed the Federalists out of those states entirely, with staggering losses of Federal troops. One report we received said you could walk for a mile on the dead and never touch the ground. Patriot losses were high as well, with over a hundred men and women giving their lives for their neighbors. Thankfully, their lives were not lost in vain, as the states are now free of oppression.

Relief supplies are beginning to land in the southern and eastern ports. Yesterday, fourteen-ship convoy from England docked at the port of Tampa, carrying relief supplies as well as unspecified military aid.

Danny looked at me. "Tampa! Maybe some help is finally coming."

The report continued. *Tampa was chosen because of its*

proximity to Patrick Air Force base, still the home of SOCOM, or Southern Command, because of their ability to provide security. SOCOM claims to have nearly eliminated all Federal forces in the state.

"That's bullshit!" I shouted. "There's still plenty of them around here!" But I was not looking at the big picture. A hundred or so Federal thugs in my neck of the woods wasn't a problem for SOCOM, but it damn sure was for us.

Mayport, in Jacksonville and home of the fourth fleet, is also receiving supplies. Naval Air Station Jax is ferrying those supplies to their final destinations. A huge amount of equipment is said to be on its way to the port after being reclaimed from bases around the globe. The Navy claims it's been a herculean effort to get the equipment loaded, but they met the challenge and hundreds of armored vehicles and tanks are on their way. Naval and Marine personnel are working feverishly to ensure that all the equipment is ready to roll as soon as they're unloaded.

In other news, a sabotage attack at the Lake City Arsenal caused minor damage and one fatality. The perpetrator was caught in the act of trying to set an explosive device. He was forced to detonate it prematurely, which resulted in only minor damage to the ammunition manufacturing plant. The terrorist was taken prisoner, and I'm sure will be questioned extensively. John laughed again. *What do you want to bet in some dark hole somewhere that bastard's being water-boarded as I speak! That's it for tonight's update. Tune in tomorrow for the news you need in these uncertain times.*

Lee Greenwood's "God Bless the USA" began to play. I really liked the song. I turned the volume down a little as I looked at Danny.

"If those Russians and Chinese get here, it's going to get really, really ugly," I said.

"Yeah, but he said they were fighting in California. Not here."

"You really think they won't try and eliminate Mayport, NAS Jax, SOCOM, not to mention, Camp Riley? They'll have to. This place will be a damn battleground."

Danny nodded. "Plus, there's Homestead."

"Exactly. All of that would have to be hit before they could even dream of landing troops."

Danny was staring out into the darkness. "You thinking nukes?"

I shrugged. "I sure as hell hope not. The only thing we can really hope for, is that they have other motives, which we know they do, for sending troops in, and that they wouldn't nuke us. It would make it harder for them as well."

"Kind of screwed up, hoping they're coming here to try and take the country, an actual invasion."

Rubbing my face, I said, "Better than being nuked."

When the song finished, I turned the radio off and stuck it back in its pocket. It's kind of amazing, something as small as this little radio opening up the world to us as it was. Information and communication are so important. If it weren't for this radio, we'd be completely in the dark. Going from a world of near instant communication with anyone, anywhere on the planet to a total vacuum, was hard to adjust to at first. Now I was on the other end of that spectrum, where It seemed odd to me to hear what was happening in other places and made me think, *that doesn't affect me.*

But that certainly wasn't the case. These things would undoubtedly affect us. The DHS was bad enough, but at least they were our countrymen. I can't imagine what Chinese and Russian troops would do. We humiliated the Russians in the eighties and ruined their economy in the nineties. Surely they would take their revenge. This thought sent a shudder down my spine as I remembered the atrocities Russian troops committed against German civilians, especially women of all ages, in a fit of retribution.

Then there's the Chinese. We've been in an economic war with the Chinese for decades. They too are capable of horrific acts. There was a lot of talk in the Before about the Chinese trying to buy up our country. It was said they needed the resources, like coal. Maybe they would make a play to try and just take it and save themselves the money. One thing was certain though, neither of these nations had our interests in mind.

Danny and I talked of these things into the night, until Perez and Ian showed up to relieve us. Perez was in his usual state and I heard him coming before I saw him. The glow from the cherry of his cigarette showed where he was, and the hacking cough gave away his approach before we even saw it.

"You sound like shit," I said as he walked up.

As he walked past me into the bunker, he said, "Maybe. But I can get better, and you'll still look like shit."

I laughed. "Touchy much?"

"Ignore him," Ian said. "He's just pissed he had to get out of bed." Leaning over, he shouted into the bunker. "He's the biggest damn baby I've ever seen!" Perez replied by flipping his cigarette out, its red tip cartwheeling through the air before bouncing off Ian's chest. Ian brushed the ashes off and replied, "Damn baby."

"How's Jamie," Danny asked.

Ian leaned his weapon against the side of the bunker. "She's doing alright. Ornery as hell. She wants to get up and do something, but Doc is keeping her in bed."

"At least she's alright. Hopefully, she gets better quick," I said.

"Yeah, I think she'll be alright," Ian said.

"Alright, I'm out."

Ian waved. "Get some sleep guys."

Danny and I walked home together. It was a quiet night and my gear was making noise. To me it seemed like a lot of noise. From my boots crunching on the ground to the nylon vest creaking and squeaking I felt like I was dragging a bunch of cans behind me. I waved goodbye at my gate and peeled off to the house. As I walked up on the porch, the dogs didn't move. I shined my light on them and had to smile. Their bellies, all three of them, were still swollen from the huge meal Thad fed them earlier in the day.

Thad laughed when he told me about it, each of the dogs eating a couple of piglets and taking yet another with them when they finally wandered off. They were so full but couldn't resist a doggie bag, pun intended. Now they were all laid out on the deck and couldn't even wag their tails! It may sound kind of odd to be feeding piglets to the dogs. I'm sure back in the Before some PETA bleeding heart would call the police and there would be a damn good chance you could go to jail for such a thing.

But if you think about it, what better use for them? Today, we don't have the luxury of going to the store and buying a sack of processed cornmeal to feed them. And I'm not going to let them go hungry, so they have to be fed. Meat is a precious resource and one not to be squandered. But I don't think I'll tell Mel and the girls about it. No doubt, they wouldn't approve.

I didn't sleep well. Every time I would drift off, I would have dreams, images of Russian or Chinese troops parading through Umatilla. It was striking to me that the images were always like the ones from propaganda videos and posters of my youth. The soldiers were always portrayed as ruthless brutes. These were the images that ran through my mind.

Finally, around five in the morning, I got up. I just couldn't lie there anymore. I was going to have to get this sleep thing under control. Getting dressed, I wandered out to the kitchen. Lighting the kerosene stove, I set a pot of water on to boil. There was a dish sitting on the counter covered with a cloth. Taking a look, I was surprised to see several large pieces of cooked meat on it. *Well this is a nice surprise,* I thought. Taking out the half loaf of bread, I sliced off a thick piece and laid a piece of meat on it. Folding it like a taco, I ate it while I waited for the water to boil.

I guessed it was bear meat and was wonderful. It was like eating a sandwich, something I hadn't had in a long, long time. I hadn't thought about a sandwich in some time. But now that I was eating something close to one, the memory of a good Dagwood-style sandwich returned to me. But at the moment, this was just as good.

Before the kettle whistled, I took it off the heat and poured a cup full. Taking a tea ball out, I filled it with the loose tea and dropped it into the cup. While the tea steeped, I got out some sugar and thought about how good it would be with some milk. Then I remembered the market visit where the old man said he'd have milk. I'd stop on the way to town and grab some, which meant I needed something to trade for it. But that wouldn't be an issue right now. We had gator meat, pork and bear. I think the old guy would probably like some more meat.

With tea in hand, I went out on the porch and sat down on the bench. The dogs were apparently feeling better now and sat up when I came out. They crowded around, all wanting some head scratching, which I gladly provided. Drake laid his head in my lap and I rubbed his ears. He rolled his head into my hand as I scratched and rubbed.

Meathead was a little more direct in his approach. He jammed his massive head into my cup, sloshing hot tea into my lap. *Shit!* I shouted as I brushed it off my pants. He smelled it and started to lick at the wet spot. I pushed his head away, saying, *little too gay there, dude.* But it was nice to sit with them.

Off in the direction of Sarge's house, I heard a diesel engine rumble to life. That meant it was time to get my stuff together for the ride to town. I went inside and grabbed my gear and hung the bulk on my body. I stepped into the bedroom where Mel was asleep, I and leaned over and kissed her.

Rolling over, she asked, "Where are you going?"

"Into town. We have to meet with Sheffield."

Half asleep, she said, "Ok. Be careful. Love you."

I patted her ass. "I will, always am. Love you too." But she was already back to sleep. I envied her. Mel could lie down and be asleep before her head was on the pillow. I used to tease her, saying she had a mercury switch in her head. All she had to do was get horizontal and she was out. Must be nice.

I walked over to Danny's and found him sitting on the porch. "You're up early," I said.

He rocked in his chair. "Couldn't really sleep."

Walking up on the porch, I said, "Me neither."

"You guys headed to town?"

Sitting down in another rocker, I said, "Yeah. We have to meet with the Captain and see what we can do about those feds out at the Elk's Camp."

"I'll be interested to see what they come up with. I'm not looking forward to it though."

Rocking my chair, I replied, "Me neither, buddy. It scares the shit out of me, actually."

Sarge's Hummer pulled through the gate and stopped in front of the house. Sarge got out with Miss kay. Then Mike, Ted and Dalton piled out as well. Kay stopped at the door on her way in the house. "You boys are up early."

I smiled. "Waiting on breakfast."

She smiled. "It'll be ready shortly."

Sarge came up on the porch, coffee cup in one hand and a thermos in the other. He took the last available chair. Mike looked around and said, "Where the hell am I supposed to sit?"

Sarge reached out with his foot and pushed his ass. "Kids play in yard, not on the porch."

Mike grabbed his crotch. "I got your kids right here!"

Sarge made a wild kick at his hand that Mike easily avoided. Mike stepped back laughing and gave the old man the finger. Sarge chuckled and said, "You're lucky I ain't had my coffee yet."

"Whatever grandpa," Mike replied.

Sarge leaned forward in a motion like he was going to throw the hot coffee on Mike. Mike jumped and ran for the door and into the house. Sarge sat back laughing. "Like I'd waste good coffee on his miserable ass."

Ted was shaking his head and sat down on the edge of the porch. I looked the two of them over. "You guys are off to an early start."

Sarge cocked his head to the side. "Shit, what the hell are you doing up before the damn sun?"

"Eh, couldn't sleep."

Sarge snorted. "Who are you kidding. You wet the bed, didn't you?" Ted's head rocked back in laughter.

With a laugh, I said, "No. I got up in the middle of the night and pissed in your coffee cup."

Sarge took a big gulp of coffee and swished it around in his mouth. Swallowing it, he asked, "Damn! You eat asparagus yesterday?" I couldn't help but laugh, as did Ted, Dalton and Danny.

"That's messed up," Danny said.

We hung out on the porch for a little while talking about the news I'd heard the night before. Sarge had some choice words about Russian and Chinese troops.

"I've always wanted to kill me a commie. I grew up with the duck and cover crap. We were told every day the Russians wanted to nuke the shit out of us. That's why I went into the army. But all I ever killed were ragheads in man dresses."

"Looks like you might get your chance now. Two flavors, borscht and Chow Mein. It's them rice-eaters I'd like a shot at," Ted said.

"I'd rather not tangle with either one of them," I said.

"Honestly, I don't want to either, Morgan," Sarge said. Waving his arm out at the scene in front of us, he added, "What we've been up against here, will be child's play compared to fighting either one of them. They'll bring all their party favors, and it'll be ugly."

We continued to talk as the sun rose and the world began to wake up. The birds began to announce to all they were awake. A flight of Sandhill cranes passed over the house making their raucous call. Large birds, they looked so elegant when on the wing. And the red crest on their heads made them really stand out.

Thad, Jess and Doc showed up and took up spots on the porch. I asked Doc how Jamie was doing. He leaned back against a post and said, "She's doing pretty good. I think she'll be fine."

Kay came out onto the porch with large platter. On it were large biscuits with meat sandwiched in them. Mike came out behind her. With a mouthful of biscuit, he pointed at the one in his hand and said, "This shit is good!" He caught himself and looked at Kay. "Oops, sorry. This is a good biscuit."

Kay smiled at him. "That's alright, Mike."

She handed me a biscuit and I looked at it. "What's in it?"

Kay straightened. "It's sausage, silly!"

I exclaimed, "Sausage! How'd we get sausage!"

"How do you think, dunderhead! We butchered a hog yesterday!" Sarge barked.

"I know. But I didn't know we had sausage making stuff," I replied. Taking a bite, I closed my eyes. "Oh, that is good!"

Mike was bouncing up and down, nodding his head vigorously. "Told you! I told you!"

"Mary and I used Danny's grinder and some spices Bobbie had; and I got some more from Mel," Kay said. Touching a finger to the side of her face, she added, "That reminds me, I need to check the rest of the houses for more spices."

"I'll do it, Kay. We'll handle that for you today," Jess said.

"Oh, you're a dear."

"I will too if it means more of this sausage!" Sarge barked. "Miss Kay, this is amazingly good."

She smiled. "Thank you, Linus."

Everyone agreed the sausage was wonderful. It was a really nice change. We take for granted what seasoned food tastes like. Spices and herbs from around the world were at our fingertips on the grocery store shelves. We never gave a second thought to what it took to get all those wonderful seasonings into our food. But let me tell you, after several months of very little spice used in our cooking, this sausage was a taste explosion!

Thad looked at the last bite of his biscuit. "I'm sure going to miss your cooking, Miss Kay."

"What do you mean you're going to miss my cooking? Where are you going, Thad?"

Thad pointed at me. "Ole Sheriff Morgan here got me shanghaied into working on the farm for a couple of days."

Kay spun around to face me, with her hands firmly planted on her hips as she tore into me. "What do you mean you got him working on the farm!"

Thad laughed. "It ain't like that, Miss Kay."

Then the realization came over her. "Wait. We have a farm?"

"Indeed, we do. We've got over fifty acres plowed and ready to plant," I said.

Thad laughed. "Yeah, *we* got fifty acres ready to plant."

Holding up my hands, I said, "Okay, okay, you and Cecil have it ready to plant."

"What are you planting?" Kay asked.

Thad rubbed his hands on his legs. "Oh, Cecil has all kinds of seeds piled up. I don't know it all, but there's going to be a lot if we can get people to work down there."

"Enough of this jawin'. Time to get this goat rope on the road," Sarge said.

"I want to stop at the market in Altoona and see if they have any milk," I said.

"Milk?" Kay asked.

Nodding, I said, "The old guy we got the butter from should have some milk this morning."

Clasping her hands in front of her face, she said, "That would be wonderful! It would make these biscuits better. I could make buttermilk."

"How do you make buttermilk?" Danny asked.

With a dismissive wave, she said, "Oh that's easy. Just a little vinegar or even lemon juice added in will make buttermilk." She winked, "and we have vinegar."

"A cold glass of clabber would be good," Sarge said. Standing up, he added, "wish we had some cornbread to put in it."

With a very distasteful look, Mike asked, "Clabber? What the hell?"

Kay smiled at Mike and patted him on the shoulder. "It's just another name for buttermilk."

"Kay I need some meat to trade for the milk," I said.

She went in the house and returned shortly with a plastic bag and handed it to me. I looked in it and saw several other bags inside containing various cuts of meat.

Kay pointed at the bag and said, "There's some sausage in there too."

Looking back into the bag, I asked, "You sure you want to trade that?"

She smiled, "We've got plenty and I can make more. We're going to be busy today canning as much as of the meat as we can. But I'll make another batch of sausage today if you guys want it."

There was a unanimous approval of the suggestion. Kay smiled and said she'd have it ready later today. We said our goodbyes and headed out. Thad was going to ride with me and Sarge and the guys had to go pick up the prisoner. Wedrove up to the end of the road to wait for Sarge and talked about the farm while we waited. Then a sudden thump on the back of the truck scared the crap out of us. We both jumped and I looked in the rearview mirror to see Dalton's face pressed against the glass with a clownish grin.

"What the hell's wrong with you? That's a good way to get lead poisoning," I shouted.

Dalton walked around to my door and leaned on the side of the truck. Looking in, he said, "Then bring that rifle up. Go ahead. Let me see."

I grabbed the rifle and went to swing it out the window. The barrel banged into the steering wheel. Thad was ducking for cover, though in my defense, the muzzle was never pointed at him. Dalton laughed at me. "That's the problem with a full size carbine in the truck. Just use your pistol."

"Yeah, yeah, I know. You need to hop in. We're headed to town to meet with the Guard."

"This about the Elk's Camp?" I nodded and he quickly climbed in. Leaning over the back of my seat and using a thick hillbilly drawl, he said, "We going to town, pa?"

When I saw Sarge's Hummer coming up behind me, I pulled out. He followed me up to the Kangaroo in Altoona. I pulled up in front of the dairy man's stand and hopped out. He was setting large jars of milk and butter out on the table. The milk was in large half gallon jars. There were also quart and pint jars of butter and cream.

He greeted me as I got out. "Mornin'! That gator meat sure was good."

"Well, I wanted to get some milk this morning." Dropping the bag on the table, I opened it and said, "I brought some more meat. This time it's bear, pork and sausage."

He reached out and picked up the bag. "Bear meat, you say?" Looking at me, he added, "and sausage?"

"Yeah, and that sausage is good too. Had some for breakfast."

The old man took the meat out and inspected the packages. "How much milk you want?"

Looking at the jars sitting on the table, I said, "How about four of them?"

The old man rubbed his chin. "I don't know."

I picked up the sausage. "This here is worth one jar by itself. I know you have to tend those cows and milk them. I know there's work in it. But there's work in this as well." Picking up the big bag of bear meat, I said, "And this is bear. It's good meat. Not to mention there's a whole pork roast in here."

"How about three jars of milk?"

I picked up a pint of butter. "Three and this."

He nodded. "Deal!" I shook his hand and picked up my jars. "You keep bringing meat, and I'll keep you in milk."

"I'll try. I have another deal I'd like to talk to you about later. But I'll have to come back for that."

"Any time. I'm here ever' day."

CHAPTER 8

P ULLING UP TO THE ARMORY, I was surprised to see a rather large crowd gathered in the parking lot. What was even better was the fact many of them were clutching shovels, hoes and rakes. They'd brought their own implements with them. Parking the truck, we got out and found Cecil. He was standing with a sergeant who was organizing the crowd into groups for transport.

"Mornin', Cecil," I said.

He stuck out his hand. "Mornin' fellas." Sweeping his arm over the crowd, he said, "Look at all of 'em. I can't believe so many people turned out."

"It's surprising. But it is the first day. Let's see how many turn out tomorrow."

"However long they work is good. We need all the bodies we can get out there," Thad said.

Sarge walked up with our prisoner. "Here's another one for the chain gang."

Cecil looked at the man. "What'd he do?"

"Killed one of our hogs. She was about ready to drop a little of piglets," Thad said.

Cecil snorted and looked directly at the kid. "I'd a shot his ass."

Robert looked at the ground and said nothing. Thad looked at him and replied, "He's the lucky one."

Cecil's eyebrows went up. "There were more?"

"There was one more," Thad said.

Cecil looked at Robert. "I guess it's your lucky day then." He pointed to where the other men sentenced to labor were standing with Shane. They were each holding a handful of chain that went down to their foot where it was wrapped around it and secured with a padlock.

Sarge looked at Mike. "Take this turd over there and have Shane get him hooked up to the shit-bird parade."

Mike pushed Robert. "Let's go. Time for you to join a gang." As Mike followed him, he started to sing, "Don't cha' know that's the sound of the men, working on the chain gang! Working on the chain, gang!"

I laughed at him. "That dude just ain't right!"

Robert kept his head down as he was guided through the crowd by Mike. He was ashamed. He was handcuffed and about to be chained to other men, right in front of the entire town. People parted as he walked past. Some of the women in the group gave him dirty looks; and more than one person asked, "What'd he do?"

Mike being Mike, began to call out. "Coming through! Make a hole! Pig thief coming through!"

Hearing what he'd done, people looked at Robert with disgust and some with possible envy. The latter was reinforced with a comment of, *who the hell has a hog now-a-days?* Mike found Shane and grabbed the back of Robert's pants.

"Got another volunteer for you, Shane."

Shane looked at him. "This your pig thief?"

Mike snickered. "The only one left alive."

Shane looked at Robert and asked, "What's your name?"

"Robert."

"Well, Robert, you'll get to know these guys real good over the next few days. Move over there on the end." He pointed where he wanted him to stand and Sean secured him to the chain with the others. "Now that everyone is here, I'll introduce you to your guards." Shane pointed to two Guardsmen. "I would like you to meet Officer and Officer. You can also refer to them as Boss, Hoss or Jefe. But you will always speak to them with respect. Understand that if you dimwits get the idea to try and run off together, you will be shot. There will be no warning shots. There will be no shouted warnings. These men will lay out the boundaries you are to remain in; and if you venture even one foot over that line, you'll be shot. Am I clear on this?"

The men nodded. Robert looked around, "What about food. Are you going to feed us?"

"You'll get one meal at mid-day."

Dave leaned against the truck they were standing beside. "What if we have to take a shit?"

"You'll have to work that out between yourselves. But you never come off the chain. One of you gets sick or hurt, you carry him. You gotta take a piss, you do it on the chain. Hell, you wanna have a circle jerk, you do it on the chain."

One of the Guardsmen interrupted him. "A circle jerk will get you shot as well."

Mike laughed, "Hell yeah it will! You guys seem to have this under control. I gotta run." Looking at the men on the chain, he wagged a finger at them. "You boys behave now."

Shane waved. "See you later."

Sheffield leaned back in his chair. "I don't like it."

Sarge shook his head; he'd expected this. "What don't you like about it?"

Sheffield patted the table. "We're going to lose people. There'll be casualties."

"Probably a lot of them," Livingston added.

Sarge nodded. "There will be casualties, no doubt. But that's the nature of the business. But with what we have, this is the best we can do."

"There's got to be another way," Sheffield said.

"Look Captain, I know you don't want to lose any people. But that's the business we're in, combat. We kill people. That's our job. It comes with certain occupational hazards."

"Like death," Livingston said.

"I know you're all gung-ho and have no issue sending men in to die. But I'd like to avoid if it all possible," Sheffield said.

Sarge leaned forward. "You think I'm cavalier! You think I don't know the cost of this!" He jumped to his feet and pointed an accusatory finger at Sheffield. "How many fucking graves have you dug! In recent days we've buried some of ours, how many of your people have died here!"

Sheffield held his hands up. "Look Top, I'm not saying you don't care. I'm sorry. I know you guys have carried the brunt of the loss here. The only deaths we've had were from illness. But this is going to be a terrible deal. People *are going to die.* I just want to make sure we do all we can to limit it. Maybe we should wait a while."

Sarge asked, "Have you been listening to the radio?"

Sheffield looked at Livingston, who shrugged. Looking back at Sarge, he said, "What radio?'

Pointing at me, Sarge said, "Fill him in on what you're hearing Morgan."

I leaned over the table, resting my elbows on it. "I've been listening to radio transmissions late at night coming from the Radio Free Redoubt. They say the Russians and Chinese are sending troops here. The UN Security Council rejected a resolution to send peacekeepers, but the President supposedly asked for help from the Chinese and Russians, and they said they're going to act unilaterally and send them."

The statement stunned Sheffield and his assembled officers. Sheffield was visibly shaken and slumped back into his chair. A lieutenant leaning against the wall behind him said, "What the fuck?"

"Yeah, what the fuck? The Russians and Chinese are sending boots. Here?" Livingston asked.

Sarge took on a softer tone. "So, you see, Captain, there is some urgency involved. We have to dislodge these assholes before the commies show up. They haven't tried much action here in town because they are obviously afraid of your force. But you let them get a bunch of commie support and heavy weapons and they'll roll over you like a fat kid on a candy bar."

"What about your higher up? Can they offer any help?" Livingston asked.

Sarge sat back down. "I've asked and I'm waiting for a response. I've asked for two Apaches. We don't know the whole picture yet. I've also asked for a clarification on the intel. Again, I'm waiting for a response."

"What the hell are we going to do? We can't fight the Chinese and Russians," Livingston said.

Dalton had been standing in the back of the conference room leaning against the wall. He'd been quiet up to now, saying nothing, just taking it all in. Now he stepped forward and slammed his fist down on the table, actually spilling Sarge's coffee.

"Shit, Dalton!" Sarge barked.

But Dalton had something on his mind. "What would you

have, you curs? That would have neither peace nor war. One affrights you, one makes you proud!"

Sheffield pointed at Dalton. "Who the hell are you?"

"Oh, that's Dalton," I replied.

Dalton straightened up and tucked his hands into his vest. "This is ugly business, but it's necessary business. Like Sarge here said, we need to deal with this now, while we stand a chance." He pointed towards the door. "You let these people get reinforced and we'll have a hell of a time dealing with them." He pointed now at Livingston. "You asked how we'll deal with them? The same way the Afghans did. The same people we lost troops to. People living a near stone-age existence. You took an oath to defend this country against all enemies, foreign and domestic. You going to allow your fear to break your oath and resolution like a twist of rotten silk? I am not afraid. I will fight! And if you are consumed with fear, get you home, you fragments!"

Livingston looked at me wide-eyed, "Where the hell did you find this guy?"

"He came nosing around one night and Morgan fed him. Now he won't leave," Sarge said. "But he's right. Sure, we've had a hard time up to now. It ain't been easy. But there's an avalanche of shit headed our way and we need to squash these turds at the Elk's Camp before it arrives."

Sheffield reached and pulled out the large drawing Ted and Mike had made of the camp. "Let's go over this again."

The plan was fairly simple. Our group would move in from the north and act as a blocking force. Though we'd only be fourteen in number, it was the best we could do. Sarge had thirty-four rounds for the sixty millimeter mortar. It was a mixed lot of high explosive and phosphorus rounds, the latter being particularly nasty. Mike would be positioned on the west side of the camp where their vehicles were laagered. Any truck that attempted to move would be taken out with the Gustav. But we wanted the trucks, or as many of them as we could capture.

When the mortar rounds started falling, the Guard would race down highway 450 and hit the main entrance and assault through the camp, pushing them towards our position on the north side. It would be up to us to either kill them or fix them in their position so the Guard could advance and destroy them. But it was a big place, and I'm certain Murphy would be out there slinking around somewhere.

"You're going to have a pretty thin line on the north side," Livingston said.

Sarge nodded. "We are. But we're going to make up for it with accuracy and volume of fire. I'll have three machinegun emplacements out there, as well as marksmen. Our people are pretty proficient now."

Sheffield stood up. "I don't think any of us are looking forward to this, but it certainly has to be done. And if what Morgan is saying is true, then we absolutely have to do it now." He looked at Sarge. "Top, I hope your people get back to you soon. Our timetable really hinges on that. If they're going to be able to help, then they'll drive the schedule. As soon as you hear anything, let me know."

Sarge nodded. "You'll know as soon as I do."

"Alright then. Once we hear back, we'll meet again to finalize the plan."

With the meeting over, we filed out of the room. Livingston came up behind me and tugged on my sleeve. "A word?" He said, nodding his head towards his office.

I followed him in and he shut the door behind me as I took a seat. "What's up?" I asked.

He motioned with his chin in the direction of the door. "Where'd that guy Dalton come from?"

"Like the old man said, he wandered in one night and never left. He's been around a while now. I like him. During the last attack on our place he jumped right in. Didn't hesitate."

"Just curious. Seems like an odd sort."

I laughed. "You don't know the half of it. He speaks several languages. He's some kind of badass when it comes to blades from what I've seen, and he has some pretty good skills. Hell, he built a forge and made some tomahawks."

Livingston tilted his head. "Sounds like a good man to have on your side. But the reason I wanted to talk with you is Shane said you were looking for a judge. He came to us for help and the Captain tasked me with it. We've had someone come into town with a group of folks. He claims to have been pretty politically connected. The guy seems pretty educated and acts as the leader of the group. Thought you might want to talk to him."

"Yeah. I want someone who can handle the civilian legal issues. It's just not right that I, as the Sheriff, have to deal with handing down punishment. We need a third party."

"They've occupied the old barber shop by the park," Livingston said.

"The one on Bay Street right there in front of the park?" I asked. He nodded. "I'll go round up Shane and Sean and have a talk with him. They'll be as much a part of it as I am."

Livingston stood up. "Sounds good. Let me know if you need anything."

The trucks pulled to a stop under the old oak trees that bordered the plowed field. People started climbing out as soon as they stopped. The three chain gang members, Robert, Aaron and Dave Rosa rode in the back of a Hummer with their guards. The chain made it difficult for the three men to extricate themselves from the truck, but they eventually managed it.

Once out, one of the Guardsmen with the name Wallner on his name tag, ordered them into a line. Looking at Robert, he said, "Alright, from what I heard this morning, you're here for stealing a pig."

The other guardsman with the name tag Lindsay laughed. "Big time criminal."

Wallner pointed to Dave, "You're here for killing your girlfriend." Then he pointed to the third man, "and you're here for setting a fucking bomb in the park with your partner."

Dave looked at Aaron. "You son-of-a-bitch! My cousin was hurt real bad because of that!"

Without warning, he punched the man in the mouth, knocking him down. He leapt on top of him and the two men began to roll around on the ground. Wallner and Lindsay grabbed them and tried to pull them apart. When a hand hit Wallner in the face, he stepped back and used the butt of his carbine to deliver a couple of blows to each man. He hit Dave between his shoulders, causing him to fall off the other man. And as the man tried to get to Dave, he was struck in the stomach. Both men lay on the ground dealing with their pain. Robert tried to stay out of the way; and when Wallner looked at him, he quickly raised his hands and turned his head, closing his eyes tight for the blow he fully expected.

"That'll be enough of that shit!" Wallner shouted. "You assholes were told this morning that if one of you got hurt you'd have to carry his ass around with you! So knock it off!" He stuck a finger in Dave's face. "And you got no room to talk! You killed your girlfriend for Christ's sake! You're just as big a piece of shit as he is!"

Cecil was gathering people together around his tractor. He

was standing on the seat whistling to get everyone's attention. Wallner looked down at the two men. "Now get on your feet and move!" Wallner and Lindsay ushered the three men over just as Cecil began to speak.

"Alright folks, quiet down so we can go over what we have to do!" Cecil shouted. The group did so. Cecil smiled broadly. "Good morning! Thank you all for coming out. I've got to be honest, I didn't think we'd get this kind of turnout."

A voice from the crowd shouted, "It ain't gonna grow itself!"

"No it ain't!" Cecil shouted back. "Any of you folks have any gardening or farming experience?"

Several hands went up and Cecil questioned them about their skills. He was pleased to learn there was a considerable amount of experienced growers in front of him. He also noticed he had a decidedly older crowd. Nearly all these people were over thirty probably, and many of them far older than that. He made a mental note of that. He let the group divide itself up into work parties with one of the experienced men or women as its head.

Once the groups were sorted, they discussed what they had to plant and let the heads of the groups pick what they wanted to oversee. It only made sense to let people grow what they knew how to. It was also a very easy process as everyone was eager and excited about getting crops into the ground. A discussion was then held as to where individual crops would be planted, and some were agreed upon to be delayed. This would be a summer garden, so there was no sense in wasting seeds by planting fall crops.

From the back of one of the trucks, Cecil started pulling buckets out. The seeds were distributed out to the groups, and they quickly moved out into the field. Soon, one end of the field was covered with people as they went to the task of first raking the grass roots and other weeds out of the turned soil. Here again, things went smoothly with the people deciding amongst themselves who would do what. The chain gang was taken to the middle of the field and put to work on three rows. They were given rakes and instructed to pull the grass out.

As the field was prepared, the grass and other weeds were piled between the rows. Cecil had rounded up several wheelbarrows. Some of the younger men would use them to collect the debris and carry it off the field. But it wouldn't go to waste. Cecil designated a spot for it to be piled up to be turned into compost.

Cecil moved about the field for the part of the morning until everyone was sorted out and things were happening efficiently. Then he picked up his shuffle hoe and went to work on a row where Thad was busy raking grass out.

While the people worked the field, the Guardsmen set up a tent and arranged their camp. From now on, it would be manned at all times. Partly to keep people out and partly for animals. There was an expectation that as things progressed, deer and other animals could become a happy problem. Anything that ventured into the field would end up in a cook pot.

After finding Shane and Sean, I rode to the barbershop with Sarge and Dalton. As I pulled up in front of the old brick building, I saw something that surprised me. Something I hadn't seen in a long time. Sitting in a barber's chair on the sidewalk under the awning was a portly man. Fat would better describe him. Not something I was used to seeing now with so many hungry people around. There were two other men standing behind him, flanking either side. In a weird way he looked like a pauper king.

"Look at this turd," Sarge said as I shut the truck off. He looked over at me. "This is your judge?"

Looking at the man, I replied, "Livingston said he wanted me to talk to him. We'll see."

We got out and approached the man, who didn't bother getting up. Not only was he round, but he also wore his pants too high for my taste. I always found it strange when someone pulled their pants up too high. Doing so put his belt buckle on the top of his belly. And unlike most people today, instead of taking their belts in, he'd obviously let his out a couple of notches. He wore a small straw hat and was fanning himself with a paper fan.

He smiled brightly as we approached. "Good morning. You must be Sheriff Carter." He offered his hand, but I had to lean over the foot rest of the chair to shake it.

"I am. And you are?"

"Name's Hyatt Hound. You gentlemen may recognize it from the company that bore my initials, H&H Insurance."

I shook my head. "Never heard of it."

He frowned at my reply. "It was a major concern here in Florida. Though we were predominately engaged in major business, so I can see how someone like yourself wouldn't know of it."

Sarge and I looked at one another. I could already see those caterpillars on his brow inching towards one another. Looking back at him, I replied, "I always looked at insurance like I did lawyers."

Smiling as he fanned himself, he asked, "And how was that?"

"Fucking thieves," Sarge spat.

Chuckling, Hyatt replied, "Most people don't understand the value of mitigating risk of unforeseen events."

"Yeah, how'd that work out for you with this unforeseen event?" I asked.

"No one could have foreseen this," Hyatt replied.

"I did," I said flatly.

With a dismissive wave, Hyatt said, "None of that matters now. I hear you're looking for a judge for this small town. I would be happy to act in such capacity. Of course we'd have to discuss remuneration."

"Remuneration, huh?" Sarge asked in a sarcastic tone.

Still fanning himself, Hyatt replied, "Well naturally. A position, especially one as prestigious as county judge will come with proper compensation."

"Let's not get ahead of ourselves. I was asked to come talk to you about your interest. But you're the first person we've talked to and there will have to be some discussion on the issue."

Hyatt stopped fanning. "I was under the impression you were the one to make this decision. And I found it odd that a Sheriff would pick a judge whom he would ultimately be subordinate to." This guy was getting on my nerves.

"You talk like a forked-tongue lawyer. I hate lawyers. Hell's full of 'em," Sarge said.

One of the men standing behind him said, "That's no way to speak to Mr. Hound."

Sarge cut his eyes at the man. "No one's talking to you, dickhead."

The man made a movement and Sarge quickly said, "If you're raising your hand, it better be to ask a question. Anything else is going to make you bleed."

Hyatt raised his hand. "It's alright, Albert. Gentlemen,

please. This is a civil negotiation. There's no need for harsh words."

"Negotiation?" Shane asked.

Fanning himself, Hyatt replied, "It only makes sense that someone of my stature will be judge." Looking at Sarge, he said, "And yes sir, I am indeed a member in good standing of the Florida Bar association. That alone should afford me considerable deference. I find it hard to believe there would be another in this meager town that could possibly be more qualified than I."

"The Florida Bar Association no longer exists. That's a moot point," I said.

Hyatt chuckled. "Dear sir, I can assure you that one of the most important aspects of reestablishing a civilized life is getting the Bar Association back to functioning."

"Where did you come from?" Sarge asked.

"We've traveled here from Boca Raton. Sadly, I had to leave behind my beloved museum, which I also curated. We've been looking for a suitable place that would recognize the considerable talents we bring."

Sarge looked at Albert. "And what talents do you bring?"

The man bristled slightly. "I'll defer to Hyatt."

"Defer to Hyatt!" Sarge barked.

"Please sir," Hyatt started. "I didn't get your name."

"You can call me sir," Sarge spat.

With a snigger, Hyatt replied, "That's quaint. You strike me as a military man. Am I to assume you are a subordinate in the local National Guard unit here in Eustis?"

"You can assume what you want. But I am not. I am a First Sergeant in the 101st Airborne."

"Ah, the highest enlisted rank one can achieve," Hyatt

replied. "That makes you subordinate to Captain Sheffield and his lieutenant Livingston."

"There you go with your dumbass assumptions again. I am not subordinate to the Captain. And First Sergeant is not the highest enlisted rank. Dumbass."

Stopping the fan, Hyatt asked, "Then who do you answer to?"

Feeling a little weird saying it, I replied, "Me."

Surprised, Hyatt began to fan himself again and said, "Now that is indeed strange. Seems to me to be a violation of several laws that a noncommissioned officer of the United States Army be subordinate to a self-appointed functionary such as a Sheriff."

"Look here, Porky. Morgan is the Sheriff, and he works directly with me in a joint effort with the Army to maintain security and provide as much aid as possible to the people here."

Hearing his superior referred to as Porky, Albert stepped forward. "I told you once to watch how you speak—" Sarge cut him off when he drew his 1911 and thumbed the safety off.

"Move one more inch and I'll turn your head into a fucking canoe."

The other man behind Hyatt drew a pistol as well, which sent all of us into action. Additional people came out of the building, all armed and pointing weapons at us. We were likewise staring down the barrel of our weapons. I shouted for them to lower their weapons. It was starting to look like the OK Corral.

Hyatt sat smugly in his chair, still fanning himself. Smiling, he said, "You see now you are not the only one with a force."

Dalton stepped forward and kicked the footrest of the barber's chair, spinning it around. He quickly drew the big Kukri blade and grabbed Hyatt under the chin and pulled his head back. Laying the blade on Hyatt's neck, he said, "You boys lay those weapons down or I'll liberate his head from his shoulders."

Hyatt squirmed in the chair and cried out in a shrill voice. "Do as he says! Do as he says!"

The men looked at one another, Albert nodded to them and they laid their weapons on the ground. With a jerk of his head, Dalton said, "Now back up." When the men stepped back from their weapons, Dalton looked at Shane. "Get their weapons."

Hyatt was still squirming, kicking his pudgy legs in fright. "Gentlemen! Gentlemen, let's not be rash!"

Dalton sheathed the blade and slapped Hyatt's bulky head, knocking his hat off. "Shut up, fat boy."

After Dalton released him and stepped back, Hyatt looked at Albert and pointed. "My hat please."

Albert picked the hat up and handed it to him. As Hyatt wedged it back on, Albert swiveled the chair back around. His face was red and he was now sweating profusely. Albert picked the paper fan up and handed it to Hyatt as well. Fanning himself furiously, Hyatt said, "There is no need for violence! This is totally unacceptable! Totally unacceptable! I will have to report this aggression to Captain Sheffield so that he may deal with you people accordingly." Pointing at Dalton, he said, "I demand this brute be arrested!"

Dalton smiled and snatched the Kukri from its sheath again. Hyatt let out a squeal and Dalton and Sarge both started to laugh as Dalton sheathed the blade. Hyatt patted his chest and fanned himself.

"I think we're done here," I said.

"I assure you sir, this is far from over!" Hyatt screeched back.

Sarge looked at Albert and pointed at Hyatt. "Earlier, you *deferred* your comment to Porky here. I'm curious if defer your dinner to him as well. I mean look at this roly-poly. How the hell can you be this fat in today's world?"

"I have a thyroid condition sir! It is not proper to disparage one's medical conditions," Hyatt complained.

Sarge laughed. "Shit. Only problem you got is that damn hole under your nose. You're obviously cramming too much into it."

"And there's a lot of shit coming out of it as well," Dalton added.

Hyatt looked at Dalton but said nothing. Looking at Sarge, he said, "What sort of barbaric town is this? If this how you treat people of my deference, I can only imagine how the common people here are treated."

Sarge wagged a finger at Hyatt. "You sure are hung up on yourself, aren't you? You think you're hot shit, don't you?"

Indignantly, Hyatt replied, "We all have our place in the world, sir!" Sarge laughed uproariously.

"I can assure you one thing. Your place is not as our judge," I said. Looking at Shane, I said, "Lock their weapons up at the PD for now."

"You can't take our weapons!" Albert shouted.

Now I laughed. "Oh but I can. You see, we have weapons and you don't. Therefore, you can't stop me." Taking hold of the star on my vest I angled it out. "Plus, I'm the Sheriff. It's my job to keep the peace. And I have a feeling you booger eaters will be trouble if you have weapons."

Finally, Hyatt got out of the chair, with much effort. He protested vigorously. "No sir, you will not take those weapons! These men provide me security and I will not be left vulnerable!"

"You're not. Shane and Sean are here to provide security in town. You waddle in here and start demanding deference. We don't know you from Adam. We need a judge for sure, but your first concern was how much you'd get paid. Service to your community is just that, a service. It should be a burden. You're exactly what was wrong with this country in the Before. I will not let you infect us with that kind of bullshit again."

Hyatt huffed, "Infect you? You, sir need to understand the need for the rule of law! People need order to live by. You can't have people, such as yourself, deciding what is right and wrong."

Sarge snorted. "Oh, we need people like you deciding for us?"

"You need educated people that can appreciate the need for the greater good."

"Then I suggest you move on and find a place where people can't think for themselves. We're good here," I said.

"Come on, Morgan. We got better shit to do," Sarge said.

"What about our weapons?" Albert asked.

"You can come to the PD in a couple of days. We'll talk about it then," Shane said.

We left as they protested, but we ignored them. Albert and the other men ran out into the road behind us as I drove away.

"Shane, don't you recommend any assholes like that again or I'll smack the taste out of your mouth," Sarge said.

Shane was shaking his head. "I'm sorry. He wasn't like that when I talked to him. He seemed like a smart guy and was nice enough."

"He was eager though," Sean said.

"We need someone from here. A local," I said.

"I thought an outsider might be better as they wouldn't have any prejudices either way," Shane said.

We dropped Shane and Sean off at the PD and headed back to the armory to find Mike and Ted.

Jess looked at the letters in front of her, then at the board. She picked up a letter and started to lay it down. Thinking better of it, she stopped and replaced in on the stand.

"Aww, come on already!" Jamie shouted.

Waving her hands on either side of her head, Jess shouted. "It's my turn! Just wait a minute!"

Jamie's head rocked back onto the sofa. "Wake me up when it's my turn."

There was a knock at the door and Doc stepped in. Jamie opened her eyes and looked up. "Oh great, nurse Ratchet is here."

Doc smiled, "Looks like you're getting back to your old pleasant self."

"Hi Ronnie," Jess said with a wave and a smile. Fred looked at her with a devilish grin.

"Hey Jess, Fred," Doc said. Fred waved. Doc looked at Jamie. "Alright. You know the drill."

Jamie let out a loud breath as she pulled her shirt up. "Come on. Let's get this over with."

Doc knelt down beside her. "Come on, it ain't that bad."

"I'm just ready to get out of this house. I'm losing my mind sitting here."

Doc removed the dressing and examined the wound. "Well you're in luck then. We don't need to dress this anymore. It's closed up nicely, so you can move around. Just take it easy for a few more days."

Jamie sat up quickly. "Great!" She grabbed her boots and started to pull them on. When she leaned over, she winced.

Doc shook his head. "I told you to take it easy."

"Yeah, yeah," she replied as she slipped her feet into her boots without tying them.

Jess looked up from the Scrabble game. "You wanna go for a walk?"

"I want to go find Perez and get a cigarette."

"I'll leave you ladies to it," Doc said as he headed for the door.

"See you later," Jess said.

Doc turned around at the door. He smiled, and with a nod, waved back. As soon as he shut the door, Jamie looked at Jess and said, "You're pathetic."

Fred jumped up. "You know he likes you. Why don't you just talk to him?"

Jess shrugged. "I did talk to him."

Jamie scoffed. "Pffft, whatever." She walked over to Jess and got right beside her. Running the back of her hand down Jess's arm, she used a sultry voice to say, "Hi Ronnie."

Jess pulled away from her. "Get away from me," she said with a laugh. The comment got a laugh out of Fred as well.

"That's talking to him, Jess," Jamie said as she picked up her carbine. Looking over her shoulder, she added, "When you have clothes on anyway."

Jess blushed. "Oh stop it!"

"Come on Jess. Let's go look for those spices Kay wants," Fred said as she grabbed her rifle from a rack by the door.

Thad had built a ready rack and put it by the front door. Everyone quickly transitioned into using it. It was easy and convenient to place your weapon on it when coming in. It was also quicker than searching the house for where you happened to set it down last when you were leaving the house. These were little changes that nobody thought much of now. Guns were a part of life, a tool. And like any tool, they needed to be cared for properly.

Jess went into the kitchen and grabbed a basket and picked up her carbine as she went through the door.

"Let's go get Mary. She needs to get out of the house too," Jess said.

"That sounds good. We need a girl's day," Fred said.

"I don't know. The last girl's night didn't end so well for me," Jamie said.

Fred snorted. "I guess you're right about that."

They walked towards Danny's house. Mary was there helping Kay. On their way, they stopped by the bunker where Aric and Perez were on duty. Fred ran over to Aric and gave him a hug and kiss. Jamie went over to Perez who was lying on top of the bunker with his hat over his eyes. Slapping him on the arm, she said. "Hey poppie, give me a smoke."

Perez lifted the hat and smiled. "Hey chica." He sat up and swiveled his legs off the side. Taking a pack from his pocket, he shook one out and offered it to her. Jamie took the smoke and Perez lit it for her. Tilting her head back, she took a long drag, blowing out a cloud of smoke.

"That is so good. Thanks Perez," she said.

When Perez was young, he suffered from bad acne. It left his face pock-marked. The combination of that and the dark skin that ran in his family, resulted in a lot of trash talk from other kids when he was in school. But the kids learned quickly that Perez was no pushover. He didn't take shit off anyone, and was quick to throw knuckles. While he won most of his fights, he took his fair share of abuse. The end result was the cartilage in his nose was nearly destroyed, and when he smiled, his nose appeared to flatten across his already wide face. To mess with his nieces, he would take his finger and push his nose flat against his cheek. They would squeal and run from him.

Perez smiled at Jamie and his silly-putty nose spread across his face. "Those things are bad for you."

Jamie smiled and blew him a kiss. "You know you love me."

Perez laughed and lit another cigarette. "Like the pain in the ass little sister I never had."

"But always wanted," Jamie replied with a smile as she batted her eyes.

The girls hung out for a bit while Jamie finished her smoke, then walked on down to Danny's house. Bobbie, Mel, Kay and Mary were in the kitchen grinding meat. Fred looked into the tub of ground meat and said, "Looks good!"

Kay smiled. "We're having hamburgers for dinner."

"Bear burgers!" Little Bit shouted.

"Sounds good to me," Fred said.

"Mary, we're going to look for spices. Do you want to come?" Jess asked.

Mary was using a pusher to force meat down into the grinder. She smiled and laid it down. "I'd love to."

Lee Ann was sitting on the sofa thumbing through an old magazine. She dropped it onto the cushion and jumped up. "I want to come too."

"Can I come?" Little Bit asked.

Mel looked at Jess, and while she didn't indicate anything either way, Mel could tell the girls wanted to get away and talk. She told Little Bit to stay with her. She was at the bar where the meat was being prepared kneeling on top of a bar stool. Picking up a piece of meat and dropping it into the top of the grinder, she said, "I never get to go anywhere."

Mel took over the duty of pushing the meat into the grinder and smiled at her. "You need to help me get these hamburgers done."

Little Bit's attitude changed and she smiled. "I can't wait! I want a hamburger now!"

Kay was beside her cutting the bear into chunks and dropping them into a large tub. She bumped Little Bit with her hip. When Little Bit looked up, Kay winked. "I want one too." Getting a happy, childish smile from the little girl.

Fred looked out the kitchen at Danny, who was down at the pond with the kids. They had a small net and a jar, and were catching tadpoles and minnows. She nodded in his direction. "He seems to be a natural with the little ones."

Bobbie looked out the window. "He's always wanted kids. They make him happy."

"He's had plenty of practice over the years," Mel said.

Bobbie looked at Little Bit. "Having the girls around was always special to him. He loves you guys a lot."

Little Bit smiled as she picked up a chunk of bear meat. "I love Danny too. He's my other daddy."

Bobbie took a deep breath and said, "What about me?" And pretended to cry.

Looking bashful, Little Bit replied, "I love you too, Bobbie!"

"Uncle Danny is more fun though, huh?"

Little Bit didn't know how to reply, so Mel helped her. "Danny does fun things outside and Bobbie does fun things inside, huh?"

"Yeah! We always do crafts together and puzzles." Little Bit's eyes went wide. "We should do a puzzle!"

"Maybe later. We have to finish this first," Bobbie said.

Little Bit looked out the window. "Can I go outside with them?"

Mel nodded. "Of course. Have fun."

Little Bit jumped off the stool and headed for the door. "Wash your hands!" Bobbie shouted.

The girls got another basket and left the house. They chattered as they walked east from Danny's house to start their search. In the back of the neighborhood the houses were sparse and located on one side of the road for the most part. Jess, Mary and Lee Ann went towards a large log home while Fred and Jamie went to a smaller home next to it.

As they were crossing the yard, Jess looked at Mary. "Looks like you and Thad are getting really close."

Mary blushed a little. "He's a nice man."

"I like him too. Thad's really helped me. He's like an uncle to me," Lee Ann said.

"He thinks a lot of you too. We talked about you guys a lot," Mary said. Looking at Jess, she said, "He told me all about your trip home." She laughed, "He said you drove Morgan nuts."

Jess laughed. "In my defense, Morgan did his fair share of 'driving'."

"What was it like? You guys walking home?" Lee Ann asked.

Jess's mind drifted back in time. There were plenty of fond memories on the trip. But they were tempered with some horrors. She looked at Lee Ann. "Your Dad showing up saved me." She laughed. "He didn't want me to go with him, but I wouldn't give up. I was in a bad place and things were going to get worse for me. But he finally gave in, and I followed him."

The girls walked up on the porch and sat down on the edge with their feet dangling over the side. Lee Ann laid her H&K across her lap and looked at Jess. "He didn't want you to walk with him? Was he mean?"

"No. He wasn't mean. He was just so focused on getting home to you guys. He thought I would be a distraction or slow him down. That's all it really was."

"Then you guys met Thad," Lee Ann said.

Jess laughed. "Yeah. Then we met Thad. I wasn't happy

about Thad at first, but Morgan liked him right away. Which was weird because we'd just had a conversation about not trusting anyone, and he brings the black Incredible Hulk along. I was scared of him."

Mary snickered. "Thad said you were afraid of him."

Jess looked at her. "Did he say anything? I mean, did it hurt his feelings?"

Mary laughed. "No. it didn't hurt his feelings. He said he was used to it. A big black man isn't many people's first choice for friends. But that's what he liked about Morgan. He said from the first moment, Morgan didn't see him as just a big black guy. He really likes Morgan."

"I know dad really likes him too. He's talked about him before. And that's kind of weird for Dad. He never had many friends. I mean, he knew a lot of people. A lot. But there were only a few he did things with. But if anyone ever asked for help, he would do what he could to help," Lee Ann said.

"He and Thad are alike in that. Thad would do anything for anyone here. After he got home to his wife and son, he was very happy. But bad things happened and he came here because he knew Morgan would look out for him. He said after he lost his family he wanted to come help Morgan protect his," Mary said.

Jess nodded. "On the road, all he talked about was his wife and son. It's like he lived for them." She looked at Lee Ann. "Just like your dad. All he thought about was you guys."

Lee Ann was thinking about what Jess said. She was mulling her perception of her father over in her mind. In the Before, he was the guy that laid down the rules that she thought were draconian and stupid. But looking back to that time, she now realized he was only trying to protect her. To instill values and responsibility in her. She was going to have to remind herself to let him know just how much she appreciated what he'd done for her.

The girls went into the house and started going through the cabinets. It took several hours for them to go through all the houses in the neighborhood. They thoroughly searched the kitchens of every house. While they were there, they also looked around to see if there was anything else they could use. In the garage of one house, Fred and Jamie found four cases of quart Mason jars. These were a fantastic score that the girls carried out to the road and stacked up to be retrieved later.

On the last street, the girls met in the road between the last two houses. The baskets were full to overflowing. They'd found so many spices and the like, that they were also packed into pillowcases. Lee Ann dropped a heavy pillow case onto the road. "How many cans of baking powder did you guys find?"

Fred laughed. "Oh my God. I think every kitchen had at least one, but usually two or three!"

"I know! What in the world do you use it for?"

Mary laughed. "For baking silly."

Lee Ann laughed. "Well duh. But what's it for?"

"It's for leavening batter. Miss Kay will be pretty happy to have it for sure," Jamie said.

Fred pointed to the now even larger pile of canning supplies. "She's really going to be happy about the jars. Can you believe how many we found?"

"We need to get one of the buggies over here and load it all up. There's just too much to carry," Jess said.

"I'll go get one," Jamie said.

"I'll come with you," Lee Ann said and ran to catch up to her.

"We'll be here when you get back," Fred said.

At the armory we found Mike and Ted and loaded up. Sarge didn't like being at the armory and wanted to get out of town as fast as possible. Not that there was much worry about anyone wanting him to stick around. As I was pulling out of the parking lot, Livingston walked up and asked, "How'd it go?"

"Let's just say he wasn't the right candidate," I replied.

Sarge leaned forward and added, "You better keep an eye on Porky. I have a feeling he's going to be nothing but trouble."

"We haven't had any trouble out of them. They came into town a few days ago and haven't bothered anyone," Livingston said.

"Our talk didn't go well. So bad in fact we took their weapons from them. Shane has them at the PD. They can have them back in a few days after they cool off," I said.

Livingston looked surprised. "What? Why'd you take them?"

"Ole Porky thinks he's king shit on turd island. And those idjits with him treat him like some kind of royalty." Sarge wagged his finger at Livingston. "Mark my words, he's going to be trouble for you."

Livingston let us know he thought we were wrong about Hyatt. I told him the man was his problem for now and made it clear to him that there was no way in hell he'd be made the judge around here. With that, I pulled away. It was time to get the hell out of town. As I drove up Bay Street, I noticed the dock along the lake was crowded with people. Some were obviously fishing while others were very obviously doing nothing.

"You know all those people lounging around out there could be out at the farm," I said.

Sarge snorted. "If they want to eat, they'll have to work for it."

"Bunch of lazy asses out there," Mike said.

"Mmm, yes. ne'er do wells," Dalton said.

As we passed the barricade, Sarge said to stop by the farm. He had something for Cecil. When we stopped, I was surprised with the activity. There were people all over the field and they certainly looked busy. Maybe we'd get some crops this year after all. Sarge spotted Cecil and called out to him, waving him over to the truck. Mike, Dalton and Ted wandered off to check out the camp the Guard set up.

Cecil wiped his forehead as he walked up. His hands were filthy from working in the dirt all day. "How you fellers doing?" He asked.

"Fit as a fiddle," Sarge replied. He looked around and leaned in close to Cecil. Sliding a plastic bag across the hood of the truck, he said, "Here, got a little something for you."

Cecil eyed the bag. "What is it?"

Leaning in as though he were confiding a secret he didn't want anyone to hear, Sarge replied, "Meat. Brought you some pork and some of that bear."

A broad smile spread across Cecil's face. "Don't that beat all. I appreciate it, Linus. I get plenty of fish here in town, but red meat and especially pork is pert near nonexistent."

"This should hold you over a couple of days," Sarge said. Then he asked, "You got a way to keep it cool?"

Cecil shook his head. "Naw. But I got a smoke box. I'll put it in there. That'll keep it from going bad, not to mention, flavor it up real nice."

"You could dry that bear meat out Cecil. I wouldn't do it with the pork, but that bear you could just air dry," I said.

Cecil picked up the bag and felt its weight. Smiling, he said, "It won't last that long, Morgan. I'll eat this up pretty quick. I've had a taste for some red meat for a while now, so I know I won't be able to ration it none."

"We'll get you some more down here. Kay also made some sausage. I'll get you some of that too," Sarge said.

"That'd be fine. Be real fine."

Sarge leaned back, resting his elbows on the hood of the truck, and looked out across the field. "It's looking good out there, Cecil. How's your help doing?"

Cecil mimicked Sarge as he rested against the truck. "You know, Linus. I really expected there to be a thin turnout. But look at all of 'em. And everyone's working hard, no fussin'. Everyone gets along and just fell in line. It's nice to see people working together like this."

"It's for everyone's good. It ain't like before. You gotta earn your groceries now. You gotta grow it, find it or hunt it down and kill it."

"I got high hopes for this patch of dirt." Cecil pointed out into the field. "You notice anything about this crowd?"

Sarge looked the people over. After a moment, he shook his head and said, "No. I see everyone working. Looks like they're all getting after it."

Cecil looked at Sarge. "Come on Top." Nodding out to the field again he said, "What's the youngest person you see out there?"

"There ain't no young people out there. I see what you mean. This is an older lot out here working today," Sarge said.

"Remember all those people we saw along the lake?" I asked.

Sarge nodded. "Yeah, there's a bunch of them in town lying around on their asses," Sarge said.

Cecil let out a long breath. "It's sad you can't get people to understand that these crops aren't just going to grow themselves."

I laughed. "Well, you know they kind of are."

Cecil chuckled. "You know what I mean."

Sarge was more to the point when he looked over at me. "Smartass."

Laughing, I replied, "Whatever, kettle."

The guys returned from their inspection of the camp. Sarge asked them what they thought.

"They've got a pretty good set up. Hell, I'd rather be here than at the damn armory," Ted said.

"Me too. Anywhere but there," Mike said.

I looked out across the field. I was wondering where the chain gang was, and spotted them on the far end. Nodding towards them, I asked Cecil, "How's the chain gang doing?"

"Oh hell, they ain't happy. But they're working," he replied.

"Looks like they don't have much choice to me," Dalton said.

Sarge snorted. "That's kinda the point."

"They got to tussling this morning first thing when two of them found out they was chained up to the old boy that set that bomb. But them guards jerked a knot in their asses quick. Since then, they've been quiet," Cecil said.

"I was wondering how that would go with the other two," Sarge said.

"That guy, Dave ain't got no room to talk. Hell, he killed his girlfriend," I said.

"There's a difference though. If he were in prison, he'd have to be segregated or the other inmates would wear his ass out," Sarge said.

Mike laughed. "Yeah, wear it out literally!"

Cecil asked, "How long you going to keep them on that chain? And what do you plan to do with them?"

Shaking my head, I replied, "I don't know."

"Shwack em'!" Ted shouted.

"That's your answer to everything," Sarge barked.

"It's the easy answer for sure. And that's probably what it's going to come down to. But while that will offer the families of the victims some vengeance, I figure making them work for the benefit of the community for a while has a better return," I said.

Sarge snorted. "You ain't turning into a damn bleeding heart liberal, are you?"

"What?" I shouted. "Kiss my ass! Dying is easy. But making these bastards work hard every day and getting something out of them before they become fertilizer, just makes sense. It's not like they're sitting around in the air conditioning and bitching about the quality of the food."

Sarge laughed. "Just checking. I can't have you getting all soft on me."

"I think making them work is a good thing. You've got a real nice visual deterrent for everyone in town. I think they should have to walk through town like that. Hell, there's got to be something in town they could do so everyone sees them," Dalton said.

"I've got those little garden plots around town. I could put them to work there," Cecil said.

Sarge nodded. "That's a good idea. That way they don't have to be transported out here every day and the folks in town can see them. They'll understand that if they fuck up they'll find themselves on the end of that chain."

"There's already folks guarding those gardens, so it wouldn't require any additional security. I think I'll talk to the Captain tonight and get that set up," Cecil said.

"Sounds like it's a done deal," I said.

Sarge slapped the hood of the truck. "My work here is done! Let's get on the road."

"What work? You didn't do shit," Mike said.

Sarge shook his head. "You wanna walk home?"

Ted laughed. "You know he'll do it! Again!"

Mike ran around the truck and climbed in. "Not this time!"

We mounted up and headed back towards home. I pulled into the plant on the way to check on the progress. One of the guardsmen providing security at the plant waved as we pulled in. Terry and Baker were buried up to their waists in a switchgear when we walked up. The sound of a ratchet banging against metal reverberated inside the small space. I stuck my head in and looked over Terry's shoulder. "What's up?" I asked with a smile.

Terry looked over his shoulder. His face was grime-covered and he was sweating. "Oh yeah. Here he is. Work on a power plant, he said. It'll be fun, he said."

Smiling, I replied, "Never said it would be easy."

Terry and Baker extricated themselves from the cabinet and looked at me. Baker brushed hair from her eyes. "This is some BS, Morgan."

"You going to let this beat you already?"

"This is going to take way more time than I first thought," Scott said as he walked up.

"What? You think you were just going to walk up to this thing and flip a switch and it'd take off and start shitting electricity?" Sarge barked.

Baker tossed a wrench into a tool bag at her feet. "We were hoping it would go something like that."

Sarge guffawed. "Shit, if it was that easy, Morgan here could have done it!"

Scott wiped his hands on a rag. "This isn't going to happen any time soon. We're going to have to go through this thing from top to bottom. It looks as though this thing has been sitting for a long time."

"Well no shit, Sherlock. Everything's been sitting for a while," Sarge fired back.

Scott snorted. "No. I mean way before that. This heap of shit has been idle for a long, long time."

I shrugged. "It doesn't really matter how long it takes. This is the only chance we have for power. If it works, that's awesome. If it doesn't, all we lost was time; and we have plenty of that."

"That's easy for you to say," Terry said. Pointing at the plant, he added, "You're not the one crawling around inside this heap of crap."

Sarge snorted. "What else you got to be doing?" Eric walked up and Sarge looked at him. "Where the hell have you been, Beech Nut?"

Eric paused and looked around, unsure. "Uh." He pointed with the wrench in his hand over his shoulder. "I was connecting the leads to the generator." Sarge didn't say anything. He stared back at the kid. Eric's eyes darted around, looking for some sort of indication of whether or not he was or wasn't doing something he was supposed to be. After a moment, he said, "I'm going to check the torque on all the bolts."

With a stern expression, Sarge replied, "You do that."

Giving the old man a quick double take, Eric did an about-face and disappeared. Sarge started to laugh and Scott said, "You shouldn't be so hard on that kid. He's scared shitless of you."

I was laughing and said, "He does have some amazing people skills."

Baker rolled her eyes. "Boys."

A low thumping sound began to fill the air. We all started looking around, craning our necks to search the skies for the source. After a moment, Mike called out, "Choppers to the southwest!"

CHAPTER 9

WE ALL SPUN AROUND AND looked to see two Blackhawks and two Apache gunships flying low and fast. They made a wide orbit around Eustis. After circling a second time, one of the Blackhawks dropped out of formation. The other ships continued to circle.

"Let's get back to town!" Sarge barked as he started to run towards the truck.

"What the hell?" Terry asked, looking up at one of the Apaches.

Sarge shaded his eyes with his hand and said, "Something is up if they're flying in here." Looking at me, he shouted, "Come one Morgan!"

Running towards the truck, I said, "Who the hell is it?"

"Gotta be someone with some serious brass in his ass to be out like that," Sarge shouted back.

I ran to the truck and jumped in as Mike piled in behind me. He was slapping the back of my seat shouting, "Go, go, go!"

As we were passing through the barricade into town, one of the Blackhawks made a low fast pass down Bay Street.

Ted had his head stuck out the window looking up. Pulling it back in, he said, "This should be interesting."

Mike slumped back into his seat and moaned. "Man, I miss

the good old days of moving in a helicopter. The way a man should ride into battle."

"Oh dry up!" Sarge shouted.

The Blackhawk that made the low pass was landing in the parking lot on the east side of Bay Street. Turning down one of the cross streets, I headed for it. People were coming out to see what was going on. The sound of the machine was getting everyone's attention. The helicopters continued landing until all four were on the ground.

As I pulled into the parking lot, Mike said, "What the hell are they all doing on the ground?"

Ted craned his head to look out the window again. "That's some fucked-up SOP right there."

The first Blackhawk to land, killed its engines. As the blades started to spin down, a man climbed out of the back. I recognized him instantly and wondered what was going on to bring General Fawcett out here. Stopping the truck, Sarge was quickly out and heading to meet him.

"General!" Sarge said as he offered his hand.

Mike and Ted were leaning against the truck. Mike snickered and said, "Suck ass. He sucks any harder, his damn eyes will cross."

Ted combed his beard and replied, "Be nice or I'll tell him you said that."

"Good to see you, Top," Fawcett replied as he shook Sarge's hand.

"Is this a social visit?" Sarge asked.

Fawcett shook his head. "No. We've got some things we need to talk about."

Sarge led him towards the truck. "I kinda figured that."

Fawcett got in the passenger seat and looked over at me.

"Good to see you again, Sheriff. Glad you're here. We've got some things to talk about."

Nodding, I started the truck as I replied, "Good to see you, too. I hope." The look he gave me didn't make me feel any better about what I was going to hear.

Sheffield and Livingston were standing in front of the armory when we pulled up. Guardsmen were running around, having been ordered to provide security for the birds on the ground. The inhabitants of Eustis were out in force at the sight and sound of the machines. It was the most exciting thing to happen in many months. As a result, people were crowding around them.

Fawcett got out of the truck and greeted the two men, who were just as surprised as we were at the arrival of the general. Sheffield ushered the general towards the conference room. We followed them in and took a seat around the table.

Sheffield stood nervously looking around the room. Sarge and I each took a seat with the old man putting his foot up on the edge of the table. Fawcett sat down and looked at Sheffield. "Have a seat, Captain."

Sheffield took a seat and asked, "What can we do for you, General?"

"We have a situation brewing that we need to talk about."

Putting his hands behind his head Sarge, replied, "Is this about the Russians and the Chinese?"

Surprised, Fawcett asked, "Where have you heard about that?"

Interrupting, I said, "I've been monitoring the radios and found an outfit called the Radio Free Redoubt that broadcasts every night. They've been reporting on what the UN has been up to."

Pointing in Sarge's and my direction, Sheffield said, "They've told us about this. But we've never heard any of these reports. Are they true?"

Fawcett leaned forward, resting his clasped hands on the table. He let out a long breath and finally started to speak. He nodded his head and said, "Indeed it is. The UN Security Council vetoed the resolution to send in peacekeepers, but the Chinese and Russians have said they are going to act unilaterally and send them." Sheffield sat back in his seat, stunned.

Sarge looked at him. "Why the surprise, Captain. We already told you all this."

"Yeah. You guys told us," Livingston said. "But it's different hearing it from the General."

Sarge looked at Fawcett. "You fly all the way down here just to tell us that? Made a special trip just for some gossip?"

"This is no gossip, Top. The Russians already have elements here."

Sheffield jumped to his feet and exclaimed, "What!"

"Sit down, Captain!" Fawcett shouted. Sheffield lowered himself back into his chair. Fawcett continued. "We know there are Spetsnaz forces here already. They're doing the same kind of pathfinding work our SF guys do. They're also linking up with Federal forces. Which is why we're here."

"We're about to deal with our local group of Feds shortly," Sarge said.

"That's what I want to know about. I've been moved to SOCOM in Tampa. We've consolidated some assets, and as part of that, I'm now down here. We're preparing to deal with the Russians. Part of that is we need to take out as many of these Federal pockets as we can."

"You say you're preparing to deal with the Russians. What about the Chinese?" Livingston asked.

"The Defense Intelligence Agency has put together a bit of

a picture of what's going to happen. We think the Chinese will come in from California and the Russians will move in from the east coast. We know for a fact they are staging assets in Syria now. There's also a lot of activity in Cuba."

"What kind of time table are we looking at?" Sarge asked.

Fawcett shrugged. "We're not sure. We don't have all our intelligence assets, satellites and such, so we don't have the full picture. But we have enough to know they're definitely coming." He looked around the table. "This is a game changer, folks. We're not going to be dealing with a mob of Federal goons with small arms and a little armor. These are going to be no shit for real battle-hardened troops. They've had plenty of combat experience in Ukraine and Chechnya."

Sarge swung his foot off the table. "Well, since you're here with all this hardware, we should put it to good use. We've been planning an attack on the camp where our local litter of Federal mutts are holed up. It was going to be a hard nut to crack because they're in a pretty big place. But with those whirlybirds of yours, we could end it pretty quick."

Fawcett thought for a moment. "I've got other people I need to meet with. But if we could help eliminate this threat now that's what we need to do." He looked at Livingston. "Can you send someone to get those Apache drivers and bring them in here? We'll need them involved in the planning of this." Livingston was on his feet immediately and left the room.

Waiting on Livingston and the pilots, I asked Fawcett, "So this is turning into Red Dawn?"

With a halfhearted laugh, he replied, "You know. We've talked a lot about that very thing in recent days." He looked up at me, "And as cheesy as it sounds, yeah, it's about to go all Red Dawn."

Sarge slammed his fist down onto the table causing several

of us to startle. "Good, by God! I've been wanting to kill me some commie bastards all my life! Shit, I thought I'd leave this Earth never having had the chance to kill some!" He smiled and leaned back in his chair. "Far as I'm concerned, bring it on!"

Fawcett looked over at him. "I know you're itching for a fight, Top, but this isn't going to be a cake walk. We're going to try and keep them out, but if they make it on the ground, then things are going to get pretty hairy."

"Oh I know. It ain't going to be pretty. But the rules of engagement are going to be on our side. These fuckers are invaders—" Mike interrupted him.

"And no quarter will be given."

Sarge looked at him and smiled. "Not an inch."

Dalton cleared his throat. "I've always been interested in the Russian Military. These are some tough bastards. It's not going to be easy. Just ask the Germans."

Sarge rocked his head back over his chair, getting an upside-down view of Dalton. "That's true. The Russians brutalized the Nazis in Stalingrad because they were on their home turf. They were fighting for their lives and it allowed them to turn the tables on the Germans." Sarge looked around the table. "Now we have the home field advantage."

"And we will be fighting for our lives," Fawcett added.

The door opened and Livingston came in with the two Apache pilots. I recognized one of them, Mark. We'd met on our trip to Camp Riley. He came in and took a seat at the table with the other pilot. Falling into a chair, Mark said, "Well, now what kind of trouble are you boys in?"

"Shit. You're just lucky we're inviting you to this party," Sarge snorted.

Fawcett sat up. "Alright. Let's get down to business. You have any maps of this place?"

The large drawing Mike and Ted made was rolled out on the table, along with a couple of topo maps of the area. The plan we'd come up with was discussed. Fawcett was happy with the initial details. The two Apaches were an ace in the hole. The plan would remain the same with our group acting as a blocking force on the north side of the camp and the Guard attacking in force through the main gate. The two Apaches would provide cover for the assault from overhead.

Mark was doing some calculations on a pad. "Our fuel is limited though. We won't be able to loiter long. You guys are going to have to push through the camp hard and fast."

"How much time can you give us?" Sarge asked.

Mark shrugged. "Maybe fifteen minutes."

"Shit. That isn't long," Sheffield moaned.

"Fifteen minutes is more than enough time, Captain. We can rain some serious hate down on these guys in fifteen minutes."

"How fast can you have your people in place?" Fawcett asked.

The question caught Sheffield by surprise. "Uh, I uh. You want to do this now?"

"We're here. You got a better idea?" Fawcett asked.

Sarge pushed his hat back on his head. "It'll take a few hours to get everyone ready."

Looking at Sheffield, Fawcett asked, "Your people know their jobs on this?"

He nodded. "Yeah. We've gone over it already. Everyone knows what they have to do."

Fawcett stood up. "Then let's get to it. We need to deal with this as soon as we can. We've got some serious party crashers coming and we don't need crap like this in the winds when they show up." Looking at Sarge, he asked, "You got enough IR strobes for your people?"

Sarge looked at Ted. He nodded. "I think we have enough

to mark our positions. There won't be one on every person, but there will be one in every position."

Fawcett nodded. "Good." He took a piece of paper from his blouse pocket and tossed it on the table. "Put these codes in your radios. You'll be able to talk to us. I'll be overhead for command and control."

Ted took the paper and wrote the codes down on a notebook. "Soon as we get back, I'll set up our radios and do a comm check."

"Roger that.," Fawcett replied.

Sarge stood up and looked around the table. "Things are going to get real interesting later this evening. Let's take care of these assholes once and for all."

Leaving the armory, I ran into Shane and Sean with the PD. The kid Micah was with them. "What's with all the helicopters?" Shane asked.

"We've got some shit to take care of," Sarge shot back.

"You going after those DHS guys?" Micah asked.

Before anyone could answer him Sarge replied, "Hell no. We don't need this kind of hardware for those shit birds."

I was wondering why he lied to the kid, but also glad. He made me nervous and I couldn't put my finger on why. I told Sean the prisoners would be returned shortly and to keep them locked up until further notice. We quickly loaded into the truck and headed out of town as the armory became a bee hive of activity.

"We need to stop by the plant and tell those engineers to get back to town. We'll need every swinging dick we can get," Sarge said.

Nodding, I replied. "I'm going to the farm first to let those guys know too. We'll need to grab Thad and take him home with us."

When we got to the farm, the people there were already gathering at the trucks for the ride back to town. It was getting late in the day and their work was done. We told Cecil and his security element what was going on. Thad quickly collected his gear.

"I'll be glad when they're gone." Cecil said. Wiping his forehead with the back of his arm, he added, "We got enough shit to worry about."

Sarge snorted. "It's going to get worse Cecil."

Cecil looked around. "Shit, Top. What the hell are the Russians gonna want with this little hole in the wall?"

"Hopefully nothing. But let's hope they don't find a reason."

Back in the truck, I headed for the plant. Terry and crew were also gathered around one of their trucks. It was quitting time for everyone. Except us, our work hadn't even begun yet. I was still processing what was about to happen. We'd been planning this, but it seemed to be far off, not imminent. There was no denying it now. I pulled up beside the group and leaned out the window.

"You guys need to get back to town. Looks like we're going to hit the armory as soon as we can get everyone in place."

"No shit? Shawn asked.

"No shit!" Sarge barked back. "Now get your asses to town!" He slapped my shoulder and told me to go.

I pushed the old truck to get us home. Everything was a rush now. I roared through Umatilla, getting curious looks from the people lingering at the old Kangaroo. The same happened as we sped through Altoona. Once back at the neighborhood, I stopped at the bunker. Everyone got out, I told them I would meet them back there with Danny and everyone from the house. Thad said he'd go get the girls, Aric and Perez were already at the bunker.

Pulling up in front of my house, I jumped out and ran in. The house was empty. They were all probably at Danny's, so I ran over there. Mel and Bobbie were sitting on the porch when I ran up. Mel quickly stood up, asking what was wrong.

"Nothing is wrong. We just need everyone to come down to the bunker. Is Danny in there?" I asked, pointing at the house.

Bobby nodded and stood up. "I'll go get him."

"Get anyone in there," I replied.

"What's going on?" Mel asked.

"That General I met with before is in Eustis. They want to attack the Elk's Camp to get them out of the way."

Confused, Mel asked, "Out of the way of what?"

"It looks like the Russians and Chinese are reportedly sending troops here. We want to deal with the DHS guys before they show up. If they show up."

"So what you heard on the radio is true?"

Nodding, I said, "It looks that way. But that doesn't mean they're coming here to Altoona. I would imagine they are going to be more interested in population centers or where there's some sort of resource they want."

"I hope they aren't coming here."

Danny came out of the house with Bobbie, Mary and my girls. Lee Ann asked what was going on. I told them all to follow me to the bunker and we would explain it. They were all full of questions, but I kept telling them to just wait until we got there. By the time we got back, everyone was there. It was quite the crowd, actually.

Sarge hopped up on top of the bunker. "Alright everyone, settle down. I know you're full of questions, but listen to what I have to say before asking any. My friend General Fawcett flew in from SOCOM." He noticed the quizzical looks he got from some. "SOCOM stands for Southern Command. He came to let us know the rumors we've been hearing of Russian and Chinese troops coming here are indeed true. They're coming. Now it ain't going to be easy for them. Our boys will give them hell. But they'll probably make it here, and there very well could be some special forces types here already."

Jess brushed hair from her face. "We already knew that. Well mostly."

"That brings us to where we are now. Why we're all standing here. As most of you know, the Elk's Camp has been taken over by a group from the DHS and some of their lackeys. These are some of the same guys that were running the camp out at the range. We've been planning a raid on the camp. With the arrival of the general, we've moved things up. We're hitting it tonight."

"Really? Tonight?" Aric asked.

Sarge nodded. "Tonight. Teddy's going to lay out a drawing of the camp and go over the plan. Our group will be acting as a blocking force. The Guard guys are going to take the hard job of assaulting the camp directly. We're just going to be there to stop anyone trying to squirt out the back door."

Ted stepped up and unrolled the drawing. "All right, everyone. Gather round so we can go over the plan.

As he said that, Doc pulled up in Sarge's war wagon with Jamie. Jamie sat in the buggy and listened to the discussion. Ted and Mike were going over the plan, pointing out the positions we would occupy. As they were covering the plan, Jamie interrupted them.

"Who all is going?"

Ted looked at Sarge, who in turn looked at Doc. Doc replied with a subtle shake of his head. Sarge looked at Jamie. "I know you want to go."

She swung her legs out of the buggy and replied, "I am going."

Sarge walked over to her. "I know you want to. Hell, I want you to. But you don't want to be a liability out there do you?"

Jamie huffed. "I'm not a liability!"

"You're not a hundred percent either. You wouldn't want one of us to get hurt trying to help you. If this thing goes south and we have to run for our lives, what are you going to do then?"

Jamie sat back in the seat. Giving up trying to get out of the buggy. She sighed and said, "You're right. I know it. It just sucks."

Sarge put his hand on her shoulder. "I know you're a fighter. This doesn't make you any less." Jamie nodded but said nothing.

"So who is going and who is staying?" Ted asked.

I looked at Mel and Bobbie. "You guys want to go?"

Mel shook her head. "I don't want you to go, much less me."

"I'm going," Lee Ann said sternly.

"What about me?" Taylor asked.

Shaking my head, I said, "Kiddo, you're in the same boat as Jamie. You need more time to heal." She didn't reply, just looked at the ground and nodded.

"We need every person we can get, but we also have to keep some people here to watch over things," Sarge said.

Pointing people out, I said, "I think Jamie, Mel, Bobbie, Taylor and Mary are going to stay. They should be able to keep an eye on things."

Sarge looked at them and asked, "Are you ladies good with that?" They nodded in reply.

Sarge tapped the drawing. "Alright then. Let's assign positions. Each position will have two people in it."

The teams would be Jess and Thad, Aric and Fred, Lee Ann with me, Perez and Ian, Danny and Dalton, Ted, Doc and Sarge would be together with Mike manning the Gustav and taking out any trucks that tried to move.

Sarge looked at Mike and wagged a finger at him. "You only hit trucks that try to move. Don't go blowing everything up. We're going to need those trucks."

Mike rolled his eyes. "I know, I know. I got it."

"You damn well better!" Sarge barked. Then he looked at Ted. "You got those radios ready?"

"Let me go back to the house and get them. We'll spread them out as best we can."

"Chop chop!"

Doc stepped up on the bunker. "If anyone gets hit, call out. I'll hang out in the center of our line so I can get to you. Do not try to come to me. I'll come to you. There will be very little medicine during the fight."

"Win the fight first," Mike said.

Mel looked at me. I grabbed her hand and said, "Don't worry."

She squeezed my hand. "That's going to be hard not to do."

Leaning over and giving her kiss, I said, "I know."

Sarge was glaring at me. "You two done? Can we continue now?"

Rocking on my heels, I looked around. "I guess you can continue."

Sarge clasped his hands in front of him. "Oh, thank you so much!"

With the teams established, they were assigned locations. Once everyone was clear on where they were to be, Sarge told everyone to go get ready. The group broke up and I walked Mel and the girls back home. Little Bit was holding my hand as we walked and I could tell something was bothering her, eating at her. I gave her hand a little tug and asked what it was. She shrugged, so I tugged her hand again.

She looked up at me. Her eyes were red, no tears yet but they were clearly on the way. "I don't want you to get shot."

Pushing my carbine around to my back, I scooped her up in my arms. She was getting so big! This wasn't as easy as it once was. "Don't worry about that. I've already been shot once and that didn't kill me!" I lifted the boonie hat on my head and turned it to the side so she could see the scar.

She reached up and touched it. "And that one was in your head too."

I bounced her. "Exactly. I'll be fine." Looking at Lee Ann, I asked, "How many magazines do you have for that burp gun?"

She carried a little messenger bag with her all the time. I guess it was kind of like a purse, only this one was a little unusual in that it carried not only the usual things a teenage girl would normally, it also contained several 9mm magazines. Without looking, she said, "Six."

"Alright. Just keep your ammo count in mind when this starts. You don't want to run out."

Once Mel and the girls were in the house I went to Danny's. I wanted to poke around in the armory we'd developed, which was now substantial. I remembered seeing a Springfield M1, and wanted it. I found the rifle in the closet and managed to find half a dozen magazines for it as well. I also picked up a Mossberg 500. It had a pistol grip stock and extended tube on it. A few more minutes of digging turned up an ammo can full of assorted buckshot.

Taking the guns back to the house, I dumped the shells into my pack and gave the shotgun to Lee Ann. "I want you to carry this in tonight."

She looked at the scattergun. "I can't shoot this thing."

Laughing, I said, "You won't have to. I just need you to carry it. This is our last ditch defense if things get really hairy."

In the kitchen, I filled the bladder in my pack from the Berkey filter and another two-quart canteen as well. Then I filled a travel mug with tea for the ride. Going into the bedroom, I went through my medical stuff and added two Israeli bandages to the pack and a tourniquet. God forbid I had to use them, but if I needed them, there would be no substitute.

Mel came in as I was putting stripper clips full of 5.56 ammo in the pack as well. She sat down on the bed. "What's up?" I asked.

"I'm worried. This is really dangerous and it's not just you. Lee Ann is going too."

"She'll be with me, babe. I'll do my best to protect her. Hell, we may not even fire a shot. When those Apaches get done, there may not be anyone to stop."

Mel crossed her arms and gave me a disbelieving look. "You really think that?"

I shrugged and half-smiled. "It could happen."

"Don't let her get hurt. We already have one daughter who's recovering. You too. You both better come home in one piece." She paused and closed her eyes. "I just couldn't take it if something happened to one of you."

Sitting down on the bed beside her, I said, "We will. I promise." I hoped I wasn't making a promise I couldn't keep.

Going out, I sat on the couch beside Little Bit. She was combing the hair of a big plastic horse. Putting my hand on her head, I said, "We're leaving, but we'll be back later OK."

She didn't look up at me, replying only with, "Mmm hmm."

I leaned over in front of her. "I'm serious. We'll be back."

She reached out and wrapped her arms around me. "You have to come back."

Holding her tight, I replied, "I will, baby girl. I will."

Standing up, I looked at Lee Ann. "You ready?"

She looked down at herself and shrugged. "Yeah, I guess."

"Alright then. Let's go."

She went over to her Mom and hugged her. Mel told her to be careful. "And listen to your Dad!"

Lee Ann smiled. "I will. I promise."

Then she surprised both Mel and me by going over to Little Bit and giving her a hug as well. They never were very close in the Before, and had bickered often. But it seemed they were getting closer now. And it was incredible to witness.

We left the house and headed down the road towards the bunker. It was dark, but I could see figures in the road. We walked quietly together. I was struck by just how calm she was about the whole thing. Looking over at her, all I could see was her outline. I said, "You know this isn't a game, kiddo. This is the real deal and will be very dangerous."

She was very calm in her response. "I know what we're about to do. People are going to die tonight." In the dark, I saw her turn towards me. "We just have to kill more of them than they do of us." It was a striking statement from her. She really did get it, and understood that we very well could lose people tonight. I put my arm around her as we walked the remaining short distance to the bunker.

We were still waiting on a few people, so I decided to turn on the little radio and see if I could catch the broadcast tonight. Ted and Mike were messing with a couple of SAWs. There were four of them lined up on top of the bunker. They would do most of the work for us tonight. Somehow they managed to come up with another one. Made me wonder if Sheffield was missing a machinegun.

I found static on the radio and checked my watch. The broadcast should start in about five minutes, so I set the radio down and went over to where the guys were working on the weapons. They both had headlamps on and were going through the machineguns.

"These things ready to rock?" I asked.

Mike looked up with a devilish grin. "Oh yeah. Ready to rain hate and mayhem."

Nodding, I replied, "It's going to be a long night of hate."

Ted stretched. "These assholes have no idea what we're about to drop on them."

With a laugh, I said, "Do unto others before they do unto you."

Sarge pulled up with Doc and Thad. Climbing out, Doc handed me a small strobe light. "Here, put this on the back of your vest. It's an IR so the Apaches can see us."

"Good, cause friendly fire isn't!" I said.

Everyone arrived shortly after that. Danny looked nervous, and I asked if he was alright. He nodded. "Yeah. I just want to get this over."

"And that's just what we're going to do tonight," Sarge said. He looked around at the group. "This is going to be some scary shit, guys. Just keep your head, don't panic. Do what we tell you to do and you'll be fine."

Ted held up a couple of radios. "These are set to talk to the Guard's radios and the helicopters. Stay off them unless you see something we need to know about. Sarge's call sign is Swamp Rat. The Guard is Eustis Six and the birds are Saber One-One and the General's call sign is Jefe." Ted handed out the radios. There wasn't enough for one in every position, but he gave me one.

Sarge looked around again. "Any questions?" When nobody said anything, he added, "Don't worry. You'll all do fine. Let's load up."

As we were getting into the truck, the radio crackled to life with the nightly broadcast.

You're listening to John Jacob Schmitt coming to you from the Radio Free Redoubt. Broadcasting to all patriots in occupied territory and those of you outside the wire. We have a mixed bag tonight, folks. On the good side, the Marines have pushed Federal forces from their positions around Atlanta. However, it came at a price. The once beautiful city of Atlanta is now in ruins. The attacking Marines were forced to use heavy artillery to dislodge the defenders. And out of pure spite, the Feds torched great swaths of the city. The fires are still burning as I speak.

Now, sadly, the bad news. We need to be vigilant, folks. We now know for a fact that advanced elements of both the Russian and Chinese forces are here. These advance units are lightly armed and have no support. If you see them, get a message out somehow. The more of them we can eliminate now, the better we'll be. If your group has the means, take them out. These are invaders. I know that sounds weird. The kind of thing we here in the greatest country on Earth never imagined, but it's here now.

A woman's voice came over the radio.

Patriots, prepare for a message. The oak tree is on fire. The oak tree is on fire.

As soon as I heard that, I looked at Danny. "Hey man, write down the numbers she's about to say." Danny grabbed a piece of paper from the glovebox and got ready. Just in time too, because the numbers came quickly.

54342 54163 93366 67696 60395 95689 64805 72476 61595 63917 26705 74223 50388 68029 39765 38995 98247 88120 79699 18962 37562 92226 87579. Please share this information with anyone in the affected area.

I was following behind Sarge and the guys who were in his two buggies. We were driving blacked out, which was strange for me because I wasn't used to driving with NVGs. I'd turned the radio off to concentrate. Plus, I was nervous as hell. We were heading down highway 42. The intent was to come at them from the back, approaching from the north where there were no roads that went directly to the camp.

The Guard was also on the move. A convoy of trucks stretched down highway 19 coming out of Eustis headed north to Umatilla. There, they would take 450 to the west and approach the main gate of the camp. During their recon, Mike and Ted noted the lack of any sort of roadblock at the entrance. There were defensive positions on either side, but the road was wide open. The Guard would take advantage of this fact.

On a dark stretch of highway 42, Sarge stopped. I pulled up beside him. He pointed off to the south. "Here's where we go in. Get your truck off the road and get everyone out. We've got to distribute the load and head for the rally point."

I pulled the truck off the road and parked it under some large oak trees where everyone got out. The buggies would be driven a little closer, but even they would be abandoned shortly. We put as many people on them as we could, but Thad, Danny, Aric and I ended up walking. It wasn't hard to keep up though, because they were going slow in the brush. Not to mention, we had to cut a couple of fences. It was not the stealthiest approach; but after tonight, it wouldn't matter one way or the other. Either they'd be gone, or we would.

At the point the buggies were to be abandoned, we distributed the load. There was the mortar and its ammunition, and the SAWs and their ammo. Mike had the Goose as well. There was a lot of hardware, and it was impressive to know we had that sort of weaponry. I was carrying my carbine and the M1. Lee Ann had her H&K and the shotgun. But we all had to carry more. I was saddled with one of the SAWs and thought about leaving the carbine. But it wasn't far to our positions and I wanted every gun I could get my hands on. Were we walking farther I certainly wouldn't hump all this shit.

Once everything was sorted out, Sarge turned to the group. "Alright guys, shit's about to get real. Absolutely no talking from here on. Move quietly and try not to make any noise. Our positions are on the edge of the camp, so we'll be kind of far away; but we don't want to give them any warning."

Ian and Ted led the way. Ian carried a SAW as well. They would range ahead and make sure we didn't walk into an ambush. I took up position at the rear of the column, keeping Lee Ann with me. From my position, I could see all the IR strobes that were with each team. They flashed randomly providing fleeting glimpses of the canopy of trees we were walking under. These quickly gave way to a large marsh. Thankfully, it'd been pretty dry lately, so we weren't wading through muck to get there.

At the edge of the marsh, we paused, everyone taking a knee. Sarge would come get one team at a time and take them to their position, then return to get another. Eventually, he got to me and Lee Ann and led us to our position. It was in a small depression with a slight rise in front of it. From where we were though, I could see most of the backside of the camp. It was a good spot.

Sarge knelt down beside me. "Alright, Morgan. When the show starts, it's open season. We want to prevent any of them getting out this side of the camp. So anyone you see out there is a target."

"Roger that," I replied as I set my pack on the ground. He patted my back and disappeared. I looked down along the edge of the marsh and could see strobes flashing. I really hope these guys don't have any NVGs. I pulled the two-quart canteen out and laid it between Lee Ann and me. "Here's some water if you need it," I whispered. She nodded, and I said, "Your weapon is for close work. Don't waste it trying to shoot across this field. I'll try and stop them farther out. But if anyone tries to make a break for it and crosses that field, you take them out."

In a quiet whisper, she replied, "Okay."

I checked my watch. It was three AM. It'd taken some time to get everyone in place. The show would start soon. We were waiting for the appearance of the Apaches to start the party. I took the time to observe the camp. There was very little movement. I saw a couple of pairs of what had to be security walking around. That meant everyone else was more than likely asleep, which was good. If those Apaches could take out the cabins with them in still inside, it would make our life a lot easier.

"When is this going to start?" Lee Ann whispered.

"I don't know. You tired?"

"A little. I was excited walking in here. Now I'm getting tired."

I patted her back. "That's the way it works, kiddo. Go ahead and sleep while you can. I'll wake you up when it's time."

She pushed her weapon out of the way and laid her head on her hands. "Okay. Wake me up."

Whispering, I replied, "I don't think that will be a problem."

I sat quiet for a long time. So long, I started questioning if this were going to happen or not. I'm not a patient person, and sitting like this was killing me. Not to mention, your ears play tricks on you, and I was forever looking behind me for guy I knew was sneaking up on me, only to see nothing. Then there was the unmistakable sound of something coming through the brush. There was no mistaking it this time.

I tapped Lee Ann on the shoulder. When she opened her eyes I held a finger to my lips and pointed to the thin line of brush behind us. I crawled around so I was facing the sound and searched the bush for any movement. The sound was getting louder, crunching and scraping. I picked up the Mossberg and trained the sight out in front of me. Then, as if materializing out of thin air, a damn armadillo wandered out of the brush just ten feet from me. I hate armadillos, and kill every one of them I find.....usually!

Lee Ann smiled, and I said, "It's your lucky day, bud."

Lee Ann cupped her mouth to keep from laughing. I held my finger to my lips again and pointed for her to turn around. With the radios came a small ear bud. As I picked up the M1 again it crackled.

Jefe to all units. Put your heads down. Saber is inbound.

I couldn't hear the helicopters and wondered how far away they were. I should be able to hear them. Then came a faint thumping. They sounded really far. The radio crackled again.

Saber one one. Swamp Rat, we've marked your strobes. Gun runs will be from the north to the south and west to east. Make yourselves small, people.

I still could only hear a faint thumping. How far can the optics on one of those things see? The question was answered when I saw a small flash speeding towards the camp. It hit one of the cabins and erupted into a massive explosion. I looked at my watch, it was 4:12 AM.

"Oh my God!" Lee Ann said, a little too loud.

I shushed her and tried to push myself a little farther into the hole. What followed was a rocket coming in every few minutes. The camp was now fully awake and people were running around. With a target-rich environment in front of me, I started to aim at the figures running around in front of the flames. I would save the machinegun ammo for when they were running towards me. For now, they were backlit by the numerous fires beginning to burn around the camp. Then the Apaches opened up with their cannons. It was a mesmerizing display as the large rounds slammed into the ground. Lying on my stomach as I was I could feel the impacts.

I took aim on a figure and pulled the trigger, and was stunned when the shadow exploded before my eyes. Several more 30mm rounds slammed into the ground around the now disintegrated body. No matter, I just picked another one. The helicopters continued their work, and then the sound of a large number of small arms entered the fight.

Eustis is through the gate. The radio crackled. It was now fully on. I glanced down the line and saw sporadic fire coming from some of our positions. Red tracers would race out from our line in short bursts. Then off to my right front, there was another large explosion. I could see men falling out the back of a burning truck. After a moment, there was a large bright yellow flash. Thick flames shot high into the sky, and even in the darkness I could see the intensely thick inky black could of smoke rising into the predawn sky.

The camp's occupants were caught completely off guard and were obviously not prepared for what happened. As the Guard pushed farther into the camp, the camp occupants started to panic and run. And they ran straight towards us. I dropped the M1 and got behind the saw. We were the last ones on our line, so it was important for me to keep anyone from getting around. Snugging the weapon to my shoulder, I squeezed the trigger.

I fired seven or eight-round bursts at the figures running towards me. They fell like grass before a scythe. All down our line now everyone was firing. Now it was a continuous steady stream of red tracers. The sound was intense. It was so damn loud. But when the radio crackled again, I heard the call.

Saber One One is Winchester.
Saber One Two is Winchester.
Jefe, Swamp Rat.

Go for Swamp Rat. Sarge's voice came over the radio with the sound of heavy automatic weapon fire in the background.

Swamp Rat you've got Tangos maneuvering to the east. We'll come over and hit them with the door guns.

Roger that, Jefe. Morgan, you see them?"

I pulled the NVGs back down over my eyes and looked to my right. There were about a dozen people running from the attack. I don't think I'd call it maneuvering, but they were certainly moving. I moved Lee Ann out of the way and shifted the weapon, opening up on them. Then I heard the Blackhawk come in and a gunner up there turned a Minigun lose on them as well. It was hellish. We cut all of them down. The sound of the Minigun and stream of tracers made me think of some heavenly demon opening his mouth and vomiting fire and death down onto those below. The sound, the sight, it was truly terrible. The last one to fall, hit the ground and tried to get back up. I stopped that with a burst to his chest. With that, my end of the line went quiet. I saw no other figures.

The radio crackled again with a terrifying message. *We're being overrun!*

It was Dalton. And while he was certainly excited, he was calm and spoke clearly.

With only four teams on the line, our positions were a couple hundred yards apart. Plenty of room for people to sneak through. Keying my radio, I said, "Our end is quiet. We're moving to support Danny and Dalton!"

I took a minute to add the last belt of ammo to the one trailing out of the SAW. Then I told Lee Ann to follow me. We ran along the marsh looking for Danny and Dalton. I heard them before I saw them. I could hear Dalton shouting, screaming at the top of his lungs. Then their position came into sight. It was above us on the crest of a small hill. I could clearly see Dalton standing up and firing. Coming up to the top of the hill, I was shocked to see so many people rushing towards them.

I told Lee Ann to shoot and dropped to the ground to get the SAW into the fight. Something must have happened to theirs as it was quiet. We started on the back of the group and made short work of them. The front part of the group made it to their position and quickly devolved into hand to hand fighting. I was trying to cover them, but couldn't fire because they were mixed up. I told Lee Ann to stay put and grabbed the shotgun and took off running.

Dalton was swinging his AK like a club, holding it by the barrel. Danny was on his back firing his pistol point blank into them. Dalton hit a man in the head and snapped the stock off his weapon. He didn't miss a beat, pulling his Kukri from its sheath and snatching the tomahawk from where it was tucked into his belt. The first poor soul to encounter him was hacked up immediately. Dalton used the hawk to hook the man's arm and pull it out of the way and force him off balance. He then smashed the head of the hawk into his face and drove the Kukri up under his ribs and into his chest. The man was done.

Kicking the body off his blade, Dalton hoisted the edged weapons over his head and screamed, "Men and lads! Wet your edges on me!" Like some sort of psycho. He then charged headlong into them. I was running towards him, firing the shotgun as fast as I could. Danny was now back on his feet and had his carbine working. I was reloading the Mossberg when a body slammed into me, sending both of us crashing to the ground.

I looked up to see a wild-eyed bearded man scrambling for the shotgun. He would get to it before I did. Then, as the sky was beginning to lighten to the coming dawn, I recognized him. It was Billy. I went to draw my pistol and it wasn't there. I groped at the empty holster and looked at it in disbelief. Then I remembered the hawk Dalton gave me. Snatching it from my vest I crawled after Billy. He was about two feet from the Mossberg when I slammed the head of the hawk into his calf.

He howled in pain. But his screaming reached a new level when I took a double-handed grip on the hickory handle of the hawk and pulled him back towards me. But I didn't think that out all the way, and he smashed a bare foot into my nose, breaking it. I lost my grip on the hawk as my head spun and my eyes watered. Rolling onto my back, I looked over to see Billy trying to get to his feet. He was close to me, so I pulled the ESEE from its sheath and slammed it into the top of his foot. He howled again as he fell, knocking the hawk free.

Picking it up with my free hand, I sank the knife into his thigh and used it for a grip to drag myself over to him. He was screaming in pain and flailing at me. I swung the hawk at his hands. It hit his right hand between the third and fourth finger, nearly cleaving it in half. He screamed again as he held the mangled appendage up before him.

I climbed on top of him, straddling him. Looking down at him, blood ran from my nose and onto his face. He took a swing at me with his left that I easily dodged. Not wanting to give him another chance, I screamed as I brought the hawk back over my head. "I told you I'd fucking kill you!"

Billy's eyes went wide as the piece of forged iron arched down towards him, slamming into his forehead. I wrenched it free and hit him again and again. I was covered in blood, mine and his. Breathing heavily, I pulled the hawk from his destroyed head. A pair of boots came into view and I looked up to see Dalton with a garish smile on his face, tomahawk in one hand and Kukri in the other. Both dripping blood. He wiped blood from his face with the back of his hand and said, "Fun ain't it?"

As I tried to get up, I replied, "I don't know about fun."

He offered me a hand and pulled me to my feet. Once on my feet, I noticed the shooting had died down. There was still sporadic fire in the camp, but it all seemed to be concentrated in one area. I could hear faint radio chatter, very faint, and realized the ear bud had been knocked from my ear. I put it back in my ear as I searched for my pistol, finding it not far from where Billy and I had collided.

I caught the end of Sarge saying to rally at the swimming pools. I looked around at the bodies on the ground and checked on Danny. He was on the ground fumbling with a bandage.

Kneeling down, I asked, "What's wrong?"

"Something hit my shoulder."

Dalton was there quickly as well and ripped open Danny's shirt. There was a small hole just below the collarbone. Dalton and I got him wrapped up and onto his feet.

"Can you move?" Dalton asked.

"Yeah, just hand me my rifle."

I handed him his carbine and smiled. "Let's go finish this."

He shook his head. "You look like shit."

I laughed. "You should see the other guy."

Lee Ann handed me the M1. I slung it over my back and picked up the SAW. The four of us made our way over to the pools where everyone else was waiting. When Sarge saw us he was surprised.

"Holy shit! What the hell happened to you guys!"

"I ran into Billy, and Danny took a round to his shoulder," I replied.

Doc quickly checked Danny out while Sarge looked at my nose. He grabbed it and moved it back and forth. It was like fire shooting through my head.

"Dammit, that hurts!" I shouted as I slapped his hand away.

Sarge giggled. "Yeah, that's broke for sure."

"Thank you for the stunning report, Captain Fucking Obvious!"

Doc said Danny would be alright for now and turned his attention to Dalton. "What the hell happened to you? There's blood everywhere. Are you hit? You hurt anywhere?"

Dalton waved him off. "I'm good Doc. All my blood's still on the inside. None of this is mine."

Doc stepped back and asked, "What the hell happened?"

I stabbed my thumb at Dalton. "Conan here went all medieval on a bunch of them."

Looking at me, Dalton replied, "I wasn't the only one."

"You finish Billy Boy?" Sarge asked.

"Yeah. He's not going to be bothering anyone else."

"I'd say so!" Dalton shouted. "You hacked his head to pieces. I've split logs with fewer swings!"

Sarge looked around. "Anyone else got any booboos?" Everyone looked themselves over and shook their heads. "Alright. This is almost over. There's a group holed up over here in the gymnasium. All of the remaining combatants here have to be rooted out; and after it gets light out, every building has to be cleared. The Guard is working on that gym, so we can all take a quick rest and wait for daylight."

We all sat down on the chairs by the pool. It was kind of strange to be sitting on a lounge chair beside a pool. But instead of coolers and floats, we had automatic weapons at our side. Of course this pool was a green swamp, but it still looked like a pool. Mike made it to the pool and flopped onto a chair. Looking at Sarge, he said, "You made me hump that damn mortar in here and you didn't even use it?"

"We didn't need it. Better that way. We still have the ammo."

Mike shook his head. "Didn't need it?"

"Oh dry up! Better we have it and not need it, than need it and not have it!"

Jess brushed hair from her face and said, "That was easier than I thought it would be."

Looking over, I replied, "Speak for yourself."

"Aric killed like six people," Fred said proudly.

"Shit, you ain't even limited out yet!" Sarge barked.

Doc came over and knelt down in front of me. "Let me see that nose."

I tilted my head back and said, "You pinch it and yours will look like mine."

He laughed. "I ain't going to pinch it."

Yeah, he didn't pinch it in the proper sense. But he mashed it around and it hurt like hell. He looked in my nose with a small light and asked, "Can you breathe alright?"

I nodded. "Yeah, it just feels like it's full of snot."

"That's blood, not snot. And don't try and blow it out. Let the clot stay there for now."

In his oh so polite way, Sarge said, "You're going to look like shit tomorrow."

I shook my head. "Yeah, well this will get better. What's your excuse?"

As the sun began to break the horizon, we were able to see more around us. It was a ghastly scene. There were bodies lying everywhere. The imagery was compounded by the smell of the burning structures, trucks and the unmistakable smell of burning fuel. Mixed in and nearly overpowered by the other odors, but still there, was the iron-like smell of blood and raw meat.

People just aren't prepared for what this really looks like. It isn't like in the movies. I could it see on our people now. Lee Ann was looking around. She was pinching her nose and had a disgusted look on her face. Fred, so proud a moment ago about Aric's body count, was now bent over getting sick. Aric was patting her back as she wretched.

Then there was Thad. He was dealing with it by not looking. He stared at the ground at his feet. Mike and Ted were oblivious to it all. They were actually eating a biscuit that Mike pulled from his pack. As though nothing happened and it was just another day.

I looked in the direction of the group the door gunner and I had taken down. They were scattered over a grassy area on a slight slope. They were over a hundred yards away and I got up and started to walk towards them. Something drew me towards them.

The closer I got the more clearly I could see them. I was struck by what I was seeing. I stopped in front of the one I'd shot trying to get up. Kneeling down, I brushed the girl's hair out of her blood-splattered face. She was young, I'd say sixteen or so. She wore only a t-shirt and her underwear. She was a pretty girl and now she was dead. Looking the group over, there were several other women, though thankfully this was the youngest. All were barely dressed, and all of them were barefoot.

Some of the bodies were chewed to pieces. Having caught the full wrath of the door gunner. The image of that red stream of death coming down amongst them returned to me. I could remember seeing them in the NVGs, but I didn't recall seeing women. Had I realized that, I have to wonder if I would have had it within me to shoot them. But in the moment, that's not what I saw.

I was surveying the scene when Sarge's voice came over my shoulder. "These the ones that were maneuvering around you?"

Shaking my head, I replied, "They weren't maneuvering. They were running for their fucking lives. And I shot them."

We stood in silence for a moment. I was staring at the side of the girl's face. Her eyes were open but it was very obvious there was no life in them. When a person dies, the eyes lose that gleam, that light. There was no light in any of the eyes of these people. Looking at the girl, I wondered what those eyes had seen. What kind of good, what kind of fun times she'd seen in her life. On the other side of that coin was the thought of what sort of horrors they'd seen. And to know that the last thing they saw was the muzzle flash from the machinegun with me behind it was too much.

Tears started to run down my face. I was supposed to be helping people. Saving them from this very sort of horror. And here, now, there was no way to deny the fact that I was the one to perpetrate the very horror I think I'm preventing.

Sarge stepped up beside me. After a moment, I heard him take a deep breath. "Morgan. When you saw these people in the dark, running, what did you think?"

I looked at him. He was looking at the bodies. "What do you mean?"

He looked at me and there was a softness to him. Sarge was always a little rough around the edges, crusty in a dry dog turd kind of way. A product of a lifetime spent in the service of his country. When he wasn't pissed off, he was usually fucking with you. But now, I could tell he was being sincere. "In the dark, when you looked down the barrel of that weapon. What did you see?"

I looked at the broken and bent bodies again. "I didn't see a group of women and girls fleeing for their lives."

Sarge stepped around in front of me and looked directly into my eyes. "I know you didn't see that, Morgan. If you had, you'd have never pulled the trigger. Hell, I wouldn't have pulled the trigger. But I didn't ask what you didn't see. I asked what you did see."

I tried to look past him, but he side-stepped, staying right in front of me and staring into my eyes. I thought about the question. I closed my eyes and saw it again, plain as day. "I saw a group of people running."

"Where were they running?"

"They were running for the bush."

"Did you think there was a damn good chance they had weapons?"

Again, I thought about the question. I remembered pushing Lee Ann out of the way and moving the weapon. I remembered falling behind it and the red tracers speeding away from me. I remembered the demonic tracers from the Minigun. At that moment, I certainly thought they had weapons. I nodded my head and wiped away the increasing tears running from my eyes. "Yes."

"And had those armed people gotten past you, do you think your friends, your daughter, could have been killed?"

Rocking my head to the side, I shrugged. "Well, yeah."

Sarge put his hands on my shoulders and I opened my eyes. He was still looking straight into mine, and I was surprised to see what could have been the beginning of tears in his. "Morgan. What you did was what anyone would have done. Do you think all those guys that come back from combat overseas have PTSD from being shot at? That's only a small part of it friend. Hell, that's a release. I've been shot at in more countries than I can remember. What sticks with you is this shit."

He stepped aside and pointed at the bodies. "This is the shit that wakes you up at night. This is the kind of shit that gives you nightmares. I know what you're thinking. I know you're thinking about your girls." He knelt down and gently closed the girl's eyes. Looking back up at me, he said, "I am too." He stood up and put his arm around me and pulled me around, away from the carnage. "The moles that have never seen combat call this collateral damage. That's bullshit from assholes that have never smelled cordite, blood, piss and shit. This will stay with you forever." He looked at me. "And it should. You shouldn't forget. It would be a dishonor to the people that lost their lives here. But you need to understand that at the time, at that moment when you pulled the trigger, you did it for a reason bigger than yourself."

I'd managed to get control of myself as I thought of what he was saying. He was right after all. I didn't do it out of maliciousness. I wasn't blood thirsty or wanting to inflict unnecessary pain or misery. But that really didn't make it any easier to live with. "I know what you're saying. It makes sense." I tried to turn back. I was going to point at those poor souls, but Sarge held me tight and wouldn't let me. "But it doesn't change the fact those people are dead because of me."

"Don't look back, son. What's done it done. And I know you're holding yourself responsible for it all. But you have to remember there was a door gunner up there with a Minigun, and he was raining some serious hell down on them."

As we made our way back to the group, I replied, "True. But that girl. She was hit, and went down. She tried to get up and I finished her. She's totally on me."

Sarge's hand gripped my neck. "Son. What's done is done. Nothing you can do will ever take it back. It's hard. Believe me, I know it's hard. I'm not going to bullshit you and tell you it gets easier with time, 'cause it don't." Dropping his arm around my shoulders, he continued. "But you have to make peace with it, for yourself. Not for anyone else. You have to know that what you were doing, why you pulled the trigger, you were doing for us. For your daughter over there. You had no way of knowing in that moment who those people were."

I nodded and wiped at my nose. It hurt like hell and I winced. "I know. I get it."

Sarge stepped in front of me, stopping me. "No. You don't, but you need to. You're not a hard man, Morgan. And I don't mean that with any disrespect, but you're not. Some people are—" I interrupted him.

"Like you?"

Sarge's head dropped. Then he looked back up at me. "Son, I've done some horrible things in my day. But I always did them because it was what I thought was right. It was what my government told me to do. And mainly, always, because it was what I needed to do for the men I was with." He paused and ran his hands through his hair. "You don't think I have regrets? You don't think I wake up at night in a cold sweat? But when bullets are flying and people are dying, there is the now. And you did no less."

His words were sinking in. While the old man always had a way with words, they weren't always like this. He was good at being an ass. At making a scene. But he wasn't as gifted at trying to express himself in a real and meaningful way. Sure, he knew how to motivate people, for better or worse. This was just a side of the old codger I wasn't used to seeing.

"I understand," I said and stopped.

Sarge stopped and looked at me. "I don' think you do. Not yet anyway. But I hope it comes to you, Morgan. You need to know that what you did, you did for us." He pointed at our group sitting by the pool. Looking back at me, he said, "You did it for all of us."

It finally sank in. Combat, a world I was not really accustomed to, was not black and white. It was a thousand shades of gray. Shit happens. Bad shit happens. Sometimes good people die. Sometimes the wrong people die. But today, my people didn't die. And right now, at this moment, that's all that mattered.

The sun was now above the horizon. Small arms still crackled not far off. For what seemed like the first time, I looked around. The scene was terrible. Bodies and pieces of bodies were everywhere. To make it worse, some of them were moving. Shading my eyes with my hand, I took it in. It was dawn, a new day. It was supposed to be a new opportunity, a clean start. Yet what I saw was far from it.

Not far from where Sarge and I stood was a man in pair of shorts and dirty t-shirt. His underwear was dirty as well; and from where I stood, it looked as though he'd soiled himself. But then I couldn't blame him. Had I been shot in my lower back as he was, the least I would do would be to soil myself. He was pulling himself with his arms, trying to get away from the camp. I looked at him as he crawled.

In a moment of exhaustion, he dropped his head to the ground. He was looking at me and I could see the small buffs of dust his breath created on the ground. Reaching up, I patted Sarge on the shoulder. I kind of understood now. More would come later. I walked past him towards the prostrate man. While he didn't lift his head, I could see him looking at me.

The look on his face was almost relief. As I stepped up to him, he let out a hard breath, blowing dust and dry grass out before him. I stood over the man. He said nothing, simply closing his eyes. Drawing my pistol, I took a deep breath. I too felt the relief wash over me. Lowering the muzzle of the XD, I pulled the trigger.

Looking up towards the pool, I could see everyone looking at me. My family, nearly all the people in this world I now cared about, were looking at me. The man on the ground was no longer suffering. I looked around and saw others. Some had fear on their faces. Some, while still alive were too far gone to care either way. I walked a few paces to a woman lying face up. The sun shone brightly on her cheek. Her eyes were closed and she gasped for breath. Raising the pistol again, I squeezed the trigger.

When I looked up again, my family was no longer by the pool. They'd fanned out and were moving across the field. The occasional pop of a pistol or rifle told me what they were doing. We'd started this. And we would end this. The thoughts of no quarter were gone from my mind. Now all I could think about was ending the suffering for these poor souls as fast as I could. Hate is a powerful thing. That is until you come face to face with it. But I guess there are different kinds of hate. I surely didn't feel any remorse for Billy. He deserved exactly what he got. Actually, if I could have, I would have taken more time with him. He got off easy.

We stopped at Billy's body. Sarge looked down at him. "Damn, Morgan."

"Shit happens."

"We caught these assholes completely by surprise," Sarge said and pointed at the body. "Look at him. He's in his drawers and no shoes."

"The other ones, over there," I jerked my head back towards the body of the young girl, "they didn't have any shoes either."

"Surprise, speed and violence of action."

I looked around at the bodies scattered across the grassy fields surrounding the camp. I saw Aric walking up behind a man trying to crawl away. He casually walked up to the man, hearing the foot falls, he rolled over on his back and held his hands up. Aric looked down at him and raised his pistol, firing pointblank into the man's face. "I think we achieved it," I said.

Sarge grunted. "Looks like everyone is getting it out of their system."

Looking around, I saw Thad. He was still by the pool with Lee Ann. I was happy to see her still there and not out participating in what was happening. The words "no quarter" came to mind. I remembered saying them; and at the time this was the very sort of thing I was thinking about. Leaving none of these people alive. But the actual of act of doing so was quite different. There's the romance and the reality. And the reality never lives up to the romance.

Thad was looking at the ground. As I got closer, he looked up at me. I smiled and asked if he were alright.

Without looking around, he said, "I can't do that Morgan."

I grabbed his shoulder. "I don't blame you, buddy."

He pointed towards a group of the cabins sitting under a hammock of beautiful oaks. "We need to go through all these buildings."

Nodding, I replied, "Yeah. You wanna go check them out?"

Thad stood up and stretched. "That I can do."

"Come on then. Let's get it over with."

Lee Ann was sitting on a lounge chair. She looked up and asked, "You want me to go?"

"Yeah, come on. You can be back-up," I said with a smile.

It was a hard thing, really. Taking your teenage daughter with you to clear buildings. But this was the new reality. This is the way it is now. It was a sobering thought that brought Little Bit to mind. She'd have to grow up fast. There wouldn't be years of video games and riding bikes with friends. Hell, there were few friends now. Jace and Edie would be it for her for some time. Thankfully though, she at least did have them, and they had her.

We went to the first cabin. The door was open. Stopping shy of it, I told Lee Ann to stay outside and keep her eyes open. Thad and I would handle whatever happened inside, she needed to be our eyes for what was happening outside.

I started for the door and Thad pulled me back. "I'll go first. You got them girls to worry about. Ain't no one worrying about me."

I smiled and looked him in the eye. "If you want to go first, you can. But don't think no one is worrying about you, brother. I am." Pointing at Lee Ann, I said, "they are and so is everyone else." Then I smiled and added, "So is Mary."

That broad smile spread across his face and he said, "Morgan, you a mess." Then he got serious. "Follow me."

The first three cabins were empty. The fourth wasn't. I went through the door first this time, making Thad alternate the task with me. The cabins were about twenty feet by twenty feet. They were nice little cabins. The Elk's had done a fine job on them. Inside were several sets of bunk beds, a small table and a bathroom. Each cabin would hold twelve people.

Throwing the door open, I stepped in, sweeping the Mossberg to the right while Thad came in behind me and went to the left. The cabin was empty and I moved to the bathroom. Snatching the door open, a woman screamed and there was a sharp crack. I ducked to my right and dropped to my knees as drywall dust fell down on me. The woman was right in front of me and still screaming. I reached out and grabbed the barrel of the .22 revolver she clutched in her right hand and twisted it, yanking it from her grip. There were two small kids in the bathtub; they too were screaming and crying.

Thad was standing over me, staring down the barrel of his AK. Without looking down at me, he asked, "You alright?"

The woman was still screaming as I started to get to my feet. Needless to say, I was a little irritated. I screamed back at her. "Shut up! No one's going to hurt you."

She reached out for the children who immediately fell into her arms. "Please don't kill me! Please don't kill my babies!"

I stepped out of the doorway and Thad leaned in. "Come on, ma'am. Ain't no one going to hurt you. You need to calm down. You're scaring them young'uns."

Thad's calm voice had an effect on her. Still sniveling, she looked up, her face wet with tears. But Thad was patient and motioned with his hand. She slowly got to her feet, clutching the crying children close to her. She shrank from his hand as though his mere touch would somehow infect her. Sensing the woman's feelings, Thad stepped back, making way for her to get through the door. She came out nervously.

I stepped out the cabin door and nodded for Lee Ann. "Go in there and try to get her to come out."

She stepped around me and looked at the woman. Kneeling down to be on the level of the children, she smiled. "Come on. Let's walk over to the pool."

The woman looked at Thad, then at me. Looking back at Lee Ann, she nodded and headed for the door. I stepped further away from the door, giving them room. As they came out, Lee Ann looked over at me. I gave her a slight nod and motioned with my chin in the direction of the pool. She nodded and guided them towards it.

Thad came out. He was watching them as they walked away. After a moment, he asked, "What do we do with them?"

"I don't know what we do with them. I'm sure we've killed whoever they depended on."

"Maybe we should just take them to town."

I let out a long breath and shook my head slightly. "And have someone inside our wire that hates us." I pointed at the little boy. "So he can grow up hating us, all the while plotting ways to kill us."

Thad looked at me. "But what do we do with them?"

"I don't know. Right now we have to finish this. That will come later."

Thad and I continued to search the cabins. We found bodies, several bodies. The damage the Apaches caused was stunning. We passed one cabin that had taken a direct hit from one of the many Hell Fire rockets. It was gone. There was part of a slab and some pipes sticking out of the ground, and that was it. Several cabins around it were severely damaged. The ones to either side were open shells. The sides closest to the blast were gone, an entire side of the cabin, just gone.

As we found wounded men, I shot them. Every one. The words "no quarter" ringing in my ears with every report of my carbine, pistol or shotgun. It was never a question when we found them. I never asked Thad to partake. He was there with me, covering me, looking out for me. But I delivered the coup de grâce. We piled weapons as we found them, just to make it easier to come back for them. We found other women and kids. Some together, some alone. Each time, we would direct them towards the pool.

Lee Ann returned and helped collect weapons. She said some of the Guardsmen were there now, bringing other women and kids to the pool as well. As we found lone children, she would take the small crying kids by the hand and lead them to the pool. I was relieved to know there was someone there keeping an eye on them. There were weapons lying everywhere. It wouldn't be hard for some woman or maybe a teenage kid to pick up a weapon and extract some quick revenge. Doc was there as well treating the many wounded. We found a number of kids and adults with wounds.

Thad and I finished searching the two groups of cabins, and walked back towards the center of the camp. There was still gunfire being exchanged at the large building in the center of the camp. It was sporadic but would flare up in intense exchanges from time to time. We found Sarge and Livingston together coordinating the assault on the building.

"We cleared the cabins," I said as we walked up.

Sarge spun around. "Find anything?"

"Some women and kids," Thad replied.

Sarge wiped grit and soot from his face. Spitting in the dust, he asked, "Any combatants?"

I looked down at my feet. "None that are alive now."

As we stood there, I dropped the mag from my carbine and looked at it. There were rounds in it, but it felt light, so I replaced it with a fresh one. I gave it a tap and a tug to make sure it was in, and tucked the other one into the dump pouch on my belt.

Thad pointed at the large gymnasium. "What's going on here?"

Livingston took his helmet off and ran his hands through his hair. "The last bunch of them is holed up in there. We're trying to root them out."

Sarge chuckled. "I keep telling them to burn the bastards out. You set that place on fire and they'll come out. They'll come out real quick."

"We're trying not to destroy this place," Livingston sighed.

Holding his arms out, Sarge spun around. "Have you looked around this fucking place?"

I looked around. Smoke was rising from several places. The

air was heavy with it. The early hour and the fact that humidity drops lower to the ground as the sun comes up was holding the smoke low to the ground. The acrid odor of plastic, wood, fuel and the general smell of structural fires filled the air. Then there was the disturbing sickly sweet smell of cooking meat. The Polynesians called humans long pig. And it was that thought, more of a mental image of the smell of cooking pork that came to mind.

As I pondered that, Ted and Mike walked up. Ted looked at Sarge. "Why aren't we burning these fuckers yet?"

Sarge jabbed his thumb at Livingston. "Ask him."

Ted looked at Livingston and took a thermite grenade from his vest. Flipping it in his hand, he asked, "How many men have you lost on these ridiculous assaults?"

Livingston shook his head. "We've had four wounded. Six KIA."

"One or two of these and this shit is over," Ted said.

Sarge looked at Livingston. "Why don't you just let us do what we do?"

Livingston fiddled with the suspension rig of his helmet. After settling it onto his head, he looked at Sarge and sniffed loudly. "Fuck it. Do whatever you want." He abruptly spun on his heels and walked way.

Ted looked at Sarge, and Sarge nodded. Turning to Mike, Ted tossed him one of the thermite grenades. Mike smiled. "Let's burn this shit to the ground."

Sarge looked at me and Thad. "You two go with them and lay down covering fire. Let's get this bar-b-que kicked off."

Mike clapped his hands and rubbed them together. Smiling like a devil, he said, "Give me a minute. Let me get a couple of things."

Sarge shook his head. "Well hurry the hell up!"

Looking at me, Mike said, "Come Morgan, give me a hand." Looking at Ted, he said, "Find me some duct tape."

I followed him as he ran back towards where the trucks were parked. He ran up to one of the DHS vehicles and unlatched a fuel can from a rack mounted on its side. I was looking at the truck that burned and a large patch of blackened, scorched ground. Pointing at it, I asked, "What was that?"

Mike stuck his head around the side of the truck. "Oh, that was a fuel bladder. When I hit that truck, it ruptured and burned."

"Shame. We could have used the fuel."

Pointing at the building, Mike said, "Run over there and grab that ladder."

I grabbed the extension ladder he was pointing at and hefted it up onto my shoulder. With these items in hand, we headed back towards the gym. Getting back to Sarge and Ted, Mike asked, "You ready?"

Ted nodded. "Yeah, let's roast these fuckers."

We made our way around to the back of the building. Ted put up a hand and we stopped. Just down the wall was a metal door hanging only from the bottom hinge. The door was riddled with holes and gashes from countless rounds. There were entrance and exit holes on either side. Mike motioned for me to put the ladder down. Ted was watching the door and Thad was watching the way we'd come from. I pulled the rope and raised the ladder up to reach the roof, expecting with every bang of the dogs on the rungs to start taking fire. While I did that, Mike took the tape from Ted and taped the thermite grenade to the side of the fuel can, carefully wrapping it so as not to interfere with the grenade's spoon.

Mike pushed his carbine around to his back and mounted the ladder and started to climb. It bounced and banged against the roof as he did. I gripped both sides and placed a boot against both rubber feet of the ladder. It didn't take him long to get to the roof. He quickly disappeared from view, and my heart pounded. We had no idea what was happening up there, not that it was likely anyone else was up there with Mike.

After a moment, he reappeared and hurriedly mounted the ladder. He came sliding down it like a fireman with one foot on either side. When he was about half way down, I heard a pop followed by a loud hiss from inside the building. When Mike's feet hit the ground, another sound came from the building, along with a bright orange flash. The sound was like a large sail being unfurled. Thick black smoke immediately began to billow from the open door. We backed away from it, keeping our eyes and weapons on it as we did so.

It wasn't long before we heard gunfire around the front of the building. I guess they were making a run for the front door. But we waited, our time would surely come. And I was right. It didn't take long for two men to come crawling out of the suffocating smoke. We immediately shot them down.

There was more shooting out front; and the flames grew too intense for us to remain behind the gym. Thad backed away, holding a hand in front of his face. "Damn that's hot."

Mike stood there with his hands tucked into his vest. "Imagine being in there."

A figure suddenly burst through the screen of smoke. His left side was on fire and he flailed about in agony, screaming. Mike quickly raised his carbine, but Ted reached out and pushed it back down.

"Fuck 'em. Let 'em burn," Ted said.

It reminded me of the World War Two movies I've watched where Japanese or German soldiers would come out of a bunker on fire and some battle-weary soldier would say the same thing.

His screams cut through me though, to my soul. No matter how much I hated someone, I couldn't let this happen. I stepped forward and quickly shot the man. He fell to the ground and continued to cook. When I turned to leave, Thad made eye contact with me and gave me a nod. I knew he'd done some horrible things, but to me it was a different situation. If I'd come home and found these men killing my family, I would feel differently. But that wasn't the case here.

We made our way back around to the front of the building. The smoke was growing thicker as the oak floor of the gym continued to burn and the fire spread throughout the building. Smoke now poured in thick choking clouds from every opening. No one was coming out now. Anyone still inside would forever remain there.

Out front, we found Sarge and Sheffield. They were organizing parties to police the camp for weapons, food and anything of use. Sheffield was telling his people what to do with what they collected when I stepped in front of him.

"We also need to take the boots off anyone we find wearing them. Collect any boots you find," I said.

Sheffield looked at me like my head was screwed on backwards. "You want to take boots off dead men?"

I shrugged. "You got a big pile of boots someplace? We're going to need them at some point."

One of the Guardsmen stepped out of the group and lifted his right foot. Reaching down, he pulled the sole away from it, exposing his sock. "I need boots."

Sheffield looked at him, then at me. "I see your point."

"Clothes too. Anything that can be used, we need to take. Anything."

"Alright people, you know what you're doing. Get to it!" Sarge shouted.

The group broke up and started going through the camp. Sarge pointed to a small house sitting across the road from the gym. It was heavily damaged by a missile strike from one of the Apaches. "Anyone clear that place yet?"

Livingston looked at it. "No. There couldn't be anyone alive in that. Look at it."

Sarge jerked his head. "Come on, let's go check it."

We walked towards the house as light columns of smoke rose from several places amongst the wreckage. The back half of the house suffered most of the damage. It was surreal to open the front door that still stood, only to see all the way out to the field behind it. All we found was a pair of feet sticking out from under a jumble of roof trusses, drywall and furniture.

But there was one part of the house we couldn't get to. The hallway going to it was destroyed. Sarge told Mike to go out and find a window into that part and to check it. Mike and Thad walked around the side of the house. We could hear them shuffling around inside and after a moment, Mike called out.

"Hey, come around here and check this out!"

Going around the house, I looked through a blasted-out window. Mike was kneeling beside a bed with a load of debris on it. A man was pinned in the bed. Sarge looked in and laughed. "Ha ha ha, I told you if I ever saw you again I'd kill your ass." He then climbed through the window.

Charles Tabor was pinned in the bed and couldn't move. He followed Sarge's movements as he made his way into the cramped space. The weight sitting on him was obvious. So much that he couldn't speak. His eyes darted between us, and from them I had a pretty good idea of what he was thinking.

Sarge sat down beside the bed and relaxed. He looked over at Tabor. "You should have just stayed the hell away when you had the chance. But no, you had to come back. Thought you were going to get us, didn't you? How'd that work out for you?"

Tabor's eyes were fierce. He tried a couple of times to say something but the weight pinning him to the bed prevented him from speaking. He was doing good to get enough breath to remain living. Mike pushed on a truss and Tabor emitted a slight sound.

With a smile, Mike said, "I say we leave him here to rot."

Sarge looked into Tabor's eyes. "Naw. I let this piece of shit get away from me once. I'm not going to make that same mistake again. This is where it ends for you sport. Your time here is over. I hope you rot in hell." Sarge reached up and cupped his hand over Tabor's mouth, pinching his nose with the thumb of the same hand.

Tabor jerked his head trying to breathe. Sarge reached up with his free hand and grabbed a handful of hair, holding his head steady. I watched as he struggled to breathe, but it was futile. In a little more than a minute, the struggle was over and Tabor was motionless. Sarge waited a little longer before pulling his hand away. He placed a finger on Tabor's neck. Standing up, he said, "This fucker is gone. Finally." Lastly, he spit on the man's face before turning towards the window. "Let's get the hell out of here."

I'd taken the life of many men today. Delivering the fatal shot that ended their existence on this Earth. But this was by far the most disturbing thing I'd seen. This was personal, Sarge used his own hand to smother the life from this man. Not that I blamed him. I hated the man as well. But I don't think I could do what I just witnessed. At least not like it happened. Sure, in the middle of a fight, like with Billy. But that's different. That's in the moment. The old man did this out of pure spite, pure hate. But I don't blame him one bit for it. I was glad he was on my side.

The rest of the day was spent cleaning out the camp. We took everything from clothes and bedding to food, ammo and weapons. We took it all. Every body I saw was barefooted. We didn't take the clothes from their backs but we damn sure took the boots if they had them. It was something I'd started thinking about when lying in my position the night of attack. I had another couple pair but there was no way to get more. Little Bit was going to need shoes soon, not that this would help her but it would help others.

Weapons and ammo were loaded onto one truck and food on another. Everything else was loaded onto a third. We ended up with twenty-seven women and kids. They too were loaded onto a truck and taken back to town. I didn't know what was going to happen to them, where they'd go, but that wasn't my problem. Thankfully, it was Sheffield's.

Around three in the afternoon our group gathered back up. Doc was checking Danny's shoulder and the girls were in a knot chattering away and laughing. It was striking to see them giggling, considering what they'd just done. But I guess it was good they were dealing with it as they were. It was yet another example of how things have changed. Not ten feet from where they were standing and laughing, was a dead man. He'd been nearly cut in half and lay on his back, face skyward and mouth frozen in an eternal scream he would never utter. But they paid him no notice. Maybe that was a way of dealing with it. I'm sure there would be some issues to come up later. I hoped they would be alright. And even more, I hoped they would be a little disturbed. Not to be disturbed as a result of this sort of thing, would be far more concerning to me.

An MRAP pulled up and the driver leaned on the horn. We

all looked up at it. The driver's door opened and there was Mike grinning like a waterheaded fool. "Look what I got!"

Sarge looked the truck over. "This thing looks nearly new."

Mike jumped out. "Yeah, I picked the best looking one of the bunch."

Sarge smiled and looked back at me. "Looks like we got us a new ride, Sheriff."

"How the hell are we going to feed that thing? What's it get, four gallons a mile?" I asked.

Sarge laughed. "It ain't that bad."

"But it's close," Ted added.

Sarge looked around the camp. Things were obviously wrapping up. The Guard's trucks were all lined up on the main road in the camp and their people were loitering around them waiting on the next order. The truck with the civilians was gone, having already been sent back to town. Sarge walked over to Sheffield and the two talked for a minute. They shook hands and Sarge returned.

"Alright, folks. Let's make like an asshole and get the shit outta here! Mount up!"

The girls were already gathered around the truck looking at it. They started to cackle and quickly moved to the back of the truck. Perez suddenly appeared carrying a sack over his shoulder. He casually opened the rear door and swept his arm with a flourish and a slight bow. "Ladies."

Shaking my head, I asked, "Where the hell have you been?"

"Out helping police up the camp," he said with a grin as he tossed the sack into the truck.

Ted laughed. "You mean looting. You old bastard."

Perez shook a cigarette from a pack in his hand and shrugged. "One man's looting is another man's policing."

"It's gonna be crowded, but everyone get in. We'll drive this back to the other vehicles. Let's go!" Sarge barked.

After everyone else was in the truck, I stepped up; and just before ducking in, I took another look around the camp. It was a far cry from what it must have looked like in its prime when the Elk's were bringing kids in by the thousands. The laughing and incredible memories that were created here were a distant memory from the destruction I now saw. Smoke rose from many places around the property as several fires still burned, and bodies were everywhere. Looking up at a lone, tall long leaf pine, I spotted a buzzard. He would certainly eat well tonight and in the days to come.

Sitting in the back of the truck as it rolled out of the camp, Perez looked at me. Touching his face under his nose with a finger, he said, "You've got a little something right here."

I gave him the finger and he laughed. Perez smiled, leaned back and closed his eyes. Mike drove us back to where we started this morning. The truck was loud and slow. It rumbled along the road bouncing us around. I looked at Danny. "How are you feeling?"

He glanced at the shoulder. "I'm alright. Doc thinks it's just a fragment."

I leaned back against the side of the truck. "Thank God that's over."

Danny grunted. "Yeah. No shit."

I looked over at Lee Ann. She was sitting with Jess and the two were laughing. It was strange to see their carefree state. But then everything went so well, for us at least. Considering what we'd just accomplished, it went well for the Guard as well. They lost a total of nine men, with an even dozen wounded. But nine people lost their lives today, nine of ours. I don't know if anyone did a formal body count on the DHS personnel. Lee Ann saw me looking at her and smiled. She waved a silly wave as if were this just a family trip and someone had pulled out a camera. I smiled, winked and waved back.

Getting back to the vehicles, Thad and Ted volunteered to drive the buggies back home. I got in the suburban and pulled out behind them. It was actually nice to be alone. No one to think about or put on false fronts for. I wasn't feeling well. I knew what we'd done needed doing, but I was feeling sick. I'd seen so many people die, some in horrible ways. Some begging and pleading for their lives. And unlike the movies, it was a messy thing.

The Apaches tore bodies to pieces and small arms caused horrific wounds. I was so over it all now. I just wanted it to go away. Spiraling down this well of despair, I started trying to think of ways to forget about it all. Something that would take all our minds off what just happened. Because, aside from Sarge and the guys who may be accustomed to this sort of thing, the rest of us were not. Every one of us would have to deal with the events of today in one fashion or another. But as this played out in my mind, I came up with an idea. Something that I thought would surely take everyone's mind off all this and maybe, if even for a little while, put a smile on everyone's face.

Pulling up to the house, Mel and Little Bit were out on the porch before I shut the truck down. Mike stopped the MRAP out on the road in front of the house where Danny and Lee Ann got out. When I got out, I saw the surprise on Mel's face. She was obviously shocked and scared. Little Bit looked at me, then up at Mel. She started to tear up when she looked at Mel, sensing her fear. I smiled, trying to alleviate her fears. She ran off the porch towards me and I scooped her up.

Holding her in my arms, she looked at me. "What happened to your face?" She asked in a timid, scared voice.

Touching my nose, I replied, "Oh, just part of the job, baby. I'm okay though."

She ran her finger across my cheek under my eye. "You've got black eyes."

Mel was there and looking me over. I smiled at her. "I'm okay." Looking over my shoulder at Lee Ann walking up the drive, I added, "She's okay too. We're both okay."

Mel wrapped her arms around me. "You were gone so long. I was so worried."

"Mommy was afraid. She kept checking the time," Little Bit added.

I grunted. "It was a long day."

Lee Ann walked up and Mel released me and grabbed her, wrapping her up in her arms. Lee Ann hugged her mother, and the two remained that way for some time. Lee Ann broke the moment by saying, "I'm fine, Mom. No one got hurt."

From the porch, I heard another voice. "You're back!"

We all looked up to see Taylor standing on the porch. She was gently making her way down the stairs. I walked over and hugged her as well. "I was so worried about you," she said.

"It's all over now, kiddo," I replied.

"Is it really over now? Are they all gone?" Mel asked.

I looked back at her and thought about her words. Gone, such a permanent choice. But I guess it was the correct one. Smiling, I replied, "Yes baby. They're gone. All Gone."

"Mom, I'm hungry. Is there anything to eat?" Lee Ann asked.

Little Bit jumped up and down. "Yes! Come in. We've got stew and bread for you! Miss Kay and Mom made it!"

We went inside and the girls all took a seat around the table. Mel asked Taylor to get the pot and put it on the table. She took me by the hand and led me to the bedroom. Closing the door, she looked at me. "We need to get you cleaned up."

I took my gear off, dropping it all on the floor. Mel took out clean clothes and put them on the counter in the bathroom. As I sat on the bed untying my boots, I heard the shower come on. Taking off my clothes, I went into the bathroom and stepped into the shower. Mel stayed with me, washing my back and hair. It was nice. Leaning against the side of the shower as she scrubbed my back then ran her fingers through my hair. Thad's lye soap was a little harsh on the hair, but it was better than nothing.

After I was dressed and slid my feet into some moccasin slippers, Mel asked me, "Is it really over?"

I thought about the question. I smiled, thinking back to a political scandal many years ago. Depends on your definition of *it*. "This is over. This part is definitely over." I took her hand and led her to the bed where we sat down. Taking her other hand, I said, "But it'll never be over. And honestly, I don't want it to. When it's over, I, you, we'll be gone. So I want it to last a long, long time. But for now, this is over."

She laid her head on my shoulder. "I just want some quiet time. I just want you and the girls and quiet."

Kissing the top of her head, I said, "Me too, babe. Me too." Standing up, I pulled her up. "Come on, let's go eat. I'm starving!"

She smiled and led me out to the dining room where the girls' voices could be heard talking and laughing. When we came through the door, they all smiled. I sat down in the middle of them as Taylor spooned out stew into bowls and passed them around. I was grateful no questions were asked about the day's events. Instead, we talked about anything else.

I ate until I was positively stuffed. But I wasn't done. I pulled the pot over and looked into it. There was a little stew still in the bottom, so I tore a chunk of bread from the small loaf on the table and used it to sop up the stew. The girls laughed at me as I hovered over the pot.

"Geez Dad, how can you eat anymore?" Taylor asked.

Smacking my lips, I said, "Waste not, want not!"

"Just lick it baby," Mel said and got the girls to laughing.

I looked down into the pot. "I can't. My head won't fit in there." This caused them to laugh even harder. Leaning back in my chair I patted my stomach. "I am stuffed. I'm going to lay on the couch like broccoli."

Little Bit jumped out of her chair. "Can we watch a movie? I want everyone to watch a movie together!"

Mel took her hand. "Sweetie, Daddy is tired. Maybe tomorrow."

She was dejected and a pout spread across her face. I smiled and looked at Mel. "Actually I would love to watch a movie."

Mel looked at her. "What do you want to watch?"

Little Bit smiled and bounced up and down. "Goonies, let's watch the Goonies!"

"Oh yeah, that's so cool. I haven't seen that in a long time!" Taylor said.

Lee Ann stood up. "I'm going to take a shower and put on my pajamas and get comfy!" She took off, scooting her feet across the floor.

Little Bit ran to the living room and got the movie and laptop out, setting it up on the coffee table. Mel told me to go sit down and asked Taylor to help her with the dinner dishes. I went and fell into the sofa, putting my feet up on the table and spreading my arms out. I was tired.

We waited for Lee Ann to start the movie. Once everyone was there, Mel brought me another glass of tea and we started the movie. I couldn't have been happier sprawled out on the sofa like I was, with Mel on one side and Little Bit on the other.

Lee Ann was sitting on the floor with her head against my leg and Taylor was curled up on the love seat.

I looked over at her, all I could see was her head poking out of the blanket she'd wrapped up in. She wrinkled her nose and smiled a childish smile. A smile spread across my face, and I reached out with my foot and wagged it at her. She pushed it away and wiggled deeper into her blanket. Looking around again, I felt so good. Gone were the thoughts from earlier. Maybe this was what would keep those thoughts away. Maybe keeping this close to me would keep those demons away. Like the guardians at the gates to my soul. I ran my hands through Mel and Little Bit's hair, my guardians.

CHAPTER 10

I WOKE UP AND LOOKED AROUND. I was confused and it took me a minute to figure out where I was. Pushing the blanket off, I stood up and stretched. Mel must have covered me and left me on the sofa last night. Shuffling into the kitchen, I poured myself a glass of tea and looked out the window over the sink. It was a bright, clear morning and looked as though it were going to be a good day. A perfect day to get what I had in mind started.

Going into the bedroom, I sat on the edge of the bed. Mel opened her eyes and smiled. "How'd you sleep?" She asked.

"Good. I need to go to town this morning. You want to go?"

She stretched. "Yeah. Can the girls come?"

"Of course."

She sat up. "Ok, let me get dressed."

I slapped her ass. "Hurry up, woman. I'll go wake up the girls."

I went and woke the girls. They were all excited about the prospect of a trip to town, especially Little Bit and Taylor. Taylor had been cooped up for some time now and was more than ready to get out. She bounded out of bed, having to catch herself, and she quickly started getting ready. As I walked out of her room, I said, "Tell Mom I'm going over to Danny's for a minute."

She was pulling clothes from her dresser and inspecting them. Those that didn't pass muster were tossed aside. "Okay," she replied.

I left the house and found the dogs in their usual place, sprawled out across the porch. I stepped over them and headed for Danny's house. Passing through the fence, an incredible aroma met me, and my mouth instantly started to water. Danny was sitting on the porch with his arm in a sling. Little Jace was in a rocker beside him eating a fat biscuit.

"How's the shoulder?" I asked as I stepped up on the porch.

He looked down at it. "Doc wants me to go to town so the clinic can get whatever is in there out."

"I'm about to head that way with Mel and the girls. You want to go?"

"Nah, you guys go ahead. I'll wait for Doc. But go in there and get you a biscuit. Miss Kay made some magic this morning."

I laughed. "It sure as hell smells like it!"

"You think it smells good. Wait till you taste it." Danny looked at Jace. "Pretty good aren't they?"

The little boy held the biscuit in front of his face as he chewed. "Mmmhmm," was all he muttered.

I laughed. "Well let me get in there and get some for us!"

Inside, Bobby, Mary and Kay were building more biscuits. Bobby was cutting them open and Mary buttered them. Kay finished them by laying a fat round of sausage on and closing them up. The ladies looked up when I came in, and all three gasped. Little Edie was sitting at the table eating her own biscuit.

"Morgan dear! What happened to you?" Kay shouted as she wiped her hands on a dish towel.

Smiling, I said, "Just the nature of the business." I started to make the old joke about, *you should see the other guy,* but decided better of it.

"Are you okay?" Mary asked.

I waved her off. "Yeah, I'm fine." Smiling, I moved to lighten the mood. "What's for breakfast? Something smells so good!"

"We made some sausage biscuits this morning," Bobby said.

"Buttermilk biscuits!" Kay added cheerfully.

"Sounds good to me. We're headed to town this morning. Can I get five to go?"

Kay smiled brightly. "Of course you can! Let me get you something to put them in."

She grabbed a plastic grocery sack and placed the five sandwiches inside and handed it to me.

"What are you going to town for?" Mary asked.

I shrugged. "Just need to check on a couple of things." I had a plan, but didn't want to share it just yet.

"Will you be home in time for supper?" Kay said as I headed for the door.

I waved over my shoulder. "We will."

Danny was cleaning Jace's face when I went outside. I smiled at him. Danny surely would make a good dad. "I'll see you guys later."

Danny nodded. "Yeah. We'll be in town later."

As I walked off the porch, Thad, Aric and the girls came through the gate. I waved at them as I headed through the fence to the house. The dogs smelled the food in the bag as I came up on the porch and sat up, ears erect and expectant looks on their faces. But this wasn't for them. Inside, everyone was dressed and ready to go. I passed out breakfast as we headed outside to the truck.

"Oh wow, this is so good!" Lee Ann said as she pushed crumbs into her mouth.

"Look at the size of this thing!" Little Bit shouted, looking at hers.

Taking a big bite of mine, I said, "Big and good. Good and big!"

We rolled past the bunker, and for the first time in a long time, no one was there. Not that there were no threats now, but they were considerably less than they were yesterday. We'd get back to security, but for now everyone needed a break, some down time. Passing Altoona, I noticed the market was busy. I'm sure some of those people had an idea what happened yesterday, we certainly made enough noise. But they were carrying on as though it were a normal day.

And I guess it was. After all, that was the whole point of doing what we did. We took out the DHS so everyone could live a normal life and not have to worry about being sniped or blown to hell at the market. So it was a normal day, and I was glad to have it. Because here we were riding down the road together as a family. Like any family headed to town. While it wasn't the old normal, maybe this could be the new normal. And that would be good enough for me.

When we passed the power plant, I noticed a couple of Hummers there, the engineers were back to work. Maybe tomorrow I would come up and offer a hand. It would be incredible if we could get the plant running again. But as with all things today, that would only be the start of the work. There would be days of work to get the power out to anyone.

I drove straight to the police department. I wanted to meet with Shane and see if he could help me set something up. Pulling up, I told Mel I needed to go inside. She said that she and the girls would go to the market on the lake. When she told me that, I looked back at Taylor in the mirror. Her last trip to the market wasn't good. I expected to hear her protest or for there to be some kind of trauma on her face. But she was smiling and looked eager.

Smiling, I looked at Mel. "You guys have fun. You have your pistol, right?"

Mel patted her side. "Yep. And the girls have their guns too."

Both Lee Ann and Taylor lifted their H&Ks up and nodded. Little Bit was the only one unarmed, and made sure she let everyone know about it. She wasn't too happy about the fact either. Turning in my seat, I said, "Kiddo, you're not old enough yet. But soon. And don't rush it. It'll come fast enough on its own, trust me."

She opened the door and jumped out. "Come on! Let's go look!"

Mel leaned over and kissed me. "When you're done, come find us over there."

"Will do."

I found Shane in the PD. He was standing in front of a large wipe-board with Cecil. The two were talking about the planted fields and manpower. When I came into the room, the two looked at me with smiles. But they quickly faded.

"Damn, Morgan. What the hell happened to you?" Cecil asked.

I shrugged. "Shit happens."

Shane hopped up on a table, letting his feet dangle. "I hear it went pretty good. You guys wiped them out."

I nodded. "We did. They're gone. All of them."

Cecil crossed his arms. "Almost all of them. They brought some back with 'em."

"Where'd they put those women and children?" I asked.

"We've got them in the old town hall. Sean is over there now," Shane said.

Leaning against the wall, I asked, "What's the plan for them?"

Shane leaned back on his hands. "Sheffield met with them last night and told them all they were free to leave."

"How'd that go?" I asked.

Cecil snorted. "Just as you'd imagine. Where the hell are they going to go? That's what they asked. And in reality, they're right. Where the hell are they supposed to go?"

I nodded. "That is the problem. But what were we supposed to do with them? Shoot them? There's some things that simply cannot be."

Cecil rubbed the gray whiskers on his chin. "And now we have people in our midst that resent us and will wish us all dead."

Letting out a long sigh, I replied, "Well, in a perfect world there would be perfect solutions."

Shane jumped off the table. "This ain't no perfect world."

"Exactly," I replied.

"So what brings you to town?" Cecil asked.

Looking at Shane, I said, "I came looking for you. I need your help with something."

"Anything. You name it."

"We've all been through a lot lately. I want to do something to cheer folks up."

"What are you thinking?" Cecil asked.

"Well, you remember the old first Friday events we used to have downtown?" He nodded. "I was thinking of something like that. Maybe in the park on the lake. I thought it would be fun to string some lights up and see if we could get a band or some folks with instruments into the band shell. Play some music, dance, just let it all go for a while."

Cecil pointed at me. "That's a hell of an idea. I think folks could really use something like that. Just a good ole time."

Shane rubbed his hands. "Yeah! Sean is part of a bluegrass

band. All those guys are still here in town. I'm sure they'd love to get together for some pickin'."

"Only thing we'd be missing was some food." Cecil said.

"I'll see what I can do about that," I replied.

"I know where there's some lights. I know what you're talking about, those strings of lights the city would drape through the trees. We can use the generator to power them and the amps and stuff for the band," Shane said.

"How long do you think it would take to set up?" I asked.

Shane shrugged. "A couple of days I guess."

"Today is Wednesday. Let's plan on having our party on Saturday," I said.

Cecil smiled. "That would be perfect."

Looking at Shane, I said, "You get the lights up and talk to Sean and see if they'll play. I'll see what I can do about food."

Cecil was smiling from ear to ear. "This'll be a hoot."

Shane looked excited as well. "Yeah. I think this will be great!"

"Let's see if we can get this put together. I think the community could really use it. I'll see you guys later."

With a wave, I left the guys and walked towards the armory. I found Sheffield in his office in front of a stack of hand-written paperwork. I guess some people just couldn't let the old ways go.

He looked up as I walked in and shook his head. "Damn. You look worse today than you did yesterday."

"Your hair looks like shit too," I replied with a laugh.

Sheffield leaned back in his chair. "What can I do for you?"

Without being offered, I sat down. "I'm planning a little party at the park. We're going to string some lights and bring in a bluegrass band to play. I think the town could use a night of fun."

Sheffield's eyebrows went up. "That's a good idea. I think

everyone could use something like that. Sounds like you've got things pretty well planned out."

I held up a finger. "Almost."

Cocking his head to the side, he asked, "What?"

"Food."

His eyes narrowed. "What about it?"

"We should have something to offer. It doesn't have to be much, but something."

Sheffield looked up at the ceiling. The wheels were turning. "We have a lot of flour. We could make bread."

That got my wheels turning. "Get me a couple sacks of that flour. I've got an idea. I'll bring the food."

He looked at quizzically. "What are you going to bring?"

"It's a secret." Without another word, I left his office.

As I walked back towards the park, I thought about what it would take to pull off what I was thinking. But if I could, it would be epic, and make for one hell of a party. Hearing a diesel engine, I looked up to see Mike behind the wheel of an MRAP. It stopped and he hopped out. The rear door opened and Sarge, Doc, Thad and Danny got out.

They walked out towards one of the small garden plots planted in town. The chain gang was there working and they stopped and looked up. The two Guardsmen watching them prodded them back to work, which they reluctantly did while keeping their eyes on the approaching group.

I walked over to where they were. "What's going on?" I asked.

Sarge rocked on his heels. "It's time to finish this thing."

Confused, I asked, "What?"

"The DHS. It's time to finish it," Sarge said.

Mike and Thad walked passed us as I said, "We did yesterday. It's already finished."

Hearing a shot behind me, I jumped and spun around. Thad was standing over a body. He looked back at me and said, "Now it's done."

The other two men on the chain gang cowered in terror thinking they would be next. I walked over and looked down at the man partially responsible for my daughter's injuries and the deaths of others. Lee Ann killed the other one. It brought back memories of beating the man. Thad was right, it was done now. I knew it would ultimately come to this. Some people just need killing, and this was damn sure one.

Looking at the two Guardsmen, I said, "Guess you can take him off the chain. Have these two bury him somewhere."

Dave and Robert stared down at the body for a moment. Then Dave looked up with relief on his face. Looking into his eyes, I said, "Don't get too comfortable." His attitude changed and he looked away. I could imagine the weight he lived under. He'd killed someone, someone that certainly didn't deserve what he'd done. And while he'd expressed remorse, that wasn't enough. In the end, his fate would be the same. And I'm sure he knew it.

Looking at Sarge, I said. "I'm going to the market. Mel and the girls are over there."

"What's this project you're working on?"

I explained the idea of the party to him. He smiled and nodded. "That sounds like a hell of an idea."

Thad asked, "What about food? It ain't a party without food."

Grinning, I moved in close to him. "I have an idea for that that I think everyone will like."

He smiled. "A party sounds nice to me."

Sarge slapped me on the back. "Come on, we'll walk to the park with you."

"Mel and them girls out shopping?" Thad asked.

With a laugh, I replied, "Who knows what they're up to."

We walked in silence for a moment. Then Thad surprised me with a comment. "You notice anything different?"

I looked around, but couldn't see anything out of the ordinary. Shrugging, I replied, "No."

"I don't mean what you can SEE."

"I know what you mean, Thad," Sarge said. "There's a different air to things now."

Thad nodded. "Yeah. It just feels different."

Sarge pushed his carbine around to his back. "Like a weight's been lifted."

Now I knew what they were talking about, and I too felt it. "I know what you mean. It was like yesterday when we got back to the ranch. No one was at the bunker. For the first time in as long as I can remember there was no immediate threat. No one had to be actively watching for what may come."

Thad smiled. "It feels good. I hope it lasts for a good long time too."

I didn't say anything, but immediately started to think of the radio transmissions about Russian and Chinese troops. What we just pulled off would seem like a cake walk compared to dealing with them. The Russians have troops hardened in the fight in Ukraine. The Chinese, well, they had sheer numbers if they were committed to it. Looking over at Thad, I said, "I hope so too, old buddy."

The market was crowded with folks. Early offerings of vegetables were showing up from those that got their gardens started early. It was good to see. Of course there were the fish mongers selling the day's catch. The lakes had been converted into quite the fishery with several boats working the waters daily with nets. In the long run, it could lead to over-fishing, I suppose; but this was a large chain of lakes and could probably take the pressure for some time.

The sun was shining and it was a beautiful day. It was nice to wander down the sidewalk. But on closer inspection, things weren't as cheery as they appeared. The sidewalks were weed-choked, and leaves and dirt were piled in the gutters. It wasn't hard to imagine that without some maintenance, the gutters would overflow, allowing water to enter the shuttered shops on Bay Street. While most of these store were empty, or at least not operating as businesses, water intrusion would ultimately lead to decay and these old buildings collapsing.

So there was a lot for the senses walking through the market and streets of downtown Eustis. The smell of the fish, the fresh earth still clinging to the vegetables. This mixed with the smell of wood smoke and meat cooking from someone offering a kabob-like skewer. Lord only knows what was on it, and I wasn't adventurous or hungry enough to try and find out.

Sarge nudged me as we approached Mel and the girls. They were at a table with a young woman selling what turned out to be soap. Looking where Sarge nodded, I saw a familiar face. "There's Porky," Sarge said.

"Yeah, I see him."

He pushed me in his direction and said, "Let's go see what he's up to."

He was talking to a group of people who'd gathered around. He looked like something from a 1930s movie about a smarmy politician. He stood with his thumbs tucked into his suspenders as he spoke as if he were campaigning for votes. We walked up behind him and stopped to listen.

"So you see good folks, you need someone experienced in such matters. You can't have a Sheriff, or God forbid, the military running roughshod over your community. And one such as myself, who's from a neighboring town and has no preconceived allegiances would be the best choice."

Some in the crowd looked at Sarge and me as Porky spoke. Seeing their attention diverted and hearing Sarge snort at the end of his oration, Porky turned, quite surprised to see us standing there.

He side-stepped and held a hand out as though he were introducing us to those gathered. "And these are the very men I'm speaking about. Why just today they executed a man in the middle of town." Turning to the crowd, he wagged a finger at them. "In cold blood, mind you! The man was chained and could not defend himself. Is this what you call justice in this town?"

A man from the crowd called out. "They shot the sum bitch that set off a bomb here. He was one of them DHS guys. Hell, I wondered what took 'em so long to do it!" His comment was met with agreement from all assembled.

"Not to mention, we didn't shoot him, Porky." Sarge said, then pointed at Thad. "He did."

Hyatt began to fan himself furiously with the ever present paper fan. Turning to face Sarge, he said, "Good sir, there is no reason for disparaging comments. I have a name of which I have previously informed you."

Sarge chuckled. "I don't give a flying shit what you think, Porky."

With Sarge's comment, Hyatt's lackey Albert stepped forward. Thad quickly pulled the shotgun from the scabbard on his back and leveled it at Albert. "Mister, this thing makes a hell of a mess this close. I suggest you back up."

I thought it was funny and smiled and figured I'd stir the pot. "He's only killed one man today. He's usually good for two."

Albert, as well as several others, backed away. Hyatt looked at Albert with disdain, then turned his attention to the crowd again. "You see? You see how these men use violence and intimidation?" Turning, he pointed an accusatory finger at Sarge. "Not to mention the unlawful seizure of private property! You still have not returned our weapons!"

Sarge jerked his head in my direction. "You gotta take that up with the Sheriff."

Hyatt looked at me and I replied flatly, "No."

"This is unjust!" Hyatt shouted, holding a finger up to emphasize his displeasure.

Looking at the crowd, I said, "Look, folks. We're trying to find someone to act as a judge. That's not my job." Pointing at Hyatt, I said, "But I'm not going to let just any spineless imp take the position. It needs to be someone of character, someone we all respect. And most importantly, someone that doesn't want it as bad as this sack of shit does.

"Think about it. Why do you think he wants to be a judge so bad? Who is he and where did he come from? We'll find someone, the right someone. I don't know what this guy's telling you, but think for yourself. What have any of us here done to you? Decide that for yourself." With that, we walked away, as did the crowd. Hyatt tried to keep their attention to no avail.

Mel was sniffing a bar of soap when we walked up. She held the bar out to me and said, "Smell it. It smells so good."

I sniffed the bar. "What is that? Lavender?"

The young woman behind the small folding table smiled and nodded. "Yes."

"Where did you get lavender oil?"

"I sold soap-making supplies online and had a lot of different oils in stock." She smiled. "Since the internet was gone, I decided to make my own soap and trade it."

Mel looked at me. "Can we get some?"

Taylor held up a bar of eucalyptus. "I want this one."

Looking at the young lady, I asked, "What are you trading for?"

She shrugged. "Whatever you have, if I can use it of course."

Reaching into a pocket on my vest, I pulled out a couple of silver quarters. "How about one of these?"

She held her hand out and I dropped one in her palm. She looked at it and said, "This is one of the old ones that is silver, isn't it?"

I nodded. "How about two of them for four bars?"

She flipped the quarter in her palm. "You know, a month ago I wouldn't have taken this. I mean, you can't eat it and no one wanted money. But now, people are starting to trade for money."

"Everyone needs soap," Mel said. "You should be able to trade this for anything you need."

The girl laughed. "You'd think so! But again, you can't eat soap. But now people are starting to look for things to make life a little easier." She leaned forward and whispered, "And starting to actually bathe." Turning back to me, she said, "Sounds like a deal to me."

I gave her another quarter and told the girls to all pick one out. Which they did. Little Bit handed the bar she picked up to me. "Smell it, Daddy. It's coconut."

I sniffed the bar. "That smells good enough to eat!"

"You could! It's all natural," the girl replied.

I laughed. "Isn't everything now?"

"Eww! I'm not eating soap!" Little Bit shouted.

Waving, I thanked the young lady for the soap and we wandered off. I told Mel I wanted to go to the clinic to check on Danny, and we walked that way. Thad and Sarge said they were going to get the truck and bring it up.

Little Bit held my hand as we walked. She looked up smiling and said, "I like coming to town, Daddy."

"Me too," Taylor added. "I've been cooped up at the house for so long, I thought I was going to lose my mind."

"I'm glad you're feeling better, kiddo. And I'm glad you're out of the house too." I said.

"When can we come back?" Little Bit asked.

I smiled. "Oh. We'll come back soon."

"What for?" Lee Ann asked.

"You'll see."

Mel looked at me. "What are you up to?"

With mock surprise, I said, "What makes you think I'm up to something?"

Mel gave me a look that screamed, *you can't fool me.* "Because I know, that's why."

Danny was sitting outside the clinic. His shoulder was bandaged with a clean dressing. Doc was laid out on a couple of large green crates with his hat pulled down over his eyes. Danny looked up as we approached.

"Yo. How was the shopping?"

Little Bit held her bar of soap out. "I got soap!"

Danny took it and smelled it. "Mmm, coconut. Smells good enough to eat."

"The lady said you could eat it. Said it was all natural."

Danny took the soap and pretended he was about to bite into it. Little Bit squealed and snatched it away. "Hey, don't eat my soap!" He laughed and tussled her hair.

He was a great uncle to the girls. He'd been there for all of them, it made me happy. "You about ready to head back?"

He looked at his shoulder. "Yeah. They dug a bullet

fragment out. Said that's all it was and I was good to go." He pointed at my face. "You should have them look at your nose while you're here."

From under his hat, Doc said, "They aren't plastic surgeons. And even if they were, I don't think they'd tackle the challenge of fixing that head."

I snorted. "Good to see you too, Ronnie."

"Well, I think he looks fine," Mel said.

Doc sat up and lifted his hat. He looked at me, then at Mel. "I question your judgment."

Danny stood up. "If you're headed back, I'm ready."

Doc lay back down, covering his face again. "Where's the old man?"

"He's bringing the truck up. You wanna ride with us?" I asked.

He bobbed his head from side to side. "Nah. I'll wait on the good humor man."

Now that was funny. "Suit yourself, brother. I've got a couple of stops to make, so we're off."

We left Doc and headed back to our truck and loaded up. As we left town, I thought about stopping at the plant, just to check on how things were going. But I wasn't really in the mood, and skipped it. I wanted to get to Gina and Tyler's. I hoped they could help with my plan for the party. I drove in a half daze as I ran through what I was thinking. The truck kicked up a cloud of leaves and dust behind us.

The roads were getting more and more cluttered with debris. This just added another thought, civil engineering. We needed to start addressing some of the issues all this crap was causing. If we wanted to start getting things back to some sort of normal, we needed to come up with a plan. Just one more thing to do. One more thing on the never-ending list of things that needed attention.

I pulled into the Publix parking lot and Mel looked at me. "What are we doing here?"

I stopped the truck in front of the Domino's Pizza. "I need to grab something if it's here."

She looked at the pizza joint. "There's nothing in there."

Getting out, I shut the door and looked back at her. "You never know."

"Grab a large pepperoni," Danny said.

I stepped through the shattered glass doors. The place was a mess, having obviously been gone through countless times. I hopped over the counter and started my search. It didn't take long to find what I was looking for. There was no reason for anyone to take them, so I knew they'd be there. I grabbed several stacks and went back out to the truck and tossed them into the back.

Mel was looking at me. "What are you doing with those?"

"I have an idea," I replied with a smile."

"What in the world are you going to do with pizza boxes?" Danny asked.

"I told you. It's a surprise."

I wheeled the truck into the parking lot of the Kangaroo Store in Altoona. Mel looked over and asked, "What are we doing here?"

"Gotta see a man about a dog," I replied as I got out.

Little Bit's head popped up. "We're getting a dog?"

"No, we already have dogs."

Mel spun around in her seat. "It's just a saying."

I walked over to the milk man. Seeing me coming, he grinned. "How are you, friend?"

"I'm good. Was hoping I could put in an order for some cheese."

He rubbed his chin. "How much?"

I shrugged. "I don't know, five to ten pounds."

His eyes went wide. "Ten pounds! What in the world are you doing?"

I told him about the party and what I was planning on making. He cackled and slapped his knee. "Now that's just about the craziest thing I've heard in a long time! Never thought I'd see it again."

"Can you help me out?" I asked.

He nodded. "Yeah, I think I can do that. Just might be a little short on milk for the day. But we can do it."

I folded my arms over my chest. "What's it going to cost me?"

The old man smiled and thought about it for a minute. "You say you're making this for everyone in town?" I nodded. He thought some more. "I could really use some twelve gauge shells. I'm plumb out and no one wants to trade any."

"What size?" I asked.

"Hell, I'll take anything I can get!"

"Alright. I'll get you some shells. Can you have it by Saturday morning?

"That shouldn't be a problem."

I shook his hand. "All right then. I'll see you Saturday morning. I'll bring the shells, and you bring the cheese."

Stopping the truck at Gina's, I told everyone to sit tight, I'd only be a minute. Little Bit protested, she wanted to go in. She knew Gina always had a treat of some kind. "No, just stay here. I'll be right back."

"What are you doing?" Mel asked.

"It's a secret."

Her face soured. "I'm really getting tired of hearing that."

Dylan came out on the porch and waved. "Hi ya, Morgan. What brings you by?" Then he was taken-a-back. "What the hell happened to your face?"

Stepping up on the porch, I said, "We took out the remaining DHS yesterday. They're all gone now. But the reason I came by is that I was hoping you and Gina could help me with something."

"Sure, anything you need. What can we do for you?"

"All those tomatoes you had. Gina said she was going to can a bunch up."

Dylan laughed. "We're up to our eyeballs in tomatoes. Why, you need some?"

"I need tomato sauce. Lots of it."

Curious, Dylan asked, "What for?"

"Let's go in and talk to Gina and I'll explain it."

Dylan jabbed a thumb over his shoulder. "She's around back. We're using a woodstove I made to can up more tomatoes."

We walked around behind the house. Gina was standing in front of half of a fifty-five gallon drum that had been turned into a stove. The cut bottom was on the ground. A door had been cut in the side to allow the feeding of wood. A large kettle sat on top of it.

Gina was delighted to see me. "Hi Morgan! Oh my gosh! What happened to you!"

Waving, I replied. "Hey, Gina. Long story, but I'm fine. I was hoping you guys could give me a hand." I was getting tired of everyone's reaction.

She wiped her hands on a dish towel. "Sure thing. What do you need?"

I looked into the pot and pointed. "I need a bunch of these."

"Tomatoes?"

"Tomato sauce, actually. We're going to have a party in town. Now that the DHS is gone and there isn't anyone we really need to be looking out for, I figured it would be nice to throw a party and have some fun. We're going to have music and there'll be lights strung up in the trees in the park downtown. All we need is some food to really make it special."

"What are you wanting to make?" Gina asked.

I told her what I had planned. Both of them agreed it was a great idea and were eager to help in any way they could. I asked them to bring as much tomato sauce or canned tomatoes as they wanted to contribute over to Danny's house tomorrow so we could get started on the cooking.

"We'll bring other stuff too. I've got lots of veggies we can use for toppings," Gina said.

Dylan pointed to a bushy green herb in a clay pot. "We've got all that Basil too."

Gina smiled, "Oooh, yeah. Fresh Basil would be so good."

"That sounds just fine. We'll be there," Dylan said.

Waving, I headed back to the truck. "Till tomorrow then."

When I got back in the truck, Mel looked at me. "Now what?"

Grabbing the key, I replied, "Time to go home!"

"Are you going to tell me what you're up to or not?"

I winked at her. "Later."

We went to Danny's house. Miss Kay would be very important for what I had planned. Bobbie was sitting on the porch while Jace and Edie played in the yard with the dogs. Little Bit bailed out to join them and took off. Lee Ann and Taylor said they were going to go find Fred and Jess. I know Taylor was ready to do something, anything, after being cooped up for so long.

Walking up to the porch, I asked if Kay were inside. Bobbie nodded, "Yep, she's in there."

I went in and sat down at the bar as Kay puttered around the kitchen. "Kay, I have an idea for something and was wondering if you could make it."

She leaned over the counter and asked, "What is it?"

"We're going to have a party in town Saturday. There's going to be a band and lights, and I wanted to have some food."

"It wouldn't be a party without food. What were you thinking?"

I smiled and leaned in closer to her. "Pizza."

Kay laughed and exclaimed. "Pizza! How in the world can we make pizza?"

Mel was beside me and looked at me like I was crazy. "Pizza?"

"Well, we have flour, so we can make the crust. We have sausage we can put on it. And Gina has a lot of tomatoes. I was wondering if you could make sauce out of it."

"Sure we could make sauce. That's easy." I could tell she was starting to think. "You know, we took all the spices from the houses around here and have plenty of seasonings. We could make the sauce easily. But what about cheese?"

I pointed to the farmer's cheese hanging in a cheese cloth from a knob on one of the cabinets. "We could put chunks of that on, like fresh mozzarella."

Kay looked at the cheese. "We'll need more cheese."

"I'll get it."

Kay looked at Mel. "You ready to start making sauce?"

She nodded. "Yep!"

"Gina is coming over tomorrow. She's bringing what we need to make the sauce and other things for toppings."

"This will be so cool. Can you imagine a pizza party?" Mel asked.

Holding a finger over my lips, I said, "Don't tell the girls. Let's surprise them."

Mel clapped her hands together and rubbed them. "Oh yeah. They'll be so excited."

"Morgan, how many pizzas do we need to make?"

I shrugged. "As many as we can."

"Let's see how much sauce we can make."

The next day was hectic. Gina came over, and she, along with Mel, Bobbie, Kay and Mary, kept the kitchen a hive of activity. I, along with all the guys, was shooed out. It was made pretty clear to me that we weren't welcome, and to find someplace else to be. Sarge was sitting on the porch in a rocking chair drinking coffee. He laughed as we were all kicked out of the house one at a time.

"I told you boys not to go in there," he cackled.

Dalton passed through early that morning and disappeared again after breakfast. From the sounds of things, he was back to work at his forge as rhythmic hammering filled the air for most of the day. But I still needed to get the cheese, and jumped in the truck for a short ride to town. Since Little Bit was busy with the kids, I left her to play. Lee Ann and Taylor were off someplace as well, I had time to myself.

On the way out of the neighborhood, I passed Ian and Jamie. They were walking together in the direction of Danny's. I pulled up beside them and stopped. "How are you feeling, Jamie?"

"Good. I wanted to go on the raid, but I guess it was best I didn't. I'll be back up to speed in a couple of days I think."

I winked at Ian. "You two have fun. Have her home before dark." They both replied with the finger and I laughed as I drove off. But it brought a smile to my face. Two people hooking up was a good thing in my opinion.

The night before I'd gone through our arms stash at Danny's and found a crap load of shotgun shells. I grabbed a couple boxes and mixed them up. Giving him number six, eight and some 00 and number four buck. I thought it would make for a good trade considering the value of ammo today. They certainly weren't making as much as they used to.

Wheeling into the market, I pulled up to the milkman's booth and got out. He smiled and waved, then gave me the fish eye. "You bring me some shells?"

I reached in and grabbed the two boxes and set them on his table. "There's a mixed lot in here." I said as he opened them and looked the ammo over.

He said, "Oh, this'll be just fine! I'm glad it's mixed up and not just a bunch of seven and a halves." He pulled a five gallon bucket out from under the table and set it down, wrenching the lid off. "This should be enough for you."

It was over half full of creamy white cheese, and looked great. "Oh yeah. That'll do just fine." As he put the lid back on the bucket, I said, "Let folks know what we're doing tomorrow evening. Tell folks to come to town for music and fun. I think everyone could use it."

He nodded. "I'll do that. Me and the missus will be there for sure." He leaned in and squinted. "Be sure and save me a piece of the pie."

Picking up the bucket, I said, "I will. Appreciate the trade as always."

He waved. "Any time, friend. I like trading with you."

With cheese in hand, I went back to the house. Danny's porch was crowded with people. It looked as though everyone was there. Carrying the bucket of cheese up onto the porch,

I was met with the wonderful smell of baking dough. I took the bucket into the kitchen and set it on the counter. Kay immediately came over, eager to inspect the product.

I pulled the lid off and she leaned her head over. "That looks wonderful. It's going to be just like fresh mozzarella. Well, maybe not exactly, but close enough."

"I don't think anyone is going to care. I mean, it's pizza!" Bobbie shouted.

Kay looked at Mel. "Alright ladies. Let's get to cooking!"

Mel looked at me with a dripping-sweet smile. "That's your cue to get the hell out of here."

I grunted. "That's all I am, huh? Just a beast of burden?"

"Strong back, weak mind."

I pointed at her and looked down my nose. "I'll remember that. I'll remember."

"Oh Morgan, you know we love you," Gina said with a smile.

I left the ladies to their work and wandered out to the porch. Sarge was in a rocking chair with his coffee cup in his hand. He was watching the kids play in the yard, a slight grin on his face. I walked over to the end of the porch. Thad and Mary were in the garden as usual. I took a deep breath and closed my eyes for a moment. It felt good.

We spent the day lounging around on the porch. There was no talk of the assault or anything dealing with fighting or trying to stay alive. We talked as though we were at any normal Saturday bar-b-que. Dylan was on the porch carving something. It looked like a small animal from what I could see so far.

"What'cha carving there, Dylan?" I asked.

He held it up to inspect his work. "It's going to be a horse when I'm done."

"Looks pretty good."

He bobbed it up and down as though it were trotting. "It's just a way to relax. Takes my mind off everything."

The door opened and Mel came out. She was carrying a large tray that she set down on a small table between the rocking chairs. Sarge looked down and asked, "What's this?"

"We thought it was a good idea to make sure it was edible before we tried to feed to it to the whole town."

Mike, who was lying on the edge of the porch asleep, instantly bolted upright. "Food?" He looked around and saw the pizza. A big smile spread across his face as he reached for a piece.

Sarge whacked him on the knuckles with his now empty coffee cup. "Wait yer turn, snot nose."

"Hey!" Mike barked. "Wait for who?"

The pie was cut into small squares. Sarge took a piece and sampled it. As he chewed, he began to smile and looked up at Mel. Giving her a thumbs up, he said, "That's a damn fine pie, Mel. Give the ladies my compliments."

We all grabbed a piece and quickly realized the old man was right. It was a good pie. But how could it not be? Fresh sauce, fresh toppings, it couldn't help but be good. I could taste the basil, it mixed well with the tomato. Such a taste after so long was a real treat. We finished the pie, making sure everyone, including the kids, got a piece. But it was more of a tease than anything. Now we'd have to wait all day to get another sample.

Now that it was no longer a surprise for the girls, they helped with the preparation of the pizzas by folding boxes and putting the pies in. There were countless requests for more pizza. Knowing we could make it now, I saw it on the menu again in the near future. That is, as long as the flour holds out.

By four o'clock, the cooking was done. Everyone was relaxed after spending the entire day lazing about. There were stacks of pizza boxes ready to be loaded. It was time to get going, so everyone pitched in to load them into the MRAP sitting in Danny's driveway. As the truck was being loaded, I went to find Dalton who had been absent all day; but the hammering let me know he was busy.

I found him at his forge. He was sitting on a stump holding a long blade. He looked up as I approached and held it aloft. "What do you think?"

It was a long thin thing that looked like it would serve well to hack the brush here in the Sunshine State. "Looks good."

He inspected his work. "Just messing around."

"We're about to head to town. You coming?"

He stood up and picked up his shirt. Shaking it out, he said, "Hell yes!"

"The ladies have made pizza, a bunch of them."

He looked at me surprised. "No shit? Pizza?"

I smiled. "Yeah. And it's damn good too."

Putting on the shirt, he shouted. "Lead on, lad and we shall sally forth!"

I couldn't help but laugh at him. By the time we got back to the house, everything was loaded and all were ready to go. Mel and the girls were waiting by the truck. Dalton hopped into the back as I got in. Looking at Mel and the girls, I asked, "You guys ready to go to town?"

The girls jumped with shouts of excitement. They all piled into the truck, and I pulled out behind the MRAP. Mike and Ted were in the buggies as well. With the addition of Gina and Dylan, we had quite the crowd. Even though we were going to a party and this was a happy occasion, everyone was armed. We traveled rather heavy with SAWs mounted to the tops of the two buggies.

As we rolled down the road, we passed many people walking

towards town. There was a steady stream of folks headed out of Umatilla. Several ATVs passed us, and a few people on horseback. As we passed an old couple riding a small donkey, Dalton laughed. "Now there's an animal I could ride!"

I laughed at the thought. "All you'd have to do is put your feet down and the thing could walk right out from under you."

The girls all laughed at the statement and continued to laugh as Dalton told the story of the last time he rode a horse. He finished it with, "The last time I rode one, was the last time I'll ride one!"

There was also an old truck rolling slowly down the road. The bed was like something from a movie about India or Indonesia. The bed was overloaded with people. Packed to capacity with standing room only. There were even smiling and waving faces sitting on top of the cab. I laughed at the sight as we passed it, and the girls all talked about it. It was quite the sight.

In Eustis, there were throngs of people walking down Bay Street towards the park. We slowed as we made our way through the crowd. Mel looked over at me and said, "I don't think we have enough food for all these people."

I nodded. "I didn't think we'd made enough to feed everyone. When it runs out, it runs out."

When we got to the park, the lawn in front of the band shell was crowded with people. There were chairs and blankets with families sprawled out on them. Children ran around playing. They were everywhere. The band was already on the stage, and I could hear a fiddle hard at work as I pulled up to a row of tables Shane and Sean had set up for us. There was a group of Guardsmen there waiting for us as well.

Shutting the truck down, Little Bit jumped out and looked at Mel expectantly. "Can I go play?"

Mel looked out across the park. There were uniformed

Guardsmen wandering through the throngs. They were all over the park, just to make sure there were no issues. She looked at Little Bit. "Yes. But stay close and don't leave the park for any reason."

Little Bit smiled. "I won't!" And she took off at a run to join in with the other kids.

Mike backed the MRAP up to the tables and everyone got out. Sarge looked around the park. After taking the crowd in, he looked at me. "You're going to start a damn riot, Morgan."

I shrugged. "I'm just trying to give a little something back to the community."

Sarge looked at Mike. "You, Teddy, Doc and Ian keep people away from this truck." He looked at the guys. "No one gets near this thing, understood?"

"Roger that, boss," Ted said.

Ian and Doc nodded, and the guys spread out around it. Jamie was in her BDUs today, in full kit. She went with Ian as they took up a position on one side. I enjoyed seeing them together and remembered the day I told them they should knock boots and get it over with. She was so pissed, it made me laugh just thinking about it. But now they seemed inseparable. It was good.

Looking at Sarge, I said, "I'm going up to the stage. I'll make an announcement about the food and ask folks to line up."

Sarge shook his head. "This is going to turn into a cluster fuck."

"You just don't trust people do you?"

Sarge snorted. "Hell no! I know people! Shit, I am one. I know what they're capable of." He wagged a finger at me. "Never underestimate the power of idiots in large numbers. And this is a damn idiot convention!"

I shook my head and turned to head for the stage. Mel took

my hand and walked with me. "Didn't know you were coming with me," I said.

"Oh, I'm not going up on that stage!" She said with a laugh.

"I didn't think you were. But thanks for coming with me."

We made our way to the stage. The sun was starting to go down and the lights in the trees came on. The crowd acknowledged it with a round of applause. A generator had been set up behind the band shell. It ran the lights and the sound equipment for the band. They'd brought in some old school amps and mics. I could tell by looking at it, the gear had seen some miles. But it sounded good.

As we approached the stage, they were in the middle of "Foggy Mountain Breakdown". The banjos were playing fast and furious. I stepped up on the stage and waited for the song to finish. From where I was standing, I could see the entire park. Kids were running, playing and laughing. Some adults were dancing. Everyone seemed genuinely happy. The lights added to the scene and made for a happy sight.

As the song finished, Mel looked at me. "You ready?"

I shrugged. "May as well be." I leaned over and kissed her and walked out onto the stage.

Approaching one of the band members, I leaned in and whispered into his ear. He nodded and stepped up to the mic. "Howdy, folks. Are you enjoying the music?" There was a round of hoots and applause. "We got someone here that wants to say a few words." He looked at me and motioned to the mic.

I stepped up and adjusted it. "Evening, everyone. Are we having a good time?" There was another round of applause and shouts. "Some of you know me, but for those that don't, I'm Morgan Carter."

From the crowd came several shouts. One above the others, "Sheriff Carter!" Followed by whistles and cat calls.

I laughed. "Yeah. I suppose. Anyway, I organized this for everyone tonight with the help of the guys from the police department. How about a round of applause for Shane, Sean and the guys that strung all these lights and set this up?" There was a loud round of applause, whistles and cat calls. I stepped to the side and swept my arm over the stage. "And let's hear it for the band!" The crowd erupted once again as I continued. "These guys sound pretty good!" The park erupted even louder and the band members nodded their appreciation.

I motioned for them to quiet down, and after a moment, I was able to speak again. "We've all been through some tough times. Our world has changed, hasn't it folks." I could see heads nodding in agreement along with a couple of shouts. "But working together, we're getting better. The park is full everyday of folks trading and bartering, things are starting to get done. But we've got more to do and the only way we can do it is to work together." There were more nods and shouts. "Like the farm. With everyone working together out there, we've got nearly forty acres planted. That's food for everyone!"

Again the crowd erupted. I gave them a minute to settle down before continuing. "To show our appreciation, and to make sure we had a real party, I arranged some food for tonight." That really got the crowd going. Trying to shout above them, I said, "It isn't much! But it is a bit of a treat."

People were looking around and shouting, "What is it? Or, "Where is it!" The idea of food excited them.

"This will only work if everyone cooperates. We need to form an orderly line at the tables set up over there," I pointed to where the tables were. "So line up for a slice of fresh pizza! But there's only so much. We made as much as we could, but I'm sure it won't be enough for everyone. So let's line up orderly and we'll do our best to hand it out."

The crowd went wild and everyone started moving. While it was a rush, it wasn't unruly. There was no real pushing or shoving. I looked at the band and motioned for them to start playing. They quickly dove into Shackles and Chains with a young lady joining in on vocals. I left the stage and walked back to the trucks with Mel. She tugged my hand as we walked.

"Good job," she said.

"Eh. Had to say something."

Back at the tables, the pizza distribution was going surprisingly smoothly. Probably because Sarge had organized the Guardsmen into a cordon the people had to walk through to get a slice. It was an impressive show of force that prevented any disorder. People in line craned their necks, trying to get a look. They talked animatedly about the thought of pizza and wondered out loud how we did it.

As Mel and I made our way back, many people shook my hand or offered thanks. Some with a simple nod, others with a slap on my back. I didn't want the attention though. That wasn't why I did what I did. I quickly made my way back to the trucks, to be separated from the masses.

Everyone was busy, cutting the pies into small pieces about three inches square. I stood beside Sarge and watched as Jess and Fred handed it out as fast as they could. Mary and Miss Kay were likewise working as fast as they could. I looked at Sarge. "Looks like you were wrong."

He grunted. "It ain't over yet."

I laughed and shook my head. I grabbed a box with half a pizza in it and handed it to Mel. "Can you take this up to the band? I want to make sure they get some for what they're doing."

Taking it, she said, "Sure."

As the crowd moved through in orderly fashion, I heard Jess say something that caught my ear. Up to this point everyone was satisfied and thankful for their single piece of pizza. "You can only have one." I heard her say, then she added, "They have to come get their own."

Looking over, I saw Albert, Hyatt's toady. I nudged Sarge and nodded at the man. We both walked over to back up Jess. Seeing us, Albert's face soured. "Why can't I get enough for our people?"

"You heard the deal. Get in line to get a piece. We're not letting anyone carry off more for someone else," I said.

"It only makes sense to allow people to take some back to others in their group. It'll make this whole thing easier, faster," Albert said.

Sarge stepped up. "You tell Porky to waddle his fat ass over here if he wants some. One piece, per person, period." Begrudgingly, Albert took his piece and wandered off. Sarge was shaking his head and looked at me. "We should have shot those dickheads. They're going to be nothing but trouble."

I nodded. "Probably. But they haven't done anything yet to justify it. We've taken their guns, there isn't much they can do."

The handout continued without issue. But we were starting to run out, some would certainly go without. Once we were down to the last few boxes, Hyatt came walking through the crowd with a number of his people. He bypassed the line and walked directly to the head, drawing a number of comments from those in line.

Seeing him, I asked, "What do you want?"

"Albert said I had to come personally to get my share. So I came to get it."

I pointed to the line still snaking its way through the park. "You have to get in line like everyone else."

Hyatt waved his hands. "This is ridiculous. I already sent my man! So I've already been in line!"

The crowd was getting irritated and began to shout and shake fists. Hyatt could singlehandedly turn what's been a very peaceful event into a damn riot. Sarge looked at him. "Back of the line, Porky." Sarge's comment was greeted with shouts from those in line. "Yeah, back of the line, asshole!"

Hyatt looked at the remaining few boxes and then down the line. Incredulously, he shouted, "There isn't enough! If I go to the back of the line, I won't get any!"

"You won't be the only one. A bunch of these folks won't get a piece. But that's the way it works. When there's more demand than supply, the supply runs out." I said.

Hyatt stamped his foot. "This is unjust! This isn't right! How can you promise these people food, and then not provide it?"

Sarge looked at two of the nearest Guardsmen. "Get this sack of shit out of here."

The two men quickly moved in on Hyatt. Using their rifles, they began to push him away from the table to cheers from the crowd. Naturally, Hyatt protested and whined, but it was to no avail. The two soldiers pushed him to the back of the line where he then stomped off.

Sarge was shaking his head. "We need to kill that fucker. Mark my words. We need to kill him."

I sighed. "You may be right. He's going to be nothing but trouble."

Ted was standing beside Sarge. He grunted. "I'll do it. Let me and Mikey take 'em out one night. It'll be fun."

Glancing sideways at Ted, I said, "Not yet."

Fred looked back at us. "Guys, this is the last one." She was holding a pizza box.

I nodded. "Give it out and we'll tell everyone."

I asked Aric to go tell the Guardsmen monitoring the line that we were out so they could start to disperse the line. Mike and Ted moved out as well and started delivering the bad news. While there were some complaints, hurt feelings more than anything, everyone behaved and those still in line broke up and drifted back to their places in the park.

The band was still playing and things were settling down. Shane approached me and said they'd planned for a big bonfire and were about to light it. While everyone was getting their food, they'd brought in wood and made a huge pile in front of the band shell. I told him it was a good idea; it would get people back into the party mood. I asked where Sean was and he said he was at the fire pit.

Sarge stepped up. "Go get him and anyone helping you and bring them over here real quick. He nodded and ran off. I asked Sarge what was up. He jabbed a thumb in the direction of the MRAP. "We've got a couple of pies in the truck still. I wanted to make sure those guys got a piece."

As we were talking, Sheffield and Livingston walked up. Sheffield looked around the park and nodded. "This was a hell of an idea, Morgan. Good job."

"Did you guys get any pizza?" I asked.

He shook his head. "No, we left it for these folks."

"Come over here and get a piece. You guys deserve it just as much," Sarge said.

Livingston looked with surprise. "Thought it was all gone."

"It is. We held a couple back for the folks working hard here tonight."

Shane and Sean returned with a couple of men that helped them. Shane pointed at the two men. "These guys worked for the city. They strung all the lights and are helping get the fire ready."

I pointed to the back of the truck. "Get yourselves a slice. We appreciate the efforts guys."

The two men thanked me and grabbed their share before heading back to the fire pit. Sheffield and Livingston grabbed a piece and were eating it when I noticed Hyatt again. He was off the side of the park, in the shadows glaring at us. I could almost hear him saying, *you said it was all gone.* Shaking my head, I turned back to the park as the fire was lit to cheers from the crowd.

I left Sarge and the guys to talk. Mel and I went out looking for Little Bit. We found her near the fire. The kid loved fire, like a moth to a flame. She was with a group of other children doing a ring-around-the-rosy around the fire as the band played. Everyone was happy. A carefree feeling swept over the park as people danced and carried on. The band kept rolling; and as the night wore on, others showed up with instruments. From time to time, someone would go up on the stage and give one of the folks up there a break.

Late in the evening, a competition of dueling banjos broke out between several players. The crowd really got into it and hooted and howled as the strings got faster and faster. The fire roared and the music filled the air. It was a truly great night. Looking at my watch, I saw it was getting on close to midnight and told Mel I wanted to go listen to the radio to try and catch the nightly broadcast.

I left her by the fire with Little Bit and went to find Sarge. He was still at the truck with Sheffield and Livingston. I pulled the little radio from my vest and turned it on. Sarge looked at me and asked, "Time for the radio show?"

I nodded. "Yeah, they should be on any time now."

Livingston pointed at the radio. "That what you've been listening to them on?"

Holding it up, I laughed. "Yeah. It ain't much, but it works."

We moved around to the other side of the truck to block

some of the sound from the band. It wasn't long before the little radio crackled to life.

Good evening fellow Patriots. You're listening to John Jacob Schmidt coming to you from the Radio Free Redoubt. Broadcasting to all of you in occupied territory and those outside the wire. Bringing you the news you need in these trying times. We have a recording we're going to play for you tonight that's chilling. We here in the redoubt are working to confirm this information. Be warned, what you're about to hear has serious implications for all of us.

A man's voice that was obviously recorded began to play. It sounded like a radio conversation.

There's smoke coming over the horizon. Thick black columns of it! We've even seen contrails from what must be rockets.

Another voice asked, *Where are you?"*

Cape Hatteras. This has been going on all day! I can only imagine what's going on out there.

Must be the Navy going at it with someone. The other voice said.

Yeah, but who?

I've heard the Russians and Chinese were coming. They must be trying to stop them.

There's another one! Another rocket just crossed the horizon!

Do you see any planes?

No, it's far off. Can't even hear anything.

This ain't good. Ain't good at all.

With that, the recording stopped, and John came back on the radio. *Folks, if this is the Navy in ship to ship battle with Chinese or Russian forces, we are in real trouble.*

We traded looks around. It was sobering news. To think we just got things settled down and we could be facing a much, much larger issue now was disheartening. I thought about what that possible future could look like as the broadcast continued.

Here at the Redoubt we're trying to verify this recording, but our preliminary findings are that it is indeed credible. Our contacts inside the DOD have been out of touch, and this only reinforces the fact they have their hands full. We've talked about this very scenario in previous broadcasts and it looks as though they are coming to pass.

If you haven't prepared yourself, your family and community for what's coming, you need to do it now. Because folks, it looks like time is running out. We are about to be in the fight for our lives. We're cutting tonight's broadcast short to give everyone more time to prepare.

A woman's voice came on next. *Good evening Patriots, standby for a message..... To our patriots under the Birch tree. To our patriots under the Birch tree. 27807 96664 40629 12071 50393 15323 15996 16341 32069 35757 19073 82868 24366 72726 77987 09349 50907 87851 15215 34264.*

When the coded message stopped, Toby Keith's song "American Soldier" started. Speaking over the intro, John said, *Now we're all American soldiers."*

At some point Cecil showed up. I realized he was there when he said, "I'll decode this later."

Looking at him, I asked, "When did you show up?"

He smiled. "I been around."

Sarge asked, "You think you have the one-time pad for this?"

"I'll go through my stack of them and see."

Sheffield looked at Sarge. "Can you try and make contact with folks up the chain? You seem to have better luck than I do."

Sarge leaned back on the truck. "Fawcett was just here. You heard what he had to say. We know this is coming; and from the sounds of that broadcast, it's already started." He looked around at all of us. "The question is, what are we going to do about it"

Shaking my head, I started to walk away. Sarge called out to me, "Where the hell are you going?"

Looking back, I said, "This sounds like a military issue. I'm going to be with my family while I have the time. From the sounds of what we just heard, things are about to change." I looked out across the park where people still danced and the music played. "There's nothing I can do about it tonight. So for tonight, just for one night, I'm going to pretend things are just fine." I saw Little Bit dancing around the fire with Mel. "Right now there's a couple of ladies over there I want to spend some quality time with. Enjoy it while you can, guys. The only day we're guaranteed is yesterday."

With that, I walked across the park, leaving them to think about it. We've had enough worry. Enough fighting. Tonight wasn't about that. I came up behind Little Bit and scooped her off the ground. She laughed and kicked and I plopped her back on her feet. Taylor was standing on the side of the fire watching everyone run and dance. I grabbed her hand and pulled her out into the swirling circle of bodies.

As we made our way around the fire, I grabbed all of the girls by the hand, pulling them out. When I pulled Fred out, she dragged Aric with her. Mary did likewise with Thad when I dragged her out. Making another pass, I pulled Jess out. She resisted, saying she couldn't dance, to which I replied, "Me neither!" As I passed Doc, I grabbed him and tried to pull him out, but he planted his heels and wouldn't budge. So Instead, I pushed Jess into him, that was good enough.

I found Mel in the crowd and we danced through the swirling bodies. Seeing Miss Kay off to the side, I guided us over to her. Leaning in, I pointed at Sarge. "Go over and get that old man out there!"

Kay blushed. "Oh, I couldn't."

Mel grabbed her shoulders and turned her towards him. "Yes you can. Go get him!"

Kay laughed and covered her mouth. Looking back over her shoulder, she shrugged and started off in his direction. Mel and I went back into the circle and bumped into Gina and Dylan. We laughed and traded partners and made a pass around the fire. Before long, everyone was changing up, and we all found ourselves dancing with people we didn't even know. The fun was infectious and much needed.

The band quickly got into it as well, calling out to change partners. It was during one of those changes that I turned to see Kay and the old man. I smiled and held out my hand. "Mind if I cut in?" I asked.

"I do!" Sarge barked. "Find your own. This one's mine." Kay blushed and smiled and the two of them disappeared into the crowd again. I couldn't help but smile at them. It'd taken long enough, but seeing that proved this was the greatest night I'd experienced in a long time. I went off to find Mel again, who I would dance with until the sun started to come up. Come what may tomorrow, I was going to enjoy this night, every last minute of it.